# The House on Lippincott

Inanna Publications and Education Inc.
212 Founders College, York University
4700 Keele Street
Toronto, Ontario M3J 1P3
Telephone: (416) 736-5356 Fax (416) 736-5765
Email: inanna@yorku.ca Web site: www.yorku.ca/inanna


Interior design by Luciana Ricciutelli
Cover design and illustration by Valerie Fullard


Printed and bound in Canada


Library and Archives Canada Cataloguing in Publication

Burstow, Bonnie, 1945-
    The house on Lippincott : a novel / by Bonnie Burstow

(Inanna poetry and fiction series)
ISBN 0-9736709-5-9

I. Title.  II. Series.

PS8603.U748H68 2006      C813'.6      C2006-900534-6

# The House on Lippincott

*a novel by*

Bonnie Burstow

ınanna poetry & fiction series

Inanna  Publications and Education Inc.
Toronto, Canada

*This novel is dedicated to everyone harmed by the Holocaust
and to victims of genocide everywhere.*

# Himmelfarb Genogram

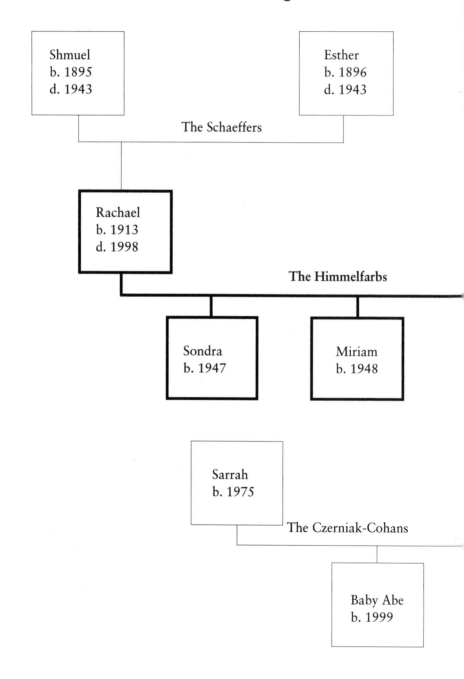

# Last Updated, April 16, 2000

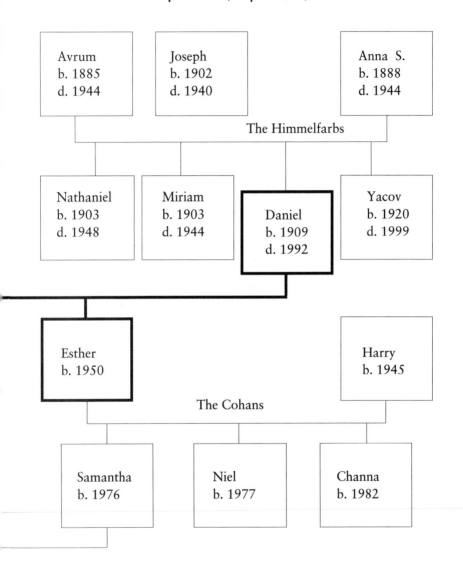

Avrum
b. 1885
d. 1944

Joseph
b. 1902
d. 1940

Anna S.
b. 1888
d. 1944

The Himmelfarbs

Nathaniel
b. 1903
d. 1948

Miriam
b. 1903
d. 1944

Daniel
b. 1909
d. 1992

Yacov
b. 1920
d. 1999

Esther
b. 1950

Harry
b. 1945

The Cohans

Samantha
b. 1976

Niel
b. 1977

Channa
b. 1982

# In the Beginning Was the Word

The narrator of this novel uses Yiddish more than most Jews of her generation because Yiddish is part of her family's dynamic, one of their ways of coping. Though far less often, she and the family also use Hebrew from time to time. There is a glossary of Yiddish and Hebrew words at the back for your convenience. If you are unfamiliar with a term but don't want to interrupt the flow by flipping to the back, try pronouncing the word to yourself. You'll often be able to grasp the sense of the sentence or guess at the meaning. Additionally, many of the terms are common exclamations which have no precise meaning and whose flavor one can gradually pick up.

"Nu" means something close to "now," "well," or "so." It can be a question, a sigh, an insinuation, the beginning of an explanation, an invitation. "Oy" is short for "oy, vey iz mir," which means, "Oh, woe is me." It is rather like a groan. A multipurpose word, "epes" means "something," also "somehow." It often denotes things beyond those listed or "anything" as in: "Pick me up cake, cookies, epes." "Kinehora" literally means "with no evil eye." The original intent was to ward away the evil eye. It is often uttered after commenting on something nice, as in, "the girls look so beautiful, kinehora." "Gotenyu" is roughly similar to "My God!" "Gevalt" is a scream, a cry, an expression of fear or shock, a desperate appeal for help. And if you can imagine the word "nothing" accompanied by thrown up hands and a declamatory tone, such is sense conveyed by "bupkes."

# Miriam's Prologue

My name is Miriam Himmelfarb. And I am the daughter of a Holocaust survivor. Nu? I wouldn't have introduced myself this way once upon a time. It is good that I do so now. It's accurate, yes? And it's urgent. It is also insufficient and what is insufficient is always inaccurate in some critical way. To be a little less "insufficient," I should clarify that I am the daughter of *two* Holocaust survivors. Not one. And while we all had trouble with my father for a while there, I love them both very dearly.

I am also a single person in a branch of a family that has had a number of branches lopped off—a node in a Holocaust-ridden family tree. That whole generation—my grandparents and their parents, sisters, brothers, and cousins—they were just stopped—just deleted. Gotenyu! Even I myself didn't include most of them in the family genogram.

You might want to take a look at the genogram. There are secrets that it hints at. And it just might help you keep your bearings in the journey ahead.

The bolded section is my immediate family. My immediate family is one of three families called "Himmelfarb." Daniel and Rachael are my parents. Miriam—the middle daughter—that's me. My older sister is Sondra. My younger sister is Esther, and to her, as you can see, goes the mitzvah of continuing the family line.

If you go up one generation to the generation of my grandparents, you will discover that almost everyone died in the 1940s, as did two of my father's siblings. For all those who died before 1945, the reason was the same. Always the same. The Holocaust.

Both of my grandmothers were German Jews of mixed descent. On my grandfather's side, both branches of the family, the Schaeffers and the Himmelfarbs, were multigenerational German Jews; the Schaeffers from Berlin and the Himmelfarbs from Freiburg. Berlin—I'm sure every-one knows. Freiburg—what's to be said about it? A geologist might tell you that it straddles the crossroads between Alsace and the Black Forest, between Switzerland and North Baden. A Jew versed in anti-Semitism is more likely to mention the well-poisoning accusations in the Middles Ages. Oh yes, and it is at University of Freiburg that the brilliant up-and-coming existentialist philosopher Martin Heidegger taught his new ap-proach to ontology—the human being as the Dasein, or location through which Being is uncovered. Dasein or There-being as being-toward-death. My mother the scholar was an avid Heidegger enthusiast once upon a time.

All four of my grandparents died in the Holocaust—my maternal grandparents Shmuel Schaeffer and Esther Schaeffer, my paternal grand-parents Avrum Himmelfarb and Anna Sondra Himmelfarb. It was for Anna Sondra Himmelfarb that my sister Sondra was named, my younger sister, for Esther Schaeffer.

My father's elder siblings were Nathaniel and Miriam, the twins. I was named after Miriam. A glance at their dates of death reveals that Nathaniel survived the Holocaust and Miriam did not. The reason is not self-evident. Indeed, both could have been apprehended, with one sur-viving and one not, yes? What actually transpired, though, is quite dif-ferent. And it can be traced back to a decision by my grandfather, zeda Avrum.

While a modest tailor, zeda Avrum was a far-sighted man who had thought deep and hard about Jewish persecution over these past few thousand years. From early on, zeda was alarmed by the changes in Germany—the Hitlerites coming to power; the incarceration of the Com-munists. One day, shortly after the passing of the Nuremberg Laws, he arched his body up high, smacked his lips, pounded his fist on the table, and announced, "The family is in enormous danger, and as patriarch, I intend to do something about it." But what to do? Where to go? How to go? While his sons and daughter were adults too, none had the finances to go very far or to help anyone else go very far. And unlike most Jews around him, zeda had this sick feeling that not a single place in Europe would be far enough. He remembered Hitler's prophecy. He thought of the Crusades. The Jews of Mainz trapped in the Bishop's palace. The York massacre. He looked inquiringly at his wife, bubbeh Anna.

Bubbeh Anna did not hesitate for a second. "The kinderlekh," she responded, eyeing him intently. "Avrum, what happens to you and me, it's not so important. We have lived. But the kinderlekh."

Zeda nodded. He went to schul to pray. When he returned, he announced that the children came first. By week's end, zeda had sold most of the family furniture and cut back mercilessly on family expenditures. The time came when he had enough money to send one of his children to safety. There was no question who it was going to be. Oy! There was no question in any of the Jewish households that I know of. It was the eldest male child, yes?

That left Miriam, my father, and Yacov. My abba was arrested very early on because of political activity. A tailor like zeda, abba had been a union man, you see, and he attended underground meetings after the unions were banned. With Nathaniel safe and abba arrested, Yacov and Miriam remained. By this time, zeda had saved enough for one more rescue. Again, the choice was predetermined. And so it was that Uncle Yacov came to North America, that Uncle Nathaniel went to Palestine, and that abba and Miriam ended up in Auschwitz. Miriam died in Auschwitz in 1944.

With my mother's family, it was altogether different. Except for eema—and she was seen as an alarmist—nobody in that family read the signs. And nobody escaped.

Like abba, eema was also picked up early on, and also on political ground—suspicions of Communist activity. That these two people, picked up so early should both survive and should keep coming across each other throughout the Terrible Times, of course, is quite unusual; and the religious members of our family have always taken it as a kind of sign.

*Image: A well fed man with an arm band. He is tall and young. He is holding a wooden club with both hands. He is striking a woman who has many of eema's features—only bald, perilously thin, weak, and younger, yes, yes, decades and decades younger. The blow is so forceful that it shatters the universe. The woman does not scream.*

Nishte fargesn! (Never forget). Eema, I promise. I will remember.

A good part of my identity is wrapped up in this story of what happened to which family member in Auschwitz or in Ravensbrück. There is more to my identity as well, of course. Who am I? And what do I do?

I am a philosophy professor at York University in Toronto. I am a feminist. I am a peace activist. I am a researcher who has conducted extensive interviews with women survivors. I am sister to two women, one of whom I would give almost anything to know better. Ah yes, and I am a woman in grieving.

Grieving—that's what is uppermost in my life at this juncture. Though it is inevitably mixed up with everything else. Why grieving? Well, there's the "obvious." There's the death in the family. But that's not the whole of it. It's also in part because of aspects of my mother's life, aspects that keep coming back to haunt the whole. My own life haunted by my parents' lives, haunted by countless lives and countless images. Lives and images that flood my mind.

*Image: A woman with no hair. Many of the same features as eema— medium height, angular face, beakish nose—only far less healthy and far thinner, and younger, decades and decades younger, before the wrinkles and the parchment overtook the smooth skin and made it hard to find the woman who was once young. The woman with no hair is squatting on a mud floor sewing, all the while squeezing a bundle between her knees. She's wearing a tattered grey schmata that's many sizes too big for her. It reeks of urine and is teeming with lice. Sweat is pouring down the woman's forehead. She peers about nervously, then quickly puts down the sewing, opens up the bundle, takes out a blood-stained rag, and mops her forehead. She sits motionless for a few moments, her eyes glazed over. Then she shakes her head brusquely, puts the bundle between her bony knees once again, and resumes sewing.*

*Image: In the dark, distinguishable only with extreme effort, a man who looks like abba only thinner, frail, and younger—much younger— is holding a bowl of very thin soup. The soup is water, water, more water. And a hint of turnip at the bottom.*

*"I'll keep an eye on your soup if you want to get your spoon out,"* comes a voice from out of the darkness—a barely audible male voice with an accent I can't place.

*The man who looks like my abba puts the bowl down, quickly opens the bundle, and takes out a strange object that is spoon on one end and knife on the other. He looks back in the direction of the soup. The bowl is gone!*

*He hears the sound of quick footsteps, first loud, then trailing off into the distance. "Low tattoo number. He's been here long enough. The numbskull should have known better," comes a different voice, same accent, the tone clearly disdainful, the words ending in a slight snicker. The man who looks like my father grimaces and slaps his forehead, like a person annoyed with himself. He stares at the number on his arm. He looks accusingly in the direction from which the laugh came. He leans forward as if about to go there. Then he stops short, pulls a scrap of paper and a button out of his bundle, and leaves, heading in the direction of the latrine. On the way, he passes two men with high numbers, stops to talk with them, then walks on. "I'll get soup," he mutters to himself. "Can always strike a good exchange with a high number." But very few are out this late, yes? And no exchanges are made.*

*Image: Naked shivering women of all ages, no hair on their heads, their bare feet in the snow, all ribs and bones, empty sacks where the breasts would have been, stand obediently in a row, trying to hold themselves straight, bracing themselves against the cold Polish wind. As the signal is given, one by one, they approach a well-fed man dressed in white. The man observes each for a matter of seconds as if assessing them, then points to the left or to the right. On this day, it appears that "right" means "work" and "left" means "gas chambers," for all of the weakest ones—including all of the women whose eyes are empty—are directed toward the left. After many have been so processed, inexplicably, a girl who appears to be about sixteen and who is comparatively healthy is directed toward the left!*

*Her eyes widen, and she whispers to the famished older figure next to her, "Why?"*

*The older woman shakes her bony head ever so slightly, not enough for it to be detected by the men with rifles to the side. Then she whispers urgently, "Shush. There is no longer any 'why.'"*

The images crowd in against each other, some merging with others, some staying intact. Some play once. Some play over and over again. Vey iz mir! Sometimes I suspect that the image gallery in my head numbers six million, but I'm not sure that this is humanly possible.

I could say that these images, these insistent realities from the past, bring me grief. And it would be true, but again insufficient. They *are* my grief, and they are the meaning that I find beyond grief, and they are me. So too is another reality, another image that presses in upon me. A frail eighty-five-year old woman. Lying in her bed. An old woman who is my mother lying in her bed. Motionless. Cold to the touch. Not to be warm again. Ah, but that reality is recent enough to be called "now," yes? And it is precisely what has just happened.

What has happened, you see—and let me be clear, it is not a tragedy, it was her time—my mother, Rachael Himmelfarb, has died. She died a few weeks ago in the wee hours of Monday, November 31, 1998. The funeral was held at Temple Ruth, that new Reconstructionist schul just kitty corner from Volya's Cheese Emporium in Kensington Market, Toronto. Over three hundred people attended the service, which was presided over by Rabbi Patricia. Family, friends, and ex-students drove to the gravesite for the saying of the Mourner's Kaddish. For seven days, we sat shiva, not working, the huge oak-framed mirror in the centre of our living room covered. In the middle of shiva, a short article appeared in the *Canadian Jewish News* entitled "Renaissance Scholar Rachael Himmelfarb-Dead at 85."

Nu? That's what happened. That's the objective truth. The facts. And like everything objective, it leaves out more than it accounts for. In this case, it leaves out loss. Loss for me. Loss of me. Loss for the world. Loss of world.

*A little girl is hiding. She turns to a second little girl who looks just slightly older, just slightly taller.*

*"Not a sound," cautions the older child. "And stop that fidgeting or the Nazis will hear you."*

*The girls are crouched down low in a little niche under a wooden staircase right at the entry to a darkened room. There is a faded red bridge table in the centre of the room. A copy of a newspaper is lying on the table. Curiously, the date on the front page reads "March 6 1957."*

These images, they flood my mind. They leave me with questions. The entire course of my life and my family's life leaves me with questions, questions as haunting as the images themselves.

As a Jew who was never in the Holocaust, what do I owe to the six million? As a woman who overwhelmingly heard men's stories throughout my formative years, what do I owe even still to the women survivors whose engendered stories were so long erased? To the women who stood naked in the snow before the gaze of the Third Reich male who sentenced them to death? To the women whose breasts were stolen from them? To the women who were bypassed when a child was sent to freedom?

How could I have faltered so badly in eema's final years? Did I protect eema and abba sufficiently when they were alive? How do I protect them now that they are no longer alive?

Who was I when eema was alive? Who am I now? That is, who is this daughter of a Holocaust survivor now that the survivor that used to be her mother is no more?

What sense do I make of this life that my family has led, this life in the shadow of Auschwitz? Giving birth in the shadow of Auschwitz. Pesach in the shadow of Auschwitz. Discovering feminism—de Beavoir, Millet, Lorde—in the shadow of Auschwitz. World events in the shadow of Auschwitz: the Eichmann trial, the Six Day War, Bosnia. Coming to old age in the shadow of Auschwitz. Daily rituals in the shadow of Auschwitz. Getting up in the morning, brushing your teeth, getting dressed, eating, drinking, going to bed, and yes dreaming. It goes on.

Funny what big questions I am asking and how minor I sometimes feel. Don't get me wrong. I don't suffer from what the psychologists call "low self esteem," nor, for that matter, from false modesty. Not remotely. I know that I'm a good scholar and teacher. I know I help people. And us Jews, we do have a sense of ourselves as beings with a mission, as beings who can change the course of history, repair the broken vessels, heal the world. We take responsibility and fight against injustice—yes, and perpetrate injustice too, let's be clear about that. The Palestinian situation is awful; there's no denying it. But the point is: I stand in a long tradition of people who know that they count. People who have stood up and been counted. Standing up for human rights. Standing up against tyranny. We even challenge God. Now I am an atheist who does not believe in God. But that is beside the point. Jews who believe in God challenge him.

Take the story of Sodom and Gomorrah. God is on an outrageous rant. The crotchety old patriarch is going to eradicate whole villages without a moment's thought. Now in the end, Abraham is unable to save Sodom and Gomorrah. But that too is not the point. He *does* confront God. "Shall the Lord of all the universe do wrong!" he protests. A mentsh this Abraham, yes? Not always and not when it comes to family. But here in this moment. A human being who had some sense of the significance of the moment and of himself *in* the moment.

I signify also, and I know that I signify. It is not an issue of absolutes. It is an issue of comparatives. And it's not a question of not understanding the importance of what I do. As eema was trying to tell me at the very end, it is a question of attending to my personal location. Attending to your own location, that's hard when you are raised in the shadow of Auschwitz. Especially for us women. You keep putting your life on hold. You keep asking: Is eema okay today? Is abba being triggered? You find yourself entertaining wishes so outlandish that you dare not utter them aloud. You keep losing sight of yourself. Even losing the sense that you have a story.

Which brings me to the matter between us. While I fell into a depression days after eema's funeral and have been struggling to get my bearings ever since, one thing is clear: There is a story here that cries out to be told, and I owe it to everyone—myself included—to tell it. This is what we are about—you and me. Nu? This is my telling, my testimony. And I'm inviting you to witness it.

Now it is a tale with a great many voices, yes? There is my mother, Rachael Himmelfarb, Holocaust survivor, mother of three, brilliant Renaissance scholar. This is a mother-daughter story. How eema and I navigated life together. How eema and I navigated death together. The unimaginable gift she gave us in those final days. It is about sisters, pulled apart by forces beyond their control or understanding. It is about abba. It is about Uncle Yacov. It is about family, five generations and counting. I share it with you in the hope that it will do us all some good. That in its own small way, it will help in tikkun olam—the healing of the world.

While I am secular, my younger sister Esther is religious; and it is at moments like these that her spirit sheds light.

May the God in whom my sister Esther believes bless you for joining in this journey. May the God in whom my sister Esther believes preserve and watch over you.

To your hearts and minds, I commend our story.

## Chapter One

# Miriam, ages 0-11 1/2

I was born at Mount Sinai Hospital in Toronto on February 26, 1948 at approximately 11:45 a.m. I weighed seven pounds two ounces. Although it was to fall out three days later, I came into the world with long white flowing hair—hair at least twice the length of my body. Nu? I am sure that there's a perfectly reasonable biological explanation for this oddity, yes? And it may well be related to the fact that I was dying in utero and only barely made it out intact. To this day, nonetheless, the more religious members of my family talk of this birth in hushed tones.

The mythology around my birth began with my mother, the atheist, who always departed from her customary level-headedness and waxed curiously prophetic when it came to this topic. You see, Jews are atheists the way no other group is atheist. Believers or not, we are part of a culture that includes specific holy days, specific stories, practices, memories; and our lives revolve around them. Not that this feature of Judaism adequately explains eema's undying attachment to this particular story.

"Miriam, my sheyneh meydeleh," she would say to me, her face lighting up, her eyes riveted to mine, "did I ever tell you about the hair you were born with? Did I tell you how long it was?"

"How long was it?" I would ask, aware that this question constituted my role in the retelling, and feeling both excited and embarrassed now that the tale had begun anew.

"Two. No, three. No, four times the length of your body. Oy, had it been a long pregnancy! Two weeks overdue I was if I was a day, yes? And every bone—nay, every sinew in my body ached. Finally, I go into labour. And the labour goes on and on. Like you couldn't have put in an appearance sooner?"

At this point, if we were close enough to manage it, she would lean forward and give a little pinch to my cheeks; then she would shift further back in her seat, chuckle at the joke she'd just made, then give me a sad sort of smile.

"Sweetie, not that any of us are blaming you," she would resume, her voice going softer, "but it was awful. We didn't think that you were ever going to come out, but then it finally happens, yes? I delivered. And I say to the nurse tending me, 'Please, bring me my baby,' and she brings you to me, wrapped in this cloth. And aside from a new tokhes to tend to, what do I see?"

Eema was an accomplished storyteller. And so, of course, she was well aware that this was the moment for the pregnant pause. At this point, without fail, she would look away, pull out a cigarette ever so slowly, light it, and take one puff, then another, then another, inhaling long and hard. Generally, she would also take this as a good time to rub her sore shoulder. You found yourself at the edge of your seat wondering what was going to happen next even though you'd heard the story a hundred times before. You would even start suspecting that she had forgotten about the story, though everyone knew that eema forgot nothing. After holding the pause to the point of agony, she would finally look you straight in the eyes and resume, "I see this tiny pink creature with an old face and with wrinkled skin, and most curiously of all, with this long flowing white hair that gave it a distinct other worldly aura. Not a regular infant. More like an ancient holy being come from out of the Old Testament to set us all right. And I think I must be going meshugah from the drugs, yes? So I give my head a good shake, and I look again. But there she is just as before—wrinkled old skin, long white hair. And suddenly, without knowing that I have anything to say, I hear myself announcing, 'It is Miriam—Miriam, the Prophet—about to deliver us to the Promised Land.'"

I don't know what the nurse thought of this announcement, for my mother's story always stopped here as if this were the natural ending—its meaning self-evident. Now that *was* typical of my mother—stopping at such a moment. Not that she always did this, but with certain stories....

There's not a lot more to be said about the day of my birth, nor the days that followed it. I was a baby with long hair. Nu? My hair fell out and I became a bald baby—not noticeably different from all the other hairless infants in the hospital. To the best of my knowledge, I delivered no one to the Promised Land. I simply put in my mandatory stay at Mount Sinai, then was delivered to my parents' house, where I proceeded to live with eema, abba, and my two sisters. Well, initially, there was only one sister—Sondra, yes? Esther came two years seven months later, but I have no memory of the time before Esther was born.

The family house where we were to live, make Pesach, and die was in this Slavic Jewish area on Lippincott St. about a block and a half from a carnivalesque thrift shop called "Honest Ed's." We had a postage stamp size front yard, with the dandelions narrowly beating out the grass. The building itself was a two story red brick Edwardian, attached on the left side only. Jutting out from the front of the house was a small wooden veranda with a weathered brown couch and two rocking chairs with mahogany trim and petit point back—eema's handiwork.

On a warm day, you would often find my parents sitting on the chairs, abba on the right, eema on the left. Abba might be depressed, in which case there would be an eerie silence, and abba would soon retire to the couch. Or he might be fuming, which meant that both of the chairs would be still; the only words that could be heard were abba's and the tension would be so thick that the world would appear to be holding its breath. On the other hand, if it was a relatively good day, chances are that the chairs would be lunging in fits and starts; and eema and abba would be holding forth on some political issue or other in such an animated way that well nigh half the neighbourhood would end up knowing where each of them stood.

"Is the Rosenburgs vat are the most important figures in America today," abba would proclaim, his hands waving, his 'w' turned into a magnificent 'v.'

"The persecution of Ethel and Julius is a symbol of the fragility of advanced capitalism," returns eema, projecting her voice as if addressing a huge audience. "Is so vulnerable, they must find traitors to unite against, yes? And who are the traitors? Who else?"

And so they would continue. In the early years before they utterly abandoned the idea of "fitting in," about half an hour into one of these exchanges, a look of caution would enter into one their faces—more often than not abba's. It was as if it were just dawning on him that they could be overheard, that they were not fitting in, and a quick change of topics would ensue.

"You like Perry Como?" abba once asked at just such a juncture, giving eema a knowing look.

"Como I like, but Crosby or Sinatra—just so-so," eema returns, seemingly casually.

From our veranda, you entered onto a central hallway leading to the downstairs rooms—first the living room, then the dining room, then the kitchen. The downstairs hallway and all of the rooms on the first floor were lined with newspaper clippings and posters of different shapes and sizes, arranged in helter-skelter fashion, some high up, some low down, some centred, some off to the side, some pinned to bulletin boards, most attached to otherwise bare walls by strips of brown masking tape. "The Rosenburgs Guilty" was the headline in one paper. "McCarthy Going for a Clean Sweep" was another. The posters were of men on strike, children starving throughout the world, women in bread lines.

Stairs led down from the kitchen to an unfinished basement, which held a workbench, a faded bridge table, and random sticks of furniture—"a good place for the children to play," eema dubbed it, and so we did. Hiding-o-seek, which was Sondra's and my favourite, and dolls, which only Esther really enjoyed. A plywood staircase with an oak stain joined the first and the second floor. The bedrooms, study, and washroom were upstairs.

The washroom was a tiny oblong space, with a big brass latch on it, so you could lock it from the inside. Unfortunately for us, the door was often latched. Nu? Abba would take in the newspaper and dammed if he wouldn't be in there for hours. "You are coming out before the Moshiah gets here? Or you are staying in to read about it in the paper?" eema would call in to him when it got to the point where three of us were lined up for the washroom.

The biggest of the bedrooms was my parents'. Directly upstairs from the living room, it had a bay window just like the one in the living room, but the window was boarded up. Sondra's room was windowless. In Esther's and my room, there was a tiny window facing north.

The house was always immaculate, with abba and eema scrubbing it assiduously to ensure that no speck of dirt could be found. Every week, they would fill the large green bucket with soapy water, grab some rags from the cupboard under the kitchen sink, go to the bottom of the staircase, get down on their knees, and wash the stairs inch by inch. Once they reached the top, they would start at the bottom again and work their way up, cleaning the knobby banister and the railing, carefully inserting the cloth into the wedges at the bottom of the posts. Every few days, they would polish the big rectangular oak-rimmed mirror on the south wall in the living room—"The Imitation Honest Ed's Special" abba called it. And every second day, they would sweep under the fridge, searching for any wayward particles of food that may have slipped underneath—eema pushing the broom, and abba lowering himself to the floor and peering under to ensure that nothing remained. "We are not animals," abba would say. "We can be clean now, yes?" eema would agree. And woe betide the child that that had forgotten to scrape and ran through the halls with muddy shoes.

Most of the walls were off-white, something eema said was easiest to live with in the long run. And the house was dark, so dark that in the evening, you worried about tripping on the way to the washroom, and even during the day you sometimes had trouble making out what people were trying to show you. One of the problems was that the green blinds were almost always down. Why? Because of abba. Always abba. Abba was deeply affected by the degree of the theft among prisoners inside the lager and the threat to existence which it posed. Of course, he knew that this was not Auschwitz. Not even close. Nonetheless, he would periodically walk through the house, poke his head into every room, and cast his eyes about slowly to see if anything was missing. Invariably, before continuing on his rounds, he would check the blinds. Let some misbeguided blind be up high enough to let in even a sliver of daylight, and he would instantly lower it, proclaiming, "Is better this vay. You never know who is trying to find out what is stewing in her neighbour's pot. Or who is thinking of stealing. Ganefs everywhere." However, the principal reason for the darkness was that there was seldom more than one light left on in the entire house—a situation arising from abba's ongoing frustration over the electricity bills. After every bill arrived, he would wave it in the air, pace up and down the kitchen, point to the section where the incriminating evidence could be found, and exclaim, "Who has such bills? Who is leaving for us the lights on?" Step out of a room for a second and neglect to flick off the switch, and even if you had not seen him for hours, even if you were absolutely confident that he was upstairs absorbed in the *Labour News International*, there he would be, bare feet and boxer shorts, yelling at you in his thick Yiddish accent, "Alvays, you are leaving on the light bulbs. Ay yay yay! You think it's a millionaire what I am? You think what I am made of gold? Here, feel," he would add, extending his vein-lined arm toward you, and not withdrawing until someone had touched it. "Is flesh. Is a vorking man's flesh. Yes? Is not gold."

While I was a brave child in some respects, I tended to be frightened once I left the cerebral realm—the realm that gave me solidity and control—and entered any other arena. The dark house was one such arena.

It was something I could not control mentally and so it scared me, yes? Additionally, the sheer reality of other people set me trembling. Combine people and darkness—two features of human existence that were inextricably linked in my mind—and I could become paralyzed with fear. I did not know who lurked in the dark shadows of our rooms and what they might do to us intentionally or otherwise. What if the people whom my abba feared were already in the house?, I would ask myself. How about the people about whom abba and eema whispered at night? And how about visitors? What if one of them had never really left at all but was there in waiting, biding his time? Had I not been a child of survivors, had abba been less furious, had eema and abba been less tormented, I might still have been beset by existential sensitivity, but my guess is that it would have been less extreme; and it most certainly would not have taken the forms that it did. Yes, and maybe, just maybe, there might have been opportunities for communication. As it was, in early childhood, I was alone in the dark, staring at disturbing scenes over which I had no sense of agency.

In the evening, I would look up from my cot and gaze at the walls for hours, transfixed by the images created by the shadows and cracks. I would see Eliahou Hanovi, the prophet Elijah, whom I had to admit through the front door every Pesach so that he could drink wine from the silver chalice set for him. There he would be, raging like abba, a mad drunken angel let loose in my room. I would turn my head to the side and my eye would catch a different constellation of cracks, and before I knew it, the cracks would disappear and another image would take shape. Thrashing about on a floor, his head writhing in agony, is this frail wisp of a man. Three muscular men in large black boots are kicking him. They start at the forehead and work their way down to the neck. Then they begin kicking a lower part of the torso that I can't quite make out. Blood is gushing from the wounds. By the time they get to the lower part, he has stopped thrashing, and he is lying there still as death.

If I was forced to go to the washroom in the middle of the night, I would be particularly frightened, for that meant a whole new set of shadows and cracks. Ah yes. And it meant passing by the Uncle Nathaniel in the dark.

The Uncle Nathaniel. Nu? That was a special feature in the Himmelfarb household. While mostly our walls were decorated with yellowing articles and faded posters, there was one colossal exception.

As long as I can remember, this huge picture of my Uncle Nathaniel awaited me at the top of the stairs. It was a waist-up painting, a self-portrait, set in a gilded frame.

Uncle Nathaniel was a muscular man in his early thirties. He had high cheek bones, hazelnut eyes, black wavy hair, and a thick curly beard. He wore a black yarmulke. At first sight, he appeared friendly enough, for he was smiling right at you. But if you looked at the picture carefully, you could detect a flaring of the nostrils, a hint of danger. At the bottom of the picture the danger was confirmed. He was holding onto something that could only be the beginning of a rifle barrel. I knew. I had seen rifles on television.

I always hated walking past the Uncle Nathaniel when I was alone. I figured that there was a chance of distracting him if there was more than one of us, but when it was just me, he was right on me, unwavering in his concentration. But what did he want? What was he up to in our house? And why did abba insist on having him here when I kept saying how scared I was?

"Abba," I said to my father one day, "I'm scared of the Uncle Nathaniel. Why can't we take him down?"

"Is family. Is important," abba answered curtly.

"But abba," I tried again.

"Not another vord about this. You hear me? Not another vord. You vant we should be a family what does not honour its relatives?"

But only Nathaniel was on our walls. Why him when no other family member was there?

*A young girl of five makes her way past a painting of a large bearded man with a rifle. As she steps, she keeps an eye on the painting and sees that the man's eyes are following her. She shakes her head, then looks squarely in front of her and continues walking. When she is about a yard away, the bearded man juts his head forward out of the painting, raises his arms, places the rifle at shoulder level in front of him, points it in the direction of the little girl, and takes aim.*

Question: If a person is flooding while she is telling a story about the past, how does she keep these current images from entering into her telling when the "current images" come from that past?

Answer: Uncertain.

I remember something else about the house as well. Whispers. It was like a crackling of leaves, a rustling sound that swept through the house almost all night long. If you listened to the rustling carefully enough, you could detect voices—my mother's voice, my father's voice. In a hushed tone, they were talking about a place. It was called "Auschwitz."

"Is Auschvitz, you are thinking of, Rachael, yah?" my father asked my mother one night in my eighth year.

"Yes, Auschwitz," came eema's voice.

"The mud? And the filth?"

"Yes, and the smell of excrement and rotting flesh mixed with the smell of bodies burning. Ach! Like an odor from Hell. You remember, Daniel?"

"Is an odor a human being can forget? Is never I'll forget."

"Where were you just now, Daniel?"

"Is boots and shoes, I vas seeing, Rachael. A dream I vas hafing. That same dream. This SS thug is making mit the boots, kicking my best friend Moshe in the head, in the neck, in the privates. Is terrible. Everywhere is he kicking. And in the next scene, is dead Moshe is. Is sprawled out on the floor, his head kicked in and bleeding. And who is creeping up but Lionel, our mutual buddy what cleaned the latrines? You remember how Lionel took messages between you and me?"

"Of course."

"And is not even looking at Moshe's face, is not reciting the Mourner's Kaddish or nothing. Is just the shoes, he is concentrating on. An exceptional pair with no rips, they are, what are both the same size and vill not need rags to make them fit. And quick as anything, he is taking the shoes. And how can you blame him? If he vaited a second longer, is someone else what vould get the shoes."

"You think that's what happened with Moshe?"

"I am thinking maybe. With mayn own eyes, I found him like that. You were dreaming too, Rachaele?"

"Uh huh," came my mother's voice.

"You were dreaming of Auschwitz. I could tell."

"I was babbling in my sleep again, yes?"

"A bisel, maybe, Rachaele."

"What was I saying?"

"Epes. Like last night. About the selections. This time, is not much you said. 'Left, right. Death, life.' Like that. Yah, and 'ashes.'"

"Daniel, their ashes—I can actually feel it on my body. Ach! Even today. It's guilt, I think. It's like they are reminding us that this happened—this unspeakable horror happened; and we aren't doing anything about it. Daniel, there are Volkswagens in every street in this metropolis—Hitler's car, no less. And look at us. We do nothing."

"Why do you talk such nonsense, Rachael? Is nothing to be done. Is no one what vants to hear about it. Not even Jews."

"Daniel, is good that I am teaching English. It is something people are comfortable hearing about. Is good that you are involved in the CCF.* It is good that we fit in. That the children fit in, yes? But what about the six million? Why after all did we live after they died if not to bear witness?"

"Is nonsense, I tell you. Is an unrealistic fantasy, one which I share, one which we all share, but except for a few choice writers what the vorld has turned into darlings and doesn't really hear anyway, is a fantasy. Think of it like this: Telling ourselves that we vould bear witness was a strategy, a vay of coping, yes? And it served its purpose."

"It was more than a strategy. You know that, Daniel."

"Maybe, but principally, it vas a strategy. It was trouble staying alive we were hafing, yah? And so vat did we do? We told ourselves that we must live to bear witness. And right away, we are more alert. Is cleaner we are keeping ourselves, despite the difficulty. Is vashing our clothes even when the vater what we had to vork with is fetid and brown. Is picking lice out of our rags. Is vatching for chances of promotion. And is surviving we are. The strategy paid off. Gut. But is a different reality what is confronting us now. Is absolutely nothing we can do now except do our labour work what vill make this vorld a better place, yes? Anyway, is late. Some sleep we should make. Gai schlufen."

"Good night, Daniel."

"Rachael, shut for me the lights. And we vill sleep. If you make with the nightmare again, you vill vake me, yah?"

The whispers came night after night. And sometimes, there were screams—my father yelling, "the Gestapo," my mother crying out, "the ashes." I could not always make out what they were saying much less what the words meant, but I always had a sense.

I would listen, stretched out on my mattress. And strange pictures would flash through my head—pictures of attacks, pictures of my parents in bed with their shoes on, pictures of ashes containing traces

---

*CCF was the predecessor of the NDP, which is the main socialist party in Canada.

of human skin falling from the sky.

How large my parents loomed in those early years! To me, they were like the gods in that thick green book eema used to read to us from—*Bullfinch's Mythology.* Their huge faces would look down from on high and frown or smile. And from out of nowhere would come decisions that struck me at the time as being of earth-shattering significance—maybe a decision that confined me to my room without food for a day, maybe a decision that brought me that special colouring book that I had longed for and lost hope of getting. I liked the stories in Bullfinch, incidentally. It made me feel just a bit less puny knowing that even grownups had to deal with giants.

By the time I was four, eema was a part-time English lecturer at University of Toronto—her specialty, Shakespeare. This was the '50s so, at this juncture, of course, as a part-timer and a woman, the only Shakespeare she got to teach was whatever play was included in the Introduction to Literature course. Now I didn't know who Shakespeare was or what a lecturer was, but I did pick up that she was something like a rabbi and that special times were set aside for people to learn from her. I knew as much because once when I asked abba where eema was, he pulled his silver watch out of his pocket, stared at it, and answered, "Is the time she meets with the students. Is learning—like with the rabbi." I also knew that she was very skilled in speaking English because abba would often ask her which word to use. I discovered later that she had spoken fluent English before the war, and indeed, she had studied Shakespeare, although it wasn't until she came to Canada that she made English her primary field. She'd been a Heideggerian, intent on writing a dissertation at the University of Freiburg on the structure of care in Heidegger's *Being and Time.* Of course, none of this was clear to me at the time. I knew nothing about English literature, or European philosophy, or dissertations, though I did know the word "Heidegger." That is, I knew that Heidegger was one of the bad words that made eema uneasy.

I remember one day, when I was five-and-a-half. Eema and I were in the living room. Eema was standing in front of the black brick-and-board bookcase opposite the mirror, staring at some books on the top shelf. Her eyes traveled from one book to another, and then back again. Then that bad name popped up again. "Heidegger," she exclaimed, "such a mistake! Vey iz mir! How could a human being that asks such questions make such a mistake!"

I had known the word "mistake" for a long time. It generally came up when I had gotten in trouble. "Eema," I asked guardedly, "I do something wrong?"

She turned to me, smiled, walked over, knelt down next to me, and stroked my hair gently. "No, meydeleh, not to worry," she responded. "Is not you. Is just a little problem I'm having with that Heidegger of mine."

"What's a Heidgger?"

"Hei-deg-ger," she said, pronouncing each syllable separately.

"Hei-deg-ger," I imitated. "What's a Hei-deg-ger?"

"Not a 'what,' meydeleh—a 'who.'"

"Who's Heidegger?" I tried again.

"Heidegger is an important man called a 'philosopher.'"

"Phil-Lo-So-Pher," I said slowly.

"Punct. And a philosopher is someone who asks questions about what is real and unreal, what is true and untrue, what is good and bad. The kind of questions that you ask, Miriam, yes? Heidegger the Philosopher wrote these books here," she added, pointing to a number of books on the shelf, most of them large and fat.

"Am I a philosopher, eema?"

Eema considered for a few seconds. Her eyes went upward then back down again. Then she sat down on the couch, reached across the table, and picked up a little yellow dress that she had been making—for the new baby down the street, she told me. And taking a spool of black thread from the pocket of her blouse, she began sewing.

"Is a very interesting question you ask, Miriam," she mused. "Some people would say no, you are not a philosopher because philosophers write books, and you have not written any books as yet. But I disagree. I think that the issue of writing is not so important as people think. No. Is *what* a person asks, *how* a person asks, how a person *answers*. I see how you search. And I would say, you are a philosopher, yes."

"Good," I answered, nodding my head in agreement. Then realizing the implication, my eyes welled up with tears; and I asked, "Will I make you unhappy, eema?"

"No, no," eema reassured me. "Is a different person you are. Not like Heidegger."

I felt better now. Eema put down the sewing, stirred the cup of tea just in front of her, and took a gulp. "Miriam, you'd like some juice?"

"No thanks."

"You have taken your cod liver oil today?"

"Not yet, eema."

"Is good that you and Sondra should remember to take your cod liver oil first thing every morning. You forget and you might get sick, no? And complications might set in. And we might end up having to rush you to emergency, kinehora."

I knew that word "complications." It's something abba and eema always worried about. I went to the kitchen, took the supplement, then went out and played hiding-o-seek with Sondra and her friends. When I returned to the living room hours later, I found eema still there, staring at the books. I had totally forgotten about her and was somewhat shaken by the realization that she had been there the entire time. She raised her head, saw me looking at her, and smiled. "Is okay," she said.

"They bad books, eema?"

"The Heidegger books?"

"Yes."

"No," she assured me, "they're good books. Very good books."

"Please don't read these books. I'll write others for my eema to read. These must be bad books because they make you unhappy. Eema, I don't want you to be unhappy."

Eema smiled at me. "Miriam," she responded tenderly, "thank you so much for your offer. But you know, meydeleh, you have nothing to worry about. I am feeling good, yes? Anyway, it's Shakespeare I read now. I've not read Heidegger in a long time and I don't intend to read him again. But tell me," she went on, arching her eyebrow, "what makes you think that only bad books make a person unhappy? My sheyneh punem, cannot good books make you unhappy? A good book with a sad ending, say? You remember how you cried when we read the section about the death of King Arthur in Bullfinch's mythology? And you think the Bullfinch book is good, yes?"

I nodded.

"Punct," she said. "And could not good books make you unhappy for other reasons? Or people who write good books but who are not nearly as good as their books would lead you to expect?"

Nu? There it was. One of eema's "thinking questions." That's what I loved most about eema. Even when I was a preschooler, she kept asking questions that made me think. She never treated me like other grown-ups did. She treated me like someone who thought a great deal and whose thinking mattered.

I left the room satisfied with my understanding of the Heidegger situation: It was good to be a philosopher. Heidegger was a philosopher. Eema likes Heidegger's books. But Heidegger has done something that has disappointed my eema deeply. I determined that I would not disappoint her.

In those days, I did not so much see eema as hear eema. Eema's gentle laughter, her carefully constructed explanations, the breathless sound of her sobs. But there were some visual features that stayed with me as well. The intense brown eyes that forever held my look, the nose that jutted out at me, commanding respect. Yes, and the conditions.

Eema had what she called "conditions." I learned later that some of these conditions dated back to Ravensbrück—the women's camp in Germany where she was first imprisoned. It was at Ravensbrück, for example, that her shoulder was injured, though she didn't say how. Other conditions such as the arthritis in her legs and hands had developed at Auschwitz. The marks likewise originated in Auschwitz.

Marks? Eema had marks on one of her arms. So did abba, though neither of them talked about it. I knew from very early on that these marks were numbers because they looked similar to the marks that abba scribbled on the scraps of paper whenever he said, "Oy, time to add up the numbers." At first, I barely noticed them. I can't remember exactly when they registered on my consciousness, but I do recall thinking of them as perfectly normal. I accepted them the way a child accepts everything. I just figured that arm numbers was something grownups had. And certainly many of my parents' friends had arm numbers. When I was five, however, I started to see more and more grownups without arm numbers. I noticed something else too. I noticed where people's eyes went.

It was a grueling summer day, and eema and I were at Loblaws, shopping cart in hand. Eema was wearing a short-sleeved white blouse—something she seldom did, but it was such a scorcher, what else was there to do? We had just picked up four extra large boxes of Tide. Eema was wanting us to get a move on, because she was already late for an appointment, but she couldn't push the shopping cart because a lanky teenaged boy was blocking her. I wondered why he wasn't getting out of the way. What could he be thinking of? Didn't he know that teenaged boys were supposed to get out of the way of grown-up women? I was a little girl and even I knew that. Then I realized that he was unaware that he was blocking our way because he wasn't seeing a woman pushing a shopping cart. He was seeing something else, yes? I followed the direction of his gaze carefully in the hope of finding out what. There could be no doubt about it. He was staring at eema's number. And there was a strange look in his eyes.

It was particularly hot that summer and eema went short-sleeved a number of times. And whenever she did, if we were out, invariably someone would behave roughly as this boy did. Now as it happened, it was right around this time that I first learnt to read numbers. For a reason that was not at all clear to me, though, I couldn't read *that* number. Let my eyes so much as drift to eema's upper arm, and inexplicably, my vision started to blur.

On the way home from Loblaws that day, I imagined going to the garage, pulling out the plywood that abba had stored there, and building a gigantic house. Eema, and abba, and all the other people with arm numbers throughout the universe would come live in it. And Sondra and I would guard the door, barring entrance to anyone likely to gawk at the numbers. And if a particularly uppity teenager turned up and looked like he was about to overpower us, we would sic abba on him.

Abba—the other significant adult in my life? Abba was a tradesman with a tailor shop in Kensington. "Daniel's Needle," it was called. He was very proud of his skill. "You vant I should make for you a coat?" he used to say, his eyes bulging ever so slightly. "I vill make for you a coat what vill make you the envy of people everywhere."

Abba was often away in the evenings. Next morning, when you asked him where he had been, he would generally straighten his back, puff out his chest, assume a demeanor of high seriousness, and say, "Where's an avid socialist to be? I was at a CCF meeting, attending to the plight of the vorking man." I imagined him in a huge room with thousands of other tailors, scribbling notes and talking about how to manage the affairs of the world.

Abba was tall, clean shaven, and had jet black naturally wavy hair. When he was fully clothed, you would generally find a cloth measuring tape dangling from his neck. His most distinctive personal feature was his large brown bulging eyes. They bulged even when he was ostensibly relaxed, but they bulged far more when he got angry. Take a monster from a horror flick and imagine him with a goiter condition, and you're beginning to get the picture. Whenever anything annoyed abba, even if only slightly, he would open those eyes wide and stare in such a way that it looked as if they were about to take leave of the sockets and fly right at you. You never knew who would be in more jeopardy from such an untimely occurrence—him or you. Nor did you care to find out.

Eema always told us that abba had once been fat, but he had lost weight because of his heart condition. You had to be careful of that heart. If he got too upset, too angry, it could mean another attack. It could also mean being yelled at, being sent to bed without supper, or being made to feel stupid.

Early on, I tended to think of abba as having two dispositions only—depression and fury. The depression was far less common, but it was terrible when it set in. He would lie in his bed for days, not coming out, not talking to anyone. Or he would mope about the house, looking defeated and muttering to himself, "Is no use. Is no point." Once in every long while, it would get so bad that I would actually long for the rage.

Then there was the rage. He would stride through the halls seemingly bigger than the house itself, yelling, threatening. Strange. Even when he didn't speak the word, you could feel Auschwitz somehow implicated in that threat.

Out of nowhere, suddenly, the door of my room would fling open, and there he would be, looking about menacingly and hollering, "Just look how messy is your room! Is an ungrateful child you are. You know what eema and I would haf given to haf such a room? And what if someone should see the mess? You haf any idea what trouble we would be in? You haf exactly ten minutes to clean it up. Is not spick-and-span in ten minutes, is such a thrashing I vill gif you, is to the hospital they vill haf to take you." Then he would pull out his pocket watch, place it inches from his eyes, and begin timing.

I would always startle and quickly begin putting everything away, praying that I would finish in the allotted time, all the while, haunted by this image of myself on a stretcher. Hours later, I would try to figure out what had happened. What's he afraid of?, I would ask myself. Is he making this up just to be mean or are we really in danger if a toy is out of place? And why can't he at least try not to be angry?

Of course, I was well aware that abba was forever struggling to control his anger. I also knew that whenever Kraft Showcase was on TV, I could count on a kind of time-out. And I took full advantage of it. I would snuggle up close to him, breathe in the reassuring scent of Old Spice, and get answers for every single question that popped into my head.

"I'm going to teach that nigger a thing or two," snarls a big hulk of a man on the Kraft Showcase.

"What's a 'nigger?'" I ask abba.

"Good question," he answers amiably, his eyes remaining glued to the set. "Is a bad vord for 'Negro.' Is a bad vord what white people use what are mean to Negroes. People are mean to Negroes just like they're mean to Jews. And Jews and Negroes haf to stick together. Remember that."

"Abba, why do people use bad words?"

"Is ignorance."

"Why is the TV world black and white?"

"Is the technology."

"Abba, what's technology?"

"Is like the sewing machine at my shop. Is the machinery vat makes things happen."

I adored abba. I despised abba. I loved his unique combination of care for the world and practicality, the way he instrumentalized everything, whether rightly or wrongly. I hated the anger. And even more than the anger, I hated the physicality—the ongoing intrusion into my space.

Nu? Somehow, abba's body was always intruding itself. In the morning, late at night, and on weekends, abba would hang about the house wearing nothing but his boxer shorts. As he talked, he would pick at the skin on his chest, repetitively pinching his flesh between his thumb and middle finger. When he slept, which was usually only a few hours a night, he would snore so loud that the brass mortar and pestle beside the coffee table in the living room would rattle. Whenever he asked you to see that his arm was not gold, he would put his arm so close that you could feel the hair on it. And he would forever flush the toilet too early; and so when you approached the bowl, a yellow fluid would be sitting there, announcing that Mr. Daniel Himmelfarb had just paid a visit.

I asked eema one day why abba had to take up so much room. Eema looked at me intently, then shrugged her shoulders and said, "Men take up room, Miriam. More than their share. It's always been. I'm hoping maybe your generation can do something about it. Meydeleh, you will push them away if they overstep, yes?"

Eema and I were in the kitchen, sitting at the table at that moment.

I had been colouring, while eema sewed. I picked up the red crayon and started a new picture. I filled a whole foolscap sheet with women. Tall women, short women, fat women, thin women, one woman after another. Not a trace of a man anywhere.

"But abba, you know, abba is special, very special," eema continued.

I pressed the crayon hard against the paper, almost breaking it. I drew another woman; I gave her a big round body, a giant head, and teeth with fangs like a cat.

"Not that abba doesn't take up more than his share of space," she went on. "Of course, he does. But there are reasons. Not altogether good reasons, but reasons."

I looked up from my drawing. I could tell from the pained expression on eema's face that she was thinking of that place again. I regretted thinking about myself when she suffered so and immediately set about providing the necessary distraction. "Eema, where are we going this weekend?" I asked.

Nu? Eema was right, of course. I knew well enough that abba was special. I remember thinking that it would be better if he weren't. Then I could have just hated him. And of course, there were moments that I did just that, but just as soon as I would settle into hating him, he would get depressed, and I would want to protect him; or he would act like a perfect mentsh and then there was nothing to be done but adore him.

It was recess at Champlaine Elementary, yes? Children of different shapes and sizes were in constant animation—running, jumping, going up, coming down, pushing, nudging, laughing, crying, cheering. A number were on the green and yellow teeter-totters, some going at a easy pace and cooperating with their partners, some jumping off and letting their partner slam to the ground. On the slide next to the teeter-totters, a large boy who had slid down too early had come crashing into a smaller boy. Next to the slide, a few particularly adventurous youth were testing their skills on the monkey bars. In random groupings throughout the yard, some girls were skipping rope, carefully assessing the situation so that they would jump in at the right moment. At the far edge of the yard, a number of boys and girls were striking their own balance between adventure and contemplation by the way they handled the swings. Jane Johnson with a few other children were standing in a circle just in front of the swings—I couldn't tell why. As usual, I was on the very farthest swing from the red brick school-house.

"Miriam, wanna join us?" I heard Jane call out. Jane was one the leaders in my class; she was medium height, with blue eyes, a pageboy cut, and a perky manner, and I liked her. So I nodded, jumped down, and ran straight over to her even though I didn't know any of the others and even though they were all older pupils. Fourth graders, I figured.

"Whose gonna be it?" asked the tallest girl.

"Only one way to decide," piped up this tall boy in a plaid shirt.

"You stand beside me," Jane urged, pulling me in next to her.

The job of determining 'it' began immediately. While everyone chanted, the tall boy whirled about, pointing to each child in turn—first to Jane, then to me, then to the shorter boy, then to the shorter girl, then to himself. And then, he'd start all over again.

The chant was one I'd never heard before:

"Eenie meanie, miny mo,

Catch a nigger by the toe.

If he hollers, let him go.

Eenie, meanie, miney mo."

I was enjoying myself during the "eenie meanie" bit. I was part of a group. I could feel an energy surge through my body, could feel my eyes and ears coming alive. Then all of a sudden, the group was broken. A single word stuck in my ear—jarring. And abba's voice was playing like a tape recorder in my brain, "Is a bad vord for Negro." The tall boy had gotten to "mo" by the time I recollected everything abba had said. "You're it!" the boy exclaimed, grinning and pointing directly at me. "Go hide."

Eema and abba always said that it was important to take a stand. I wanted to, yes? I also wanted to "go along" and cringed at the idea of making a fuss. I saw myself "going along." I saw myself agreeing to be "it" and hiding in the rusty old incinerator at the other side of the schoolyard. Then I saw myself in a courtroom. The benches are filled with Jews and Blacks watching a case, all of them murmuring under their breath, all of them shaking their heads in dismay. My parents are the judges. Their skin is brown. They are sitting side by side behind a tall mahogany desk, each holding a wooden hammer, and each wearing a black robe and a white wig. Her voice distant, her eyes glassy, eema instructs me to rise. I get to my feet. Abba pounds the wooden hammer with such force that it smashes the desk into smithereens. "Is guilty," he bellows.

I looked around. Still in the schoolyard. It was not too late.

"No," I answered, "I won't do it. I won't be it."

"Don't be a spoil sport," scolded Jane. "You're it and you have to go hide."

"Don't want to."

"You gotta."

"This is a free country; and I don't gotta do nothing."

"Yes, you do."

"No, I don't."

"What's wrong with you anyway?" Jane asked, her face wrinkled in distaste.

"Don't like the word 'nigger,'" I blurted out. "It's a bad word. And Jews and Negroes have to stick together."

Jane looked confused. The tall boy made the crazy sign with this finger. Had I gotten something wrong?

The next day was Friday, and everything was just fine. Jane even asked to borrow my pencil; and during recess, we played hopscotch together as if nothing had happened.

Then came Monday. Again, nothing extraordinary occurred as I arrived at school. Jane greeted me, and we talked about our weekend, as usual. Miss Nerum, our teacher, called the class to order and taught us reading. When we finished reading and turned to spelling, the big hand on the red clock on the wall was at the twelve. We worked on some difficult two-syllable words. "Across" was one, because of that extra "c" that didn't belong but always kept creeping in. Then we examined some three-syllable words; I can't remember which. Then the big hand reached the six; and it was recess time.

I walked out, headed for my favourite swing, and hopped on. I closed my eyes, not wanting to see anyone and enjoying the sightless climbing. When I opened them again, I spotted some kids in front and to my left, pointing at me. I could tell that they were talking about me, yes? I pumped higher and higher, hoping that I might pump right onto another continent, which I didn't, or that they would go away, which they didn't. Eventually, recess draws to an end. Out comes Miss Nerum with the big brass bell. Ding dong. Ding dong. She rings it again and again, calling all the children back into school. Then she turns around and starts walking toward the front of the school, all the while ringing. "Thank God. Saved by the bell," I whisper to myself, starting to calm down and pleased at the half joke I was making. I stop the swing, hop off, and brush off my tunic.

27

As I head toward the school, the trouble begins. Jane Johnson places herself in my path. The tall boy joins her, stretches out his arms, and blocks my way. Then most of the kids from the other day and four or five extra form a circle around me and join hands. "Ding, dong; ding, dong," the bell keeps ringing. As the bell continues, they circle to the left, chanting in unison:

"Eenie meanie, miny mo,
Catch a Jewess by the toe.
If she hollers, let her go.
Eenie, meanie, miney mo."

All I can see are hands joined together, and everything going about in a whirl, while I get dizzier and dizzier. I don't really know what the verse means, where I am, or why my ears are ringing, but I know that I'm in trouble. Then the strangest thing happened. Similar things have happened since so it no longer seems odd to me, but this was the first time.

I am higher than my body. I am looking down, as if from the top of the telephone pole, calmly surveying the scene below. I can see Miss Nerum rounding the corner, yes? I can see the kids surrounding me with joined hands. I see my body struggling to stay standing. Then I see it running at one of the sets of joined hands—Jane's and the tall boy's. It is breaking through. It is running straight past the teacher, not seeming to notice that Miss Nerum is calling out, "Miriam." It is racing past Honest Ed's. It is taking the turn at Lippincott and Bloor without slowing down. It is approaching the house, opening the door, running into the washroom, and turning the latch.

Next thing I know, I am lying down. And it is dark. Abba is sitting on the chair next to my bed.

"You are feeling better now, Miriam?" he asked gently, reaching over and stroking my hair with his hand.

"Yeah, abba," I answered. "Something happened at school. Am I in trouble?"

"Sha, sha now. Is no trouble you are in. I talked to Miss Nerum. And is all straightened out. Is a difficult situation what you handled as best you knew how. You, eema, and me, we vill talk later. Right now, is good what you sleep."

"Thank you, abba."

"You vant I should sit here tonight while you sleep? Is not good what you should be alone right now." And he did. Every time I opened my eyes, there he was, sitting next to me, protecting me. The cracks and the shadows didn't have a chance that night.

The next day, I was allowed to stay home. For the most part, I was fine, though strangely, the ringing of the telephone was starting to bother me. "Miriam, something wrong?" Esther asked.

"Don't worry about it, Esther," I answered.

I could never get enough of Esther. Esther was the baby of the family— "the shrimp," Sondra called her. She was small and plump, and she had dark brown hair that smelled like lilacs whenever eema washed it. This warmth would course through me whenever her freckled face would peer up at me and she would lisp the name "Miriam." And how protective I felt whenever she got confused or hurt! Like the time that she scraped her knee tripping on the sidewalk and I rushed her to the washroom, washed off the blood, applied iodine, then stayed with her for hours, telling her tales about the knights of the round table. "Was their table bigger than our dining room table, Miriam?" she asked, her green eyes glistening.

"A hundred times bigger," I answered, blowing on the knee to make it feel better. She was my little sister, no?

By the time I was eight I was keenly aware that Esther's role wasn't an easy one. Somehow, she was always discounted. And she was frequently confused because conversations in the Himmelfarb household were distinctly geared toward an older mind. I kept seeing Esther trying to follow, then giving up and fretting, then doing whatever she could to please, often to little avail. And I kept discovering that confusion was harder to help her with than scraped knees.

Esther commonly turned to me for comfort. When something upset her, she would bury her head in my lap or reach for my hand and hold on really tightly as if I could save her from whatever life brought her way. With that tiny hand in mine, I would sometimes feel like one of the gods in Bullfinch. Very large, very powerful, very adult. At other times, I would feel like a little child myself, a child who had somehow been mistaken for an adult and who was bluffing her way through the part. Esther's physicality, Esther's entrance into my space, incidentally, did not bother me the way abba's did. It was gentle, mutual, even reassuring. But I was worried about Esther's reliance on me. What if I made a mistake and hurt her? Like Heidegger did with eema?

People make mistakes and hurt those who love them, I noticed. Many a time I would see eema visibly upset and glancing up at the kitchen clock every few minutes, then abba rushing through the front door, avoiding eema's eyes, and muttering, "Is a mistake. I lost track of the time." Clearly, this was a world of mistakes and of people getting hurt. It was a dangerous world, where one wrong move had serious consequences. Did that explain what was going on with Sondra? Did I make a wrong move? And was that why Sondra was so distant?

Unlike Esther and me, you see, my older sister Sondra and I never touched, though once upon a time, we had. And oh how I missed those early years when Sondra and I put our arms around each other and hung onto one another at home, in the car, and at the Plautsnickis. With longing, I remembered how we would tire, then cuddle, and fall asleep in each other's arms. How we huddled together for warmth. I remembered this funny noise we once made by puffing out our cheeks and blowing onto each other's skin. When Sondra blew, at first it felt warm; then it got cold again. Oh yes, and I remembered the last time that curious right foot of Sondra's had sprung into action.

I was six. Sondra and I were both on the couch in the living room. I had measured out the distance carefully and positioned myself well beyond the reach of the deadly foot. I doubted that anything would happen because eema was sitting right opposite us, but a kid could hardly be too careful. Why only yesterday Sondra had kicked me in the knee. I meticulously re-measured the distance between us on the couch. It would do. If Sondra was offended by how far away I was sitting, so be it. Giving how ornery that foot had become, taking chances made no sense.

"Time to practice the three times table," eema announced, her hand smoothing out the wrinkles in her skirt.

"Okey-dokey," said Sondra.

"Sondra, what's three times six?"

"Eighteen," answered Sondra.

"Excellent. And what's three times seven?"

"Don't know," said Sondra. "Geez! None of the kids know numbers that high."

"Miriam?" asked eema, turning to me.

"Twenty-one," I answered.

Quick as can be, Sondra leapt to the centre of the sofa and landed a particularly nasty kick on my left shin.

"Ouch," I yelled.

"Stop kicking your sister," insisted eema. "Sisters are not for kicking."

Sandra backed off. Eema grimaced and went on to a new lesson. I was hoping that eema wouldn't ask me another question, for I only had two legs and one of them was already smarting; and for a while, she didn't.

"Miriam," she asked about ten minutes later, "how do you spell 'walk?'"

"Don't know."

"Sweetie, you knew yesterday."

I could never disappoint eema. And so I spelled it out. And sure enough, that right foot of Sondra's got me again.

"What's going on here?" asked eema.

"Nothing," I muttered.

"It wasn't 'nothing,'" said eema, turning to Sondra. "Sondra, we'll talk later, because something is clearly bothering you. But sweetie, there's two problems here. The first is that people are not for kicking, yes? They're for loving. The second is, when I tell you to do something, you have to obey. It's the way things work between adults and children."

"But I *did* obey," protested Sondra.

"You kicked Miriam just now," insisted eema, looking frustrated. "It doesn't matter what Miriam says. I was here, yes? And I saw it."

"But I stopped just like you asked. You didn't say I couldn't *start* again."

A slight smile flickered across eema's face. Then her face got serious, and she looked squarely at Sondra. "Sondra, don't start kicking Miriam and, if you start, stop immediately."

"But when *am* I allowed to kick Miriam?" Sondra asked, clearly feeling hard done by.

"Never," said eema. "It's never okay to kick Miriam. Or Esther," eema added. "Or anyone else," she inserted a few seconds later. "But let me tell you two a story about an ingenious little girl that was angry and found the cleverest ways to deal with that anger."

Sondra did as eema instructed. She never did kick me again. I wasn't sure exactly when it happened or why, but as time went on, Sondra stopped cuddling as well. And now there was almost no physical contact between us.

We never hugged, or kissed, or brushed each other's hair, as some sisters do. And I could swear that Sondra resented it when eema and I hugged. She would tolerate the goodnight kisses, but let eema and I engage in a gratuitous hug, and she would wrinkle up her nose and make this dismissive guttural sound, which I hated. Then she'd say, "Miriam, do you always have to act like such a baby?"—which I hated even more. Nu? I wasn't overly fond of any of the names in Sondra's repertoire— "baby," "eema's favourite," "nimrod," "Public Enemy Number One." Nor did I like it when she stuck her tongue out at me.

"Why does Sondra hate me?" I asked abba one day.

"Vey iz mir," he answered. "Where did you get such an idea?"

"She gets so angry at me," I pointed out.

"Kids get threatened by each other. And when a kid is threatened, she says mean things. But is threatened, she is. Is not hating."

I didn't want to hurt his feeling, so I didn't correct him, but I was pretty sure abba was wrong. Why would Sondra be threatened by me? After all, she was the popular one, the beautiful one. She was absolutely dazzling, yes? And when she walked down the street, perfect strangers would turn their heads to look at her. And she was the one with the charm. "Such a charming child," the grownups would say.

Ten-and-a-half months older than me, Sondra was much taller; and she had short blond hair. She was what abba called "the beauty in the family"—slim, fair, teeth that shone, I suspect because she was forever brushing them. And it wasn't just physical beauty. She exuded this confidence and looked like somebody who was really going to do something with her life, yes? And, indeed, she had theatrical aspirations.

"When I grow up, I'm going to be an actress like Sarah Burnheart and I'm going to tour the world," announced Sondra, one day in her nineth year.

"You just might at that, meydeleh," responded eema.

"You vouldn't like that kind of life in the least," insisted abba, eyeing Sondra intently. "Is like my mother, you are," he reasoned. "Is a stay-at-home type."

I was baffled by abba's pronouncement, for Sondra was not in the least a stay-at-home type. Every Friday night, she would sleep over at a friend's house. And she went to the movies once a week. I couldn't quite put my finger on what was happening, but it was clear that Sondra and bubbeh were associated in abba's mind, yes? And there seemed to be no way for Sondra to wiggle out from under that association. Similar problems arose with the names "Miriam" and "Esther"—and not only with abba. It was as if there were special obligations from the past embedded in our names.

When I wasn't upset with Sondra, I secretly looked up to her and not just because she was my older sister. She had something critical that the rest of us lacked—an ease in the world. Not that she isn't surrounded by the Holocaust, I told myself. She is, and she knows it. And not that she never gets frightened, for she does. But she bounces back. Once the danger passes, it is as if it leaves no trace, and off she is again enjoying herself. And, indeed, Sondra did seem to be exceptionally resilient.

✡

Having just bought two bags of jawbreakers from old man McPherson's candy store, Sondra and I were strolling down the block side by side, no particular destination in mind. I was concentrating on the jawbreaker in my mouth, and Sondra was daydreaming, I suspect about Sarah Burnheart. Suddenly, there was the street bully—this older kid, Ivan Dziadecki—his left hand in his trouser pocket, his right hand skimming the top of his shortly cropped hair. Before I could alert Sondra, he was in our face. And without so much as a warning, he poked my shoulder. Then he poked Sondra's and hollered, "Ya watch your step, ya understand? My folks have lived here way longer than yours. This is *my* sidewalk. My pa's taxes and my grandpa's taxes paid for it. So next time you're on it, make room. Now out of my way *or else!*"

Uttering nary a word, we scurried past him single file, our eyes fixed on the sidewalk. When we were a few yards away, we could hear him bellowing, "Kikes! Not bad enough they own all the banks and everything! They think they own the sidewalk too!" I looked at Sondra. She was trembling. She wanted to get home right away to talk to eema and abba. So we did.

Abba told us, "Is an anti-Semite, Ivan is. Anti-Semites hate Jews. Oy, this is a world of anti-Semites."

Eema said, "ach!"; then gave us one of her serious looks and explained, "Anti-Semites think that Jews are rich, yes? They think we own everything. They think we are forever plotting to keep everyone else poor."

I shook my head in bewilderment. Clearly, we didn't own everything. I couldn't figure out how such a terrible mistake could have been made, or why it wasn't corrected, or what I was supposed to do with an entire world that hated me. I got up and paced the hallway. I was worried. But not Sondra. When I left to go for a walk about an hour later, I found Sondra thoroughly engrossed in a game of marbles with the children on the street, her hand skillfully directing a moony toward a cat's eye, a smile on her face.

That's my sister, I thought to myself with pride. Nothing rattles Sondra for long.

*A tall, thin, middle-aged woman is sprawled out on the couch in the living room, her left leg draped over the edge. The woman vaguely resembles Sondra—only her hair is red and unkempt, her teeth yellow, her pants and shirt wrinkled; and dirt is building up under her finger nails. She has been dozing, but lets out a grunt, then starts to cough convulsively. The cough wakens her. She abruptly opens her eyes. She gazes about uneasily, as if unsure of her location. Her face relaxes and she seems about to trail off once more, but then she coughs again. She clears her throat, rubs her eyes, and sits up. In front of her on the coffee table is a partially drunk mickey of bourbon and an ashtray with a pile of smoldering butts. She reaches over, picks up several choice butts one at a time, examines each carefully, chooses the longest, puts it in her mouth, and inhales deeply until the butt begins to glow. Hacking some more, she reaches for the mickey.*

There was something else that drew me to Sondra too. She had a certain creative flair. She brought her own twist to whatever interested her—the games she played, the presents that she bought, even the jokes that she told.

"You and the shrimp wanna hear a new knock-knock joke?" asks Sondra.

"Yes siree," I answer.

"Okey-dokey, but first let's check the time. What's your watch say?"

"But I don't have a watch," I point out.

"Never mind. There's probably enough time for this joke. So let's just start. Okay?"

"Okay."

"Knock knock," she begins.

"Who's there?"

"Abba."

"Abba who?"

"Abba time ya had a vatch."

Despite the friction between us, Sondra and I spent considerable time together. Sondra was the obvious one to play hiding-o-seek with. Esther didn't like the game at all. And whenever us kids had to make an important decision, which we frequently did, the task tended to fall to Sondra and me. Like that time that one of the campers' children told us that we were insufficiently prepared and we had to make a decision forthwith.

The campers, they were this crowd to which eema and abba belonged. Couples with children. And the husband, the wife, or both—generally both—were Holocaust survivors. Mostly, death camp survivors. The majority Polish. There were sixteen adults in all.

My parents were never so relaxed as when we were out with the campers. Eema's arthritis would not bother her quite so much. And abba's brow would unfurl. And how the lot of them would reminisce!

"Remember that weirdo Kapo at Auschwitz II, the fat toothless one what was always smiling?" asks the woman camper sitting next to eema at the picnic table.

"Wasn't that Crazy Alma?" eema inquires.

"No," answers the woman. "Crazy Alma was the Kapo attached to the Munitions Factory. Remember? She had a scar just above her left eye, and she was always swearing to kill the person what did it."

"Yes, you're absolutely right," returns eema.

"I remember Crazy Alma," pipes up a third, excitedly thumping her hand on the picnic table. "You can forget such a person? She was still attached to Munitions in my time. A sadist if ever there was one!"

Generally, the men would sit at one table, the women at another, and each would tell Holocaust tales. "Organizing" and "barter" stories were particular favourites. "Organizing"—that was the agreed on name for specific skills that were absolutely critical to surviving in Auschwitz, namely: stealing, smuggling, tricking. Eema summed up the situation succinctly: "You didn't organize or barter? You didn't live."

A good four, five times a summer, we would picnic with the campers and their children. Sometimes, I'd hover near the men's table, sometimes the women's, waiting, hoping. Nu? You'd just never know when something extraordinary was about to be shared.

✡

Picnic day again. And we were at our regular haunt—Christie Pits. The grass freshly mowed, the park had a clean crisp look. The sun was peeping through the branches of a nearby ash, creating bursts of light amid the shade. In the distance, you could hear dogs barking and the sound of children squealing, while closer by, a gentle blend of Yiddish and English singsong graced the air.

I was nine-and-half. Sondra and I were sitting at the men's table, partly to listen, partly to eat. A blue sheet covered the table. And before us was an enormous spread—Montreal bagels, creamed cheese, lox, pickled herring, potato knishes, blintzes, gefilte fish. I excitedly went between different foods, enjoying the mixture of tastes, only stopping long enough to refill and to flick off the odd fly. Every time I emptied my plate, Mr. Plautsnicki would say, "A little more of everything, Miriam?" And I would nod. And he would load up the plate again. The men had been speaking about organizing, but my attention was divided between the topic and the food until abba began talking.

"Daniel," a man with hairy legs in Bermuda shorts said to abba, "I swear you were one of the best traders at Auschwitz."

"No question about it," agreed a second man.

"C'mon, you old ganef," pleaded the man in the Bermudas excitedly. "Tell us one of your trading stories."

"If you insist," abba answered, a huge grin appearing on his face. "Let me see now," he said, rolling up the sleeves of his blue plaid shirt. Then he looked at that first man, and began, "Vas the main camp at Auschvitz. Vas March of 1943. And vas especially hungry I vas. Vas about three quarters of an hour before curfew, and what did I have left to eat? Just one bowl of turnip soup, what vas even more vatery than usual. So, I say to myself, 'Daniel,' I say. 'Is time to effect a judicious trade.' Now, of course, as everyone knows," he added, casting his eyes from man to man, "you can only trade judiciously with men what have high numbers."

All the men nodded.

"Why were high numbers important, abba?" I asked, already finding this story more intriguing than the blintzes.

"Because," answered abba turning toward me, "the higher the number, the less time a man's been at Auschvitz; and the less time a man's at Auschvitz, the more easily he can be tricked into making a bad deal."

"Anyvay," abba continued, looking back at the men again and fingering a bagel, "Vat do I do? One by one I skim these little bits of turnip out of my soup. And I sit myself directly in front of a man with a high number, and I ignore him. I just look at my turnips, yah? 'What do you have there?' asks the man after a few minutes. 'Is turnips. Is an absolute rarity in the camp,' I answer. And I smack my lips and look like I am about to eat them; quick as anything he is offering me two rations of bread for the turnips. I do not agree at first, but eventually, I gif in. Then I take the leftover liquid, call it 'turnip soup,' and offer to trade it to another high number for one slice of bread. He is a Jew from France; and he is uncertain. Why? Because he sees how vatery is the soup. But I say, 'Is chowder, you expect? You think this is Paris? Is Auschvitz.' And he too makes the trade. Gut. So is now *three* rations what I have. Next, I split one of the bread rations in half; I take one of my whole rations and one of my half rations, and I look around for someone with *thick* turnip soup. And I find one. 'Is nice looking soup you haf there,' I say. 'A bit on the thin side, but very nice. I'll gif you one ration of bread for it. You interested?' He says, 'two rations; and you haf a deal.' 'Is not worth two,' I inform him. 'And is no man here what has so much bread. But I'll tell you what. I'll gif you all the bread what I haf. One and one half rations of thick bread for your vatery soup. A hungry man can live for days on one and half rations of thick bread.' He says, 'no.' So I turn avay and walk off without a vord. He follows. And right avay is he saying, 'please.' And I am saying, 'I really can't.' And he is agreeing to my second offer; and I am saying, 'I changed my mind,' and continuing to valk away. And so what happens? Eventually, I turn around. And I trade him one ration of bread for his thick turnip soup. And so it is I turned one bowl of *thin* turnip soup into one bowl of *thick* turnip soup and two rations of bread."

Most of the men laughed so hard that tears rolled down their faces. To my surprise, though, this heavy-set man next to abba was frowning. What was more surprising, Sondra was looking away. Now I don't think abba noticed Sondra, but he did take note of the heavy-set man. Glancing at him from the corner of his eye, abba shrugged his shoulders awkwardly. Almost instantly, Mr. Plautsnicki turned to the heavy-set man and announced, "You know, David, Daniel is famous for more than just trading and smuggling."

David nodded. "Of course. We all know he helped other inmates. Sorry. Didn't mean to be a Moshekapoyer," he added, turning to abba.

"Not to worry," answered abba, his face softening.

"Tell you something I'll bet you don't know," Mr. Plautsnicki continued. "Daniel was instrumental in establishing a very important rule among the inmates in his Block."

"Didn't know that. Which rule?" inquired David.

"The bread rule."

"What's the bread rule?" I asked excitedly.

"The rule that stealing food from fellow inmates was not organizing but a life-threatening transgression," replied Mr. Plautsnicki.

"And that anyone caught in the act would be soundly thrashed," added Mr. Cohan.

The man in the Bermudas stepped forward and slapped abba on the back. "Gut for you, Daniel. Oy! As unpleasant as it was to punish a starving man for stealing, the bread rule was simply necessary."

Now I was too young to realize no one exactly invented the bread rule, as important as abba's contribution undoubtedly was. Nor did I appreciate the moral conundrums involved. Nu? I was simply excited because this was exactly the type of information I'd been looking for—or at least one of the types. I played everything over in my head. I saw abba dipping a strange looking spoon into a bowl of watery soup and skimming out tiny bits of turnips—bits so small you could barely recognize what they were. I saw abba gazing at these little pieces and smacking his lips as if they were a magnificent feast, while a man with a high number peers over abba's shoulder, his eyes on fire, his legs trembling, his mouth drooling. I saw abba, shaking his head, saying, "Is enough," then summoning together the men in his barracks and announcing, "*We need to make a rule.*"

I immediately made a mental note: "Daniel Himmelfarb: brilliant trader and creator of the bread rule. Bread rule made by Daniel Himmelfarb: From this day forward and for all eternity, stealing bread from other inmates is not to be considered organizing."

I had many such notes on abba, yes? Unfortunately, I had very few on eema. Nor did I have many mental pictures. Women campers just didn't reveal as much. I knew that eema was also highly regarded. But I didn't exactly know why.

"Rachy," exclaimed Mrs. Weitzman at the women's picnic table a few weeks later, "I swear you were one of the bravest women in all of Auschwitz II. How did you do it day after day? Such chutzpah! Personally, me? I would never haf had the nerve."

I was all ears. This could be the breakthrough I was waiting for. I was hoping to find out what marvelous thing eema had done. But no such luck. Eema glanced pointedly in the direction of Sondra, Esther, and me, then looked back at the women and shook her head. And immediately, a change of topics ensued.

Once it was clear we weren't going to find out anything more about eema, I exchanged looks with my sisters. And the three of us trundled off in search of the other children.

We found everyone on the ground about thirty yards from the women's picnic table, listening intently to Harry Cohan. Most of the kids were sitting cross-legged; one had her legs extended in front of her, a couple were lying on their stomach, their elbows pressed against the ground, their heads resting in their hands. Slightly higher than everyone else, Harry was sitting on a small boulder, his legs draped over its craggy form.

Harry was a tall eleven-year-old with dark brown hair and a firm squared jaw. He always wore a blue yarmulke and thick black-rimmed glasses. I tended to notice Harry's glasses because he was the only person I'd ever come across with glasses as thick as mine. On this day, he had on a red polo shirt and a dusty pair of jeans that were threadbare at the knees.

Harry was the oldest of the campers' children. He had a lot of credibility with us because he had often given us helpful tips in the past—stuff like what to do when someone calls you "a dirty Jew."

"Look at them without either fear or anger in your face," Harry had suggested, "and say, 'I know you don't like Jews. Lots of kids don't.' And if you can, walk away. But not while the kid's talking, right? And not too fast and not too slow."

At the time, Moshe had said, "Know something, Harry? I usually like what you say. But this advice sucks big time." A few months later, though, Moshe swore that Harry's advice had saved him from getting whooped.

And so if Harry talked, we listened.

As we got closer, it was clear that something was up, for none of the other kids were making a sound. Nor was anyone budging an inch. Not to squirm as they usually did, not to itch, not even to wipe their noses even though some noses were visibly dripping. And everyone's eyes were fixed on Harry. As we sat down, we could hear Harry conclude, "So, you see what I am saying? As Jews, you need to be prepared. You need to choose a hiding place."

"Why would we need a hiding place?" Sondra asked.

"Cause of the Gestapo," answered Harry.

"But the Gestapo have been gone for years," I point out.

Harry shook his head. "It's like this," he said, looking at Sondra. "According to the newspapers, the Gestapo have been gone since 1945. Not so. The Gestapo have been laying low in order to trick everyone into thinking everything's okay. They've been at work all these years, building up their organization. They're on their way to Toronto, and while they're after us all, they'll begin with survivors. Won't be long now before they'll turn up at each of our houses. And it's up to us kids to handle the situation. The grownups, they've all swallowed the line about the Nazis being gone."

I look at Sondra. Sondra looks horrified; I suspect that I do too, for I can feel terror gripping my body and there's this bitter metallic taste in my mouth. I look around. I can tell by the widened eyes and raised shoulders that everyone's frightened, but most are staying focussed. It's as if they all know that we have a task to do. I determine to stay focused as well and be as grownup as possible.

"Harry, don't get angry. But how do you know all this?" I inquire.

"My older cousin Ruben told me," he assures me. "Rube knows stuff like that. And he's seen one of them with his own eyes—a big muscular guy who came early to prepare the way."

Everyone gasps.

"He actually seen them!" exclaims Moshe, his eyes widening.

"Just as sure as I'm seeing you now."

"Geez. Jesus H. Christ!" exclaims Moshe, his jaw dropping.

"How did Rube know the guy was Gestapo?" I ask. "And how will we recognize one when we see him?"

"Can tell by the boots," Harry informs us, again looking at Sondra. "They've these big boots and they're always clicking their heels."

"What do the Gestapo want?" asks Sondra.

"They want Jews back in concentration camps," answers Harry. "It's a new roundup. They'll be beginning with one parent, in some cases, both parents. They may be picking up children too, though Rube didn't say for certain."

"Why *one* parent?" Moshe inquires.

"Not quite sure," Harry answers, turning to Moshe. "But I think it has something to do with space. Once they kill off the first load, they'll have room for others."

Sondra eyed Harry intently. "You have a plan, don't you?"

Harry nodded.

"Harry, tell us what to do," Sondra implored.

Harry rose to his feet, placed his hands on his hips, and looked from child to child. "The kids of each family need to decide on two things," announced Harry. "First, choose a good place to hide. Second, choose which parent you're willing to sacrifice to save the other. Cause they'll ask you, see. Nazis always ask stuff like that. They may take both anyway. But if you don't come up with a name, they'll snatch both for sure, right? Anyway, it's up to you. We don't have a lot of time. So, go now. Divide up by family, and make your decision. You—Sondra, Esther, and Miriam—the Himmelfarb girls, in one group," he specified, pointing to the three of us, "and you two Plautsnickis in another, and so on. Moshe, you're alone; so you can stay here with my family and we'll help you out. The rest of you, take off. I'll keep a lookout for the grownups and give three short whistles if any are heading your way."

A few more questions were asked and answered. Then slowly, most of the group dispersed as Harry had asked. Of course, some of the younger ones started crying so hard that they needed help. And the Rothstein brothers were in real difficulty since both of them were under seven and understood little of Harry's explanation.

I motioned to Sondra that we should go away and talk. Sondra nodded. I took Esther's hand and the three of us left. We walked for about twenty yards in a kind of stunned silence until we came to a green picnic table. Then Sondra raised her right hand and said, "far enough." And we all sat down—Sondra and I on opposite sides of the table, Esther nestling up next to me.

For what seemed like an eternity, no one spoke. I looked around. It was starting to darken. You could still make out the shapes of trees. You could distinguish tables. And you could identify figures sitting, crouching, lying. There were adults and children and infants. Yes, and this grey poodle was gobbling up garbage a few yards away. And a few feet further along, Blacky—the Boston bull from next door—was sniffing another dog that I couldn't quite make out. But everything had this unreal look, like in a dream.

"Nazis in Toronto after all this time!" I finally exclaimed. "How could this have happened?"

"It's horrible," said Sondra, shaking her head.

"They could be here at this very moment," I noted.

Sondra nodded. Then she startled as if she had spotted something. "Oh God! That man over there!" she exclaimed, her eyes darting sideways to indicate a man in a black shirt about five yards to her right.

I forced myself to look. "No boots," I pointed out. She sighed with relief.

Then I started scanning the grounds nervously. "One of them could be right behind that tree over there," I observed in a hushed voice, pointing with my little finger only to a large craggy oak about six feet to our left. "He could be hiding behind the trunk, waiting to catch us off guard."

Sondra and I shifted our heads ever so slightly, scrutinizing the oak from different angles. We didn't spot anything important. Just some blight here and there, and this broken-off branch next to it that had me worried for a moment. Finally, I went up and examined it. Then I checked behind the one other tree nearby—a birch, if I recall rightly. Then I returned and reported, "Coast clear."

"I'm scared," whimpered Esther.

"We've got to stop this. We don't have time for anybody to be scared," said Sondra firmly, straightening her back and sitting up tall. "Harry said for us to make a decision. So let's get down to business."

I gulped down a mouthful of saliva and forced myself to stay calm. "Okay, let's start with the hiding place."

"What do you think?" asked Sondra.

"How about the attic?" I suggested. "We can get to it from the ceiling in Esther's and my room. All we have to do is stand on a chair."

Sondra considered the suggestion for a few seconds, then answered, "No way. It'd take too long. Anyhow, that's where Ann Frank hid. So that's the first place they'd look. I'd say the basement. There's that tiny room where abba keeps the wine. Whatchya think, Miriam?"

I nodded. "Yeah, sounds right. Not the wine room, though. They're bound to check anything with a door. Maybe the crawl space under the stairway. When they come down the stairs, they'll be looking in the opposite direction, and they'll miss us. And by the time they return to the stairs, they'll probably have given up."

"Agreed. Now for the hard part."

"I don't wanna do *that* part," I said, shaking my head repeatedly. "Sondra, we just can't. It's too awful."

"Harry said we have to or we will lose both of them."

"No. I don't care what Harry's reason is. You just don't choose between people. And certainly not between eema and abba."

"You wanna lose them both?" asked Sondra accusatorily.

"Sondra, *I don't want to do this.*"

"Me neither. But it's better to lose one parent than two. So let's just get it over with, okay? So, who do we sacrifice, and who do we save? You vote first, Miriam."

"No."

"Miriam, don't do this to me," pleaded Sondra. "I'm upset too, but we haven't time for this. Harry said there's no time."

"No."

"Don't be such a baby," she called out, glaring at me.

"Eema," I heard myself stammer. "I vote that we save eema."

I didn't know where that voice came from, for I hadn't intended to answer again. I instantly know that I have betrayed abba. An image comes into focus in my mind. Two Gestapo officers are hauling off abba, who is shouting, "Is my daughter Miriam what has turned me in." Then that image fades. And it is replaced by an image which is to haunt me ever after, but this is its first appearance: Abba is stretched out in a coffin, his eyes glazed over, his left hand clutching his heart. I open my mouth, intending to say, "I take back my vote." Instead, to my surprise, I hear myself asking, "How do you vote, Sondra?"

"I vote to save eema as well. So, it's decided," she declares.

The reason that Sondra considers the decision made is that we seldom include Esther in complex decisions, because of her age. But it has all happened so quickly. And the solution appalls me. I don't know what to do because Sondra almost never agrees to reopen anything that she has declared "decided." I glance at Esther and among other things, it dawns on me that there's still a chance of keeping faith with abba. A slim one, I know. But I decide to go for it.

"Esther has to be allowed a say," I state firmly, looking directly at Sondra. "It's just too important a choice to leave Esther out. And it needs to be unanimous. We can't just outvote her on a question like this."

Sondra nods. I turn to Esther. "Esther," I ask, speaking as gently as I can, "you understand what Harry was saying just now?"

"I know it's important. And I know you and Sondra are picking between eema and abba."

"And you know that abba and eema both love you dearly and always will no matter what?"

"Yes."

"Do you want to vote? Sweetie, you really don't have to," I assure her, noticing the tears welling up in her eyes and beginning to regret involving her in this mess.

Esther nods and whispers, "I vote for eema too." Then she bursts into tears and buries her head in my lap.

The decision is made. Now, there really is no going back.

The three of us sit together for some time, saying nothing. I can sense a kind of bond between us, a terrible bond that holds us together and separates us from every other human being on earth. I look at Esther, see her lip quivering, and wonder how she's going to manage. I look at Sondra. Her head high, she seems calm just like she did but an hour after we'd been bullied by Ivan Dziadecki. I feel this strange combination of respect, resentment, and dread. Then I start worrying about the Nazis. In the rustling of the leaves, the buzzing of the flies, and the panting of the dogs, I hear Gestapo officers whispering. And I am relieved that Sondra is here.

Now the events of this day were to have consequences, yes? And the very first of these was an inordinate amount of time spent hiding. In the last half of my tenth year, throughout my eleventh, and part of my twelfth, Sondra and I were forever hiding under the stairs. Esther never joined us, for how she hated hiding! Sondra initially maintained that it was our responsibility to help Esther better appreciate the danger. And so a good six, seven times, we sat Esther down and explained the situation as we saw it. Fortunately for poor Esther, though, after a few months, we could see it was of no avail, and we resigned ourselves to hiding without her.

If we heard an unusual noise, Sondra and I would exchange looks and head toward the basement. "Don't make a sound," Sondra would whisper.

"Hold your breath if they get too close," I'd answer.

We would crouch down low in the crawl space. And there we would stay, often for a whole hour at a time, convinced that we were hearing the click of Nazi heels.

"The nazis are still there. You hear them, Sondra?"

"Sha. No talking. Not a sound."

I am eleven years old. I am with my sister Sondra in a cold, dark, musty basement, hiding under the stairs. I can feel the freezing moist air seeping into my limbs. I can't see much, though I am aware of the brown paint peeling away on the wall next to me, and I can see green and black mold growing everywhere. The mold is taking different shapes, yes? It looks like a man hitting a woman. It smells like something rotting in a coffin. Another more acrid smell is filling my nostrils and is making me dizzy. Wouldn't you know it? Abba left the cap off the turpentine like last time. The middle finger on my left hand has turned white again. My throat is raw, my nose is clogged, and I am having trouble getting air. Could I suffocate here? Why am I hiding anyway? How can I strike a deal with the nazis to leave eema alone if I don't come out and talk to them? Or are abba, eema, and Esther in a safe hiding place too? If Sondra and I come out and let them take us, will the nazis give up looking for everyone else? Would they then let eema and Esther be? Maybe even abba? And will that make up for betraying abba? And what will they do to Sondra and me then? Will they load us onto a train headed for Auschwitz? Will we pass through a gate with the words "Arbeit Macht Frei" (Work Makes You Free)? Will they work us till we drop? When we are too weak to be of further use, will they herd us into one of those special shower rooms, close the door, and turn on the gas? Maybe, just maybe, we could handle that if we knew that our deaths would be taken as payment in full and that Jews would finally be left in peace. Nu?, I told myself. I am a practical person who is almost an adult—less than two years from batmitzvah age—and I think I can accept such a death as a reasonable sacrifice if that would be the end of it all. If it could be agreed on once and for all that the imaginary debt of the Jews was cancelled now and for all time. But what if it were not the end? What if it were only another beginning?

Two-and-a-half years had passed since Harry Cohan had conveyed this important information to us. And Sondra and I were still hiding. Pesach of 1959, however, marked something of a turning point in the Himmelfarb household.

✡

We were sitting around the large knotty pine table in the dining room. Eema and Molka Plautsnicki, her best friend, sat opposite Sondra, Esther, and me. Abba sat by himself at the head of the table.

Mrs. Plautsnicki was a fat squat women with dark hair and a just hint of a moustache. On some days, she smelt like Gerkins pickles, on others, like malt vinegar. When abba was out at one of his CCF meetings, she and eema would talk for hours in the kitchen—"schmoozing," they called it. And without fail, within half an hour of Mrs. Plautsnicki leaving, the phone would ring. And who would it be? Mrs. Plautsnicki, of course, needing to speak to my mother on a matter of grave importance.

Mrs. Plautsnicki and her husband were both campers. She was one of the very few Jews who had escaped the Warsaw Ghetto during the final days when the uprising was over and the Germans were searching through every last bit of rubble. I never exactly liked her because she tended to ignore us kids. But I couldn't help but be in awe of this woman who had survived Warsaw, who had hidden in that collapsing ghetto amid fires and shooting, who had bent over so as to fit, then inched her way through the long sewage tunnel until she reached the Aryan side.

Mrs. Plautsnicki was on her second marriage. Her first husband, apparently, had left her after a few months. Years later, she married a Christian widower who was also a survivor and who had two adolescent children. While Mr. Plautsnicki was a dear and while this marriage lasted, I could see that it wasn't a totally happy union. Mrs. Plautsnicki would frequently come crying to eema about family tsores, yes? And every few years, come the second seder, the original family and Mrs. Plautsnicki would go their separate ways—I imagine because they quarreled at the first seder. Hence, her solitary presence at our table.

This year, the seder table was perfect. A wine glass was set for everybody, Esther included. The silver chalice for Eliahou was centred in the middle on the table. Between the chalice and abba, eema had placed a new blue and white seder plate, which had a spot for everything—the covered matzo, the horseradish, the shankbone, the charoset, the roasted egg, the parsley.

Abba was dressed in a dark brown suit, a crimson bow tie, and a black yarmulke. One of the comfy beige chairs from the living room had been brought in and he was sitting on it. Leaning against a red velvet cushion, he was reading from the Haggadah—speeding through the Hebrew a thousand words a minute. Mostly, I couldn't follow, but I knew the odd word, "moror," "matzo," and my heart leapt up whenever they were uttered.

"Borey p'ree hagafen," came the all-important phrase. I always started smiling whenever he recited this prayer. I knew what it meant. Not the words, of course, because we were never taught Hebrew—that's not something that happens in families trying to fit in—but what it signified. I lifted my glass and gulped the wine straight down, enjoying the warm glow that spread through my body.

Abba's brow furled, and he leaned toward me. "Miriam, you are all right?" he inquired. "More careful you must be. If you drink so quick, the wrong vay the wine goes, and you could choke to death, kinehora."

"I'm okay, abba," I answer.

"But you vill be careful, no? I don't vant any more of my family dying. There has not been enough death already? I haf survived Auschvitz so I will haf idiot children what will choke to death?"

Not again! I thought to myself. Why can't he ever just let things be? Why does he have to drag Auschwitz into everything? Auschwitz. I hate that word. I hate him. If only he'd died at Auschwitz like most self-respecting Jews, we could be spared all this. If only he could just—I recoiled instantly at this terrible thought, then recoiled at my own state of mind. Then I found myself in trouble. I was shaking inside. I couldn't figure out an acceptable way to get through the evening and I didn't like the way that was taking shape at that very moment. It was the schoolyard experience all over again, only with considerably less provocation. I didn't want to be up on the wall looking down, though there I was. I determined to settle back into my body.

Miriam, I told myself. Move your thumb. Can you feel it moving? Try again. Now move it again. And again. Now the other one. That's better. Now focus, Miriam. You can do it. I know you can. Right now, just focus on being here. You are sitting on a chair. Feel the chair. It is soft and firm at the same time. There's a plate right in front of you. Look at the plate. It has a blue design on a white background. Can you see it? Good. As soon as you can, shift to the realm of thought. Focus on eema's "thinking questions." Eema's "thinking questions"—you know how intriguing they are. Just let yourself go with them and they'll create a buffer. But not yet. First, focus on abba. Can you see him? Good, now say something to abba. It might not be too late.

"Abba, I'm sorry. I'll be careful," I finally answered.

"Is right avay you should answer a person what is talking to you, young lady. Is only courteous. And is an example, you haf to set. And is not only with courtesy but with the drinking of wine too." "Look at the little pisher there," he went on, pointing to Esther. "She sees you gulping the wine, and what do you think she's going to do?"

I'd been noticing Esther off and on. She had turned toward abba because she'd been mentioned. She'd been bored earlier. Now she was watching nervously. Her upper lip started to quiver. I reached over and squeezed her hand under the table. She squeezed back.

I wasn't worried about the gulping. Abba wolfed down food all the time and it hadn't hurt him. But Esther might start bawling any second.

And abba—if he got more upset, what would happen to his heart?

"Daniel, your heart," eema cautioned just at that moment.

I saw an image of abba lying in a coffin. He was dressed in his dark brown pants, crimson tie, and yarmulke, but he had no shirt on. His face was blue. His mouth had formed a silent scream. The skin had pulled away from his chest, exposing a heart with a huge tear in it. Blood was gushing from the wound.

Abba read some more Hebrew. The coffin disappeared. Abba kept reading for at least an hour. Every so often, he stopped to speak about Moses—about how Moses was once a prince but was a socialist at heart and so had walked out on Pharaoh and joined the working class.

"Is the real meaning of kosher," proclaims abba.

"What do you mean?" I ask.

"Slavedriving your vorkers. Is not kosher," abba answered.

Sondra and Esther began fidgeting. Abba exchanged looks with eema. They'd noticed that they'd lost most their audience. I wondered whether abba would resume reading now or eema would pick up the ball. I was rooting for eema.

"Nu, my darlings?" eema began. "It is written that Moses delivered the children of Israel to the Promised Land. Now we can understand Promised Land in different ways, yes? It can be a real place. Or it can be how we feel about one another. Or how we treat one another. What do you think a Promised Land might be like?"

"I know. I know. It's Israel. So it would be like Israel," answered Sondra, looking confidently at eema.

Eema scrunched up her eyes like she always did when she was trying to think her way out of a corner. Then her face relaxed, and she answered, "Yes, good, Sondra. That is what we are told. So, we will stick with this answer for awhile, yes? So, what is Israel like? What is this Promised Land?"

Sondra replies, "A place where Jews live."

"Jews, absolutely, there are. You are perfectly right, Sondra. There are many other people in Israel too, though, no? There are Arabs and there are Christians."

"Who are Arabs?" I ask, noticing that Esther has lost interest again and guessing that she does not remember this term.

"The Egyptians in the story of Moses are Arabs," observes eema, nibbling on some matzo. "And many other groups are Arabs."

"Arabs are evil," says Sondra. "Like, they enslaved the children of

Israel and wouldn't let them go. Right, eema?"

"Is not so simple," eema answers.

"Maybe they're good people who made a mistake, like Heidegger," I suggest.

Eema looks at little taken back, then laughs good naturedly. "Yes, meydeleh. Is one possible answer. And there are others. What if everyone made mistakes? And what if the Haggadah is not right? Or what if it is just not the *only* story?" she asks, her brow arching. "Everyone has different stories. My sheyneh punems, what if this story is just the way that certain Jews make sense of that time in history?"

No one has ever talked to me about Pesach this way before. And for a moment, I am shocked by what eema seems to be suggesting.

"But isn't the story in the Haggadah true?" I ask.

"You're always interested in truth, Miriam, yes? And that's gut. But if I had to give a yes-no answer, I would say, no, the story is not true."

"Eema," I ask with a real urgency, holding her look, "why do we tell this story if it is not true? What use is it?"

The story that we used to read about Romulus and Remus and the beginning of Rome, is true?"

"No, I don't think so."

"And you learned from it even though it isn't true, yes?"

"Yes," I answer slowly. "I did learn something. I learned that human beings underestimate animals and that we too are animals."

"Gut," says eema. "And so this untrue story, it is useful?"

"Yes, eema."

"And this untrue story, it is true in a way too, no?"

A "thinking question." Good. I can see where eema is heading. Truth is not simple. There are different kinds of truths. And there are different kinds of stories. And....

Abba cleared his throat. "Rachael," he interjected, looking at eema, "back to Miriam's question we should be getting, yah? Who are the Arabs? Is a simpler question than the nature of truth."

Eema smiles at abba and nods. Then looking at Sondra, Esther, and me, she continues, "So in the Bible stories, the people from Egypt were Arabs. The people from Jericho, they were also Arabs. Who else do you think were Arabs?"

"Everyone except the children of Israel, right, eema?" Sondra responds.

"Yes, good, but not exactly," replies eema, making a wavy motion with her left hand. "The Jews were one of the Arab tribes. Listen to me my sweeties," she says, leaning forward, the way she often did when she wanted us to take special heed. "Jews were Arabs who had developed their own set of ideas and own holidays. A different set. Yes? Not a better set. Just different."

"Are Jews really Arabs?" asks Sondra, her eyes widening.

"Originally, yes."

"But if Jews are really Arabs," I ask, "why do Jews and Arabs fight?"

Eema looked pleased with the direction that the conversation was taking. She began to say something about Jews taking over the land, adding, "Of course, sweeties, we must make concessions seeing as so many of these Jews were affected by the Holocaust, yes?"

I understood the part about the land. I didn't understand what the Holocaust had to do with it, and so I asked eema.

She looked toward abba. Abba caught her eye and nodded. Then, leaning forward and eyeing us intently once again, eema responded, "My sheyneh punems, never use your pain, or your tragedy, or your people's tragedy as justification for mistreating others. But be understanding about people who do. Be understanding, of course, while opposing it, for it must be opposed, no? That said, let me answer your question. About half a century before the Holocaust, at a time when enormous harm was being done to our people, a movement to establish a Jewish homeland in Palestine began. It was called 'Zionism,' yes? As the anti-Semitism worsened, more and more Jews became Zionists. By the Holocaust, most Jews were passionate about Palestine—were intent on turning as much of this land as possible into a Jewish state."

"Because we needed the land, right eema?" asked Sondra.

"Oy, Sondra. Food, freedom—these are needs, yes? Not a particular stretch of land."

"So why?"

"Well, because they felt that considerable land would be necessary if Jews throughout the world were to have some place to go when danger struck. Because this land had been taken from them, and ever since, century after century, they'd wandered through Europe, meeting with appalling treatment everywhere—forced to become Christians; driven out of the country; annihilated. Because Hitler had come close to finishing them off once and for all, and the world did nothing. Makes a kind of sense, Sondra, no? The problem is, another people—the Arabs—were also native to this land. And most of Jewry had become European."

"Become European, what's that mean?" I ask, somewhat confused.

"Jews had been in Europe for so many generations they thought like Europeans and did not understand the Arab world. So what did they think? They thought the Arabs would be happy to have a Jewish state because the standard of living in the area would rise. Is sad looking back on it, meydelehs, because many of the Zionists were socialists committed to building a society with peace and brotherhood for all. Anyway, how did the Arabs respond? Most said 'no' to Jewish statehood. What else would they have said? And Palestinian and other Arab leaders began organizing politically and militarily. Now, far-sighted Jewish philosophers like Hannah Arendt and Martin Buber said that Arab wishes must be respected; and they called for the creation of a bi-national state."

"Not sure what that is, eema," I asked.

Eema took out a cigarette and lit it. "A combined Jewish-Arab state," she answered. "Actually, Arendt even suggested sticking with the yeshuv, where Jewish culture had thrived, no? And indeed, the Buber and Arendt position had been the position of a high percentage of the earlier Zionists. Meydelehs," she added, her hand raised, "not all Zionists favoured Jewish statehood. Far from it. But what could be done? The bi-national Zionists had already lost."

Just at that moment, Esther lifted her empty wine glass high in the air and grinned at eema. Eema reached over and patted Esther's cheek. Then she launched into a description of the acts leading to war, speaking of Jews, Arabs, the British. "And as the British blocked ships of Jews desperately trying to enter Palestine—many of them Holocaust survivors," she concluded, "the settlers became adamant that a Jewish state was the only conceivable solution, and bloodshed the only possible way."

"The settlers," I observed, "they fought because they cared about the victims of the Holocaust, right?"

"Is not straight forward. Let me tell you something, Miriam. This settler society, it had very mixed feelings about the victims of the Holocaust."

"Eema?"

"They saw the Holocaust as enabled by Jewish passivity and dismissed the lot of us as spineless shtetl dwellers who went obediently into the camps. In fact, a contrast between us and them was strangely implicated in what transpired."

"How?" I asked, astonished that such a thing could come to be.

Eema sat back in her chair, took a puff on her cigarette, then caught my eye. "They defined themselves in opposition to us. If we were meek, they were going to be bold. If we spoke Yiddish, they would speak Hebrew. If we were thinkers, they were going to be warriors. If we asked what was good for humanity, they asked what would guarantee the survival of the Jewish people and saw ruthlessness toward this end as a kind of virtue, no? And so the terror and the massacres began. And it continues to this day."

Images of blood-stained corpses began flitting through my mind. "That's horrid. All of it," I exclaimed.

"Is terrible what has happened here," said eema. "Yet I tell you just as surely as we are sitting here, it is the legacy of two thousand years of Christianity. And it is a legacy of the Holocaust. You cannot terrorize and almost wipe out an entire people and expect that they will still act well. Of course, they are still obliged to act well. And, of course, we want to believe that they'll do just that. That they'll act like mentshes who say, 'We know first hand what bad treatment is, and so will treat others properly no matter what.' Punct. Now, don't get me wrong; some will act very well indeed. And, for sure, thousands of Jews did and still do, yes? But I tell you, meydelehs, frighten an entire people badly enough, and that people will fix on some solution to the problem of group survival. And how will they see any people who pose a formidable obstacle to the solution which they now regard as a matter of life and death? As a lethal enemy, of course. And how will they regard any attack which they themselves perpetrate against this other people? As self-defense. And how will they regard the attacks which this other people perpetrates against them? As proof of villainy and a warrant for massacre and never-ending expansion. Even when this other people have claim to the land, even when it too has been victimized by the twentieth century, even when the two peoples are relatives, as Jews and...."

"Ach," she continued, shaking her head sadly. "I haven't a clue how this mess is ever going to sort out. Maybe it will resolve itself in a decade or two. But when something begins this badly..." she added, clutching her stomach. She did not finish her sentence.

It wasn't at all clear that eema would be able to continue, she was that distressed. But Mrs. Plautsnicki reached over and put her hand on eema's shoulder and, after awhile eema nodded and smiled. Then she passed around some matzo with charoset on it; and she began talking about biblical times again. She used a term I hadn't heard before—"sibling rivalry," I think it was. She was saying something about Abraham sending Ishmael out into the desert. She was trying to explain how Jews and Arabs initially became divided but I cannot recall her point exactly because my mind was drifting.

I was back again on the question of truth. If truth were not simple, I asked myself, did that mean that we should avoid questions which lend themselves to yes-or-no answers? And if a story was a given group's attempt to make sense, how were we to manage a world with so many groups and so many conflicting stories? Jewish stories? Arab stories? Christian stories? White stories? Negro stories? Did all the stories have a kind of truth? Were the stories equally true? Were they always equally true? As one story becomes prominent, what happens to the other stories? As you focus on the truth of one, is there any way at all of seeing any truth in another? As I pondered these questions, I could hear eema's voice in the distance. "So, Miriam, let me ask you," she was saying, "if it was up to you to deliver us to the Promised Land, would you think that your task had been performed properly if it led to Jews and Arabs fighting?"

I refocus as quickly as I can. I am not sure where this question is coming from or what went before, but I'm well aware that fighting solves bupkes. "A Promised Land where people kill each other is no kind of Promised Land at all," I respond, confidently.

"Exactly," she affirms. "So maybe next time, we won't leave everything up to your brother Moses."

At this point Mrs. Plautsnicki begins to howl with laughter. When she laughs hard, her whole upper body shakes and now was no exception. "Good one, Rach," she shrieks, slapping her hands together, her upper body shimmying in all directions. "I must remember that."

I feel myself turning red. A joke is clearly being made, but I don't get it.

"It's okay, Miriam," eema reassures me. "Is a little joke, no? But a serious joke. You remember we were just talking about Moses?"

"Yes, eema," I answer, feeling on safer ground.

"Moses had a sister and the sister's name was Miriam."

"Same as my sister," pipes up Esther.

"Exactly," says eema. "And Auntie Molka and I—we sometimes wonder about Moses's sister Miriam. But is nothing for you to worry about, Miriam. This is a story about Moses. Moses, not Miriam. And abba is about to tell us more about Moses." As she ends, she glances nervously in abba's direction.

Abba is shaking his head. His eyes are beginning to bulge. He has been drumming his fingers on the table for the last few minutes, but the drumming now stops abruptly. "You think we haf all the time in the vorld to get through the Haggadah?" he bellows. "And why do you talk such nonsense about Miriam? Liberation is a vorking man's job. Is a socialist's job. And Judaism is the story of Moses. Like anyone's ever heard of the idiot sister? And what about my brother Nathaniel? He escaped Germany and fought in the Var of Independence so that his sister-in-law could badmouth the var to his nieces?"

At the time I did not understand the part about Uncle Nathaniel, but weeks later I learned that he had engaged in terrorism. A member of the Stern gang, he had blown up buildings, killed Arabs, and attacked the British to secure Palestine for the Jews. And while abba was uneasy about Nathaniel's methods and sometimes rejected them altogether, he nonetheless tended to regard Nathaniel as a hero—a liberator of the Jewish people. What I did pick up at this point is that eema and abba had quite different takes on the Middle East generally and Uncle Nathaniel in particular.

"Daniel, I mean no disrespect for Nathaniel," eema responded. "He was a Jew in a dreadful era who did what he thought he must to secure the safety of his people. And is terrible that his heart gave out at such a young age. And Daniel, I really do apologize for pursuing this touchy issue for so long. Is Pesach though, abba," she went on, looking at him tenderly. "Is a time for different interpretations, no? And is a time for the family to be happy together."

"Happy together? Yes. Is gut," replied abba, his voice getting lower, his eyes beginning to settle back into their sockets. "Sondra," he inquired, peering at her, "you are happy, yes?"

"Yes, abba."

"And you, Miriam?"

"Yes, abba."

"And my little Esther?"

"Yes, abba."

"Is gut. Is important. I saw you making with the frowns a few moments ago, Miriam," he went on, turning toward me. "I don't vant what you should frown. Not ever. Six million Jews were unhappy. Is enough."

"Abba," eema interjected. "Is maybe a good time to tell the children the story about the bread, yes?"

"Like, isn't that the story about how you and abba met?" asked Sondra, beginning to perk up.

"That's it," said eema.

"Yes, please," Sondra urged, turning to abba. "Abba, tell us the story again."

Abba beamed with pride. It was one of his favourite stories, and it paved the way for one of his favourite comparisons.

"Is latrine duty at Auschvitz II what I vas going to, yah?" he begins. "Not that this vas my assignment. Absolutely not. But it was covering I vas for my good friend Lionel, what vas sick and would be given less leeway than myself, what was a skilled tailor. But that's besides the point. Anyvay, I approach the latrine, and who do I come across but this woman what is skin and bones? Is looking like she is caput—finito. Two, three veeks tops for that one, I estimate. Is not really bothering me, I am ashamed to say. After all, is not the least unusual, because this is Auschvitz, yah? And is everyone what is skin and bones. And is every fifth one what is caput. You learn not to care—least vays, not about people what are so far gone. Is a strange thing, not caring. On one hand, is a curse. Is letting the Hitlerites win. Is letting them reduce you to a thing what valks and eats and speaks but has no heart. On the other hand, is a blessing. You care too much and is zero chance you'll survive. Is even zero chance you'll be any help to the people what actually have some possibility of making it. So, is defying Hitler. Is resistance. Is gut strategy. Anyvay, in my mind this remnant of a woman is already caput. But I make small talk regardless just to be polite, you understand. But is she returning small talk? Nein. Is talking about Marx, she is. Is talking Engels. Is talking Shakespeare. Is talking Heidegger. And is making plans for the embetterment of the vorld. A caput woman, and she is making plans! Think of it! And I asks myself, 'Himmelfarb, you schmuck!' I ask, 'you vill let such a woman die?' And right avay I am answering, 'no.' So what do I do? No matter what I am starving myself, just like that, I gif her one half of my bread ration. One half and not a crumb less. Not a millionth of a crumb less. And right avay I am stepping up my organizing so is more I vill have to share. Now, as often as I can, I make a point of meeting her or sending her food through Lionel, yah? And even if organizing is yielding nothing, is always something I gif her."

Abba cleared his throat. "And what makes this story a good and fitting Pesach story?" he asks. "Is a good and fitting Pesach story," he answers, "because is a story about life, and bread, and blessing. You see the point what I am making? Is a similar kind of thing—eating unleavened bread and giving half of your bread ration to a woman what is starving. In both cases, is a mitzvah."

*Image: In the middle of a reeking wasteland is a gigantic ditch, overflowing with excrement and buzzing with flies. At regular inter- vals, narrow planks cross over the ditch. On the planks crouch dozens of underfed women in various stages of undress, all of them holding onto their tattered clothing, all of them relieving themselves. They are squeezed together so tightly that each soils the next, but nary a soul comments.*

*On the ground in front of the ditch sits a woman in rags, seemingly oblivious to the others. The woman looks like my mother, only younger, much younger, and without any flesh. The woman's ribs stick out; she has no breasts; and her face and hands are covered with running sores. She is gobbling up a piece of muddy bread—stuffing it down her throat just as quickly as she can. When only a smidgen remains, she holds it in front of her eyes and stares at it. A look of horror spreads across her face. Then she glances to the right. An emaciated man sits there, smiling at her. She nods, clenches her teeth, but does not smile back.*

Now to this day, I'm not exactly certain why abba was comparing the shared bread and the matzo. Whether eema understood or not was unclear, but she did nod. However confused we were by this customary comparison, of course, Sondra and I were enormously proud of abba for making such a sacrifice and told him so repeatedly.

"Abba, with everyone all together, is maybe a good time also to tell the girls about the *great news*," eema suggested, catching his eye.

*Now* abba had everyone's attention. Even Esther sat up in her chair and turned toward him.

"Is a big change what is coming to the Himmelfarb household," announces abba solemnly. "You remember your Uncle Yacov, what vas here visiting four years ago last February?"

Sondra and I reply that we do. Esther looks confused.

"Is very important," says abba. "Is not much family we haf left. And Uncle Yacov is a fine man what is coming all the vay from New York city to live with us. At the tailor shop, he vill be vorking with me. Coats and jackets, we vill be making together. Is gut news, yes?"

"Yes," we reply in unison, nodding vigorously and honestly excited at the prospect of a new addition to the household.

"Is he really coming?" asks Sondra, barely able to contain her enthusiasm.

"Is coming absolutely," responds abba. "Is a train ticket already bought and pocketed."

"Oh abba, when? When is Uncle Yacov coming?" she persists.

"Is two veeks from yesterday," answers abba.

Abba hunched over the table again and began pouring over the Haggadah, his index finger moving swiftly over the text. "Baruch ata Adonoi," he began. And there we were, back again in the familiar seder. But I wasn't listening now—not even for the few words I knew. I was thinking about Uncle Yacov, whom Sondra and I decidedly liked. After all of this time, why was he moving in with us? And what would it be like having a *live* relative around?

My thoughts drifted to abba's story. I felt touched at the thought of abba giving half of the few scraps he had to a woman that he didn't even know. I tried to picture the story, starting from the beginning. My first attempt was absurd, and I couldn't help but smile at it. I saw abba in his brown suit attempting to exchange small talk with eema, dressed in her white-laced frock. "Is a nice day you're having, yah?" he asks. "Fair to middling," she replies. "But never mind that. Nu? Let me tell you about my latest theory about Shakespeare's *The Tempest*." No, I said to myself, dismissing this image. It obviously didn't play out that way. They were at Auschwitz. And so they would be dressed very differently. They would be by a latrine. And no one would be talking as if everything were all right. I started over again, making the necessary adjustments in critical parts of the opening image. I turned the clothes into ill fitting rags. I made both people gaunt and yellowing. But the image was still wrong. There was something else that had to be built in. Abba had always emphasized the fact that eema was caput. What did a caput woman look like? And how did he figure out that she was caput? No, that's not how the story went. He didn't *figure* it out. He knew it straight off. Like he *recognized* something. Something he'd seen many times before. Now the recognition that she was dead already couldn't just be based on how thin or sick she looked. Abba himself had told me that people in obviously dismal shape sometimes made it through selection and lived. What was it about her that instantly told him that she was a goner? I made my image of eema bigger so that I could get a better look. I peered into her eyes the way I had so often done throughout my childhood. As the image got bigger, her eyes went vacant. She wasn't looking back! Was that what he saw? Did she have vacant eyes? Had she lost all will to live? That felt right.

Abba had often spoken of the musselmen—those skeletal beings whose divine spark had already been extinguished and who walked about Auschwitz with vacant eyes.* They did nothing to protect themselves— never organized, never learnt which duties were lighter, never thought about which people to avoid, never tried to stretch their rations to day's end, never spoke to anyone. Come selection, they would invariably be sent to the gas chambers. And once killed, nothing would change, for in short order, dozens more musselmen would spring up, indistinguishable from the ones that went before. All slouched over, all in a stupor, all with empty eyes that showed nary a trace of life. Although abba only spoke of men—always men—and although eema never discussed such details, it only made sense that if this terrible descent happened to men, it must have happened to the women. And it must have looked the same. Or at least similar.

With this concept firmly in mind, I began the story again. I tried to imagine abba approaching and initiating small talk with a female musselman. I couldn't do it. The problem wasn't the shift from man to woman. It was the small talk itself. Indeed, it was any kind of talk. Abba had always been clear that no one ever talked to the musselmen because they never responded. I focused on the image of the female musselman that I had just conjured up—a famished frail woman with empty eyes, a woman from whom the spark had departed, a woman who had lost all interest in life, all connection with the people around her, with nature, with her very body, with existence itself; and I tried to imagine her speaking about her plans to improve the world. Again, I couldn't do it. It didn't come together. I tried again. No use. No matter how many attempts I made, I couldn't make the imagery work.

I felt discouraged. No. More than that. I felt disappointed in myself. Some years back, I had concluded that it was my responsibility as their daughter to understand eema and abba. It seemed to me that being a good daughter to parents with such an appalling history meant appreciating what they had been through at Auschwitz. Appreciating it—not

---

*Like everyone who has written about the musselmen ever since, I am indebted to Primo Levy's original description. For Levy's description of the musselmen, see Primo Levy, Survival at Auschwitz (New York: Simon and Schuster, 1996).

getting angry at abba and wishing him dead the way I had earlier. I often thought about the importance of understanding and tried to contrive ways to understand better. There were even times that I wished that I had been at Auschwitz myself. If only I had been there with them, if I had been in the work groups, in the lice-ridden bunks, at the infested latrines, I would tell myself, then I would truly be able to understand them as they deserved to be understood. Now, I could not even understand a simple story. I asked myself what was wrong. Why couldn't I make the images work? What was I missing? Was the small talk of a different nature? Was it perhaps not small talk at all?

Eventually, though very very slowly, my mind shifted to other parts of the evening. I saw six million Jews with six million frowns all commanding me to be happy. I saw Moses marching up to Pharaoh and announcing that he was the foreman and that the workers were officially on strike. I saw Ishmael and Hagar shaking their heads and walking off into the desert. Then an image that had not obviously been part of the evening popped into my head. I saw myself at one day old, hair trailing down my body.

Interesting, I remember thinking as I got to the part about the hair. Where did that come from? Yes, of course! Eema's question about the Promised Land and her joke about not leaving everything up to my brother Moses—it was connected to her story about my birth. Eema had been telling the same story about my birth as long as I can remember, but I never took in the reference before. When eema announced that I was the prophet Miriam come to deliver everyone to the Promised Land, she was telling a new kind of story. A new kind of Pesach story. And I was in her story. But why? And what, if anything, was the nature of its truth?

# Chapter Two

## Miriam, ages 11 1/2–15

*On an upper bunk on top of a muddy straw mattress lies a woman who looks like my mother, only younger, much younger, and so thin that she appears more like a skeleton than a live human being. She is wearing a stained grey schmata with multiple tears and is lying on her right side. Her right hand pushing into the mattress, she tries to turn over, but is unable. She glances about nervously, taking in the starved bodies that press in upon her—the spindly legs, arms, and trunks that hem her in and cut off movement on all sides. A long wheezing sound issues from her clogged nostrils as she sniffs the putrid air. Then she goes still.*

I was just beginning to drift off when I felt a tugging at my right arm. I opened my eyes to find Esther peering into them, imploring, "Can't get to sleep, Miriam; tell me a story."

"No, way," I mumbled, rubbing my eyes and yawning. "Oh, aw right, but just one: The Story of Uncle Yacov." I proceeded to tell Esther about how the Himmelfarb family rushed to the train station seven days hence to meet Uncle Yacov, about Uncle being the very first passenger to step off the train, about there being such merriment as nobody has seen before in the history of the world and no one will ever see again, and how we all lived happily ever after. Did I believe that the real Uncle Yacov story would follow the storyline I had just developed? To some extent, yes. Nu? I was eleven-and-a-half years old; and how I wanted to believe in fairy tales!

Next day over dinner, abba announced that Sondra would be moving in with Esther and me. "This vay Uncle Yacov will haf his own room," he explained. "A grown man, he needs his own room. Is gut, yah?" About an hour later, abba and Sondra carried Sondra's cot into our room, eema instructing, "a little to the right" and "angle it up further, Sondra."

Despite the assistance, the narrow hallways made navigating difficult, and at one point Sondra nicked the wall with the edge of the cot. Abba abruptly slammed down his end, rushed by Sondra, stared at the nick, ran his finger along it, then put his hands on his hips and glowered at her. "How can you be so clumsy!" he shouted. "You vant we should have a big hole in the vall, kinehora? You vant the vall should cave in; and we should spend all our money repairing it; and we should haf no gelt what for to pay our bills; and we should haf to move out; and we should end up in rags on the streets like has happened with some other DPs; and Jews what haf been in the country longer should whisper to each other, 'You heard about the Himmelfarbs? Such tsores! But what else vould you expect from greeners?' That's what you're vanting, Sondra?"

Eema knelt down and examined the damage, then turned to abba and said, "Daniel, is nothing. A minor nick that I can repair tomorrow." And after a few more protests by abba and a few more reassurances by eema, Sondra and abba picked up the bed again and, before long, Sondra's bed was safely in my room—a reality, I should point out, that did not exactly please me, for I was comfortable with just Esther.

I immediately thought of my Uncle Yacov story and smiled at my mistake. I had told Esther a simple happily-ever-after story. And already, it has proved inadequate.

It is 6:00 p.m. erev the Great Arrival. The family is seated at the dining room table. His sleeves rolled up, abba is carving the chicken. As Sondra begins gushing for the umpteenth time about how wonderful it'll be to have Uncle here, the phone rings. Abba gets up and heads for the kitchen to answer it. Minutes later, he returns and sits down, a scribbled note in his hand, a puzzled look on his face.

"Daniel, something wrong?" inquires eema, leaning forward.

"Ay yay yay! Such a bruder!" exclaims abba, shaking his head. "Alvays with Yacov, is something wrong. Gut thing he wasn't at Auschvitz, no? We'd haf ended up in the furnace for sure."

"You spoke to Uncle?" asks Sondra. "Abba, he's coming, isn't he?"

"Is not so simple," groans abba. "Better I should read you. Is vord for vord I wrote it down. Is a telegram from Uncle Yacov."

Abba clears his throat and begins reading: "Unforeseen complications. Stop. Unavoidably delayed. Stop. Still coming. Stop. Don't meet train. Stop. Don't call. Stop. Vill write shortly and explain everything. Stop."

"What does it mean?" asks eema, her eyes widening. "Why is Yacov delayed? And why can't we call?"

Abba shrugged his shoulders. And he slumped further back into his seat.

The letter which was supposed to clarify everything arrived about three weeks later, by which time Sondra was back in her own room. While abba never showed us it, saying he'd lost it, on the day of its arrival, he did announce, "Is gut news. I haf heard from your Uncle Yacov. Is delayed on business, he is. Is coming for certain in a few months, yah?" Abba's account is accurate as far as it goes, but it does not cover the totality of the letter, nor the spirit of it, nor for that matter, whatever else abba knew or suspected.

As the family member into whose hands abba entrusted the family documents, I have a copy of this letter that abba claims to have lost. And it seems only right to introduce it at this juncture.

The manuscript in my possession is a pen-and-ink letter scribbled on three sheets of lined yellow paper. The handwriting slants dramatically to the left, as if it were looking backward. Having seen Uncle's writing on many occasions, I have no doubt as to its authenticity. The text reads:

Brother, Shalom:

What a shame about the last minute changes! Just like your baby brother to screw up at the eleventh hour, no? What can I tell you—you oversized baboon? An unfortunate matter—a business matter, if you will—has delayed me. There are difficulties with the accounts which I need to straighten out before coming. But not to worry. It will all work out. I will send you a longer letter when I have time and explain in detail. By the by, I've already given up my flat, and should you wish to write me, I would suggest writing care of my attorney and best friend Lionel Avromson, whose address you have.

What a meshugener brother you have that he should get his accounts into such a mess! I am sorry for any inconvenience that my carelessness has cost you. I know what a wonderful opportunity you are giving me and I will try to be worthy of it.

In the meanwhile, Daniel, let us give thanks to Hashem, master of the universe, knower of all things, that I will be arriving in Toronto within the next six months. Thanks to Hashem, we will work together as brothers should at the older brother's shop. What is happening is so wonderful I feel like a giddy bridegroom on the day of his nuptials. I keep having to pinch myself to ensure I'm not dreaming! After so much tsores, the family will be together again. Bless you, brother, and bless Rachael, who is a good and kind woman. No posthumous victory for Hitler here!

You'll give my love to everyone, yes? Kiss the girls for me and tell them their doting uncle cannot wait to come and kiss each of them in person and hear all about their lives.

About that other matter, Daniel, remember you are head of the family, and you have to start acting like head, though I say nothing against Rachael, for she is a fine woman and a good mother. Is it wrong for a devoted uncle to ask that his little Sondra, Miriam, and Esther go to temple as Jews do? I say nothing against the choices that you and Rachael make for yourselves. What you and Rachael went through in the Shoah I will never fully understand and if anyone has earned the right to choose for themselves, it is surely you two. Indeed, as you know, I weep daily for your sufferings. I am plagued with guilt at having been spared. Each morning, my tfillin on, I pray for your happiness and I would not wish to burden you in any way. Consider this, though, Daniel. If the Holocaust has taught us anything, it is that we are Jews; we are the witness people; and there are forces in the universe bent on our destruction. Let us not do the enemy's work for them. Hashem has not saved us from utter destruction so that we can destroy ourselves. And there is no surer way for us to destroy ourselves than for the youth to lose their way.

As the only uncle left, of course, it would be a mitzvah for me to accompany the girls to temple. And then you and Rachael will not have to bother your heads about it. What is out of sight is out of mind, as the poets say. By the by, have you given any serious thought to the girls transferring to that labour Zionist school? While Rachael rejects Zionism, it's what their bubbeh and zeda would have wished. And how about Shabbat? Naturally, I was delighted when Sondra made that arrangement with the Rothstein daughter to celebrate Shabbat at the Rothsteins every Friday. Better still would be bringing Shabbat into her home. But enough. It is not my decision. You have the wisdom of Solomon and I know will choose wisely.

May we dance at three weddings for three beautiful girls; may your babies have so many babies that Hitler's design comes to naught; and may we all be rejoice together at the coming of the Moshiah,

Yacov

The letter with the fuller explanation which Uncle Yacov promised is not in the family archives. From this absence itself, I draw no conclusions.

The next relevant document in my possession is a telegram which arrived about four-and-a-half months later and which reads, "Yacov arriving tomorrow 18:07 Union Station;" the memories associated with it are of a frenzied moving of furniture; eema asking, "how come with no notice?" abba throwing up his hands and exclaiming, "is not the most predictable man in the vorld;" everyone dragging themselves out of bed at 7:00 a.m. the next day; the house being scrubbed from top to bottom, then the family rushing out to meet the train.

✡

The man before us was approximately five feet ten inches. He appeared to be in his late thirties or early forties. He had abba's black wavy hair and thick lips. His beard curled and waved in every imaginable direction, as if each small section had a will of its own. He wore a gray tailored suit, a huge gold Star of David, and a blue yarmulke with milk white beads at the bottom. Unlike abba, he was slender, though muscular, and his body moved with grace, almost as if he were dancing. Although he did not have abba's eyes, his own were every bit as memorable—very soft, very gentle. And how they glistened!

Uncle looked far past us into the crowd at the far end of the platform. Certain who it was because of the eyes and barely able to contain myself, I eagerly called out, "Uncle, over here."

Uncle saw me, but seemed uncertain. Then he spotted abba and a deep sigh issued from his lips. He placed his hands together as if in prayer, looked toward the sky, and with his eyelids almost touching, murmured, "Hashem be praised." Then he hurried to abba and embraced him for a long time, saying over and over again in a voice that shook with emotion, "Brother, you are my Promised Land. I have arrived at last." Afterward he hugged the rest of us, yes? Then each of the kids grabbed a suitcase or a shopping bag. And the six of us squeezed into abba's battered-up chevy and headed home.

That evening was magical. Presents were distributed all around. Uncle gave Sondra a set of three books on Jewish history, all of them in fine black leather, all in Hebrew. A wonderful present in some respects, I thought, but Sondra doesn't know Hebrew. None of us do. And, anyway, everyone knows that Sondra is hardly a reader.

"By the time I finish teaching you Hebrew, you'll be able to read them like a pro," Uncle Yacov assured her, smiling.

"You're going to teach me Hebrew?" asked Sondra.

"Absolutely. You are the eldest."

I received a Star of David, a silver star set in a Newfoundland stone. I would normally have preferred books over jewelry, but there was something mesmeric about this blue and silver piece. Clearly, it affected Sondra the same way, for she couldn't take her eyes off it.

For most of the evening, we sat in the living room nibbling on peanuts and popcorn and laughing as Uncle Yacov regaled us with one funny story after another. He told a story about a fat Jewish sailor caught in a snow storm. He told several stories about a group of shrewd prisoners in cell block C that outsmarted every single warden pitted against him. His delivery was precise; his voice so soft and mellifluous I could have listened to him for days. Then the clock struck ten, and eema announced, "time for bed, my sheyneh punems," and the three of us let out a collective groan.

"Not to worry, princesses," said Uncle, winking at us. "First thing tomorrow, your favourite uncle is going to tell you a particularly clever joke. One about herring heads." He paused. Then glancing toward eema, he added mischievously, "unless of course, the boss over there lets us get in one more tonight."

Abba coughed nervously.

"Please, eema," Sondra and I coaxed.

Eema caught abba's eyes and the two of them nodded. Flashing a smile, Uncle took a cigarette from his package of Camels, lit it, pursed his lips, and blew a couple of smoke rings. Then he smacked his lips and focussed.

"Once upon a time," he began, running his fingers slowly through his beard, "there was a goy named Ned. Now Ned was a decent enough soul. But he was what is called 'a schtick idiot.' Not very bright, don't you see? And poor man, he knew it. One day, after having been tricked by the neighbourhood children, who were all considerably brighter than him, he decided to become smart himself. He made a list of every smart person he knew. And it was then that he discovered the strangest truth."

"What did he discover?" asked Sondra.

"He discovered that every single bright person he knew was a Jew. He concluded that there was only one bright group in the world—Jews. So as you can see," Uncle added, a deep grin spreading across his face, "old Ned was not a complete idiot after all."

The story was irritating me—especially Uncle's last comment. Eema had read us literature by Moslem sages. Two of my school-teachers—Miss Nelson and Mr. Shkwarok—were brilliant and both were Christians. And despite the mistake he'd made, eema had always insisted that Heidegger was the world's finest philosopher. So how could Ned conclude that only Jews were bright? And more to the point, why was Uncle Yacov agreeing with him? Mental note: Uncle Yacov: very kind, very generous, wonderful story teller, possible bigot.

"Anyway," continued Uncle, "fortunately for Ned, he knew one of the men on his list well enough to turn to him for help. That man was Chaim Kaminsky, owner of the local fish store. So, off goes Ned to Chaim's Fish Store. And he asks, 'Chaim, why is it Jews are brighter than everyone else?'

'Herring heads,' responds Chaim.

'Herring heads?' asks Ned.

'Is an old Jewish custom,' explains Chaim. 'We eat them because there's a special oil in the herring head that makes us smart.'

'And if I eat herring heads, will I become smarter?' asks Ned.

'What else?' replies Chaim. 'You think the head of a dead herring can distinguish between a Jew and a goy?'

Every day for the next five months, Ned treks over to Chaim's Fish Store and buys a herring head. And every evening he cooks and eats it. And every so often he says to Chaim, 'but I don't seem to be getting any smarter.' And every time, Chaim smiles and answers, 'Just wait.'

Now one day when Ned is in the fish store, he sees the customer ahead of him—old man Finkelstein—buy a whole herring.

'How much for the herring?' asks old man Finkelstein.

'Ten cents,' responds Chaim.

Ten cents!, Ned thinks to himself. How can that be?

His cheeks flushed, Ned rushes up to Chaim, and he says, 'Chaim, what's going on here? How come I pay more for the herring *head* that everyone else pays for the *entire* herring?'

'See,' says Chaim, 'you're getting smarter already.'"

A quiet laughter fills the room. Even I laugh, though I wonder how Uncle got me to when I didn't want to. And now it really is time for bed. And so the three of us kiss Uncle on the cheek and trundle off.

Next morning, I leap out of bed fully intending to tell eema about my misgivings over the herring head story. When I arrive at the kitchen table, abba is popping bread into the toaster, eema is pouring the orange juice, and Sondra and Esther are already seated.

"Sha," cautioned eema, sitting down and putting her finger to her lips. "Uncle had chest pains all night and he's just fallen asleep. We don't want to wake him. You remember our telling you about his bad heart, yes?"

"Is he in terrible pain?" I asked, instantly ashamed of being critical of him.

Abba nodded and sat down. "Is not good—chest pains. I am hafing sometimes too, but is not so bad as Yacov. For him, is like a five hundred pound truck what is sitting on his chest. Miriam," he added, his forehead wrinkling, "someone was leaving the kitchen light on all night long. And everyone is saying is not them. You left it on, maybe?"

"Pretty sure I didn't, abba. Maybe Uncle."

"Yah, yah, of course, Yacov. Is okay."

"Abba, why is Uncle's pain worse than yours?" I prodded, taking a sip of juice.

"And why not? Is a different person. Also, in the last few decades, is a harder life what he's led. Vat can I tell you? Money problems galore. Yacov and money, is not a gut mix. Also guilt. Alvays is Yacov feeling guilty because he never vent through the Holocaust. Is a happy man on the outside, yes, but deep inside, is carrying around this guilt. About me, he is feeling guilty. About eema, he is feeling guilty even though he didn't even know her pre-Auschvitz. Also, about our sister. Others too. Anyvay, we are his family. Is no one else he has, no parents, sister, vife, lady friend. Is up to us to help him feel better. So ve vill make allowances and be kind."

"Of course, abba," said Sondra. "Oh abba, poor Uncle Yacov!"

"And we'll do things as Jews for Uncle Yacov's sake because he vants what we should make Jewish."

"What kind of things?" I asked, hesitantly.

"Jewish things, epes."

I feel bad for Uncle Yacov and want to help. At the same time, I suspect that "Jewish things" is code for "going to synagogue." I remember my one and only synagogue visit a few months earlier:

Eema, Sondra, Esther, and I were upstairs in the women's section. While we were allowed to pray, that was it. We watched from a distance as old men, young men, and veritable children wrapped themselves in the wonder of the prayer shawls, proclaimed the sh'ma, approached the bimah to read. We watched as the men waited with growing anticipation, their breath held, their hands quivering, their faces yearning, while the Torah was removed from the wall, then carried through the room. We watched as men and boys rushed to the aisle, reached out with loving fingers, touched what they saw as the word of God, then brought those sanctified fingers to their lips, a look of profound joy in their eyes. We watched and did sweet bugger all. We were not actors. We were not even full-fledged spectators.

I had seen plays. Actors address the action to the audience. But nothing was addressed to us. I remember looking at these holy men and wondering: Why do they even have us here at all? How can they do such injury to their mothers, their sisters, their daughters, their wives? A mistake like with Heidegger? Perhaps. But what do you do about a mistake that is repeated century after century?

"Abba," I finally blurted out, "I'd be happy to do Jewish stuff. But please don't make me go to synagogue. Don't like it."

Abba's eyes started to bulge. "What's not to like?"

"I don't want to upset you, abba, but it's … How do I explain it? A men's space."

"What is the girl meaning?" asked abba, turning toward eema. "Men's space—schmen's space! Like there isn't a gallery for women and girls? Who has ever heard such meshugahs?"

"Trust me on this one, Daniel," urged eema, her eyes meeting his. "A special gallery removed from the main action is not everyone's idea of being included. And you know as well as I that Yacov will insist on Orthodox."

"Is head of this household, I am and I say that she goes."

"Daniel!" protested eema, a pained look in her eyes.

"Head of the household—is just a phrase, yah?" he mumbled apologetically. "Is not to be taken seriously."

"Never mind. A mistake, I understand. But Daniel, do consider. If Miriam doesn't want to go to temple, who are we to insist? We don't go ourselves. How can we force Miriam? As loving parents, as fair minded people, as socialists, how can we?"

"Socialists?" considered abba for a second. "Yes, yes, is a contradiction for sure," he chuckled. "A socialist agnostic forcing religion on the proletariat."

"Let me make a suggestion. Yacov can go with Esther and Sondra if they wish to go. Otherwise, he can go by himself. And we'll do other things together."

"Is not okay that a fine uncle and a decent vorking man should go to schul by himself. He is the uncle. I am the father. And I say it is not okay."

"Abba, I'd like to go," Sondra offered.

"Me too," piped up Esther.

"Punct," concluded eema, handing Esther the pitcher of juice. "Is settled. Sondra and Esther will go to temple with Yacov. Miriam will stay home with us. Yes?"

To my relief, abba nodded, and his eyes began to recede.

"Additionally," eema went on, starting to rub her sore shoulder, "there is one thing we can do as a family that should make Uncle Yacov very happy indeed. Meydelehs, it's something I promised your father and Miriam, there's no male space involved here—least ways not the way we'll do it. Uncle Yacov loves Shabbes. We will start having Shabbes dinner. In some ways, it's an opportunity. I remember Shabbes dinner in my childhood home in Germany. The chicken stewed in its own juices, the family together, the singing of nigguns, the lighting of the candles. A time when the business of life stops and space is made for reflection and renewal. Even for an atheist like me, it is good."

"What's a niggun?" I asked.

"Hmm. Something you'll find interesting. A song without words."

"And what about the Hebrew lessons I'm supposed to have with Uncle Yacov?" asked Sondra, turning to abba. "I can start taking them, can't I?"

Abba nodded and began to beam. "Is gut that you are learning Hebrew from your uncle. Tell you a secret, Sondra. Your Uncle Yacov has alvays gotten immense comfort just from being with you."

"How come, abba?" asked Sondra.

"Is the spitting image of bubbeh you are," he answered, his eyes scanning Sondra's face. "The nose, the eyes—all bubbeh's. And Uncle Yacov misses bubbeh so. What can I tell you? When he was your age, the kids vould pick on him because he vas so sensitive. So—what do you call it today? Artsy fartsy. And bubbeh, she'd comfort him. But poor bubbeh, like everyone else, is gassed she vas, yah? And so who is to comfort Yacov now?"

"Abba, you said that I was a comfort to him. I can comfort Uncle, can't I?" Sondra urged, her eyes meeting his.

"And why not?" answered abba, beaming even more.

✡

I entered the dining room dressed in my green corduroy jumper and new Mogen Dovid. "Gut Shabbes, Miriam," everyone said, their eyes alight. "Gut Shabbes, abba; gut Shabbes, eema; gut Shabbes, Uncle; gut Shabbes, Sondra; gut Shabbes, Esther," I returned.

It was the first of many Shabbeses. And what an evening we had! Throughout dinner, Uncle Yacov hummed and taught us melodies we had never heard before—songs without words that carried us to the soul of the earth: "Di di, di di di." We discussed the meaning of rest, what it is to make holy, our responsibility to repair the world. A banquet was set out before us—chicken, cholent, gefilte fish, tsimmes, chopped liver, wine. No, not "set." We had made it together. And while, traditionally, such banquets are disproportionately women's labour, as in all work in our family, abba did his fair share, as did Sondra, Esther, and me—grinding the fish bones, basting the chicken, polishing the three piece silver candle set, setting the table. Riddles were asked and answered. Uncle Yacov told us stories about a man called "Rabbi Nachman"—stories that made your brain turn inside out and made your fingers tingle. But that is nothing—nothing compared to the lighting of the Shabbes candles, with which Shabbes began.

The lighting was the centre of it all, the prime mover, the secret essence; and to my delight, that essence was female or female-like. Eema was right. All the maleness in the room was temporarily suspended. The room changed—changed utterly. And the power was the power of woman.

Eema had always made quick work of the candles at Pesach, but not now. A white lace kerchief lying loose on her head, her head slightly bowed, eema lit the three long white candles one by one. "*Baruch ata*

*Adonoi Eloheynu Melech Ha-olam asher kid-shanu bemitzvotav vitzivanu l'hadlik ner shel Shabbat,"* eema chanted. Her voice reached back across the centuries so that you could see red tents teeming with women; you could feel the sandy wind in your face. And as she chanted, the strangest thing happened. Her eyes all but closed, her fingers spread out, and her two hands circling about the flames, she drew the air to herself and out again, to herself, and out again, to herself and out again. It was as if she were creating and being created. It was as if all of us were being purified. With each circling of eema's steady hands, you felt lighter. Every time the outstretched fingers completed its figure, another layer of worry disappeared into the flames. Into the flames went the Uncle Nathaniel; into the flames went Eliahou; into the flames went Ivan the anti-Semite; into the flames went the segregated schuls; into the flames went the billowing furnaces of Auschwitz; into the flames went eema's and abba's nightmares; into the flames went the bickering, the putdowns, the possessiveness, the jealousies, the petty mindedness of the everyday world. And twenty-four hours of holiness began—holiness so sweet that I wept next evening when abba placed the scented metal spice box on the table and lit the braided havdalah candle, and slowly, unavoidably, we were ushered back into everyday life.

Nu? Don't mistake me. I did not then and I do not now forsake atheism. But I am no idiot. I know holiness when I see it, hear it, smell it, feel it, taste it. I do not believe in God. But like every other member of my immediate family from that day hence, I believe in Shabbes.

From that very first Shabbes, I identified Shabbes dinner with eema, though there is no question we would never have begun it without Uncle. I was grateful to him for introducing it and knew that by conventional standards, he played a major role in the proceedings, and yet his role seemed strangely tenuous to me, partly because he didn't light the candles, partly because of the whole issue of work. While he told stories and led us in nigguns, Uncle didn't help prepare the meal. Nor did he help clean up afterward. I soon discovered that he didn't contribute manual labour to other meals either. Nor did he pitch in when we cleaned the house. Eema, abba, Sondra, Esther, and I would be on the floor scrubbing, in the kitchen bending over the stove. Uncle would be stretched out on the living room couch, slurping coke from a bottle and leafing through the *New York Times*. At first I figured that he was just taking time to get used to the place. But as the weeks went by, Uncle

Yacov continued as before, even when his health was just fine.

I asked abba about it. "Your Uncle Yacov, he has such trouble doing things. Is guilt about the Holocaust," abba explained. And indeed, Uncle was frequently depressed. Even when he was in a good mood, though, he didn't help.

I didn't have to ask eema. She made her views clearly known. And the differences in perspective quickly became a source of conflict in the household. "Yacov should help around the house," stated eema, loading the dirty clothes into the washing machine. "I know many men don't, but I can't accept it. A grown man should do something."

"Enough already," abba snapped. "Woman, alvays are you cvetching about mayn bruder. Can't you see the man's in trouble?"

"Eema, Uncle contributes," objected Sondra, her voice rising. "He teaches me Hebrew, and he takes Esther and me to schul. So, why you always on his case?"

Now and then, eema also voiced other concerns about Uncle. And you could see why, yes? Charming though he was, at times Uncle seemed to be purposely getting at her.

Mr. and Mrs. Plautsnicki were over. The grownups had set up a bridge table in the living room and played a few games—with abba and Uncle partnered off against the Plautsnickis. The rest of us had been hovering about watching, now checking out abba's hand, now Uncle Yacov's. In the middle of the third game, an argument broke out.

"You didn't signal! How in the name of God was I to know you were out of hearts?" yelled Mrs. Plautsnicki, waving her hands in the air.

"Wrong. One hundred and one per cent wrong! Didn't you see me discard a four of hearts followed by a three of hearts?" countered Mr. Plautsnicki. "By every convention I know, that means I'm out of hearts and it was up to you to lead with a heart first chance you got."

"You did nothing of the sort," screamed Mrs. Plautsnicki. "And how can you yell at me after all I've been through? Rafal, you've forgotten about the ghetto, maybe?"

The argument continued for some time. Finally Mr. Plautsnicki leaned back in his chair, pulled out his pipe, and said, "Tell you what. We've had a few good games. We're getting hot under the collar. The kids and Rachael are probably bored stiff by now. Let's pack in the cards and sit down together, and maybe we can prevail on the maestro over there to tell us one of his stories."

And so it is we all ended up sitting around the living room stuffing our faces with bridge mixtures, guzzling bottle after bottle of coke, and listening to abba's stories about organizing. After about the third story, Uncle Yacov said, "Daniel, I'll bet Rafal hasn't heard the one about how you saved Rachael. C'mon on, you oversized baboon, tell it."

"Is later, I'll tell it, yes?" answers abba, taking another swig of coke.

"Later? Rafal will be gone later. Tell it now."

"I think maybe not this time," says abba, looking uncharacteristically nervous.

"Oh c'mon."

"If you insist, but let the records show, is under protest."

As abba begins the story, I think back to the last time he told it. I recall my difficulty making the images fit. I decide to try once more. Maybe if I make eema something short of a musselman, I conjecture. I start to picture the scene again, focusing as before on eema. I put a bit of expression in eema's eyes, but not too much. I make her almost skin and bones, but not quite. I glance over at eema to see if the image which I'm concocting is conceivable. And I notice something unusual. Eema's head is turned slightly away from abba and she is frowning. But why? Whenever abba tells this story, eema and abba always exchange endearing looks. Why not this time? Is it because Uncle suggested the story? Is it perhaps improper for a brother-in-law to initiate telling such a story? Or is eema simply tired of it? Or has it something to do with the de Beavoir critique eema's been telling me about? Like the story is masculinist? As I ponder these questions, abba gets to the point where he says, "And I asks myself, 'Himmelfarb, you schmuck, you vill let such a woman die?'" The tale has about three minutes left to run, but at this very juncture Uncle shifts in his seat, looks straight at eema, and grins.

Eema turns white and begins to tremble. She quickly excuses herself, murmuring, "My apologies. I have a headache and have to lie down. Please, everyone, you'll go on without me, yes?"

Later that night, as I lie in bed, I hear eema chastising abba. "Daniel, what did you tell Yacov? What did you say about us and the bread?"

"Gornit," answers abba.

"You must have said *something* even if only by insinuation," she persists. "Daniel, how could you? You had no right. None whatsoever."

"You're right. I'm sorry. Like a schmuck, the other day, I am talking sloppy. You're uncomfortable, Rachael?"

"About Yacov knowing and about you taking such chances, how else would I feel? Also, about company hearing the story. I'm at fault here too, but this solution of ours, it really was just for us and the kinderlekh."

"Punct. I von't tell it in company. And I'll be careful around Yacov."

"Rather you didn't tell it at all."

"Is no good any more, Rachaele?"

"I'm sorry. You tell it so beautifully, yes? And the kids adore it, and for a long time I adored it too. Oy, Daniel! We find ways to make peace with the stuff of our lives, and we want to believe those ways will work forever, but...."

A few minutes later, I heard heavy crying—I think both of them were sobbing. And now I was really worried. Clearly, something was wrong with the story. And something seemed to be happening to abba and eema.

Nu? Eema and abba continued to have problems. And they weren't alone. As time passed, most of the relationships in our household became strained. What particularly distressed me were my growing problems with Sondra.

Within two days of Uncle Yacov moving in, the Hebrew lessons began. Uncle and Sondra would go to the basement to study, usually for about an hour. At the beginning, there were two lessons a week. I expected them to go down to one because Sondra had always hated studying. To my surprise, though, they increased to four or five.

"Uncle Yacov," I asked one day at the breakfast table, "can I study Hebrew too?"

"Later, sport," replied Uncle, a wry smile on his face. "I'm a one-pupil-at-a-time kind of teacher. And right now," he added, casting a sideways glance at Sondra, "it's the princess over here."

"How 'bout if I just listen?"

Sondra glowered at me. "You just can't stand me knowing something that you don't, can you? Well, Miss Smartypants, *I'm* the Hebrew scholar in this family; and there's nothing *you* can do about it."

"Meydelehs, meydelehs," implored eema, "there's enough of Uncle Yacov to go around. Yacov, maybe you and Miriam could do something together? You'll give it some thought, yes?"

"I will indeed," agreed Uncle Yacov, nodding.

I was pleased at the idea of doing something with Uncle, for he really was fun, but eema was not reading me correctly. The person I was most worried about missing out on was Sondra. Our relationship was disappearing and I was trying to grab hold of something. Then one day, it was as if it had slipped out of reach.

We were sitting at the kitchen table. Abba and Uncle had been schmoozing about a high ranking Nazi who had escaped Germany at the end of the war when abba said, "Is full of Nazis South America is and, I'm telling you, is Nazis here in Canada too."

"Here too, abba?" I asked.

"Absolutely! The Canadian Jewish Congress may tell us we've nothing to vorry about. But vat do they know? Big shots! Alvays are they making with the pronouncements as if they are the ultimate authority on Jewish affairs! And alvays they are underestimating."

"But, abba, are Nazis really here now?" I asked, my heart pounding. "I mean—right here, right now."

"Is exactly what I'm telling you. Right here. Right now."

A chill went through my body. I got up and drew Sondra aside. "Basement, now," I whispered.

"What for?" she asked.

"To hide from the Nazis."

A mocking smile spread across her face, and she walked away.

Later that day, I started getting glimpses of Nazis everywhere—under the dining room table, behind the half closed washroom door, on the wall right next to Eliahou. I decided to hide. I got up and headed for the basement. I turned the green door knob, flicked on the switch, and started to descend the stairs.

"That you, Miriam?" came Sondra's voice.

"Yeah."

"What do you want?"

"To hide."

"Not now!" she exclaimed. "For Pete sake, Miriam, Uncle and I are studying."

I left, went to my room, crawled into bed despite the early hour, and drew the covers over my eyes. Next morning, I got up hoping to clear the air with Sondra. But when I started to speak to her at breakfast, she up and walked away again. I checked the basement and washroom for Nazis, then went to school, got absorbed by Mr. Shkwarok's speculations on the Quebec Act, and somehow forgot about them. By mid afternoon, however, I started to get spooked by abba's words again.

When I returned home, I headed straight for the hiding place. I felt a strange apprehension as I passed through the kitchen and approached the basement door. I turned the knob and pulled. It didn't budge! I tried again. No use. Locked. As I stood there vacillating between fear and confusion, I could hear Sandra's and Uncle's voices, though I had no idea what they were saying.

Another slap in the face from a sister who despises me, I recall thinking. And how it galled me!

Months passed and my relationship with Sondra continued to deteriorate. Nu? On several occasions, that door was locked. Sondra never hid with me again, which meant I was now under those stairs alone. And these days I almost never got to see her. She was always studying.

I took comfort in the thought that at least there was no malice in anything that was happening. But how could I be sure?

✡

"Hi there, Harry," I called out, as I approached Bloor and Brunswick. Harry Cohan was standing there at the corner, his hands in his pocket. He was wearing his customary jeans, yarmulke, and glasses, though he also had on a brand new pair of blue sneakers. He immediately asked about everyone in the family, but he was especially interested in anything to do with Sondra. One story led to another and before I knew it, I ended up telling him how distant she'd become.

"With me too, Miriam," Harry confided, shrugging his shoulders. "And I really don't get it. One minute she's dating me and seems to like me. Next thing I know, she won't even give me the time of day."

"Yeah, I wondered why you were never around lately."

"Anyway, glad I bumped into you. Gotta go now, Miriam. Got an appointment with Rabbi Israel. Gut Shabbes."

"Gut Shabbes."

I continued on my way, but two minutes couldn't have passed before I heard someone shouting, "Miriam." I turned around. Harry was running toward me, his face flushed.

"What is it, Harry?"

"Just one more thing. This is embarrassing," he adds, catching his breath. "You say Sondra won't hide from the Nazis with you, right?"

I nod.

"I don't know how to put this," he stammers. "So I better just tell you straight out. About six months ago, I started getting suspicious. So I pressed my cousin Ruben for more details, right? And he confessed. He'd made up that stuff about the Nazis. The whole megileh. He was just trying to rattle my chain. I don't know what's wrong with that character," he adds, shaking his head. "I could always trust him before."

For a moment, I say nothing—I am that shocked. "You mean we've been hiding for nothing all this time?" I eventually exclaim.

"Fraid so. I'm sorry, Miriam."

"So, the Nazis *aren't* coming for our parents?" I ask, eyeballing him.

"Right."

"I feel like a complete idiot."

"Join the club," says Harry, smiling sheepishly. "I told everyone. Had little kids terrified that they were about to lose a parent."

"Harry, I know you didn't do it on purpose. You made a mistake. But I don't get it. You've known for how long now? Half a year, right?"

"Uh huh."

"Why didn't you say anything when you first found out?"

"But I *did*. That's what's puzzling me. I phoned Sondra first thing. How could she not have told you?"

I was stunned. I didn't want to think about it. And so I mouthed a few platitudes, then changed the topic and kept plying Harry with questions. How was Moshe? What did he think about the crisis in the Congo? Anything to avoid the central issue. Eventually, Harry took his hands out of his pockets, like he usually does when he is about to leave.

"Harry," I asked, catching his eye. "I'm confused about something else to do with the Nazis—something abba said the other day. Could you give me your opinion?"

"Sure. Shoot."

"Abba says there's Nazis here. You saying he's wrong?"

Harry shook his head. "I looked into the question after that huge blooper with Ruben. There's Nazis here all right. Some came at the end of the war. Some were born here. And, y'know, they have it in for us. So we need to keep an eye on them. But a mass roundup of Jews? No. They don't have the strength or the numbers. That was just us kids scaring ourselves. Get it?"

"Yeah, thanks."

"Anyway, Miriam, gotta go."

I watched Harry take off south on Brunswick and disappear around the corner at Sussex. Then I headed home. When I got to the porch, I sat on one of the rocking chairs and swayed back and forth, mulling over the situation. Sondra could have forgotten about the phone call, I assured myself. After all, she's so distracted by her Hebrew lessons these days almost anything's possible. Then I recalled that mocking smile on her face that last time I had suggested hiding. Who was I kidding? She remembered all right.

In my imagination, I saw Sondra and Uncle sitting opposite each other at the bridge table in the basement, their shoes touching, a conspiratorial look on their faces. A Hebrew text lay open on the table, but they are ignoring it. "You means she's really hiding?" asks Uncle, a twinkle in his eyes. "Just as often as she can," answers Sondra, breaking into gales of laughter. "By the way, you aren't really going to do anything special with that loser, are you?"

It was a cold blustery evening in early January. There was a damp chill throughout the house and a number of the windows had frosted over. Abba had just headed off for a CCF meeting, and the rest of us were sitting around the living room—Sondra and me on the couch, Uncle Yacov and eema on the lounge chairs. I can't recall where Esther had gotten to, but perhaps she was on her bed reading the prayer books that Uncle had recently bought her. She was doing that a lot these days.

For awhile, Uncle kept flipping through this book on Jewish history, mumbling away to himself. But eventually, he put down the book and began looking at me curiously. Then his eyes starting to sparkle, he said, "Miriam, you're interested in family history. Well, that's something you and I can do together. I used to listen for hours to your zeda talking about the family."

"What would we actually be doing, Uncle?" I asked, surprised that he was keeping his word after all.

"You could create a family tree. I could tell you anecdotes—stuff like that. Actually, I could give you a detailed account of the Himmelfarb clan. We could work on family history before breakfast every Sunday. Just the two of us. What do you say, sport? Deal?"

I peered over at Sondra to see if she had a problem with the arrangement. There was no expression on her face, almost as if she were unaware that anything had been said. I thought nothing of this, as she often seemed vacant lately.

"Deal," I declared, delighted at the prospect. I had always wanted to learn more about the family. And if Sondra and I weren't relating, I told myself, at least I could get to know Uncle better.

"And sheyneh punems," said eema, her eyes moving between Sondra and me, "as long as Miriam's learning about one side of the family, why not also learn about the other? How about us women getting together and talking about the Schaeffers and the Panofskys? We can start with the Panofskys, yes?"

The first history lessons with Uncle Yacov were full of great great great grandparents. It seems the Himmelfarb males were tailors as far back as anyone could trace. Great great great grandfather Zachariah Himmelfarb owned a tailor shop much like abba's. And it must have been after his shop that abba named his own, for that earlier shop was called "Zacs Nodl," which is Yiddish for "Zac's Needle."

Listening to eema, I discover that my maternal great grandmother Andzia had originally come from Poland and that a number of the early Panofsky women were midwives. Not only did they bring babies into the world, they knew about plants, about herbs, about the special properties of different metals, and patients came from far and wide to take their treatments.

"Your great great bubbeh Tzedakah was known throughout Europe for treating rheumatism with the application of magnets," eema informed me. "And true to her name, she never charged anyone. You know what 'tzedakah' means, sweetie?"

"No, what, eema?"

"Righteous giving. The women gave. Women do."

By late February, I had taken on a new identity. I was the family historian. I started to create a family tree. I would help my generation and the generations after me know who we were and where we came from. The Nazis wanted to erase us from human history? I would set us down on paper for everyone to see. And I wouldn't make mistakes. I would be reliable. I would get it right.

To my delight, Uncle was particularly knowledgeable. And he explained all the details with such art that I thoroughly enjoyed learning from him. Uncle seemed to enjoy himself too. Of course, I was worried for him whenever we touched on the relatives killed in the Holocaust, but except for moments here and there, Uncle seemed to enjoy the lessons as much as me. "Lesson time again, sport," he would say, rubbing his hands together, his eyes twinkling. "Such a mechayeh!"

✡

"Let's see how the family tree's progressing," urged Uncle, clearing a space in front of him.

Uncle was seated across from me at the kitchen table. Essays by eema's students were strewn about the table, a number of them filled with red ink notations. Eema had obviously been up marking late into the night.

I went to my room, came back with the diagram, and handed it to Uncle. He held it up and examined it carefully. His eyes traveled from one section to the next, every so often stopping to focus. At one point, his eyes stopped moving entirely, and a tear rolled down his cheek.

While I had seen Uncle upset during our lessons before, not like this. "Uncle Yacov, I'm sorry," I exclaimed. "Didn't mean to bring back painful memories."

He said nothing. Just continued to stare. Then he cast his eyes downward and shook his head, slowly, sadly. A few minutes later, he moved his chair along side mine, placed the diagram in front of us on the table, and started eyeing me intently.

"You've nothing to apologize for, Miriam," he finally says. "You're doing me a good turn. You know what? The work you and I are doing together is the best thing I've ever done in my life. Hashem knows, I'm not a particularly good man—not like your father."

"Uncle..." I start to say.

"No, Miriam. Trust me on this one. I know what I'm talking about. But what you're doing—the mitzvah of remembering—this is good. You don't go to temple," he adds, "and that's a problem no matter what your parents say. But whatever happens, remember this. You are doing holy work. You are doing Hashem's work. And I bless you."

"That why you're crying, Uncle?"

"Partly."

For a few moments, he is silent again. Then he resumes. "The family tree you have there," he notes, gesturing toward it with his eyes, "you've done a fine job. A very fine job, indeed. But it won't stand up to scrutiny."

"What's wrong with it? Just tell me, and I'll correct it."

"There," he indicates, his index finger pointing to the section of the diagram covering his family of origin. "Someone's missing."

I bend forward and examine the section carefully. On the top level are Avrum and Anna S. Himmelfarb—my zeda and bubbeh. On the next level are their children—Nathaniel, Esther, Yacov, and, of course, abba. Seems right.

"I don't understand. Who's missing?"

"Your great Uncle Yosef," he replies, another tear rolling down his face.

"I've never heard of any Uncle Yosef," I exclaim, even more perplexed than before. "Who is he?"

"Your zeda's youngest brother. But he was much younger than your zeda. So young, he was like a brother to me. You see your Uncle Nathaniel there, who was born in 1903?" he asks, pointing to the Nathaniel node on the family tree.

"Uh huh."

"Well, there's only one year difference between great Uncle Yosef and your Uncle Nathaniel."

"What was great Uncle Yosef like?"

"An absolute mentsh! And so bright! He wrote poetry. He sang. His head was filled with exceptional images—nightingales that flew on one wing but never missed their mark, frogs that recite Torah."

"What happened to him?"

"Gassed," says Uncle, rubbing his eyes.

"Oh Uncle, I'm sorry. When?"

"1940."

Uncle Yacov's eyes glaze over, and he seems lost in thought. I don't want to disturb him. So I quietly begin working on the family tree. I pick up my pen and add a new node for great Uncle Yosef. I add the date of his birth—1902. I add the date of his death—1940. I want to get a sense of his death in relation to the others so that I can place him in the larger picture. So I examine the death dates of each of the other family members who've been gassed: zeda Shmuel and bubbeh Esther—1943, Zeda Avrum, Bubbeh Anna, and Auntie Miriam—1944. Everyone else's dates are 1943 or 1944. The 1940 date means that great Uncle Yosef died three or more years earlier than the other relatives. Now if I could just recall the Holocaust dates that abba taught me, I could figure out why great Uncle Yosef was killed so early. And then it hits me. He couldn't have been killed in 1940. The annihilation of Jewry didn't even begin until 42. Uncle Yacov must have the date wrong. I look up at him. He's eyeing me closely. I get the feeling he's been watching me for some time.

"You've noticed, haven't you?" he asks.

"You mean about the date?"

"Yes."

I nod. "What's it mean, Uncle? How could great Uncle Yosef have been gassed before the Wannsee Conference?"

"Miriam, we always talk about the Holocaust as if only Jews were gone after. But there were a handful of other groups. Don't for a moment think they're as important as Jews. But there were others."

"Uncle, I don't wanna upset you further," I respond, "but abba and eema taught us different. They taught us that all the groups are equally important."

"They taught you about other groups?"

"Yeah."

"Which ones?"

"Let me see. Political prisoners, gypsies, homosexuals, and ..."

"Pu, pu, pu," says Uncle, making a spitting gesture. "Forget about the faggots and the other sexual perverts," he snaps, his voice suddenly stern, a look of disgust on his face. "What those people do is unmentionable. You hear me? It's an abomination. It's against Hashem's commandments. And, trust me," he adds, his finger wagging an inch from my face, "nary a one of them is ever going to see Hashem's face. But never mind about them right now. There's one other group you should know about," he continues, his voice softening, his hands settling down—"mental patients. Abba and eema ever mention them?"

"Oh Uncle, were they killed too?"

Uncle nods. "In 1939, the Nazis began rounding up mental patients. And under the guise of treatment, hundreds of thousands of mental patients were gassed. And Hashem forbid, at the hands of the psychiatrists no less! Oy, Miriam!"

"And that's what happened to Uncle Yosef?" I ask, horrified.

Tears are flowing down Uncle's face at this point, though no sound comes from his lips. "Sport, as Hashem is my witness, we didn't know," he eventually goes on, his voice quivering. "The Nazi shrinks, they sent us this phony death certificate. What was it they said Yosef died of? Oh yes, pneumonia," he continues, his upper lip curling. "Some diagnosis, eh?"

"It's horrid, Uncle. But I don't understand. How come no one's told me about great Uncle Yosef?"

"What can I say? After the war, us brothers, we'd get together and reminisce sometimes, you know. 'Nu? Remember the day Esther first wore makeup?' we'd say. 'Remember abba's prayer shawl?' But Yosef, we'd never mention."

"But Uncle, why not?"

"We were ashamed, I guess, of him, of ourselves. Whatever the reasons, it was as if Yosef had never existed. As if his name had been stricken from the Book of Life."

Uncle went quiet once more, his skin assuming a distinctly ashen hue. Then he got up, placed his hand on my shoulder, and murmured gently, "Sport, you'll excuse me for a moment."

Minutes later, I saw Uncle and abba huddled together in the upstairs hall. I couldn't make out much—just abba throwing up his hands, exclaiming, "ay yay yay," and "oh, Yacov," and calling for eema.

I sat there staring at the diagram and thinking of the terrible things that happened to Uncle Yosef—being removed from the family, being gassed, having his name stricken from the Book of Life. And I pictured this huge black book. It was made of leather of the finest quality. Each letter was over a foot high. Each page was larger than the kitchen table. It was opened at a page marked "H." In the centre of the page in huge golden letters—all of them capitals, all of them shining like the light of a thousand suns—appeared the name "YOSEF HIMMELFARB." Then suddenly, without notice, the letters disappeared, leaving nary a trace behind.

Who was responsible?, I asked myself. Who had stricken the name from the Book of Life? The Nazis bore primary responsibility for sure. They had killed Yosef, no? But as Uncle's words suggested, it was not in their power to completely erase him.

Eema and abba had often spoken of our responsibility to bear witness to what happened to people in the Holocaust. Nothing of the sort had been done for Uncle Yosef, and surely that was part of the problem. But it wasn't just this responsibility that had been shirked. And the Holocaust wasn't the whole of it. The family—abba, Uncle, eema, and others—had failed to witness Uncle Yosef's very existence. They'd kept quiet about Uncle Yosef for decades, and in the process, they'd turned his life into nothing. But there was something more as well. There had to be or I wouldn't be feeling so guilty. They had somehow implicated us in Uncle Yosef's tragedy. Not knowing about him, we ourselves were not doing our duty—were not bearing witness.

It had never occurred to me that either of my parents would keep anything this significant from me. If I wasn't told about this, what else wasn't I being told about? Were there any other murdered family members that weren't being talked about? Another aunt? Another uncle? And if there were no other relatives, what other secrets lay hidden? Then I thought of Sondra and what she was hiding from me; and I thought of Harry's cousin Ruben. And I imagined a world filled with Sondras and Rubens.

As the world of Sondras and Rubens was taking shape in my head, I could hear footsteps on the stairs—soft like a woman's, not pounding like abba or Uncle. Then eema appeared in the kitchen, her black night gown on, concern flickering in her eyes.

"Sheyneh punem, you okay?" eema asked.

I shook my head.

"You're upset about Yosef?"

"Yeah, but also about it being a secret."

"Yes, my meydeleh," she says, sitting next to me. "Secrets are hard, very hard."

"It's not just hard, eema."

"Sweetie?"

"It changes everything. How do I know that no one's tricking me or withholding information? And if I can't trust you and abba, how can I trust anyone?"

Eema bends over me, places her hands on either side of my face, and stares into my eyes. "Miriam," she says firmly, "look at me. What do you see?"

"You, eema."

"There's love for you in my heart. Can you see it?"

"Yes."

"I can't say you'll never be tricked in your life. I can't even promise never to keep secrets from you, but ..."

That's not what I want to hear. I can feel tears streaming down my face.

"Oh sweetheart," she says, her hands cradling my head, "it's life. Parents can't always tell their kids everything. But I can promise you I will always love you."

"I know what you're saying, and it sounds right. But what if you keep something secret that you shouldn't? And what if ...?" I stop, unsure if I should go on.

"What if...?" eema prompts.

"What if I'm trapped in a world where nothing is what it seems. Not even...?"

"Not even me, sweetie?"

I lower my eyes and only very gradually raise them again.

Eema is silent. Seeing the pain in her eyes, I feel guilty and try to think of a way to take back what I've just said. I'm just about to say something when she begins again, slowly, thoughtfully, "About secrets, we will try to be more sensible. You're older now and we can tell you more, yes? But still not everything," she adds. "As for the world, that's harder. I was in a place once where things were not what they seemed."

"Eema, I'm sorry," I interrupt. "I've no right talking to you this way after all you've been through. I don't want you having nightmares. It's no big deal. Let's just let it go."

"No big deal, meydeleh? Obviously, it's a very big deal. So, hear me out. At Auschwitz, very little was what it seemed. People were told they were going to take a shower. And, in actuality, they were going to the gas chambers. The Nazis posted this huge sign telling everyone about the importance of washing. Meanwhile, they were forcing us to drown in our own filth. And in this world where nothing was what it seemed, people were thrown back onto more primitive parts of themselves, and in the process many of the inmates too stopped being who they seemed. Some inmates would pretend that they wanted to help you when they were just trying to catch you off guard so that they could steal your bread, no? Not because they were awful people, meydeleh, but because they were desperate."

"So how did you know who to trust, eema?"

"You do your best to distinguish. You listen to your kishkeh, and you watch very carefully. Is the person usually doing what she says? Does she generally consider you? You use all your faculties to distinguish the trustworthy from the untrustworthy. And still you're forced into making a leap of faith. Why? Because there are no certainties; and yet you cannot live as if everyone is either a knave or a coward. So, what do you think? Abba and me, do we generally act with your interests at heart?"

I nod.

"Meydeleh, see if you can hold onto that. If not, it's not the end of the world. We'll simply look for something else for you to hold onto, yes? One more thing, meydeleh. Remember, no one is consistent. Not any of us. So you have to cut us some slack."

With this, eema kissed my forehead, informed me that there would be a family meeting in the living room in an hour, and left. I went outside and paced for awhile, promising myself to do something for great Uncle Yosef, vowing to be more sensitive to eema.

When I arrived in the living room, everyone was already there and everyone was fully dressed, except abba, who was shirtless. Abba motioned for me to take a seat between Sondra and Esther on the couch. And once I was seated, he told us all about Uncle Yosef, apologizing profusely for saying nothing sooner. "Is my fault and is not okay," said abba again and again, his voice teeming with anguish. Sondra and Esther looked confused. A good part of the time, eema was also registering surprise.

"You mean it was in T4 he was killed?" eema eventually asked, turning to abba.* "Is that why you seldom mention him?"

"Punct," says abba, picking at this chest and avoiding her eyes.

"Daniel, no one is judging you. We all just want to understand, yes? Why were you keeping it secret? He was a victim like everyone else."

"Is ashamed we were. Also, I didn't vant mayn kinderlekh vorried. I didn't vant them asking: Are we going to inherit it? Then, too, I am scared myself. If it runs in families, what about my own strange thoughts?"

"Daniel, I didn't know," says eema, her eyes seeking out his. "I'm so sorry."

"I am asking myself, is it schizophrenic I am too?" he continues. "And I am not vanting to think about it. And so I am pushing poor Yosef further and further from my mind."

"We all have strange thoughts, Daniel," says eema gently. "Strange doesn't mean meshugah. And these strange thoughts, they're sometimes our wisest thoughts, no?"

"What strange thoughts did great Uncle Yosef have?" asks Esther.

"Is not remembering I am," answers abba, shrugging. "Is so long ago."

"He thought animals had special powers," Uncle Yacov offers, looking over at Esther. "Thought frogs recited Torah. Asked birds for advice."

---

*"T4" is the code name for the annihilation of those deemed physically or mentally disabled.*

"Sounds like a spiritual man to me," suggests Esther, a timid smile on her face. "You don't have to worry about us, abba. I wouldn't mind being like him."

Esther seldom says anything; and so this declaration of hers catches the family by surprise. Everyone looks at her in astonishment.

"I agree with Esther," I affirm, casting a quick glance at abba to ensure that his eyes have not started to bulge.

"Me too," says eema, also glancing at abba, then going over and giving Esther a hug. "A man who communes with nature. A man whom animals trust. A zaddic if ever there was one. We should find a way of honouring this remarkable relative, no?"

For a moment there, abba's eyes begin to bulge, but then they settle back and he starts to smile.

"I'd like to light a yarhzeit for him. Can I, eema?" I ask.

Eema checked with abba and uncle, then went to the kitchen, and brought back a yarhzeit candle. Eema gave it to me. I looked at Esther, took in the meaning of the imploring look on her face, and handed it to her. Esther lit the candle. And we all went silent.

Now in our family, we often got to light yarhzeits, yes? A yarhzeit for both bubbehs and zedas, a yarhzeit for Auntie Miriam and Uncle Nathaniel, some fourteen yarhzeits for abba's and eema's various cousins. A yarhzeit for abba's friends Moshe and Lionel. The yarhzeit for that mysterious woman called "Roza," whom eema clearly cared for but never spoke of. And now, after all these years, a yarhzeit for great Uncle Yosef.

It felt good going to bed that night, knowing that the candle for Uncle Yosef continued to burn. Next day, I sat by the candle and watched it get smaller and smaller. As it started to flicker, I closed my eyes and pictured the big black book. It was opened at "H." And there in the centre of the page was the name "YOSEF HIMMELFARB."

In the next few weeks, I made a point of thinking about great Uncle Yosef. I asked myself, did he ever fall in love? And if he were born today, what would happen to him?

Abba insisted, "Is fine, he vould be. Such good treatments they haf these days! Is marvelous!"

Eema said, "Vey iz mir! How can you say that, Daniel? What's so marvelous? E.C.T.? Drugs? And for what? Respecting animals?"

Uncle Yacov didn't comment, but in light of what he had said to date, I was pretty sure that he agreed with eema, which was strange, since they didn't agree on much. Not even on the history lessons, which eema declared "temporarily postponed." Actually, she never really explained why they were postponed even though I repeatedly asked her.

I wondered what Sondra thought about Yosef, but there seemed to be no point asking. Nu? The yarhzeit and my talk with eema had helped me with everyone else, but the Sondra problem continued to haunt me. It wasn't just her saying nothing about Harry's call. It's that she had written off the entire family. Correction: The entire family except Uncle.

At first, I thought it was only me. I would come into the room and say "hello," and she would just sit there as if I were invisible. Then one day I noticed she seldom talked to eema any more. She didn't even seem interested when eema had meetings with us to discuss important topics, such as our changing bodies. "Sheyneh punem," said eema, looking at Sondra and smiling tenderly, "you know that you can come to us with anything, yes? You're in trouble. Something's bothering you. No matter what it is, you can come to us." Sondra just rolled her eyes.

✡

We were sitting around the kitchen table listening to Uncle's jokes and nashing on chopped liver and crackers, Uncle in his blue sports jacket, eema in her old brown moo-moo, the rest of us in jeans. Esther had overloaded a cracker and gotten liver all over her face and we were all giggling. The radio was playing quietly in the background, but none of us were paying it any heed. Uncle Yacov had straightened his tie. He was about to tell us another joke when, suddenly, abba put his finger to his lips and said, "sha," which we did. Abba reached over to the radio and turned the knob to the right. "Repeat. Late breaking news," announced a deep male voice. "Official sources in the Ben Gurion government have just confirmed that Israeli security apprehended Nazi Adolf Eichmann in Buenos Aires on May 2. Eichmann is now in Israel and is expected to stand trial."

*Image: Two middle-aged men sit facing each other at either ends of a small oak table. The taller man is puffing incessantly on a cigarette. Directly in front of the nonsmoker is a document labeled "Memorandum: impending large scale deportation of Jews from Paris." He glances at a section of it, shakes his head slowly, then looks up abruptly. "I've*

*pointed out the contradictions in your testimony three times," he states
impatiently. "You still maintain that the problems specified here were
nothing but technical transportation problems?" The smoker clears his
throat and carefully flicks an ash into a tray. "Thank you for asking,
Herr Hauptmann," he eventually responds, his tone polite, his eyes cold
as ice. "As I have stated, the memorandum is about shipping. Evacua-
tion and transportation pure and simple. Nothing to do with killing,
Herr Hauptmann."*

Eema and abba looked at each other for what seemed like an eternity and said nothing, their expressions shifting between anguish, worry,
and relief. Finally eema reached over, touched abba on the shoulder, and
said, "Daniel, it'll all come out now. And that is good. But how could
they just go in and grab him? I mean, what will the world say?"

"The vorld?" echoed abba.

"Oh Daniel," she exclaimed. "The six million—they have been
waiting so long!"

A look of yearning entered onto abba's face. Tears rolled down his
cheeks. And eema and abba got up and held each other.

For some time, the family went between laughing, and crying, and
hugging, and conjecturing. And for the rest of the day, we kept asking
each other, "When will the trial be? What will the witnesses say?"

Starting the following day, eema and abba bought every newspaper
they could lay their hands on—comparing, contrasting, underlining,
making notations. And every Sunday they would clip the week's articles
on Eichmann, taping some to the walls, removing others from the walls,
and pasting certain articles into a large green scrapbook bought spe-
cially for that purpose.

Like everyone else, I read every Eichmann story word for word. I
remember my amazement at the sheer volume. "Jews is news," abba
explained. Even more than the number, I remember being struck by the
differences in perspective. I read the *Canadian Jewish News*. I was informed that Eichmann's apprehension was nothing less than the redemption of Israel. I read the *Daily Star*. Snatching Eichmann violated international law, it declared; moreover, trying him for breaking Israeli law
can't be legal, for the state and its laws didn't even exist during the Third
Reich. Was this another one of those instances of different truths, each
with their own validity?, I wondered.

Clearly, uncle didn't think so. "Goyishe news!" he exclaimed, as we sat around the dining room table one evening. "Why are they objecting to Israel infringing on Argentinean sovereignty when the Argentineans themselves no longer object?" he asked, pointing with irritation to a lead article in the *Globe*. "Anti-Semites—all of them! If the Argentineans were objecting, that would be different."

"Is agreeing with Yacov, I am," mused abba, nibbling on a piece of cherry strudel. "But you know the real story here? That tiny little country. Is such a good security they haf, they can track people down anywhere. Vorld class army too."

"Daniel, please," implored eema.

"And even if Argentina did object, so what?" persisted Uncle. "The Argentineans are knowingly protecting people who have committed crimes against humanity. The Nazis are living openly. Everybody knows about it. And no one's been doing anything."

"But Yacov," exclaimed eema, "to just go into another country like that? Without authorization!"

"If I remember rightly, Rachael, you've done things in your time without authorization."

Eema caught his eye and quickly shook her head. Once again I had the feeling of hearing something I'm not supposed to.

"And what about the question of venue?" asked eema, her brow arching. "You really think the man should be tried in Israel?"

"And why not?" countered Uncle.

Months passed by and newspaper after newspaper continued to be scrutinized. While they had other concerns too, one monumental objective motivated eema's and abba's reading—trying to figure out whether or not Jews were going to be in trouble in what they called "the court of public opinion."

"If people don't accept the trial," eema warned, "mark my words. Synagogues will be desecrated throughout the world."

At first, it looked like we were in trouble. I could see that from the slant in the stories. But then the story lines started to converge. And it was clear. The synagogues would be safe.

For survivor families like ours, the Eichmann trial represented a major breakthrough. For it led to a kind of public scrutiny of that period. Don't mistake me here. It's a disruptive narrative that the general public had no intention of coming to terms with, and especially not with respect to Canada's role. Nu? No one asked: how come Canada let in less Jews fleeing Europe than any other country in the industrial world! No one asked why Ottawa's much celebrated politician—the indefatigable Charlotte Whitton—had toured the nation after the war began, imploring authorities to keep our sort out. No one asked how it is that Canada let in more Nazis after the war than any other country save Argentina. No. None of that. No one even asked why Canada kept the doors barred to Jews long after the war, leaving people like my parents lingering in European refugee camps until 1948.

Additionally, while the trial created a bit more space for Jewish survivors to tell their story, it did not create the space we hoped for. Nor was it long before people like my parents were silenced again.

All that said, it was a beginning, an exciting dizzying beginning. Nu? A window was opened. And there was a period there where the country stopped and took notice. I remember. The country turned on their televisions and watched with shock and compassion as survivors like Canada's Sylvia Grottner and Avi Schwartz described details of the camps—the mud, the lice ridden bedding, the showers out of which Zyklon B came. And we watched with them.

The campers and their children would get together in the Plautsnickis' living room; we would sit there, holding each other's hands, our eyes glued to the set.

"That's it. You tell them, Sylvia," Mrs. Plautsnicki would say, pounding her chubby fist on the table.

"Exactly as I remember," said eema, a tear rolling down her cheek.

Jews who had lived in Canada longer stopped calling abba and eema "greeners." Yes. And there were even moments there when non-Jews actually approached us and raised the issue of the Holocaust.

It had just snowed. Eema and I were out for a walk, enjoying the freshness. Turning onto Major St., we saw Mr. Morrison in his green parka and orange scarf, shoveling the walkway between his house and the black cast iron gate at front. As we neared the house, he spotted us, called out, "Mrs. Himmelfarb," and approached, shovel in hand.

"Mrs. Himmelfarb," began Mr. Morrison, panting from all the exertion, "I was listening to the commentary on CBC. You know, on the upcoming trial and all. It really did happen, didn't it?"

"The Holocaust?" she asked.

"Well, the gas chambers."

"Yes, Mr. Morrison," answered eema, holding his look. "Hard to believe, I know, but it really did."

"It's not that I didn't know," he explained, an embarrassed look on his face. "I knew. But not in a real way. You know what I mean? Excuse me if I'm intruding," he added, lowering his head.

"You're not intruding," eema assured him, giving him a warm smile. "And if there's ever anything you want to ask, please feel free."

Though they had never been to our house before, Mr. and Mrs. Morrison came to one of eema's and abba's parties about three weeks later. The Morrisons became fairly regular visitors after that. In retrospect, they were part of the good changes that took place in our household after Eichmann's apprehension. And then, there were the other changes.

I had a bad cold. My throat was raw and my own hacking kept me awake. I had just drifted off. Suddenly, I was jolted back into consciousness.

"Oy Gott! Look at Dena. She can't walk straight. She's not going to pass," came eema's voice, desperate, urgent, most of her words in Yiddish.

"Rachael, wake up," came abba's voice.

"Dena, lean on me. We can fool them."

"Rachaele, is okay. Is me, Daniel."

"Gott! They know about the dynamite."

"Rachael, is no dynamite."

"What's going to happen to Roza?"

"Rachael, is no Roza. Is no crematorium. Is no Auschvitz. Is at home we are with our children."

"At home?"

"Mit the kinderlekh, yah, in our house on Lippincott."

"Oy! I've woken you again. So sorry, Daniel."

✡

I often worried about eema during that period, yes? Though except for those nightmares, she went on as before—making dinner, settling disputes, preparing classes. I worried about myself also, for I had difficult moments. I kept getting this terrible feeling that Eichmann was there, watching, ready to pounce. I saw him in the cracks on the bedroom wall. He was sneering, a notebook in his hands, the word "Juden" on his lips. When I looked at the Uncle Nathaniel, the eyes of Adolph Eichmann glared back—intent, distant, plotting. And Eichmann, alas, was only the prelude.

✡

It was October 30 1960—just after dinner. Uncle, Sondra, abba, and eema were in the living room playing bridge, and I was in my bedroom room studying, when the phone rang. Minutes later, abba burst into my room, a look of urgency on his face. "Come quickly," he urged. "Is doing a call-around, the campers are. They say the Hitlerites are on TV."

When I entered the living room, the bridge table had already been folded up and placed against the book case. Scattered about the carpet to the left of the television lay an assortment of pink scoring pads, a red felt pen, and cards facing in every direction. Eema was sitting right at the edge of her chair, the fingers of her right hand digging into its arm, her eyes fixed on the set. Uncle was leaning forward in the new brown lazyboy, his lips twitching. Esther and Sondra were on the sofa looking perplexed. Crouched just in front of the set, abba was switching channels with lightning speed, yelling, "You bastards! Where the fuck are you?" I joined my sisters on the sofa and held my breath. And suddenly, there it was.

It was *Newsmagazine*. Norman Depoe was hosting. A handsome man in a well-pressed blue suit sat cross-legged, facing Depoe, a swastika emblem on the arm of his jacket. He was puffing on a corn pipe and nodding amiably. Behind him stood a group of men, most of them middle-aged, all wearing swastika armbands, all facing the viewer, all looking very solemn as if they were officiating at a public ceremony of unprecedented national importance. Behind the lot of them stood a large swastika flag, though I don't recall what or who held it up.

"Abba, swastikas," I exclaimed, horrified that such signs should be displayed.

"Sha," said abba, glaring at me.

"Abba, who is that man?" asked Esther.

"Is George Lincoln Rockwell, head of the U.S. Nazi Party," answered abba hurriedly. "Now, sha."

Unfortunately, none of us did "sha," and so none of us heard Rockwell's exact words. But there was no mistake about it. Rockwell was announcing the existence of two divisions of the Nazi Party in Canada—one of them actually in Toronto.

I felt my heart sink. They were here after all. And this time it was for real. And they were setting the agenda, making the announcements, summoning the press.

"We'll organize. We'll apply pressure, no?" said eema, eyeing abba.

"What organize?" bellowed Uncle Yacov, rising to his feet and waving his arms about. "Just create intelligence. Find out who they are. Find out where they are. And kill the sons of bitches."

"Sha!" insisted abba, his eyes beginning to bulge.

After the program, eema drew Uncle aside, and a quarrel ensued. I could tell they were fighting by the way their arms kept waving, though I couldn't quite make out what was said because abba was talking at the same time. Then Uncle disappeared, as did Sondra. And eema and abba started making phone calls.

"They didn't haf anyone better to interview?" abba shouted into the receiver. "What are you meaning 'free speech?' Vey iz mir, they displayed svastikas! Vas on national television! National television, no less! Freedom like that we had in the Veimar Republic. And just look where it led." Abba nodded, then stopped nodding abruptly. "Legal, you say? Punct, if it's *legal*, then let's make it *illegal*. Only with Moses is the law written in stone."

You might think that the family would have gone into shock that night. And on some level, we did. Nonetheless, a kind of clarity and calm set it. There were tasks to be done if we were to keep track of the nazis, if we to raise public awareness, if we were to change Canadian law. And despite the pellmell of the first hour or so, we immediately set about them.

That very night eema and abba and some of their friends held an emergency meeting in our kitchen and struck a committee called "Committee to Investigate Nazism in Canada"—CINC, for short. And a few days later, eema joined a Toronto-based action committee as well. Uncle Yacov joined a different committee, though he never did tell us its name. And I understand that Harry and some of his friends got involved in the youth group Antifa Toronto. Nu? A threat had been identified. And people were beginning to mobilize.

Not that most Jews in that era got involved or even understood. Like most other Canadians, most Jewish Canadians downplayed the significance of the neo-nazi upsurge. I remember our next door neighbour Mrs. Schachter stopping eema on the street and asking, "Rachael, why make such a big megileh of it? Is a momentary flash in the pan. This is Canada, after all." As if the Canadian landscape hadn't included le Fasciste Canadien, or the Swastika Clubs that had harassed Torontonian

Jews and Blacks with impunity, or the hundreds of Whittaker's brown shirts who had marched fully armed through downtown Winnipeg! Fortunately, though, there were Jews who knew Canadian history better. Not surprisingly, for the most part, those Jews were survivors like my parents.

Of that group, a tiny percentage were political and acted. Eema, abba, and many of their friends were among them. And our house was a hub in the operations.

Committees would meet in our dining room—on weekends, on evenings, sometimes even in the middle of the night. While eema declared these meetings "adults only," Sondra, Esther, and I were well aware of what was going on, for no matter where you were in the house, you could hear the deliberations loud and clear.

"You know what the nazis are saying? That we invented everything just to frame Eichmann!" Mrs. Plautsnicki exclaimed.

"What do you think about rewording the petition this way?" eema would ask. "Here, take a look."

I helped in mail-outs—stuffing brochures into envelopes, attaching labels, licking stamps. At first, the tasks themselves kept me calm. What with the meetings, the mail-outs, the newspaper clipping, and the emergency calls, however, the time eventually came when I started to feel as if our lives revolved around the nazis.

Now the early sixties were *all* difficult years for survivor families like mine, but 1963 was particularly daunting, yes? In 1963 the Canadian neo-nazis began stepping up their activity, prod on by leaders like John Ross Taylor, and John Beattie. And while the committees were actively monitoring, we weren't prepared for what happened. Not organizationally, and just as significantly, not psychically.

One Sunday, her face ashen, Esther grabbed my arm, pleading, "Miriam, come." She led me to a series of buildings on Bloor St. not far from Christie Pits—a few grocery stores, a drug store, and a Max Milk. "See, Miriam," she said, pointing. Five different buildings had graffiti scrawled all over them. The letters were huge and red, the style—Gothic. "Hitler was Right," read one. "Communists are Jews," read another. It was weeks after the walls were repainted before Esther would venture to Bloor by herself.

"Miriam, I need something at the store. Don't make me go alone," Esther would plead.

"It's okay, Esther. I'm coming," I would answer.

Late one afternoon, abba bolted through the front door and rushed into the kitchen, the large vein in his forehead twitching, this shopping bag full of neo-nazi pamphlets in his hands.

"Rachael," he cried out, looking straight at eema, "is awful it vas."

"I know. I know," said eema, rushing over to him and stroking his cheek. "It was on the news."

"Ay, yay yay!" he exclaimed, his eyes widening. "That I should live to see such things! Better I should haf gone up the chimneys with my parents and sister!"

"You were there when it happened, Daniel?"

"At King and Yonge, yah. And is thousands and thousands of pamphlets what came raining down upon us. How could the nazis haf pulled off such a stunt?"

As summer approached, I could feel it all becoming too much. It was frightening to see abba so vulnerable. Every so often, for no ostensible reason, he would turn around and stare behind him, his eyes searching out one direction, then another.

I started looking back with a certain nostalgia to that earlier period when I was hiding. However real the threat had seemed at a time, there was a piece of me that had always known I had a part in creating it. Now it had a cruel solidity. Whether I hid or not, the nazis were there. Whether I was ready or not, new incidents would occur.

Nu? I was shaken. I knew I was shaken. But I didn't know what to do.

One very partial solution occurred to me in late May: Don't compound the problem by thinking about the Holocaust. But how can I avoid the Holocaust, I asked myself, when the nazis keep bringing it up? When abba, eema, and Uncle keep bringing it up? When most of the people who hang out at our place keep bringing it up?

I hatched a plan. Take refuge in Shabbes. Let everyone talk about the Holocaust six days a week. And let Shabbes really be the day of rest. I took the plan seriously and immediately began dissuading people from discussing the Holocaust on Shabbes. Separating out one day a week, of course, is no easy matter.

✡

The grass was passing the nine inch mark, a good part of it in seed. While the lilac bush just behind the house was beginning to fade, the air was still alive with the echo of its purple sweetness. The spireas next to it were in petal, white and wonderful and smelling like orange blossoms. Dandelions and ragweeds were sprouting up everywhere—in the grass, in front of the rickety green fence dividing our house from the Schachter's, in the cracks in the side walk leading to the garage. And if you put your head close enough to the ground, you could see armies of white ants on the move.

Uncle and I were sitting facing each other on the grass, him in blue corduroys and a straw hat, me in black shorts. We were at the far end of the yard near the garage, just out of reach of the sprinkler, which abba had turned on earlier. The sun was just beginning to bear down. And the grass was glistening from the freshly dropped water.

I had this raw ticklish feeling in my throat. Allergies, I figured. But no matter. It was good just being out with Uncle. He'd been depressed for the last few days and had been in bed with heart palpitations almost the entire week before. So I hadn't seen nearly enough of him.

The two of us were singing nigguns together and clapping our hands in beat. "Di di di, di di di, di di, di di di," we sang. Of course, the singing made my throat worse, but what did I care? It was Shabbes. The sun was warming my body. The lilacs were swaying in the breeze, sending out wafts of sweet perfume everywhere. A couple of the sparrows perched on Mrs. Schwartz's maple tree next door had begun to chirp. And we were chirping with them.

"Uncle, I'm so glad you're feeling better," I said during a pause in the singing.

"Thanks, sport. Nothing like Shabbat to raise the spirits, eh?"

I nodded and coughed.

"By the by, Miriam, you ever give any thought to beginning the history lessons again?" he asked, shooing away a fly that had just landed on his arm. "I'm more than willing."

"Thanks for the offer. At some point, absolutely, but not now. I'm finding it hard enough just to keep up with what's happening."

"You mean the neo-nazis?"

"Yeah."

"They upset you, don't they?"

"Uh huh."

"Wanna talk about it?"

"Can't we just sing, Uncle?"

Uncle spit out a grass sprout he'd been dangling from his lips. We sang for another thirty, forty minutes, now and again stopping for a moment because of my cough. Every so often Uncle varied the beat or shifted the melody, his head nodding ever so slightly as he led us into each new refrain. Then he closed his eyes and said a blessing for the grass, for the lilacs, for the birds, for the family. "And please give our Miriam the strength which she needs in these trying times. Amen."

When Uncle opened his eyes again, he looked at me intently. "Miriam," he said, "we're all upset about the neo-nazis. But the important thing is, we're doing something about it. We're acting. And when righteous people act, Hashem gives them a hand."

"Not sure I believe that, Uncle."

"You're like your mother—a non-believer. But, you know," he continued, beginning to stroke his beard, "belief is a strange thing. You have a choice. You can believe if you want to. But you can't get there with your head. You have to do things that create belief—read the Bible, go to temple, light candles, pray. You have to take Judaism personally and act as if. You remember what the Haggadah says? 'When God led me out of Egypt.' Me! Not some Jews thousands of years ago. Say it, Miriam. Say, 'when God led me.'"

"Please, Uncle, I don't want to."

"I promise it won't hurt you. Just say it."

"No, Uncle, please."

"Okay, okay, don't say it," he muttered, shaking his head. "But do this for me, Miriam. Remember Hashem first thing as you rise in the morning. Remember Hashem as you eat the food which He has provided. Remember Hashem as you go to school. Remember Hashem as you turn in at night. Remember Hashem as you think about the neo-nazis. Remember, it is Hashem who gives life to us. And it is Hashem who sustains us. And it is Hashem who gives us the power to stand up to Rockwell and Taylor and all the nazis yet to come."

"Uncle, can I ask you something?" I inquired, hoping to change the topic. At this point, I was willing to settle for a neo-nazi discussion. It's not that religion *per se* turned me off. It was hard to put my finger on why, but it was creeping me out every time Uncle said "Hashem."

Uncle nodded.

"Remember that day that Rockwell was on *Newsmagazine*? You and eema were arguing about something."

Uncle nodded again, reached into his left pocket for his package of Rothmans and his lighter, pulled them out, lit a cigarette, and took a big drag. "That's better," he murmured, his facial muscles relaxing and the smoke drifting slowly out his nostrils. "Let me see now. That was over a year ago. Now what were arguing about *that* time? Ah yes, tactics," he answered, tossing the package and the lighter onto the grass, then starting to run his fingers through his beard. "We were arguing tactics. The way I see it, you do what you must to protect your people. Your mother? She doesn't see it that way. She doesn't want violence happening. She's not even too keen on our breaking the law unless we announce our intention first. What a joke! Announcing your intentions first! Totally eliminates the element of surprise."

"You're involved in violence, Uncle?" I ask, a wave of fear passing through me.

"Between you, me, and the lamp post, yes," responds Uncle. "But of a limited nature. Of a strictly limited nature. Mostly, I'm a peaceful guy, a law-and-order kind of guy. But, sport, not every one is law-and-order like us. There are people out there who are inherently violent and who do everything they can to break the law, or side step it, or abuse it. Toward what end, you might ask? To get the Jews, of course. And I say, if we have to break a few arms and legs to deal with them, so be it."

"Uncle!" I exclaim, truly shocked.

"You think your eema's any different?" asks Uncle, his eyes fixed on me. "She draws the line in a different place, but if circumstances are bad enough, she doesn't stand on ceremony, if you know what I mean."

"I don't mean to offend you, Uncle, but eema would never break anyone's arms or legs," I answered, feeling the blood rush to my face.

"Easy there," says Uncle, his voice going gentle again. "We haven't really broken any limbs. And Hashem knows, I would never criticize your eema. She is a decent woman and good mother. And what that woman did in the Resistance! Such courage!"

"What do you mean, Uncle?"

I realize even as I ask the question that I am heading further and further into the territory that I promised myself to avoid. But my mind flashes back to that picnic with the campers: The women's picnic table at Christie Pits. Mrs. Weitzman saying, "Rachael, I swear you were one of the bravest women in all of Auschwitz II." I had waited years to find out what Mrs. Weitzman meant.

"Like your abba, she got people's names crossed off lists so that they didn't get sent to their death," Uncle answers, his voice sounding more and more distant. "And she was even peripherally involved in an important action. If I remember rightly, she was a direct link to the Sonderkommandos."

"Sonderkommandos"—that was the word that sent everything tumbling. I knew who the Sonderkommandos were. Abba had talked about them once. They were special prisoners involved in the gassing. They had appalling tasks—leading inmates into the fake showers, removing the corpses from the air tight room, loading the bodies into the furnaces. I'd had nightmares about them often enough.

Now, I am aware of getting dizzy, very dizzy. And something is happening to my vision. I can barely make out Uncle any more. I see a young man in striped camp fatigues, wooden shoes though no socks on his feet, a gas mask on his face. Large brown rats are scurrying about him. He is walking in the direction of a door with a large peep hole. He moves stiffly, mechanically, like a robot. He reaches the door, opens it, and disappears inside. A few minutes later, the door swings open again, and out he comes. He is dragging some*thing*, or rather, some*body* by a leg. It is a pile of skins and bones that must once have been a man. The dead man's flesh is strangely pink. Red and green spots appear throughout it. Out of its left ear trickles a stream of blood.

The image fades and another takes form. I see eema. She is thin—very thin—and decades younger. She is in a dark room. She is bending forward, whispering something into the ear of a man in striped camp fatigues. Someone is watching them. I can't make out who it is, but I can see eyes peering from behind a large gray cart. I need to warn her. Let her know.

I hear myself yelling, "eema."

Uncle's voice is louder now. I can't catch everything he says because his voice is muffled by the sound of someone yelling. But I do hear him ordering, "Miriam, get down on your knees and pray. Pray to Hashem, and He will help you."

I have a vague sense of watching myself being lifted. I hear someone screaming. And eema's voice keeps coming in snatches. She is saying something to somebody. Something about her being safe and everything being okay.

I am stretched out and in motion. A large metal structure keeps getting closer and closer. The metal structure is a furnace or an oven or something like that. A man in striped fatigues is loading three corpses into this oven. A corpse of a older man with scales and sores throughout his body. A corpse of a child—a girl a few years younger than Esther. A corpse of a young woman. I look carefully at the last corpse. I can't see it clearly, because somebody has just removed my glasses and placed them in a huge stack of spectacles—men's, women's, children's. But there's a red birthmark on the face that would seem to suggest it is me.

I am inside my body now. And that body is inside something metallic which is pressing in on me on all sides. Something is right up against me, yes? It feels like the back of a body, a body smaller than mine. Oh, how it reeks! First, it is dark. Then there are bursts of blinding light. It is hot, so very hot. I can feel my body catching fire—first my head, then my chest. I can hear eema's voice breaking through the flames, urging, "more ice, Daniel. We need to bring the temperature down."

The flame is blue and yellow and white. I am disintegrating. I am turning into ash.

"Wipe her forehead again," comes eema's voice.

I feel something on my forehead. It is cool and moist like a glass of lemonade at high noon on a scorching summer day. How can something be cool and moist when it is burnt to a crisp? How can a body feel at all when it is dead? Think, Miriam. For God's sake, think.

Absolutely no way, I reason. Therefore, I must be alive.

The next few days, my throat was raw, and there was this throbbing pain behind my left eye and a heavy weariness throughout my body. I was drifting back and forth between that scene of horror and a safe comfortable room. More and more often, though, I found myself in the bedroom that Esther, Sondra, and I shared.

I had never exactly appreciated life before. While I had good times, without question, and while Shabbes was generally an exception, I felt victimized by my existence and rather resented being saddled with it. Those days of recovery were different. Exhausted though I was, I trembled with delight at just being around. Everything seemed so fresh, like I was seeing the universe for the first time. I looked forward to the next sight, to the next sound.

"The light bothering you, Miriam?" came Sondra's voice gentle and fresh, crispy clean just like the collars on abba's newly starched shirts. Was she talking to me again, or was I imagining it? Or does it even matter which, I asked myself. What a funny face Esther is making and how kind of her to entertain me! Isn't that Dr. Nostick's chubby red face looming over me, asking me to open my mouth and say, "ah." So beautifully red and round that face of his. And here's eema, good old eema, coming to the bedside with soup, going on about a viral condition that had taken a sharp turn for the worse because of my having a shock, her face all contorted as if such things actually mattered. As if the world would miss a beat one way or the other. And now she's smiling. Amazing.

I slept and woke, slept and woke. Slowly, I became more aware of the rest of the house. The time came when I could take in daily conversations—what was going to be served at supper, when abba was coming home. Stunning—all of it!

One day, the sweet simplicity of it all gave way. When eema came to my room, she was in a rush, and gone was that wonderful smile that had come to her face every day during my convalescence. The day passed. And evening settled in.

I heard Mrs. Plautsnicki and eema schmoozing in the kitchen. They were speaking in a hushed tone as if worried that someone would overhear them. To my surprise, they weren't talking about the Plautsnicki household. They were talking about ours. A couple of times my name was mentioned. Then Sondra's name. Then Uncle Yacov's.

"You sure that's what you saw?" asked Mrs. Plautsnicki, a few minutes later.

"I'm not sure of anything, but this is my daughter."

"Only one thing to do," declared Mrs. Plautsnicki. "You know as well as I do, Rachael. Anyway, it isn't as if he hasn't been a shitload of trouble since day one."

Then Mrs. Plautsnicki said something about somebody having always been a strange religious bird.

Later that night I could hear my parents' voices. They were yelling at each other.

"They're my daughters," screamed eema.

"Is my daughters too, they are. And is my bruder. I haf survived Auschvitz so I should be granted the unique opportunity to lose yet another family member!"

"Daniel, I've talked to Molka."

"Vat am I caring what yenta you are talking to? Is a bruder. Is the only member of my family I haf left. And on sheer speculation!"

"I'm sorry, Daniel. I truly am. You think I want to do this?"

I couldn't make out much more after that—just the odd word—something about a worker, something about money, something about cutting back on meetings and not having them at the house. Something about not talking about the Holocaust so much. No matter. They'd obviously gone on to new topics. And I'd already heard enough to know that Uncle was in trouble. Clearly, eema was upset with Uncle for talking to me about her work in the Resistance. And I had to let her know that it wasn't Uncle's fault.

I dozed off again. I dreamt eema and Sondra were facing each other in the hallway just outside the washroom. Her hands on her hips, her eyes smoldering with rage, Sondra was shouting, "You bitch. You God damn fucking bitch." I awoke thinking only a few minutes had passed, but eema came in just as I started coughing and said something about it being Thursday afternoon and my having slept for over thirty-five hours. "Sweetie, you'll try getting up maybe, and coming to the kitchen?" she suggested.

Eema helped me into my bathrobe. I went to the washroom, then headed to the kitchen and sat down before a bowl of piping hot chicken soup. I wasn't so tired any more.

"Where's Uncle tonight?" I asked, slowly sipping the warm broth.

Eema sat down across from me, reached over, and ran her fingers through my hair. "Meydeleh, we'll talk about Uncle more later," she answered softly. "You're just finding your legs again, and I don't want you getting upset. But you need to know that Uncle will be moving out."

"Moving out! When?"

"Tomorrow."

"You're sending him away, aren't you eema? But it's not fair. It's not his fault. I asked him what you did in the Resistance."

"Is distressing, I know, sheyneh punem. I feel terrible about it. And we'll talk more about it later. But, sweetie, listen to me. I don't want you blaming yourself. There's lots of reasons we needed Uncle to leave. Anyway, he's got opportunities in New York, yes? And he's excited about them."

"He's got opportunities?"

"So he tells us," answered eema.

She was being evasive, I realized. She knew as well as anybody that Uncle's word could hardly be taken at face value. But she was hoping I wouldn't pick up on it.

"Sondra know?" I asked.

"Yes," answered eema, looking at me inquisitively. "Esther too."

"It's just that Sondra'll miss him more than the rest of us," I explained. "I mean, what with the Hebrew lessons and all."

"You're right about that. She's bound to have a hard time." Eema caught my eye and added, "I know you two barely speak these days, but you'll try to be extra sensitive to her, yes?"

I nodded. "He'll visit, won't he, eema?"

"We'll see."

"I'm well enough to see him off at the station."

"Actually, you're not. But it makes no difference. He's getting a lift to New York in exchange for sharing the driving."

"But I will see him before he leaves?" "Just when *is* he leaving?" I asked seconds later.

"8:30 tomorrow morning. He had to go to the shop to tie up some loose ends just now, yes? But he told me to assure you that the two of you would have a good heart-to-heart before he leaves. Here, sweetie, have some more soup," she added, refilling my bowl.

I waited up till 11:00, but there was no sign of Uncle. I set my alarm, got up at 7:30 sharp next morning, dressed in minutes, and came downstairs. There was no Uncle in the living room. And there was no Uncle in the kitchen, just a sealed blue envelope with my name on it propped up against the salt and pepper shakers on the kitchen table. The writing slanted to the left, so there was no question who it came from. Eema said something about being sorry, about having no idea he would just take off. I was disappointed. I stuffed the letter into my shirt pocket, not ready to face the series of excuses I anticipated it containing. And I sat down.

About ten minutes later, Sondra slouched into the kitchen and sat at the table. Her hair was in tangles; and her eyes were red and puffy.

"Sondra, I'm really sorry about Uncle. I know how close you were," I offered, turning toward her.

"You're a baby. You know nothing. Just fuck off," she snapped.

Eema looked like she was going to say something, but clearly thought the better of it and started serving the poached eggs.

Come 8:30 that evening, I still hadn't brought myself to look at the letter. Esther and I were alone in the bedroom. Esther was sitting in the middle of the carpet, leafing through one of the prayer books that Uncle had given her. I was in bed flat on my back, staring at the family tree. I looked up and was about to say something about Uncle when in came Sondra. Without a word to either of us, she sat down on the chair in front of the desk, her back toward us.

"Miriam, I miss Uncle," Esther whimpered a few minutes later, a tear rolling down her cheek.

"We all do, Esther," I say. "Especially Sondra," I add, glancing over at Sondra.

For a while, no one speaks, though now and again Esther and I smile half-heartedly at each other.

"It's partly your fault, you know, Miriam," observes Sondra, her body stiffening, her back still toward us.

"Agreed."

"Doesn't matter anyway," continues Sondra. "Nothing does."

"Really am sorry, Sondra."

Again, we go quiet, though this time it is Esther that breaks the silence.

"Sondra," says Esther, "since you moved in with Miriam and me, the three of us have barely spoken. No special kids' meeting—nothing. Member the good old days when we used to have meetings?"

"Yeah," recalls Sondra, cautiously turning her chair about.

"Remember that day when we pinched a pack of cigarettes and smoked the whole thing?" I ask.

"Absolutely," Sondra says, beginning to grin, "and like, how about the time we took the kitchen clock apart, thinking we could put it back together?"

The three of us reminisce for some time, exchanging knowing looks. For awhile there, we are even chuckling. Then Sondra straightens her back abruptly and says, "I've a better one. Remember that time Harry Cohan told us that the Nazis were coming and we had to give up one of our parents?"

Now Sondra had yet to say a word about Harry telling her that his cousin had made it all up. I wondered if she's going to say something now. I hoped so. Then maybe I could start trusting her again. I'd like that. It would feel good having my older sister back. Already it was feeling good.

"Well, guess what?" says Sondra, turning toward me. "We're voting again. Miriam, how do you vote?"

"I don't understand," I stammer, staring at her in disbelief. "What exactly we voting on?"

"What else? On who to save from the Nazis. As the eldest, I'm calling for a new vote. I *am* still the eldest, you know."

"Oh c'mon, Sondra. We're getting too old for this. And you know as well as I that there's no point."

"You vote first," she insists.

"Not this time."

"Just to clarify the rules, no vote will mean your original vote stands. So what is it?"

"I'm not doing it."

"One vote for the bitch," announces Sondra.

"Sondra, for God's sake!" I exclaim.

"And your vote, squirt?" she asks, looking over at Esther.

"Eema," answers Esther, a stunned look on her face.

"Big surprise! Two votes for the bitch," sneers Sondra, holding up two fingers. "It's looking good for the bitch, isn't it? You think you can save her. But no. It has to be unanimous; and this time, it isn't. So the bitch is done for."

I can't bring myself to say anything to Sondra. I just want to get out of that room. I get up and am about to go when Esther asks, "Sondra, how come you're voting for abba this time?"

"Abba? Is that what you think? Fuck, no!" exclaims Sondra, waving her hands in the air, a wild look in her eyes. "Screw both of them. Screw the bitch *and* screw the bitch's husband."

"I don't understand," says Esther, her eyes scrunching up. "There's only two people to choose between."

"If the Nazis are coming for that generation, that means *all* of that generation. That means Uncle too. So that's who I'm voting for. I'm voting to save Yacov. I'd far rather save him than either of those losers."

I can't even look at Sondra now. I know I promised eema, but there are limits. "I'm out of here," I call out, heading for the door. "Esther," I add, turning toward her, "you know there's nothing to worry about. It's just Sondra messing with us. Eema and abba are safe."

Esther nods.

"We'll just see about that," threatens Sondra.

I turn around and walk out. I make it to the porch, sit down on one of the rocking chairs, and start to rock. I feel nauseous almost instantly and so put my feet on the floor and bring the chair to a stand still. I consider returning and trying to talk some more, but I don't have the heart for it. I am starting to feel weak again. My legs are getting rubbery and it is hard to keep my eyes open. I should probably be going to bed, I realize, but how can I possibly go back in that room again?

Bit by bit, I go through my memories of the last week, hoping to make sense of what has happened, but I can't. Then I remove the letter from my pocket, tear open the envelope, and begin to read.

"Sport, Shalom," it begins:

My sincere apologies for not waking you. I know that I promised. But you've been very sick, and I couldn't bring myself to deprive you of the rest you so clearly needed. You will forgive a doting uncle who has always only wanted what is best for his beloved nieces?

I am sorry about upsetting you the other day. As I told you years ago, I am not as good a man as your abba, though Hashem knows, I try.

I'm off to New York. As your parents, I'm sure, have mentioned, I've been offered a wonderful position there. It's still in the hush-hush stage, so I can't go into details, but I'll tell you more shortly. Give me a few months to get settled and I will write. And what letters us two historians will exchange!

By the by, I will always think back fondly on our history lessons together. You have given me back my Uncle Yosef, Miriam. And Hashem knows, I'm eternally grateful for that. Such a mitzvah! Whatever happens, whatever is said or not said about me and my time at the house, you will remember our lessons, yes?

I continue to respect your work. I pass responsibility for the history of our family to you. Keep records, Miriam. Keep the family tree up to date. And find ways to tell our story.

I hope you will try temple again. In this regard, don't blame Hashem for the shortcomings of a foolish Uncle. And who knows? Temple could surprise you.

Can I impose upon you by begging one more favour, sport? The princess—she's taking my leaving very hard. You will look out for her, won't you? You have a heart as well as a head. You have always been my favourite niece, and I know you will be kind.

May Hashem watch over you. May Hashem shower blessings upon you. And may the two of us dance together at your nuptials.

Your doting Uncle,
Yacov.


P.S. Incidentally, I don't mean to be uncharitable, but if that Cohan boytshik should start dropping by again, I wouldn't give the s.o.b. the time of day. As I told your sister at the time, Harry spoke to me incredibly rudely on several occasions during my first years at the house. I pride myself on being a fair judge of men, and I can read that man like a book. That young man has no respect for his elders or women either for that matter. And ultimately, a Jew who respects neither elders nor women does not respect himself, his tradition, or his people. And there's just no saying what damage he could do.

I stared at the letter for some time. How could Uncle possibly call me his favourite niece when I so clearly was not? And what in the world had happened between him and Harry? Exhausted, I repocketed the letter, went to the living room, and flicked on the television. And in short order, I fell asleep on the couch, wondering about Harry and watching a rerun of "Leave it to Beaver."

## Chapter Three

## Miriam, age 15 1/2

I awoke in the morning, sprawled out on the sofa, a kink in my neck, Uncle and Sondra on my mind. I peered about, sat up, and began pressing on the kink with my finger—first gently, then harder. No, it hadn't been a bad dream. Uncle was gone. Harry had not treated Uncle properly. And that meshugahs with Sondra! Gotenyu!

My relationship with Sondra was feeling close to the breaking point. Nonetheless, remembering my promise to eema, I got up and tried to talk to Sondra. Again she turned her back on me.

The next few days were not as bad as I'd anticipated. Sondra shot poisonous looks at eema over the dinner table, but what's new about that? And Sondra's hair was in tangles, as if she just couldn't be bothered, but that too had become common enough. Then after about three, four days, there was a small change. Sondra began addressing eema on occasion. "Lila tov," she said one evening as she headed to the bedroom. "Eema, what time is it?" she asked one morning at breakfast. I wondered if she would refuse to come to Shabbes dinner given its association with Uncle. But come she did, even donning a red taffeta dress for the occasion. Could it be we were returning to normal?

Normal! Who was I kidding? Ever since Uncle's abrupt departure, nothing in this household any longer felt normal. Oy! It was as if the entire house was haunted with the presence of Uncle not-being-there. Uncle was not-there at the Shabbes table as the family sang nigguns. Uncle was not-there on the couch as we dimmed the lights and switched on the CBC news. And Uncle was not-there when we passed that room that he'd occupied lo these past several years. What added to the sense of haunting, while Sondra had moved back into her old room, she had not repositioned a stick of furniture. There was the bed smack in the middle of the room, the chestnut drawers to the right, yes? There was

109

the rectangular mirror on the wall, slanting dramatically to one side just as Uncle had left it. What spooked me more, when it came time to clean the house, Sondra would actually pull an Uncle Yacov on us. She would grab a newspaper, stretch out on the sofa, and begin to flip through it just as he had, totally ignoring the fact that the rest of us were bent over the broom, sweeping, or down on our knees, polishing.

I glanced at eema the first time this happened. I saw eema take note, suck in her lips, and say nothing. I didn't dare look at abba.

Abba was beside himself. "Where could it be?" he asked, pacing back and forth between the coffee table and the television. "Does a broach doesn't valk off by itself?, I ask you. Is leaving the blinds up you were, Miriam?" he checked, coming to a halt.

"No, abba. Honest."

"You mean that emerald-studded piece, abba?" asked Esther.

"Yah, your eema's favourite broach, what I gave her to celebrate our first anniversary in the new land. You saw it?"

"Sorry, abba. No. Just asking."

Abba resumed pacing. "One of you girls must haf left for us the blinds up. You left the door open too, maybe. And some schmendrik is looking in, spotting, and taking. Ay yay yay! Ganefs everywhere!"

"Daniel, don't upset yourself," urged eema, giving him a warm smile. "I'm sure the girls did nothing of the sort. Just relax and give it time to show up. The rest of you too, no worrying."

We did as eema suggested. But a week and a half later, there was still no sign of eema's broach.

✡

It was almost Shabbes, just an hour or so before sundown. I was rifling through the top drawer of my dresser, searching for my Mogen Dovid. I kept it in the small black box it came in beside the other boxes and just in front of my underwear and socks. I spotted the other boxes instantly—the blue box with the assortment of thread, the see-through box with the hair clips. But not *this* one. I removed each piece of clothing one by one, but no. I opened all the other drawers. I searched the rest of my room—the closet, the book shelves. Nothing!

The family was in the dining room beginning to set the table. I must have been more agitated than I realized, for while I'd intended to say nothing about it, within seconds of arriving, I found myself blurting out, "Eema, my Mogen Dovid's missing."

"Sorry, meydeleh. Let me see now. You've checked your drawers?" asked eema.

"Several times."

"And the closet?"

"Yeah, and the bookcase, and the table."

Seeing my distress, in short order eema turned the family into a search party.

"We'll take a quick look now, Miriam," she said, turning to me. "If we don't find it by the time the roast is done, though, sheyneh punem, just put it out of your head; and we'll sit down together as a family and make Shabbes. And we'll do a more thorough search on Sunday, yes?"

"Thanks, eema."

"Okay, let's be methodical," eema resumed. "We'll each search one room, yes? Esther, you take yours and Miriam's room. Sondra, how about you schlepping yourself to the dining room? Miriam, you check out the washroom. I'll take the basement. And Daniel, how about you going through Sondra's room?"

Except for abba, who stopped to make himself a cup coffee, everyone set off immediately. Almost before it started, my search of the washroom was interrupted by Esther. "Miriam, I need to go badly," she pleaded, her voice urgent. I left. Standing in the hallway, I heard a sound in Sondra's room. I figured it was abba and that he had already started searching it. But no. The footsteps are too soft. And I can still hear abba shuffling about in the kitchen. A minute later, the door creaks open, and out comes Sondra.

Sondra sees me looking at her and quickly places her hands behind her back, then heads straight for my bedroom, announcing, "With the shrimp busy in the washroom, figured I'd check out your room. Hey, you can thank me later." As she turns to enter my room, I can see her hands cupped behind her back. She is hiding something, but not well enough. A piece of silver chain is visible between her knuckles. Not realizing I've detected it, Sondra carefully closes the door behind her. Seconds later, she thrusts the door open again and enters the hallway, holding the Mogen Dovid up high and proclaiming triumphantly, "Hey, everyone. Look what I found." I stare at her in amazement as the whole family comes running.

"Way to go, Sondra," exclaims Esther, exiting the washroom and

111

giving Sondra a thumbs up.

"Mazel tov!" yells abba, nearing the top stair. "You found it where?"

Sondra turns to abba. "Was in the top drawer of the dresser after all. It's like you always said, abba. Miriam'd lose her own head if it wasn't screwed on!"

"It was in Miriam's room?" eema inquires, eyeing Sondra curiously.

"Yeah, eema. What can I tell you? Like, I opened the top drawer and *voila*, there it was."

"In plain view?" asks eema, her brow arching.

"Uh huh. That's Miriam for you. The dingbat really should learn how to look, don't you think?"

"Enough now, Sondra. You found it. And Miriam has her Mogen Dovid back. And that's the important thing. And now we can all make Shabbes, yes?"

We returned downstairs. And before long, we were sitting around the dining room table, the candles blessed, and ample portions of roast, tsimmes, and knishes on our plates. I sat there, cutting the beef into bite-sized pieces, galled by Sondra's chutspah. Then inevitably, it began dawning on me: If Sondra was the explanation behind my missing Mogen Dovid, she was probably also the explanation behind eema's missing broach. I considered saying something—not now, of course, because it was Shabbes—but Sunday maybe. But I decided against it. Sondra knows she was almost caught, I reasoned, and with any luck she now realizes that stealing is too risky—if indeed, it was stealing. After all, Sondra could have simply borrowed it without permission. So why upset everyone needlessly? Why not give Sondra a chance to slip this back as well?

Another week went by, but eema's broach did not materialize. Sondra had started being surly again, but I figured she was feeling better regardless because she was dolling herself up; and it seemed to me that she was once again socializing a lot, because whenever I bumped into her outside the house, she was always on some guy's arm. Initially, I thought that these were all dates, but no, it soon became clear that she was going steady with Harry Cohan. Actually, Harry was dropping by regularly these days.

Abba didn't seem to mind, which was a relief given his usual response to our dating. I suspect it's because Harry was the eldest of the campers' children and had always commanded a certain respect. Me? I was a little wary because of Uncle's letter, but I had always looked up to

Harry, and so didn't know what to believe.

"Sondra," I asked one day when we were alone in the kitchen, "Uncle and Harry never really hit it off. He ever say anything to you about it?"

"Whatchya mean?"

"Well, you know, about Harry being rude to him."

"Oh that," she groaned, rolling her eyes. "Forget about it."

"I was a bit concerned, is all."

"Like I really believe you!" she exclaimed sarcastically. "You've always had the hots for Harry, and wouldn't you just love to break us up!"

I was bewildered by Sondra's accusation and a little offended, but I said nothing.

Abba's tolerance of Harry continued. The two of them even started playing chess together. One evening as we were hanging out in the living room, abba offered to take us all out to the movies on Sunday, actually including Harry in the invitation.

"Is important we go out. It'll help us take our minds off Uncle, no?" explained abba. "And Hershel, you come too," he added, turning toward Harry.

Harry thanked abba but looked awkward, as if unsure what to do. He glanced at Sondra, who was sitting next to him on the sofa.

"No way. Harry and I have other plans," asserted Sondra, grimacing.

Abba turned red, threw his hands in the air, and rose from his seat. "Other plans, other schmans. Like the family isn't good enough to go to a movie with? For this I have survived Auschvitz! So that I vill haf children what are too busy to spend time with their abba and eema!"

Sondra went pale and sneered, but said nothing. Harry looked strangely calm, like he was used to these kinds of outbursts.

"Sondra, we can always change our plans," Harry offered, smiling amiably at her. "I mean, for a family outing and all."

"No, no. It's okay. The two of you, enjoy yourselves. And you'll join us another time, yes?" suggested eema.

Harry shot a quick look at Sondra, then nodded.

Abba stared at Esther and me. "So how's by the rest of you? You are also busy people what cannot possibly make time for family because you haf plans?"

Eema, Esther, and I thanked abba profusely, repeatedly assuring him that we were delighted at the prospect of going. And abba quickly calmed down and returned to his seat.

Now I don't recall what movie we saw, though I do remember that Tony Curtis was in it. And he kept batting those sexy eyelashes of his. Also that abba's heart started to act up.

As I sat in the dark, looking up at this huge close-up of Tony's long eyelashes, I distinctly heard abba groan.

"Daniel, you all right?" whispered eema.

"A bisel heart ache. Is nothing."

"We'll go home, yes?"

"Rachaele, is not right to drag the kinderlekh to the movies only to schlep home again. Anyvay, is not a big pain. Honest."

"Alright, Daniel, but you'll let us know if it gets worse."

Abba was feeling a bit better by the time the film was out; he offered to take us out for milkshakes like always, but eema was not about to take any chances. So we headed to the parking lot, got in the chevy, and took off home—abba, driving, eema beside him, Esther and me in the back.

Most of the way back, Esther was gushing about Tony, but I wasn't exactly paying attention. I had opened the window for air and was watching the sky darken as we road along Queen then headed north on Spadina. How the lights of the establishments gleamed against the grey brown air outside! How the streets stirred with life! Adults stopping to say, "Hi there, Marg, Lila, Jack; whatchya been doing with yourself lately?" Teenagers hanging around on the corner and exchanging tales of erotic adventures. People flowing in and out of the shops. It started to drizzle, and the smell of freshness began teasing my nostrils. Then the rain got more steady: Drop, drop, drop. And the people began rushing. Whoosh! Splash. Abba turned on the windshield wipers. The wipers leapt into motion. Swoosh. Swoosh. Swoosh. Swoosh. Mechanical arms that had taken their orders and cared not what they struck down in the process. They followed orders. They followed orders. They followed orders. They proceeded relentlessly—up, then down again; up, then down again; up, then down again. I saw a bug flattened when they first started, and now it stuck there—a black smudge splattered against the pristine glass. What else? What if a miniature person was caught toward the bottom of the windshield?, I wondered. A tiny person could get crushed by these wipers. She would have to make herself as small as possible and pray that the wiper would miss. She would be afraid to go to sleep, for fear of stretching out and the merciless arm getting her. If there was food a stretch away but that stretch extended her into the danger zone, she would have to time her movement ever so carefully. How much time did she have? One-and-a-half seconds? Two seconds? Was that was it was like being at Auschwitz? Waiting, watching, timing, knowing that at any moment you could be wiped out?

By the time we pulled into the driveway, it was pouring heavily.

"Vey iz mir," groaned eema, looking about at the three of us. "No one is dressed properly. We'll catch our death for sure."

"Let's make a run for it," suggested abba, taking the key from his pocket.

Although we were out like a shot—onto the curb, into the yard, onto the porch—we got drenched anyway.

Eema immediately scurried to the washroom to get towels; abba headed for the living room to get some whisky. "Is gut for my heart," he pointed out. Esther and I stood shivering in the hallway, waiting for eema to bring the towels. Seconds later, a piercing scream came from the living room. Gotenyu! Abba's heart! Esther and I rushed to the living room where we took in a scene we were not in the least prepared for.

Abba is standing in the middle of the room, white as a sheet, his eyes bulging, the large vein in his forehead pulsing. Harry is on the couch, half sitting up, half crouched over, his shirt buttons undone, a look of horror in his eyes. Harry quickly sits up straight and begins buttoning his shirt, in the process exposing the person under him. Stretched out on the couch is Sondra, not a stitch on, her skirt, blouse, bra, underpants, and socks lying in a pile on the floor in front of her, her hands reaching toward Harry's buttons.

In rushes eema. She looks around at everyone, her eyes widening. The green and the red towels in her hands drop to the carpet.

"Sondra, please stop," urges Harry, moving her hands away and retreating to the far corner of the sofa. "Sondra. They're home. Oh, Mr. and Mrs. Himmelfarb," he exclaims, looking up at abba, then eema, "I'm so sorry. It's all my fault. What you must think of me!"

"Is vearing a yarmulke but is no Jew what you are," bellows abba, pacing back and forth. "Does a Jew act this vay? Does a Jew disgrace a daughter in her parent's house? And after I made you welcome and everything. And you," he snarls, glaring at Sondra.

Sondra shrugs her shoulders, grabs the bottle, and takes a swig.

"You mind if I take the bottle now, Sondra?" asks eema, approaching her.

Sondra shrugs her shoulders again. Eema bends over Sondra for several moments, running her fingers through Sondra's hair. I keep expecting Sondra to swear at her, yes? But Sondra is quiet.

"I'll be right back, so everyone please give me a moment," says eema. Eema picks up the bottle and heads out of the room. She quickly returns with Sondra's beige coat and drapes it over her. Then she comes over to Esther and me, touches each of us on the shoulder, eyes us meaningfully, and says, "Meydelehs, I know you're upset, but this is something for abba and I to discuss with Sondra and Harry. You'll go to your room now, yes?"

Esther and I nodded. As I started to say goodnight, abba knelt down, picked up the bra, glared at Sondra, and threw it at her, shouting, "Just look at you—you slut! Is a posthumous victory for Hitler for sure." There were tears in his eyes.

"Girls, go now," urged eema, catching my eye.

Esther and I went upstairs. Though I knew I shouldn't, I immediately laid down on the bed and listened. I could see that Esther was listening as well.

I could hear Harry stating repeatedly that it had all been his idea and that he had plied Sondra with liquor. And I could hear abba threatening Harry.

"Daniel, calm down. No one's going to throttle anyone," I heard eema say. "Harry shouldn't see Sondra for a while, and maybe we'll re-evaluate later; but we're not going to make a big megileh out of this. And we're certainly not going to hurt the boy. Nor are we going to call our daughter names. I'm going to put on the coffee. Sondra is going to go to her room and get dressed. And the four of us are going to sit down and work something out, yes?"

"*Now* she wants to talk!" exclaimed Sondra. "Like she throws out Uncle without so much as a how-do-you-do; and she's getting ready to throw out my boyfriend; and she thinks we can just fucking strike up a conversation."

"Sondra, I understand you being angry about Uncle. We can talk about that later. And about Harry, we'll see. Right now, you'll get some clothes on, yes? And everyone, please lower your...."

I couldn't hear much more after that—just mumbling and every so often abba yelling out, "Di beyner zolen im oysrinen," which roughly means, "May his bones be drained of marrow."

About an hour later, Harry left. For awhile, Sondra and eema were whispering in Sondra's room. Then Sondra yelled, "just leave me alone," and eema's and abba's door closed.

"How could he do such a thing!" I heard abba exclaim a short while later.

"Daniel, your heart," urged eema.

"Never is that mamzer setting foot in this house again. Imagine shikering her up so that he can take off her clothes and God knows vat else! And in her parents' own house!"

"But he took responsibility. And Sondra's no child."

"Yah, yah. And that's another thing. How could she let him? Rachaele, is it like with Yosef, you think? Is it sick she is, maybe? Is needing to see a psychiatrist?"

"No, Daniel."

"Is after her bubbeh Anna we named her. Remember, Rachaele? Her bubbeh what died at Auschvitz. Ay yay yay! My poor mother! Is this why she told my abba to save the next generations? Is this why she said, 'Avrum, vat happens to us is not important, but the kinderlekh?' So that she should haf a namesake what becomes a whore? But if Sondra is sick in the head and is needing a doctor, that's different."

"Daniel, she's angry and she's a teenager. Not a crazy kid and not a bad kid."

"She's a whore."

"Sha. And please, don't call our daughter names any more."

"Oy, that I should live to haf a daughter to shame me."

"Daniel!"

"No more names, I'm hearing you. But is such tsores, Rachael."

"Of course, sweetheart. But we've had far worse tsores and can handle it. We are no weaklings, you and me. Come. Let's turn off the lights and get some rest. The tsores, it'll wait for tomorrow. Gai schlufen."

"Gai schlufen, my Rachaele."

I repositioned my pillow and pulled the blue flannel blankets over my head. I recalled Uncle Yacov's warning about Harry. And I imagined the windshield wiper continuing on its relentless course downward.

Next day, eema and abba argued over whether or not Sondra should see a shrink. Abba was in favour, eema, against.

"The two of you can just forget it," snarled Sondra. "And eema, don't you dare pretend to be on my side. I heard you talking about dragging the family to see a family therapist. You think I don't know what that's all about?"

By Monday evening of the following week, abba and eema had finally agreed on the length of time that Sondra and Harry were to stay apart. Esther and I were in our bedroom doing homework when they told Sondra. So we didn't hear the explanation, but we most certainly heard the aftermath.

"You can't be serious!" screamed Sondra. "What hypocrites! Like you guys never had sex? Give me a break!"

"Young lady, is no vay to speak to your parents," roared abba.

"Abba is right," came eema's voice, steady as usual. "You're angry with us, Sondra, yes? Punct. It's okay to be angry. And we want to hear about it. But directly, not sniping like this. As for your point, abba and I have never claimed we don't have sex. Nor are we stopping you and Harry. You are sixteen now, yes? And you feel certain things; that's perfectly normal and we understand that. You and Harry want to have sex in two months' time, and you're able to do it responsibly, that's your business. But meydeleh, don't combine it with drink. Use the birth control that I bought you and no sex on the living room couch. It's public space, yes? What you did, it's disrespectful. And disrespect, we won't tolerate."

"No sex on the living room couch," repeated Sondra, mimicking eema's tone of voice. "Now how's someone with as few brains as little ole Sondra possibly going to remember anything as complicated as that! Oh, yeah, I know. I'll just have to keep repeating it. No sex on the living room couch. No sex on the living room couch. No sex on the...."

"Sondra, enough," said eema.

I was pretty sure Sondra was skipping school at this point because whenever I arrived home after four, she was always there, stretched out on the couch. One day I entered the living room expecting to see Sondra lying there as usual. While she wasn't around, she must have been in the living room recently because I could smell her perfume. Also, the television was blaring, and only Sondra ever put it that loud. I decided to turn it off before abba arrived and gave us all shit over the hydro bill.

As I approached the set, I detected a slightly charred smell in the air. I followed the scent to the large bookcase directly opposite the mirror. I couldn't figure out why the bookcase would be giving off a charcoal-like odor and decided to investigate. I checked the top shelf. Yes, the Shakespeare texts were all there and all fine. So were the other literary texts—Chaucer, Marlowe, Milton, Johnson, Pope, Wordsworth, Coleridge, Yeats, Eliot—all looking like they should. I quickly perused the shelf directly below it and then checked for specific books. De Beavoir's *The Second Sex*—looking good. Sartre's *Being and Nothingness*—perfect. Heidegger's—oh no! The text was there all right, but the cover was badly burnt and there was something wrong with the pages. I picked up the book and examined it more carefully. Half-burnt pages here and there, whole pages torn out, paper turning into black film, ashes everywhere. I felt sick. To desecrate the one thing that eema cherished most—the book she didn't read but that joined her with the philosopher that she used to be before the camps, before the roundups, before the universe lost its centre and everyone went stark raving mad! I placed the book back, noticed the tell-tale signs on my hands, rushed to the washroom, and turned on the tap.

I wanted to warn eema, yes? But when eema arrived home, I couldn't bring myself to say anything. I kept waiting for eema to enter the living room, but she didn't. She went straight to the kitchen to make dinner. "Miriam, come set the table," she called out a short time later.

Throughout the meal, Sondra repeatedly taunted eema. Abba exploded, then calmed down, exploded, then calmed down. Eema tried one futile approach with Sondra after another. Not able to stomach it any longer, I excused myself early, went to my room, and pulled the pillow over my head.

That night, eema had a nightmare.

"Mamenyu! The books! Save the books!" she screamed.

"Rachaele, wake up," came abba's voice. "Is only a dream."

"Book burners! Gevalt!"

"Rachael, is okay."

"Oy! Help us! Can't anybody help us? Can't anybody see what's happening in this God forsaken land?"

She had come across the Heidegger book, I realized, and it had thrown her. And I could have prevented this.

Next morning, when I looked at the bookcase, sure enough, the Heidegger book was gone. That's it, I said to myself. Sunday's eema's birthday. So I won't say anything until Sunday's come and gone. But just as soon as it's over, I'll tell eema what really happened with my Mogen Dovid. And from now on, I'll protect them from Sondra no matter what.

119

I glanced over at the neatly wrapped present on the table in front of me and smiled to myself. Esther and I had pooled our money and bought it for eema over two weeks ago—*Bartlett's Concordance to Shakespeare.*

"Want to go in on the *Concordance?*" I had asked Sondra.

"Nope. Believe it or not, I already got her a present," Sondra had answered, smirking.

I was sitting at one of the orange booths near the window of the Jaffe Restaurant. Everyone else was waiting at home for Sondra. Then they were to meet me at the Jaffe Restaurant at 6:30.

The Jaffe was this happening Jewish establishment on Spadina, just south of College—a cherished haunt of downtown Jewry in the sixties. Eema's favourite Jewish restaurant. Mine and abba's too. We loved the mouth-watering knishes and blintzes. And we could stare for hours at the walls. They were covered with photographs of famous Jews, all standing next to Abe, the balding proprietor.

I glanced up at the large white clock on the wall. 7:02. Everyone else was decidedly late, but I didn't care. It was exhilarating just breathing in the buzz around me.

A family of three was looking at a picture that had recently been added to the collection on the wall. It was of a rabbi called "Avromi Schach." The rabbi had a beard and peyes—that is, unshorn sidelocks and ear ringlets. His eyes were almost as big as abba's and there was this look of ecstasy on his face.

"Nu?" said the young man, grinning. "Did I tell you that Rabbi Schach was a great man or what! There he is, front and centre on the famous Jaffe wall!"

"He really is. Look, Sarah," urged the middle-aged man, pointing.

"I see. I see. Kinehora! Our own rabbi! Who would have believed it?" asked the middle-aged woman sitting opposite him.

At a nearby table sat a man with a nose like eema's and a black yarmulke. He had been listening to the conversation with clear enjoyment, making no attempt to hide the fact that he was relishing every single word.

"Landsman, you know Avromi Schach?" he finally asked, smacking his lips with delight.

"Avromi? Of course, we know. North-end Winnipeg Jews, we are. How could we not know Avromi?" answered the woman, looking at the stranger and smiling.

The man clapped his hands and grinned with delight. "Me too," he announced. "I'm not even from Winnipeg and even I have heard of the wisdom of the great Avromi Schach. Even got to meet him a few times, Adoshem be praised. Such a rebbe!"

The father looked at him invitingly and moved to make room at the booth. "You'll join us?" he asked.

"Don't mind if I do," responded the man with the long nose, rising from his seat and joining the family of three. "Why, I can tell you a Rabbi Schach tale that'll knock your socks off!"

"And what's wrong with me? Am I chopped liver or what that I can't tell a Rabbi Schach story right after yours?" chimed in an older woman with white hair, sitting at the counter. "What, you think cause I'm an old woman that I don't hear when a new zaddic appears?"

"Of course," exclaimed the father. "We will eat challah and we will hear everyone's story, Hashem be praised."

Three quarters of an hour passed like it was a second as I listened to tales about this exceptional rabbi that was getting the university youth high on Torah. The father of the family had just mentioned a friend of Rabbi Schach's—a Rabbi Avi—when in walked eema, dressed in a gorgeous new black pant suit, then Esther, then abba. Esther sat next to me, and eema and abba sat on the side opposite.

"Where's Sondra?" I asked.

Abba caught my eye and shook his head. So that's why they're late, I realized. And she hasn't even shown eema the courtesy of turning up!

"Do you know what Reb Avi did last high holidays?" asked the old woman with the white hair, continuing her conversation with the family.

Overhearing this, eema's eyes instantly lit up. "Did I hear you say 'Reb Avi?'" said eema, turning around and exchanging looks with the old woman.

"Avi, yes."

"You mean the singing rabbi? The one with the guitar? Such a mentsh!"

"Who'd like to know?" asked the old woman amiably.

"Introductions, absolutely. I'm Rachel Himmelfarb. And this is my husband, Daniel. And these are my daughters—Miriam and Esther."

"Such sheyneh punems. Glad to meet you all. Chavela Fenster, here. Just a minute. You aren't by any chance *the* Rachael Himmelfarb?"

"*The* Rachael Himmelfarb?"

"The famous English professor who spends so much time with her students? You are, aren't you?" she asked, eyeing eema intently.

"Well, not so famous."

"Not so famous!" exclaimed Chavela. "Sha, everyone. Have I an announcement to make or what!" she asserted, rising to her feet. "In a million years you'll never guess who we have among us tonight—*the* Rachael Himmelfarb. My granddaughter Golda—may she never marry that farshtunkener Mordechai—was failing English until she met this brilliant scholar here," she said, pointing at eema. "And now she gets straight A's. The time this woman spent helping my granddaughter, the day should have so many hours. A lomed vovnik, this woman."

"A lomed what?" I asked.

"A lomed vovnik," Chavela repeated, her eyes narrowing. "One of the thirty-six righteous people on whom the well being of the world depends. What, you a teacher and your children don't know such things!" she exclaimed. "But then again," she added, looking at eema, her eyes twinkling, "who am I to question what a lomed vovnik does or does not teach her children? Am I right or am I right?"

A slender man at the counter had been eagerly watching the exchange. "Rachael Himmelfarb!" he now chimed in. "Aren't you the prof who gave that public lecture at U. of T. last spring about women protagonists? What was it called? Oh yeah, 'Women Heroes.' No. 'Women *Anti*heroes in Elizabethan and Jacobean Drama.'"

"Guilty as charged," confessed eema, blushing and beaming at the same time.

The young man rose from his seat and approached eema. "Professor Himmelfarb, I'm Arthur Donan," he went on, "and I agree with everything you said that day. Just about everything. May I shake your hand?"

And so the evening went. The birthday dinner was a smashing success—Sondra or no Sondra. We laughed, and ate, and sang, though every so often an anxious look crept across eema's face, and every so often, she excused herself and went to the pay phone in the front.

Eema was delighted with the *Concordance* and made a kind of game of it. Someone in the restaurant would pick a word at random and eema would look it up, then read us the first three entries under it. We were having such a good time we probably would have stayed a lot longer were it not that eema was worried about Sondra.

As we drove home, the incident in the living room flashed through my mind, and I started getting this sinking feeling. Everyone else must have been apprehensive too, for we were uncharacteristically quiet. I held my breath as we came into the house and entered the living room. But I was instantly relieved. Everything was quiet, everything in place. We sat down. And abba quickly got us started on a few rounds of "For She's a Jolly Good Balebosteh." While we were singing, I looked at abba and noticed the huge rings around his eyes. Had he been up all night with heart pains again? Was he having heart pains now?

"Abba, you look so tired," I said. "Maybe you want to lie down."

"Is okay, Miriam," he answered, smiling sweetly at me. "Is a birthday. So we vill sing a bit longer, yah?"

"Oh no you don't," cooed eema, cradling his head in her hands. "Abba, you can barely keep your eyes open. I'm the birthday girl, yes? And I get what I wish. And what I wish is that my wonderful husband should go to bed while he can still walk. Noodnic, you think I don't know you've been struggling with heart pains all night?"

Abba kissed eema on the cheek, excused himself, and staggered toward the staircase. I heard him drag himself slowly up the stairs, open the door to his room, and switch on the light. Then the whole neighbourhood must have heard as he shrieked, "Rachael, Rachael, for God's sake."

Eema turned white. "Just stay here," she ordered as she rushed upstairs.

A short while later, abba went to the washroom. While he was there, I heard eema descending the stairs. I stepped into the hallway to see if there was anything I could do. Eema was on the bottom stair, used condoms in her hands.

"Meydeleh, no point trying to hide what's going on," said eema, holding my gaze. "There's four kids on our bed upstairs, including Sondra, yes? Abba and I have gotten their clothes on, but they've been drinking so heavily they're barely conscious. I recognize one of the boys. Alf Dennis. And I'm calling his parents right now to come and get him. You'll make some coffee, yes? And when you're finished, take it up, and see if you recognize either of the others."

Though eema had prepared me, what a shock it was entering that room! Sondra and three older boys—not one of whom I recognized—were draped over the bed. While the other kids were unconscious, one of the boys was groaning and looking about, dazed. There were puddles of puke all over the carpet. Beer bottles were strewn about. And there was spilled beer and shards of broken glass everywhere.

"Esther, bring me up a basin of water and some Old Dutch," I yelled.

I looked at the clock. 8:00 a.m. I could hear eema and abba moving about, probably rustling up breakfast. I dressed and hurried downstairs.

"Miriam, thanks for all your help last night," said eema, as I stepped into the kitchen. "You must be exhausted. Stay home today, yes? Abba's called in sick and me, I won't be going in."

"Okay, eema. It'll give me a chance to work on your carpet some more."

I quickly gulped down some breakfast and headed to their bedroom. About an hour into the scrubbing, I heard Sondra yawn. Worried what might happen, I put down the scouring pads and joined eema and abba in the living room. And it wasn't long before a haggard-looking Sondra shuffled into the room. She was carrying a small package wrapped in silver paper.

"Sondra, your head must feel awful. Want some fruit juice?" offered eema, her voice a bit strained but still gentle.

Sondra sat down on the couch and said nothing.

"Is deaf you are?" bellowed abba. "You answer when your eema speaks to you."

"Abba, not so loud," cautioned eema. "She has a hangover, yes?"

"Hangover? I'll gif her from hangover," abba growled.

"What's everyone in such a snit about anyway?" Sondra said, slowly rubbing her forehead and talking ever so quietly.

"Meydeleh," began eema, "you were very drunk last night. So I'm not sure how much you remember. Alf Denis, Michael Lowes, and Christian Kaminsky were over and you must have all been having sex."

"So?" asked Sondra.

Abba looked like he was about to scream at Sondra, but he caught eema's eye and clearly decided to try to let her handle the situation.

"Sondra, you remember our agreement?" eema continued.

"Agreement! Is that what you call it? Anyway, to answer your question, yes, I remember."

"Well?" asked eema, looking at Sondra intently.

"Well what?"

"You didn't keep it."

A smirk came over Sondra's face. "Really? That's not my take. You said no seeing Harry for two months. Well, Harry wasn't here, now was he?"

"You know what I mean. About sex."

"I know *exactly* what you mean, eema," continued Sondra. "And as far I can make out, I followed your instructions to the letter. Don't see Harry, you said. I didn't. Take birth control, you said. I did. Oh yes, and the ingenious one—no sex on the living room coach. Well, you tell me, seeing as you were the sober ones, or so I assume. Was I anywhere near the living room couch?"

Eema's eyes narrowed, and her brow raised. "No, you weren't. But you know, Sondra, we have a problem here and playing around with words won't solve it. If having sex on the living room coach with one boy is disrespectful, having sex with three boys in abba's and my bed is far more disrespectful. And what do you want me to do? Not notice that you chose my birthday as well as my bed? Obviously, you very much wanted me to notice, yes? But you know, meydeleh, as serious as all this is, it's not what's most important here. What's important is that something is profoundly distressing you, yes? Something's wrong when a kid starts sleeping with everyone she can lay her hands on. You are my daughter. I love you. And I want to understand. And I know it's not just about our asking Uncle to leave—the problem began earlier—but why don't we start there?"

"If you think I'm going to spill my guts to you, think again."

"Maybe to somebody else then?"

"Not on your life."

"And not even turning up for your eema's birthday or buying her a present or anything," piped up abba, rubbing his chest.

"Oh, is that what's eating you?" asked Sondra. "Eema, I'm sorry. I really should have given you this on your birthday. But please accept it now in the spirit in which it is intended." "Eema, happy birthday," she announced, getting up and handing eema the small package.

While eema let Sondra put the package in her hands, she did not stretch out her arms to receive it. She just sat there, a worn look on her face.

"What's wrong? Aren't you going to open it?" asked Sondra.

"I'd rather talk first and open later."

"You say you care about what's important to me. *This* is important to me."

Eema gave Sondra a faint smile and started removing the silver wrapping. Inside was a small blue rectangular box. Eema took the lid off the box, revealing a strange array of uneven bits—green slivers of something or other, tiny irregular chunks of silver, a clasp of sorts. For a split second there, I couldn't figure out what it was. Then I saw eema startle and exclaim, "Gotenyu!" And it came to me.

Eema shot a nervous glance at abba. Then her eyes and facial muscles relaxed and she looked at Sondra again. "What do you want me to say, Sondra?" she finally asked. "I don't like that it's broken and I especially don't like that you did it. I didn't like what you did to my Heidegger book either. But I'm far more concerned about what's broken between us. You want to shock me, yes? I'm shocked. You want to hurt me? I'm hurt. You want me to make feel your fury? I can feel your fury. Now what?"

"Wouldn't you like to know!"

Abba's eyes had been bulging for some time. Now his face went blood-red. "Ach, is a ganef and a sadist what you are," he yelled. "All this time we are asking where is eema's broach? And never do you say, I'm sorry, eema, but I took it. And then vat do you do?"

"You object to stealing, abba?" asks Sondra, staring him straight in the eye. "Now how can you of all people possibly object to stealing? You—the man famous for stealing. You, the man of a thousand stories. What did they call it again, abba? Oh yes, 'organizing.' Well, I'm my father's daughter now, aren't I? Just look how good I am at organizing!"

"We took from Nazis and gave to Jews," abba stammers, shaking his head in disbelief.

"*You* took from authorities; *I* took from authorities," counters Sondra. "And abba, if I remember right, some of your stories were about tricking Jews into unfair trades. Not exactly your model little Holocaust socialist, now were you?"

Abba groans as if she's hit a nerve.

"Meydeleh," eema intervenes, "none of us are perfect. But ninety per cent of what abba did is make sacrifices and help other inmates."

"Ninety per cent? Really, eema. Interesting figure, that! Why don't you tell us about the other ten per cent?"

Eema turns white. Sondra shrugs her shoulders. Seconds later, Esther nervously steps into the living room and sits down.

Sondra smiles broadly first at Esther, then me. Then she stands up and positions herself in the middle of the room, facing eema. "You know, eema," she begins, "for years, your precious little meydelehs—Esther, Miriam, and me—we had this little game. The Nazis were coming, and we could only save one of you. The question is: which of you were we going to...?"

"Sondra, don't," I interrupt, feeling the blood rush to my face. "For God's sake, just how much punishment do they have to take!"

"What's the matter, little sister?" asks Sondra. "Getting a tad nervous, are we?"

And that's when I said it. "You do this, Sondra," I threaten, "and you're no sister of mine. I mean it, Sondra. Take one more step in this direction, and I'm through with you."

"Now wouldn't that be a loss! Boohoo," taunts Sondra.

"Miriam," says eema, eyeing me sadly, "Sondra's going to do what's Sondra's going to do. You can't stop her. And we'll be left with what we're left with. She's still your sister and she's my daughter. Nothing changes that."

"You heard me," I insist, glaring at Sondra.

"As I was saying before I was so rudely interrupted," Sondra continues, her voice raising, "we used to try to figure out who to save and who to give to the Nazis. Abba, why don't you ask Miss Goodie-Two-Shoes over there who she decided to turn over to the Nazis?"

I can see the shock on eema's and abba's faces as they turn to stare at me.

"I... I..." I stammer.

"And don't forget your other sheyneh meydeleh over there," continues Sondra, pointing to Esther. "What! Cat got your tongue? Okay, let good ole Sondra tell you what happened. Miriam and Esther were all for giving in abba and, to tell you the truth, so was I initially. But eventually, I decided I wouldn't save either of you, but especially not you," she adds, looking straight at eema. "Cause you're a out-and-out bitch, now, aren't you?"

Eema winces but says nothing.

"Hey, any Nazis around?" Sondra calls out, her voice projecting as she were on the stage at Carnegie Hall, her arm making a grand sweep. "The bitch of the century—Rachael Himmelfarb—is here. Come, take her to the gas chambers. Hurry up now. We wouldn't want to keep the poor little Jewess waiting any longer, now would we?"

Abba can contain himself no longer. "What kind of meshugener hunt are you!" he screams, waving his hands in the air.

"Not meshugener enough to stay in this Holocaust madhouse one more second," bellows Sondra.

"That a daughter should speak to her eema this vay! Is unheard of! Go to your room this instant!"

"Go to hell—Holocaust hell, if you'd prefer!" snarls Sondra, tearing out of the room. "I've had it with all of you. I'm out of here. And I won't be back. Not ever."

I hear Sondra grab a coat from the rack and the rack come crashing to the floor. A few seconds later, the front door slams.

The expression of anger is gone from abba's face. Suddenly, he looks frightened, vulnerable, years older.

"Stop her! Call the police!" screams abba, rising to his feet.

"Abba, she's sixteen," I reply. "It's legal for her to leave."

"Call a meeting of the Resistance. Get Lionel here immediately. Immediately," repeats abba, pacing back and forth.

"Daniel, darling. We're here. In Canada," eema reminds him.

"Call Moshe too."

"Daniel, we're in the house on Lippincott."

Abba stops pacing and stares at eema. He looks confused for a moment; then his eyes open wide and his face sinks. "Oh no," he exclaims. "Mayn kind! I've lost mayn kind. Our first born what came to us in the d.p. camp. You remember, Rachael?"

"Oy, Daniel, I remember," whimpers eema, tears welling up in her eyes. "Daniel, help me. I don't know what to do."

Her whole body shaking, eema rises and approaches abba. Then eema and abba fall sobbing into each other's arms.

Hour after hour, abba and eema sat in the living room, saying nothing, waiting for the front door to swing open or the phone to ring. Eventually, I motioned to Esther and we headed to the kitchen to make tuna sandwiches and coffee to bring to them.

"Don't be so hard on Sondra," urged Esther as she globbed the mayonnaise onto the challah. "She'd never have acted that way if she weren't hurting."

"She's forced me to choose. It's not like I ever wanted to."

Abba and eema never touched the sandwiches. They just continued sitting.

As evening settled in, abba's breathing grew more laboured and sweat was trickling down his face. Eema began taking note and fussing over him. "Daniel, you're not looking good. You should lie down, yes?" she urged him. At one point, eema knelt down and pulled back his socks. She startled as she saw the swelling at the ankles.

"Daniel, it's serious. Easy now, sweetie, we have to call an ambulance."

"No hospital," groaned abba, terror flickering in his eyes.

Eema stroked abba's arm ever so gently. "Sha, sweetheart," she urged.

*Image: On a straw mattress, lies a naked man, his ribs jutting out, his eyes bulging, his lips aquiver. He is in a small room, crammed with mattresses, all of them soaked in urine and crawling with lice. Right at his side, pressing up against his arm, lies a corpse. The corpse is not much thinner than him. A rat is gnawing at these shriveled bits of flesh that must have once been its toes. The man peers over and takes in the corpse, then shakes his head. He glances toward the entrance to the hut and spots a rusty bucket overflowing with excrement. Using his arms as a wedge, he starts to rise and falls back again, starts to rise, and falls back again, starts to rise, and falls back again. A greenish brown liquid comes oozing out of him, staining his body, mixing in with the urine in the mattress, adding to the swill on the floor. He looks down at his feet and grimaces. He sweeps his arm along the ground at the side of his mattress, as if searching for something. He calls out, "Doktor," but no one comes. A short while later, a plump man dressed in a filthy white frock passes by.*

*"Doktor, my shoes, what's happened to them?" asks the man.*

*The man in white continues walking as if no one has uttered a word.*

*The man with the bulging eyes looks about. He sees writhing bodies, semi-conscious bodies, dead bodies. Then he notices a middle-aged patient in the far corner sitting up and eyeing him.*

*"The staff's way of getting good shoes," the middle-aged man explains, shaking his head. "Mostly, everyone dies here. The place is a cesspool, no? But it's all the same. You live. You die. Either way, they have your shoes."*

The waiting was difficult. That old image of abba in the coffin kept flashing through my mind. Eventually the ambulance turned up. Abba was screaming, "Get away from me—murderers," as they laid him on the stretcher and carried him down the stairs.

"Daniel, I'm here," eema kept calling out.

Esther and I started following, but eema turned around and instructed, "Meydelehs, please stay. Sondra might call, yes?"

Eema phoned from the hospital about an hour and a half later, though she had little news except that abba was being examined. Shortly after 11:00, the phone rang again. It was eema, saying that abba had been admitted to hospital and that he was calmer.

"His heart, isn't it?" I ask.

"Yes."

"I should have stopped her. I'm so sorry."

"Sha, now. Let's just be here for abba."

"Eema, I didn't want to give either of you into the Nazis. I love abba. I...I...."

"Meydeleh, I can't think about that right now. But understand, we're your parents. We've known you all your life. You think I don't know how much you love your abba? I know. And sheyneh punem, if anything should happen to your abba, give the man some credit; he knows too."

"Eema, you okay?"

"Hanging in there. You and Esther?"

"Yeah, though we're scared. What if we lose abba?"

"Someday we'll have to face that, yes? But my guess is not today, sheyneh punem. He's doing better; they are calling it a minor heart attack. Miriam, I really think he's going to be okay."

"Thank God! Just a sec while I tell Esther."

"Miriam, hold on. Did... did...?"

"No, eema. No word from Sondra."

Abba didn't die, but he was hardly okay. He was in the hospital for almost three weeks. Oftentimes his shoulders would be raised, his breathing stopped, his eyes opened wider than I thought humanly possible. And every so often he became totally disoriented. The pain, the hospital, the staff themselves were all pulling him back to the camps, the infirmary, the horror that was Auschwitz.

Eema and I kept telling everyone we could grab hold of, "Listen! It's important no one remove the man's shoes. He's a Holocaust survivor; and it'll terrify him. Please, put it in his charts, and explain it to the other staff." The orderly, the nurse, whoever, would nod and leave abba's shoes alone. But no one ever passed on the information. So abba was at the mercy of every new orderly, nurse, and doctor on duty.

One morning eema and I arrived to find abba sitting up in bed, staring at his naked feet and whimpering, "Rachael, I'm done for. Caput." Eema tried to reassure him. I immediately bent down to hunt for the shoes. I arose to find abba's anguish turned to terror as this condescending young nurse sauntered into the room, this humungous needle in hand, and announced, "We're having a hard time today, aren't we Mr. H.? Well, here's a little something to take care of that."

Next day, I sat in the hospital cafeteria thinking about how fragile it all was—that safe world which my parents had constructed for themselves. For abba especially, but for eema too, despite her remarkable strength. It depended on personal routines that could be counted on, discrete practices that had to be maintained. Added to this, as was becoming progressively clearer, it depended on us children being there and not turning on them, for we were the hope, the continuity, the ultimate victory over Nazism, but only if we stuck by them.

There and then I vowed I would never walk out on them. And I would do everything in my power to ensure that neither of them ever ends up in a place like this again.

## Chapter Four

## Miriam, ages 15 3/4-24

It was two-and-a-half months since abba had returned home and life was no picnic—not for him, not for anyone. Vey iz mir! He had slipped into one of his depressions, and it wasn't lifting. Day in and day out, he just laid around the house in his boxers, picking at his chest, hanging his head, muttering about Auschwitz. Eema as well had had a kind of collapse. Nu? She could tough out any kind of emergency, but there was a price to pay. She had used up energy she didn't have. She would schlep home from work, barely able to keep her eyes open. She would nap while Esther and I rustled up dinner. And in the middle of the night, she would murmur the name of that woman that she always lit a yarhzeit for—Roza.

Knowing that we had two depressed people on our hands and not sure what else to do, Esther worked particularly hard at making the food as tempting as possible. Succulent strips of beef in a bed of onions and garlic, kinehora, piping hot chicken soup with fluffy golden matzo balls floating about and maybe just a hint of carrot and celery. But neither of them would take more than a few bites. By early evening, abba would drag himself to bed, groaning, "Is too much. Too much." And eema would sit in the living room just staring into empty space as if waiting for Sondra to materialize.

Then slowly, things began to shift. Abba started perking up, putting on his trousers, going into work. To my great relief, he even began shouting at us all once more. And eema was starting to get a second wind.

"Let's go the movies tonight," suggested Esther one day.

"But what if Sondra..." began eema.

Esther and I held our breath as eema paused.

"Why not?" she eventually answered, her eyes clearing. "Abba, get off your tokhes for a change; go get a paper, and we'll see what's playing, yes?"

Eema and abba never exactly recovered. Ever after, from time to time, I would find eema weeping for no apparent reason. And a week didn't go by when Sondra's name wasn't mentioned or there wasn't some reason to haul out her childhood photographs and examine them one by one. At the same time, somehow or other, sometimes with great relish, sometimes not, everyone in our family did get about the business of life.

Eema began teaching full time, I suspect to take her mind off Sondra; the department begrudgingly accepted her, though they never let her forget that she was junior, and they never let her teach her specialty. What? A mere woman allowed to teach Shakespeare! Not in that era!

It would have been far too controversial to teach the history of literature course from any kind of consistent women's perspective, and so eema didn't go that far, but she did always ask: How are women being portrayed? Students got interested and she ended up giving more public lectures. Before long, bright young women were dropping by our house regularly. Of course, back then Toronto was hardly the diverse city it is now and so the vast majority of the women were white, but not all.

"Professor Himmelfarb," asked a young white woman in faded jeans.

"Rachael," eema corrected, passing the strudel around.

"Rachael, what do we do about being *ensoi?*"

"It's like any other occupation, isn't it?" suggested this Black political science student named Ayanna. "They've invaded us. Reduced us to a body that is for-them and taken over that body. So we need to find ways to resist—just like Fanon in Algeria."

"Resist, absolutely, Ayanna," asserted eema, nodding emphatically. "Couldn't agree with you more. A form of colonialism, just as your example suggests. The question is: How do we resist from moment to moment as we go about our daily lives?"

Abba was uneasy with the direction which eema was taking. And when his socks were not washed on time, he would go on this tirade about "you women." But he didn't make as big a fuss as I was expecting, maybe because he secretly saw the parallels with the class struggle, maybe because he too was involved again.

He'd gotten over the initial shock of the CCF turning into the NDP and had joined the executive. A *groser knaker* socialist—a socialist big shot—eema was now calling him, yes? Comrades would seek out his advice. And his old cloth measuring tape dangling from his neck, he would spend long hours in political meetings.

Esther too had taken up her life and was now taking initiatives that were to inform her adult years. Although it now meant going alone, almost every Shabbes, she went to schul. And she had started volunteering at Mount Sinai and would frequently talk about growing up and becoming a social worker.

Still, I found myself worrying about Esther from time to time. She'd put on weight and had developed a touch of arthritis. Moreover, she often seemed out of sorts; and with me at very least had become uncharacteristically aloof. It was as if she was going through her own private tsores and didn't want me intruding. Now whatever else was bothering her, it was clear that she missed Sondra and Uncle, because now and again she would turn to me and ask, "Miriam, think we'll ever see either of them again?"

Actually, the family had gotten a card from Uncle in early January of 1964. It reads: "My dearest Daniel, Rachael, Sondra, Miriam, and Esther: Happy Chanukah. Do hope this reaches you in time. May the mitzvah of Hashem's light illuminate the path before you. Your loving uncle and brother, Yacov." No account of what he'd been up to. No return address. Bupkes.

From Sondra, we heard nothing. Nor could we figure out much about her, though we made repeated inquiries, putting ads in the local papers, approaching her friends. We knew she had dropped out of school, for the principal had called the second week, complaining, "Mrs. Himmelfarb, this time Sondra's absenteeism has gone way too far." I had wondered at first whether she was in touch with Uncle Yacov, but Uncle's card seemed to suggest otherwise.

Sondra's departure was monumental in the life of our family. While eema and abba had pulled themselves together, they had been badly shaken. And what Sondra's leaving brought home to them was that there was a terrible truth in the Holocaust message: There really was no safety, no baseline, and at any moment they could find themselves in Hell.

In my own way, I too was affected. Without anyone intending it, there was a kind of tightening of the screws, for I was now the eldest and there were now only two of us left to make up for a lost generation. The problem is, I was rapidly approaching adulthood; I needed to explore the universe, and yet somehow I bore this tremendous responsibility for eema and abba.

It wasn't so much the fierce pull toward eema and abba that was problematic, for it was my lot; nor was it reaching out toward life, for that was a developmental need. It was not having a clue how to do justice to both and having no one to show me the way. Nu? There were no instructions on how to be a child of survivors—no books, no workshops; the campers and the campers' children were no longer meeting with any regularity; and Sondra, who might have served as a model, had fled.

The next decade of my life was largely shaped by conflicts over needing to stay and needing to leave, over allegiance to my family and a hunger for the outside world. Now this was the period when I most reached outside the family. At the same time, this was the period when the world of ideas decisively beckoned to me. I was becoming a scholar, a philosopher, yes?

When I was eighteen, I became preoccupied with Heidegger. While he was presented in my U. of T. philosophy class as nothing but this respectable existentialist philosopher, I wasn't buying it. For years, I'd been replaying that scene in my head—eema frozen in front of the Heidegger book, groaning about this terrible mistake. I quickly discovered what Heidegger had done. Joined the National Socialist Party. I could only imagine what eema must have gone through. Her mentor of all people! What I didn't know is whether or not his philosophy itself was tainted. Using *Being and Time* as a reference point, I set myself a question: Was there something about his mode of thought that predisposed Heidegger to make this unspeakable error? And what follows, was anything wrong with his philosophy?

At first, I could find bupkes. Then I started to notice something. There was no place for individual human beings in Heideggerian philosophy. We were simply there to serve Being. If philosophies that were overly individualistic could lead to the atrocity that was capitalism, maybe the absence of individualism led to something even worse.

Over time, the treatment of T. S. Eliot also began to concern me. As I read through poems like "Gerontion," I could sense a kind of anti-Semitism in them. And yet no one was discussing this—not in class, not in the critical commentary. Now it was precisely this issue that first brought Lanie Unger into my life.

✡

It was English 101 at New College, and I was seated in the middle of the eighth row. At the front of the lecture hall stood Professor Dunstan—a silver-haired man clad in a burgundy robe. As the bell rang, he straightened his spectacles and leaned into the lectern. "Now class," he announced, "open your book to 'Gerontion'—page 39 of the *Selected Poems.*" I opened my book, took one additional look at that poem, and shuddered. Determined, I raised my hand.

"Miss Himmelfarb?"

"Professor Dunstan, I have problems with 'Gerontion.'"

"Yes, the classical allusions can be difficult."

"It's not that," I explained. "And it's not just 'Gerontion.' But I can start there." Glancing down and finding the passage, I began, "Listen to this line: 'The Jew squats on the windowsill.'* Now I'm not trying to be funny, but I've never known a Jew to squat on a windowsill. And why *the* Jew?"

"You don't like how Eliot portrays Jews in specific poems?"

"I think something's wrong with what the line is saying."

"Strictly speaking, poetry doesn't say anything. Poetry explores feelings, situations, poses, intuitions."

"But the intuitions are from a certain vantage point. And surely poets bear responsibility for their vantage points!"

"You suggesting that Eliot isn't acting responsibly?" continues Professor Dunstan, his brow wrinkling. "I put it to you, Miss Himmelfarb, that he's being eminently responsible—to a tradition. Judge him in these terms, and he acquits himself brilliantly."

"I can't understand being responsible to an anti-Semitic tradition. Surely Eliot has a more basic responsibility."

Professor Dunstan said something about the importance of taking artists on their own terms. Then the lecture resumed.

I sat through the rest of the class, convinced that I had achieved nothing and disappointed. When it finished, without a word to anyone, I rushed over to Victoria College for my philosophy seminar and took my customary seat at the far end of the large oak table.

Within seconds, in walked Lanie Unger, her usual green bag slung over her shoulder. She nodded at me, but instead of sitting in her usual seat, she took the seat next to mine.

A first-year student like me, Lanie was a tall woman. Five foot ten inches in socking feet. Her face was moon-shaped and she was on the

---

*See T.S. Eliot, Collected Poems, 1909-1962 *(London: Farber and Farber 1963)* p. 39.

heavy side, but in a rounded sensuous sort of a way—zoftig, as abba would put it. She always wore bright colours. Today, she had on an orange caftan that trailed to the floor and gave her a distinctly regal air.

Lanie carefully placed her shoulder bag under the table. Then she turned to me and smiled. "Miriam," she asserted, "I fucking admire what you did back there in Dunstan's class."

"Thanks," I responded, smiling back.

"You put into words something many of us have been talking about. It's just with everything being the way it is, none of us really thought such issues could be raised. Incidentally, do you know about Ezra Pound's fascist sympathies? And like, did you know that Pound was Eliot's mentor?"

"I've heard about Pound's fascist sympathies, but no, I didn't know that. Was he really Eliot's mentor?"

"Absolutely," stated Lanie. "Now Eliot had no such sympathies. Nonetheless, you can actually trace the literary influences. You know, my roommate Joe Boxer has this book that...."

"Miss Unger and Miss Himmelfarb, please," interjected the facilitator.

Lanie and I quickly became fast friends. We had much in common, though she was far more counter cultural than me. She was a north-end Winnipeg Jew whose family was left wing like mine. Her grandfather had been involved in the Winnipeg General Strike, and her mother had been instrumental in introducing the first birth control clinic in Manitoba. Lanie was an actress, but not like with Sondra. She could have cared less about touring the world or people adoring her. She was dedicated to political theatre—theatre that could change the world.

Along with six other counter culture types, she lived in this co-op about a block and a half north of Bloor, on Albany Street. Often when I was over, all of us would hang out in this living room, which in those days would have been called "groovy." The furniture was mainly bean bags, though some stacked orange crates doubled as a table.

Many is the riveting discussion we had in that room: "What does the intellectual owe society?" Lanie would ask.

"I take my cue from the French existentialists; intellectuals have a responsibility to take stands on the issues of the day," I would assert.

"But do you agree with Camus or Sartre?" asked Lanie's roommate Don.

Now it was in this very room that the idea of my moving out was first raised. "Got a vacancy coming up," announced Lanie, as we lay stretched out on the bean bags, passing around this extra fat joint. "Meems, you interested?"

"Sure am, but give me some time to mull it over."

Much as I wanted to, of course, I couldn't accept the offer. Not with eema and abba still reeling from Sondra's departure. Not that it would have been easy even had Sondra stayed.

"It's not like I can just take off like you, Joe, and Don," I explained to Lanie on the telephone that evening. "You know how survivors are with changes like that."

"The other campers' children," Lanie asked, "they all still at home?"

"Well, Ben and Moshe have taken off, sure, but most haven't. And you know what, Lanie? Except for Sondra, not a single daughter has."

After I hung up, I made a decision: I'd wait another year or so, see how eema and abba are doing, then reassess.

✡

It was a countdown to war and Jews everywhere knew it. On May 15, Egyptian troops started amassing near the Golan Heights.

"It's going to be war," groaned eema. "Gotenyu! If only the yeshuv hadn't gone for statehood! This was bound to happen, no?"

"But we're a state just like any other state," bellowed abba. "They attack us and we haf to defend ourselves."

"They haven't attacked," eema observed.

"No, is just putting out all that artillery for fun!" exclaimed abba sarcastically.

On May 21, Syria announced, "This is a battle of annihilation." On May 22, Egypt closed the Straits of Tiran to Israeli ships, cutting off the route to Asia, blocking oil from Iran. On May 28 Nasser declared: No co-existence with Israel.

"What did I tell you?" asked eema. "And how else do you expect the Arab states to respond?"

By May 30, the armies of Egypt, Jordan, Syria, and Lebanon were poised at the borders of Israel, with the armies of Iraq, Algeria, Kuwait, and Sudan not far behind. "We will wipe Israel off the map," vowed President Adur Rahman Aref of Iraq.

For two weeks, we talked about nothing else over supper. The question on everyone's mind was: what would Israel do?

Abba was clear. "Israel has to fight. Is no choice."

Eema was full of reservations. "I don't want our people massacred or the economy destroyed," she sighed, shaking her head, "but neither do I want anyone else attacked. I want something to be worked out."

"What's to vork out?" asked abba, shrugging his shoulders. "They've said no to negotiations. And they're surrounding the state."

Eema closed her eyes and said nothing.

A few days later, as we were sitting around the dining room table, abba declared, "Is time. Israel has to strike."

Eema shook her head.

"Is a tiny little state what is surrounded," shouted abba, glaring at her. "They haf announced our destruction, yah? What are you vanting? People should do nothing like in Germany!"

"Daniel, it's not the same thing; and you know it. The other campers, I expect this from them. Not you."

"What's your solution, I'd like to know? Why, my brother Nat ..."

"Who said I have a solution?" wailed eema. "It's a mess. I don't see anything happening here except war. But I'm hoping against hope. Daniel, it's real lives on all sides. Real men, women, children."

Tears came to their eyes, and they got up and hugged.

I glanced over at Esther. For some reason, she was checking her watch nervously.

"Gotta go," she finally declared, rising from the table.

"Go where?" asked eema, smiling at her through the tears.

"Tell you later. I'm late."

As Esther bolted out of the room, eema shot me one of her what's-going-on-with-your-sister looks. I had no more clue than she did and so shrugged my shoulders.

I talked to Lanie on the phone for almost an hour that evening. She had relatives in Tel Aviv and was scared. Afterward, I joined eema and abba in the living room. We sat around for hours, nashing on peanuts and discussing possible scenarios. Around 11:30, we could hear whispers on the porch. Eema went to check. To my surprise, she was gone over ten minutes. And when she returned, Eric and Esther were with her.

Eric was Harry Cohan's younger brother. Clear resemblance. Same squared chin, same jet black hair, but his features were softer. He didn't have glasses and he wore khakis—not jeans.

"Abba, you remember Harry's brother Eric?" began eema as they entered the living room.

Abba took one look at Eric, and his eyes began to bulge. "What are you vanting here?" he shouted, waving his hands about. "You're vanting to have hankypanky with one my daughters in our living room, maybe! I haf survived Auschvitz so that Israel should be viped out and the farhstunkener Cohan boys should put their schmecks in each of my daughters?"

"Daniel, remember your heart. And be fair. Eric's done nothing."

Abba stopped shouting, but his eyes did not settle down. Eema placed her hand on his shoulder, then went to the kitchen to make coffee. Eric and Esther looked away nervously and said almost nothing until eema returned.

"Nu?" said eema, handing everyone a cup and eyeing each of them in turn. Then Esther and Eric began explaining their appearance on the porch at this late hour.

Though they were frequently interrupted by abba, who fired one question after another, Eric and Esther eventually got their story out: They were both very sorry to be turning up at this hour. Eric had simply walked Esther home because it was late. No, they weren't dating or intending to date. Yes, they really were at a committee meeting. Yes, Harry was involved. And no, the committee had nothing to do with turning teenaged girls into prostitutes.

"You see," Esther explained, "Israel is calling on young Jews from around the world to come to Israel immediately. Everyone's expecting a long war. Israelis will be busy fighting and there'll be no one to harvest the crops. And if no one harvests the crops, our people will starve. Honest, eema, no volunteer will be fighting or contributing to the war in any way. Just tending to the crops."

"And the meeting this evening?" asked eema, her brow raising.

"The second I've attended," answered Esther nervously. "It's just this committee that's been set up to recruit volunteers and, well, you know, support them."

"Can't go. Case closed," ruled abba, looking Esther right in the eyes. "Is not safe."

"No, Mr. Himmelfarb, neither of us are going," Eric clarified. "It's only for people 21 to 35. We're just helping in the effort. There's passages to be arranged, provisions to be bought."

"I see," said abba, his face beginning to relax. "So Esther," he asked, looking over at her, "how did you come to hear about such a thing—a meydeleh like you?"

"From Eric. He's in my class and we talk."

"And I got involved because Harry's one of the main organizers," offered Eric.

"Is Harry going?" asked eema.

"Sure is," answered Esther. "He's already applied for a passport and visa. And Eric and I, well, we're sort of his support crew."

"I'm not sure the plan will work," eema mused. "The country's on the brink of war. He's not likely to get the documents quickly enough. And once war's declared, who's going to get through?"

"We expect his documents any day now," answered Eric. "You have to understand. We have inside people. And they'll make sure the applications are processed quickly."

"You don't think the Canadian authorities will obstruct when they see all those Canadian citizens suddenly going to Israel?"

"It's just a couple of people per major city," replied Eric. "And it won't exactly be clear they're heading for Israel, if you know what I mean."

"I see," said eema, nodding.

Eric left a few minutes later. Everyone else continued talking. Eema and abba were uneasy that Esther had said nothing to them.

"I wasn't sure how either of you would react to my being involved," explained Esther. "And eema, it's something I have to do."

"We respect your feelings, sweetie," answered eema, holding her look. "And you're old enough to make all sorts of decisions for yourself. But we're your parents and the thing is, we've a right to know what's what."

By 2:00 a.m. a decision was reached. Eema and abba wouldn't interfere with Esther's involvement as long as she was straight with them and did nothing illegal. And Esther would be more up front in the future.

"Esther, you okay?" I asked, once we were alone in the bedroom.

"Yeah. Thanks," she answered, reaching down and removing her shoes.

"Love you."

I wasn't sure what else to say. On one level, I was proud of my little sister. She was doing something, yes? And after all, the situation was dire. Israel was surrounded on all sides with nations committed to driving the Jews into the sea. And it's not like any of the volunteers would be fighting. Nonetheless, I had serious misgivings. What if every Canadian volunteer meant one more Israeli freed up to join the war? What if every volunteer meant one more Arab shot, one more community bombed?

"Esther, I don't..." I began to say.

Esther got out of her bed, came over to mine, and stood there, facing me. "Miriam, I love you and eema very much and always will," she said. "And I'll always learn from you. You're the smartest people I know. But that doesn't mean I agree with you. I've never agreed with either of you about Israel. We're not the intruders you and eema seem to think," she went on, eyeing me intently. "Just like the Arabs we've been in the Middle East thousands of years. It's hardly our fault we're dispersed because of centuries of persecution. And the tiny piece of land on which Israel sits, this is the land of Abraham, Isaac, and Jacob. Adoshem gave the Arabs much more land, but he gave us this one tiny piece; and it's ours and ours alone. And all of it. Not just the part that the U.N. allowed us. And you know as well as I do, Miriam, there's nowhere else in the world where Jews can be safe. But please, let's not talk about it. We'll just get into an argument and, of course, you'll win—what else?—but that won't change how I feel."

Esther went over to the light switch, then looked at me pointedly. I nodded, saddened at the realization that a scene not unlike this one was being enacted in many a Jewish household throughout the world. Then Esther turned out the light.

"Miriam, you still up?" came Esther's voice a few minutes later.

"Yeah."

"Miriam, Eric is really terrific. You should have seen how he helped Harry at the meeting. They're awfully close, you know."

✡

Everywhere I went—to the library, to Lanie's—people were talking about "the situation."

"Himmelfarb, what do you think's going to happen—you know, with the situation in the Middle East?" asked Joe.

"We have a situation on our hands," declared Moshe, rolling up the sleeves of his red denim shirt, "and we just have to attend to it like the warriors we used to be. And don't you give me any of your Arab-loving meshugahs, Miriam Himmelfarb. Got to be warriors now—not victims. The blood of six million Jews paid for this land. Israel is the redemption of the Jewish people. And any Yid who says different is a traitor and an anti-Semite."

"Moshe, it's not that simple. And I'll thank you not to call me an anti-Semite."

On June 4th, we awoke to discover 465,000 troops, 2800 tanks, and 800 planes surrounding Israel.

On June 5th the dye was cast. Israel attacked Egypt.

I wasn't prepared for what happened next. Six days of war, and Israel emerged with triple the territory. Homes, communities, cities, whole regions seized! And here we were thinking that the war was going to last a long time and that Israel was in trouble!

"Eema, how could this be?" I asked, astounded. "Israel had to have been planning some kind of a land grab. How else could they have managed it in six days?"

"Is okay," assured abba. "Is no ganef. Israel vill return the land."

I thought about all the times Israel had returned land in the past and I felt better, but I was still apprehensive.

A month passed. And there was Israel—still holding onto the land. "Why with the long faces?" asked abba one evening. "You think the crisis isn't over? The crisis is over. They've seen to it, the Israelis."

"But people's homes, people's land!" exclaimed eema.

"Not to vorry," answered abba "Is a vat-do-you-call-it? Like the poker piece."

"Chip," I offered.

"Punct. Is a bargaining chip, this land, farshtey? It'll force the Arabs to make a deal, yah? You gif us peace and we'll gif you your land. Is a brilliant strategy. It'll all be resolved in one year, two years tops. And everyone'll be happy. Jews. Arabs. Everybody. Mark my vords."

It was a difficult summer. Except for eema and Lanie, I was having trouble liking anyone during that period, myself included. I would run into friends like Moshe; and they would spout off biblical justifications for keeping the land. Or they would tell these blatantly racist jokes about what bad fighters the Arabs were. What distressed me every bit as much, some of my friends on the left kept depicting Israel as a European colonial power pure and simple. And I didn't know what to say because it was true and it wasn't true; and so I felt guilty no matter how I responded. And sometimes even when I agreed wholeheartedly with some left analysis, I could hear distinct anti-Semitism mixed in with it. "The Jews" did this. "The Jews" did that. And then it got worse.

I was at Lanie's stretched out a bean bag, and I'd just said something critical of Israel when her roommate Don looked me squarely in the face and gibed, "How can you be so soft on them! Those goddamn Israelis, they're nazis pure and simple!"

"You can't honestly say there's no difference!" I exclaim.

"Try me," retorts Don.

As the summer progressed, the impasse in the Middle East deepened. I remember. The Israelis kept refusing to return the Occupied Territories. Arab leaders met at Khartoum and emerged united and adamant: No to peace with Israel. No to negotiations with Israel. No to recognition of Israel. Israel answered back, "Land for peace." The lines in the sand were drawn. And for the time being, Israel was the victor. But at what cost, and for how long? I asked myself.

Many a time that summer I thought of the Palestinians—their homes stolen from them, the children going hungry, the word "no" on their lips. I thought of the Arab peoples—ancient proud civilizations, who had found themselves underdogs in the twentieth century, who resented this intrusion into their territory, and who were planning our annihilation. And I thought of the Israelis—Jews who had been persecuted for centuries, who didn't want it to happen again, and who somehow had no concept of Jews doing wrong. And I thought about myself, sitting there and doing nothing, caught between two peoples and two narratives. Between the descendants of Isaac and the descendants of Ishmael. Me, Miriam—the daughter on whom eema had always pinned some strange hope. As if this daughter of the daughters of Sarah could deliver any one to any kind of Promised Land!

Whether my thinking back then has any practical meaning, I'm not prepared to say, but as I sat in the living room pondering the situation one evening, I found myself taking a very different turn. My mind was reaching back through history—further and further back, before the U.N. resolution, before the yeshuv, before the diaspora, before the City of David, before Jews and Arabs as we know them today. And I started telling myself a mythical story about two hapless brothers and their families just like I had always told myself stories since early childhood, in this case, one filled with questions and dilemmas. It may well be that the tale has gotten polished over the years and the original story which I told myself was rougher, but this, nonetheless, is how I remember it: Two brothers—Ishmael, son of Abraham and Hagar and Isaac, son of Abraham and Sarah—are friends despite the terrible difference in their mothers' positions. Nu? Every day as the sun rises, just after the morning meal, they roughhouse with each other just outside the big tent of Abraham their father, throwing each other to the ground, laughing, then picking each other up, as their mothers watch on, beaming with pride at their beautiful sons. One day as Sarah, mother of Isaac, lifts up the flap to the red tent and gazes out at the boys, the smile disappears from her face. She is worrying about something, but what? She rushes to the big gray tent, her eyes searching for Abraham, the patriarch. Spotting him, she looks at him guardedly and urges, "Husband, cast out the servant Hagar with her son; for the son of this woman must not inherit with my son Isaac."

How could Sarah say such a thing? Has she lost sight of who the boys are to each other? Does she look down on Ishmael because he is the son of a servant? Or is this an old wound speaking? Is she perhaps remembering the theft of her *own land*—her *own body* that was stolen from her when Abraham pimped her to Pharoah in exchange for sheep, and oxen, and asses? Is this what happens when women are disposable?

And what about Abraham? Why does Abey heed Sarah now when he usually ignores her? Is it unacknowledged guilt for having prostituted Sarah? And how can he even consider treating his own child so? Does patriarchy require absolute rule, single potentates, single lineage? Has he thought about it at all? Or is this some kind of mindless repetition of the betrayal by his own father, who handed him over to Nimrod and allowed him to be cast into the fiery furnace?

And what about God? Why is God telling Abe to do as Sarah has requested? And why does God tell everyone who will listen that Hagar and Ishmael must be sent away and that there will be two utterly separate nations—the nation of the Jews and the nation of the Arabs? In all his omniscience, has he no idea where this will lead? Or is he not omniscient after all? Is this just another empty male pretence? Or is God, perhaps, a racist at heart? Or was it never God in the first place? Is it something other than the voice of the non-existent God that has been speaking?

What are Hagar and Ishmael feeling as they stand in silence, their heads bowed as the Patriarch orders them to leave? How will they make sense of what is happening?

What does Sarah think about as the night passes? Why doesn't Abraham struggle? Is there to be no reflection, no heart-to-heart talk, no self-examination, no last minute realization, no ultimate reprieve?

As the sun rises next morning, one little boy sits alone in the sand, bereft of half his family, soon to be dragged to a mount and bound up as a sacrificial offering by a patriarch who cannot distinguish between the voice of his own pain and the voice of the spirit. As the sun rises, a woman and child set out for Beer-sheba, nothing but a few pieces of bread in their sacks, a small skin of water slung over the woman's shoulder.

It is three thousand years. And behold, the children of Hagar and the children of Sarah are in trouble. The children of Sarah fight the children of Hagar as if they are not kin. Many a mother weeps over the dead body of her child. What can we do for these grieving mothers? And how many more mothers must grieve?

And what's happening with the two brothers? In the midst of the fighting and hatred, in the midst of curses and blows, do they remember those days long ago when they frolicked together in the sands near Kadesh? As the tanks roll in and as the bombs drop from the sky, do they ever yearn for each other?

What's going on?, I wondered, waking with a start.

"Nein! Nein! Nein!" abba was shouting. "Is too much! Is my youngest daughter, and I'll not haf it."

"Daniel, I've lost one daughter," came eema's voice. "I'll not lose another. Maybe it's a phase she's in, maybe not. Either way, we can't jeopardize our relationship with her. She says she loves him. And basically, he's a good kid, no? And they're only talking about dating."

"Gevalt!"

"We'll lay down rules. They break the rules? We go back to the drawing boards. Come, Daniel, we'll invite him for Shabbes, yes?"

My eyes having adjusted to the dark, I glanced over at Esther, eager to find out what gives. The paradigmal heavy sleeper, she was stretched out on the bed, oblivious to everything, despite the din around her.

✡

"Miriam, got a moment?" asked Esther, approaching my desk.

"Yup."

Esther sat down in the chair next to mine. "Ever been in love?" she asked, a sheepish look on her face.

Now for a second there, I wasn't quite sure what to say, because I was aware that I probably was in love with Lanie, but I wasn't confident that Esther would understand. Then, getting excited for her, I exclaimed, "Oh Esther, you have something to tell me, don't you?"

"Miriam, I'm in love. I really am," Esther announced. "I want this man more than I've ever wanted anything. And I need you to feel good about it."

"Of course I feel good about it."

"Been in love with him for years, but it looked like it wasn't meant to be and I accepted that. But now that I'm older.... He's coming for Shabbes dinner this Friday night and...."

"I'm so happy for you, sweetie, but I'm not quite following. Why was the age thing so important?"

"Because of the age difference, ninny."

"You're not talking about Eric, are you?" I asked, suddenly realizing my mistake.

"Is that what you thought!" exclaimed Esther, looking at me curiously. "No. It's Harry. Since he got back from Israel, we've been spending every Sunday afternoon together."

I hadn't seen it coming. Stunned, I answered, "Mazel tov."

"I know I should have told you sooner. You'll forgive me, won't you?"

"Consider it done." Seeing her face cloud over, I added, "Stop worrying, Esther. Really, there's nothing to forgive."

"It's not that. I'm worried about Shabbes. Abba is just barely agreeing to it. He could take offence at almost anything. We could really use your help."

"Of course I'll help. And what I suspect will do you a whole lot more good, I'm sure eema will help you."

"But his heart. And if he starts thinking about Auschwitz and Sondra and everything."

"Eema and me, we'll be right there ready to calm him down, though I'm not sure it'll come to that. After all, abba's good about things he's agreed to. And it's not as if you're walking out on him. And remember, he was always fond of Harry."

"That was before."

I nodded.

"Meems, got any advice?"

"Well, I'd phase in the relationship slowly. Oh yeah, and ask Harry to dress up for Shabbes. Stuff like that impresses abba."

For a moment there, Esther looked easier. She thanked me and started to rise. Then she sank back into the chair, her brow wrinkling again, tears welling up in her eyes.

"Oh Es, there really is something else bothering you. What is it?"

"Miriam, is it a sin?"

"A sin?"

"I mean he *was* Sondra's boyfriend and all."

"He was. But I'm not sure what that means to you."

"Well, isn't this a bit like, you know, coveting my sister's man?"

"That was a long time ago. And clearly, Sondra never really loved him. And guess what! Strange though it may seem to you, she dumped the guy—just like she dumped the rest of us!"

Esther nodded.

"You think about her a lot, don't you?"

"All the time."

"You know, Esther, forgive me if I'm on the wrong track, but if part of this guilt is over having a crush on Harry when Sondra and Harry were dating, you should know, Harry was the golden boy. All the girls were meshugah over him. It was like this developmental stage for the campers' daughters."

A hint of a smile flickered across Esther's face. I wondered if Esther was picking up on the fact that I'd also had feelings for Harry and that feelings like this always leave some kind of residue.

"Must be hard for you knowing they used to be together," I continued.

"A little, I guess. Mainly, I don't want to be a bad sister. Miriam, don't you see? I don't want to be the reason our sister never returns."

"You've never been bad to anyone in your entire life. Anyway, Sondra isn't exactly returning. And we've no reason to believe she has any interest in Harry at this point."

"You're probably right," she answered, sighing.

"Let me ask you something. Any chance any of this unease over Sondra is really left over feelings about that other thing—you know, what happened the last time Harry was over?"

"You mean Sondra and Harry on the couch?"

"Yeah. Harry ever talk about it?"

"Not much. Only to say he's sorry and hopes the family can forgive him. And as Adoshem is my witness, I really do forgive him. You do as well, don't you, Miriam?"

"I'm working on it."

"Work hard, Miriam," urged Esther.

We fussed and analyzed for the rest of the week. And at least twice a day

Esther would come rushing to ask me some question that began, "but what if abba…?" Nonetheless, we weren't in the least prepared for what actually transpired.

It wasn't just Harry that was dressed to the nines, though he looked like a perfect gentleman in his smart green vest. Abba himself had on his good brown suit. And he never once removed his shirt. Throughout dinner, abba kept calling Harry "Hershel." I kept waiting for the other shoe to drop.

"So, Hershel? How did you find being on a kibbutz?" asked abba, looking genuinely intrigued.

Harry started talking about kibbutz life. Later on, abba asked him about the war. What was it like being so close to the fighting? What special emergency measures were introduced? What did people think was going to happen next? As Harry talked, you could tell he supported the Occupation. Eema winced a few times, but kept her cool. Abba, on the other hand, seemed enthralled.

"Is a courageous young man, you are, Hershel," abba declared, reaching for a second drumstick, a look of admiration on his face. "Not every man can valk into a situation like that. I've seen in it your vork in that anti-nazi group too. Is called what?"

"Youth against Nazis."

"Yes, that's it. Is fine vork you do. Mazel tov."

It was beginning to look as if no one was even going to mention that there was ever a problem. We polished off the meal, eating all the chicken, most of the rice, and all but one of the knishes. Then Esther plugged in the kettle, and we retired to the living room.

Once again Harry began talking about the kibbutzim—how the children were all raised communally. A safe subject, for it was part of the socialist dream. Then he launched into a discussion of religious instruction—a distinctly precarious topic in this household. I opened my mouth, fully intending to change the subject. And it is then that the most re-markable thing happened.

"Hershel," began abba.

"Mr. Himmelfarb," responded Harry, looking straight at him.

"My wife and I haf been talking, yah? She tells me I've been an absolute schmuck when it comes to you. Eric must have told you the meshugahs I've been spouting. Is not the kind of man I vant to be. All my life, I'm a socialist. Like you, I am someone what fights for a better vorld. I've a bad temper, though, yah? And it gets in the vay. And is apologizing I am. I'm apologizing to you as one good man to another."

"Mr. Himmelfarb, you had cause. I acted very badly," acknowledged Harry.

"Let's say that we all acted badly, Hershel. And epes, we'll leave it at that."

Harry and abba got up and approached each other. Harry reached out his hand as if to shake abba's. Abba grabbed Harry and gave him a hug. Then they both sat down.

"You'll start coming around to the house again, yah?"

"Thank you, Mr. Himmelfarb."

"A few rules, though, young man. No running off with my daughter. No sex on the living room couch. And you'll play chess mit me once a week, and you'll let me beat you every single time, yes?"

I was so proud of abba I could burst. At the same time, I was in something of a dilemma. I'd started the evening intending to help Esther with abba. No help was needed. And now I was the only one uncomfortable, because I was the only one who knew that something bad had gone down between Harry and Uncle Yacov. And I was the only one who could add up the mistakes: The Nazis coming. Offending Uncle Yacov. Sondra on the living room couch.

Needing to get away and think, I got up. "I'll take care of the dishes," I offered.

"A wonderful meal," Harry immediately exclaimed. "So I hope you'll have no objection if I refuse to be a male chauvinist pig and if I share in the mitzvah of clean-up."

"By all means," I answered, feeling just a little cornered.

Harry followed me into the kitchen. As we were scraping off the plates, emptying the chicken bones into the waste bin, Uncle's words kept echoing in my head. I just had to find out what happened. I turned to face Harry. "Harry, forgive me for asking and forgive the timing, but it's been niggling away at me. Something happen between you and Uncle Yacov?"

"You can say that again," Harry snorted, anger in his voice.

"The two of you had some kind of fight?"

"That we did. Can't talk about it though. I promised Sondra a long time ago."

"I respect that."

"I'm sorry, Miriam. But I really can't."

There was an awkward pause. After a few minutes, I broke it, asking him, "you ever hear from her after she left?"

"Actually, yes. It was when your father was in the hospital. Out of the blue I get this call from Sondra. Says she needs money pronto."

"Let me guess. You gave it to her. And she never returned it."

Harry shrugged his shoulders.

"Hear anything after that?"

"Well, sort of. A mutual friend of ours bumped into her in Vancouver about a year ago."

"Was she okay?"

"Yes and no."

Clearly, Harry knew something but didn't want to say. And I didn't want to press him. But there was one more thing I needed to check out.

"Look, Harry, Esther is my sister," I began, "and I don't want to see her hurt. And so I'm just going to ask you straight out. You don't by any chance still have feelings for Sondra?"

"Not like you mean."

"And you wouldn't ever, well, take advantage of Esther?"

"I would never do that," answered Harry, looking distinctly uneasy.

I nodded. Then Harry and I loaded the plates into the sink. As I began running the water, he observed, "You don't trust me the way you used to. Can't say I blame you. But I've always valued our friendship. You'll give me a chance to win back your trust, won't you?"

"Yes, of course," I responded, turning around again. "Sorry, Harry. I know how all this must sound."

I didn't mean to stare, but I couldn't help it. It was like turning back the clock. Something about his expression, the way his eyes met mine without either intruding or backing away. He looked earnest, honest, like the decent kid I remembered from childhood—the one we all looked up to and adored. I could feel my doubt lifting. I could feel a strange sadness tingling just behind my eyes, clutching at the back of my throat. So I did have feelings for this man despite being in love with Lanie. For a moment I felt uncomfortable and then the discomfort lifted; and I could feel my commitment to protect their relationship getting stronger.

"Incidentally, thanks for the tip about dressing up," he went on. "I think it helped."

"Harry, abba's been an absolute mentsh tonight. But you and Esther should probably go slow regardless. You know what it's like with survivors."

"Tell me about it," laughed Harry.

151

Harry and Esther did indeed proceed slowly—so slowly, in fact, that by the third year, I was starting to worry. I was concerned for the two of them because they needed to be getting on with their life together, yes? But to be clear, I was concerned for myself as well. Harry and Esther being a couple, it seemed only right to let Esther move out first. But gotenyu! They weren't budging.

"The two of you thinking of getting hitched soon?" I asked Esther one day.

A touch of sadness came across Esther's face. "We want nothing more than to be husband and wife. Be we're leaving it a bit longer."

"Because of eema and abba?"

"What else?"

1968 and 1969 were busy years for the family. There was a huge proliferation of fascist groups in the city and Harry again became involved in anti-fascism. For a while I too was active politically. I attended numerous meetings of Shalom Now—this Toronto organization devoted to peace in the Middle East. By the time I was in my final year at U. of T., however, I found little time for politics.

As November 1969 rolled around, I considered doing my M. Phil. in philosophy at Leeds even though it would mean moving out before Esther. With Lanie's encouragement, I applied. When I told the family that I'd been accepted, only Esther and Harry were favourably disposed. Abba paced the hall nervously. Now Eema said all the right things: "A wonderful opportunity. Meydeleh, I support you wholeheartedly." But her eyes clouded over. And three times that night, I awoke to hear her shrieking, "Oy! Not another one!" So come morning, I resigned myself to staying.

I began my M.A. in philosophy at U. of T. in the fall of 1970. Did I do my M.A. thesis on the Heidegger question I'd been researching for years? No. Nor on anything else with such clear substance. Though I didn't consciously plan or even reflect on what I was doing, it was as if I had made a decision to distance myself however I could from my Holocaust-ridden life. The thing is, where could a child of a survivor go when she had the family I had, the commitment, the love? She could hardly jump ship. But she could perhaps find a spot—a corner—in which to hide. And where better to find such a corner than in the aloof reaches of scholarship?

I had always been mesmerized by language. How words work in the world. The way Sondra said, "Go to hell—Holocaust hell if you prefer;" and abba found himself in Auschwitz. I now made language my primary focus. The fact that I tied the Holocaust into my thought, however abstractly, just made the slippage away from it all the harder to detect. Eventually, I decided to do my thesis on performatory utterances in oppressive regimes, with Nazi Germany as my primary example. And before long, I had drafted a twenty-four page proposal. Now while I suspect both abba and eema spotted the all-too-obvious flaw in my thinking, only abba named it.

✡

Eema was sitting on the beige chair in the living room, pouring over my proposal. I had just sat down and answered some question she'd asked about performatory utterances when abba burst into the room, lowered himself into the lazyboy, and said, "performatory vat?"

"Performatory utterances, abba," I answered. "It's what my thesis is about. It's statements, well, which are true by virtue of being uttered."

Abba's eyes began to bulge. "Don't you talk down to me young lady. You think I know from nothing just because I've never been to university?"

"Daniel, she didn't mean anything," assured eema, looking up from the manuscript. "We all know you're an extremely bright man."

"Absolutely," I asserted.

"Is better," he announced, sitting back in his chair, his eyes receding. "So, Miriam, how do they vork, these performatory utterances of yours?"

"Well, take promises," I began, eyeing him nervously. "I say, 'I promise,' and a promise is, in effect, made."

"And Israel says the country is at var and the country is at var," piped up abba.

"Exactly, abba. Anyhow, what I'm seeking to demonstrate is that a clear sign that a society is becoming oppressive is a dramatic increase in the range of utterances that become performatory. The Germany example is an obvious one for me to take up. In come the Nazis, yes? And a whole new range of performatory utterances enter linguistic space."

"Say more," invited eema.

"Okay. Take the so-called Jewish question. The Nazis announce, 'Jews are not citizens,' and instantly, Jews are without citizenship. Or take the disabled. 'These people are life unworthy of life,' says Hitler.

And the disabled are as good as dead."

"But why the whole megileh?" asked abba, shaking his head. "We think the vay you think, and is caput we are. No. No. Is no good at all. For this you go to university—to play with vords! It makes no difference what fancy schmancy terms you use. You still haf to resist. And resistance is still about real men, women, children changing orders, setting off explosives, smuggling people in and out, organizing."

Of course, abba was absolutely right, yes? Nonetheless, I hid the validity of his objection from myself because I didn't want to see it. Additionally, I somehow turned abba's "not understanding" into a need for me to move out imminently. I told myself that I had no choice but to leave if I were to have a chance of becoming a first-rate scholar. In actuality, of course, this urgency had nothing to with scholarship and everything to do with being a Holocaust survivor offspring who desperately wanted to fly the coop while convinced she had no right.

Not wanting to let my resolution flag, that very day, I broached the issue with Esther.

"Go for it. It'll be okay," she assured me. "Harry and I aren't getting married for a while. And meanwhile, I'm fully capable of holding down the fort."

"You sure?"

"Uh huh."

"Where will you go?" she asked, looking up from her book. "Oh, I see," she exclaimed, a grin breaking out on her face.

As Esther was well aware, I wasn't about to desert eema and abba by leaving Toronto, and there was only one place in Toronto I wanted to be—Rochdale College.

A cement high rise on the south-west corner of St. George and Bloor, Rochdale was one of the most formidable counter cultural scenes in North America. A broad range of people who loosely identified as hippies and freaks had flocked to it from across the continent—potheads, draft dodgers, artists, activists, students like myself who hungered for something different, though to my knowledge, no other child of survivors. What was every bit as significant, Lanie was now there.

The second of the offspring to move out, I did so far more carefully and tentatively then Sondra. Having checked with Lanie and discovered that there was a vacancy in her Rochdale commune, one evening over supper, I raised the idea of moving there as a remote possibility only. Eema must have already seen this coming and decided to back me, for she immediately offered to help with the rent. I examined her face carefully. A smile. No clouding of the eyes. She genuinely appeared to be okay.

Abba, on the other hand, was adamantly opposed. "Ay yay yay!" he exclaimed, his eyes bulging as he stared at me from the other end of the table. "Is this what you're vanting, Miriam? With all your learning, you should become a potskull like vat's-her-face?"

"Pothead," corrected eema, reaching for the bottle of king-sized coke.

"Abba, her name's Lanie," I said. "She smokes up, sure, but only in the evening."

"Punct. I should have a daughter what smokes up every evening. And do you really need to be spending more time with this Lanie person?"

Esther and I exchanged looks. And eema raised her left hand just slightly, motioning for me to let the topic drop.

Over the next couple of weeks, eema commented on Rochdale a few times, always watching abba as she did. "A couple of my students are there and really like it," she interjected. "It's not as wild as the papers say. It's an experience, yes?" she pointed out. "It's only a fifteen-minute walk away. Anyway, Daniel, she's twenty-three. You want we should stand in her way forever?"

Eema had clearly gauged it right.

"So, Miriam," abba announced one day over breakfast, "You're going to Rochdale? Is gut. Just promise: No drugs; and you'll not break your eema's heart but vill come home regularly for Shabbes, yah?"

"Every Shabbes, abba," I answered excitedly.

Every night for the next few weeks I was plagued by a repetitive nightmare: Men in green uniforms and swastika armbands had broken into the house. As he entered the living room, abba would spot them. A look of horror spreading across his face, he would yell out, "Miriam, helf mir! Helf mir!" But I was nowhere to be found. The dream rattled me, but I proceeded with my plans regardless. And on August 1, 1971, with eema weeping and abba groaning, "oy gevalt," I moved into the fourteenth floor commune at Rochdale—the commune with the weathered barn boards on the walls.

Throughout my time at Rochdale, a week didn't go by when abba didn't cry about his diminishing family. And many a time I would enter the Lippincott house to find both of them fretting about Sondra. Not surprisingly, therefore, the nightmare kept returning. And whenever it did, I would feel guilty and consider moving back. Nonetheless, knowing that Esther was there, I would let myself stay.

I did all the things that youth typically did at Rochdale—get involved in theatre, smoke up, create art. Once the buzz of the first few weeks subsided, though, what I found myself valuing most was the friendships. And of these, none was more significant than my growing relationship with Lanie. Again and again, Lanie and I would stay up to the wee hours, confiding in each other about family problems, about our thoughts about the future, also, about our fears of physical intimacy. "I know they'll die some day," I remember telling Lanie, "but I just can't imagine being alive without them."

"While screwing's terrific, I have this idiotic hang-up over guys coming down on me," Lanie acknowledged, her eyes fixed on mine. "Meems, you think it'd make any difference if it were with a woman?" I felt encouraged by Lanie's sexual queries, for she had indirectly raised the possibility of something happening between us—a real possibility, I thought, given she's not going out with anyone. Then there was this unexpected development.

One day, as my Caribbean roommate Joe and I were on the floor putting the final touches on this giant puppet head, he glanced at me and said, "Miriam, you'll never guess who Lanie's started balling! Animal Al, Vice-president of the Dog Shit Committee."

"No kidding," I answered, trying to sound as calm as possible.

Lanie broached the topic herself around 3:00 p.m. the following Friday. It was an opportune moment, for the two of us were sitting at the harvest table in the dining area and no one else was home.

"Miriam, you cool about Animal Al and me?" she asked, looking up from her copy of the *Tuesdaily*.

"Cool."

"You know I love you, Miriam," she continued, taking my hand in hers. "And so if it did start to bother you, I would stop. So help me, Meems," she added, looking me straight in the eyes, "I would stop in a heart beat."

I nodded, tears coming to my eyes. I felt as if we had arrived at one of those critical moments. It seemed to me that Lanie thought so too, for she looked at me intently and brought her face within an inch of mine. I could feel the warmth of her breath on my cheek, and I could smell the sweet tangy scent of her body. For a second there, I thought something was going to happen—that she would ... that I would.... But neither of us did. And as I sat there waffling, the phone rang. I hesitated, realizing it would be Shabbes in a few hours. What if eema or abba needed something? Then again, what if I was just chickening out and using Holocaust survivors as an excuse?

"Don't move. I'll be right back," I whispered to Lanie, rushing to the hall to answer. It was abba, checking as he always did after my health. Was I taking care of my cold? I should be more careful, or I'll die of pneumonia, kinehora. And had I seen any good movies lately? Oh yes, and could I maybe pick up some chopped herring, a bottle of Manichewitz, and a bisel coleslaw?

Eventually, I was off the phone and back at the table. There was no Lanie. I could hear the rattling of pots and pans in the kitchen. She had started dinner. I sat down and waited in silence for about twenty minutes.

"Lanie, you want me to skip Shabbes tonight?" I finally called out.

"No, enjoy yourself," she answered.

Lanie and Al were an item for a couple of weeks. Then it was Lanie and Jim. Then she began sleeping with Wolf as well—the guitar player from an ashram on the third floor. Lanie was almost always at one of their ashrams now. So there seemed to be no point hanging around the kitchen waiting for some elusive moment to return. Myself? I slept with Jeff for a couple of months there, but it was nothing serious. Of course, I repeatedly promised myself to tell Lanie how I felt. But the fact of the matter is, I never did.

That year I finished my masters. And I entered year one of my Ph.D. in the fall of 1972. In short order, I determined to do my thesis on Saussere's theory of signs. Something even more removed from the Holocaust, yes? For the next couple of months, I plotted out the thesis while continuing to enjoy those special moments which Rochdale kept offering up. My Rochdale days, however, were rapidly coming to an end.

The Rochdale breakaway was rather like being a door attached to a giant spring. I had managed to swing open, to venture forth. But I had already reached as far as the spring would permit.

✡

I was in the in-house grocers shopping. I surveyed the goodies as I placed them on the counter: crunchy granola, marble halvah, coke, and six packages of potato chips. Yes, that should hold us if we get the munchies again. Noticing that the political buttons jar in front of me was brimming over, I began searching through it. I was hoping there'd be something spoofing Nixon what with the election just days away and it being painfully obvious that Tricky Dicky was getting back in. And sure enough, I spotted one. "Don't change dicks in the middle of a screw," it read. Jack—a fellow actor who always wore tie-dyed—was on shift that day, and he nodded with approval as I pinned on the button. "See you at rehearsal tonight," I said. Then I paid him and caught the elevator up.

As I entered the commune, the phone was ringing. I quickly plunked the bags of groceries on the floor and grabbed the telephone. It was Esther.

"Miriam, can you come over?" she asked, alarm in her voice.

"Yeah, of course. What's up?"

"Miriam, he's turning blue. And I'm scared."

"Abba?"

"Yes. We told them about our being engaged yesterday. They seemed to be taking it all right. Then today, this thing happened with the television. And then abba started pressing Harry about our plans and Harry ended up blurting out that we were thinking of living in Israel, and well, you can imagine! Oh, Miriam!"

"What thing with the television?"

"Just come."

"I'm on my way."

I grabbed my jacket, bolted out of the building, and flagged a cab. As we drove to Lippincott, the old image of abba in the coffin kept flashing through my head. If only I hadn't moved out!, I thought to myself. A sense of dread came over me as the cab pulled up. I handed the driver a five spot and hurried to the front door. I turned the knob. As the door swung open, I could hear abba shouting, "What for are they going to Israel? Gevalt!"

"Abba, we only said 'maybe,'" came Esther's voice.

Good. He was alive.

I held my breath as I entered the living room. I was relieved to see that everyone was there—abba and eema on the beige chairs, and Harry and Esther on the couch. But something felt off kilter. And then I took it in. There was this large empty space where the television should be. But why? I exchanged looks with Esther. She looked frightened.

Though everyone else said hello, abba only barely noticed me. He got up and began pacing the room frantically, utter desolation on his face. "Oy!" he exclaimed. "Is all gone. Mayn mameh, mayn tateh, mayn shvester, mayn bruders, mayn tokhter Sondra, mayn tokhter Miriam, and now mayn tokhter Esther."

Eema rose and put her arms around abba. "Miriam and Esther are here, Daniel. They're not dead. And they haven't gone anywhere. Look. Look, sweetheart. Miriam's home, yes?"

"Abba, I'm right here," I announced, going over and putting my arm on his shoulder.

His face turning blue, abba shrieked, "Is dead, is everyone. Or worse than dead."

"Abba, I'm not dead. It's Miriam. Look at me," I insist, holding his head in my hands.

Abba's eyes light up with recognition, and he smiles faintly. "I'm sorry, Miriam. Is gut you're home."

"It's okay, abba. We're all here. And everything's going to be fine."

Abba tries to walk to his seat, but starts to weave back and forth.

"Sweetie, you having heart pains?" asks eema, grabbing hold of him.

Abba nods.

"You'll let Harry and Miriam help you to bed, and I'll get some pills, yes?"

Abba agrees. His eyes wide with astonishment, Harry rises; and Harry and I each take a shoulder and half carry abba up the stairs.

"Let me," says Harry, as he lays abba down. Harry loosens abba's tie and unbuttons his shirt, while abba groans. Harry glances at the shoes, then looks up at me. I shake my head and he lets them be.

A second or two later, in comes eema with the pill bottle and a glass of water. With her help, abba swallows two pills, though they don't go down easily. Then eema reaches down, pulls back abba's socks, and checks his ankles. No swelling. She listens to his breathing and nods. It's sounding fairly regular at this point. And while he is pale and trembling, he's looking better. If we could just keep him calm.

Eema begins humming a tune I don't know. And slowly, a smile comes to abba's face.

"Is damn gut we were, Rachaele, no?"

"Damn good."

"How many times did we train newbies to organize goods from

Canada? And how many comrades were saved that were slated for extinction?" he asks in Yiddish.

"Countless," replies eema.

"Miriam," he observes, looking up as if noticing me for the first time, "you here? Is Shabbes already?"

Abba closes his eyes, and a few minutes later, drifts off.

Harry kisses eema on the cheek, looks at her earnestly, and whispers, "I'm going downstairs to check on Esther. Call if you need us." Eema sits down on the bed, bends over abba, and begins stroking his head. I go to the kitchen and make her some tea. When I return, I place the tea on the night stand, then sit down in the blue chair near the door and wait. After about fifteen minutes, eema sits up straight, eyes me gratefully, and whispers, "Meydeleh, you've no idea how happy I am to see you. Did Esther call?"

"Yeah, but eema, what happened?"

"When abba found out that Harry and Esther were thinking of going to Israel…" she begins, her eyes darting about the room.

Reading the signs, I get up and fetch the cigarettes, ashtray, and matches.

"He just started screaming. You know what it's like, Miriam," she continues, lighting a cigarette, and taking a long drag. "It brings back the other losses. If only he hadn't pressed Harry so hard, but he was upset about the television, yes? And…."

"Eema," I interrupt. "Exactly what happened to the television?"

"Don't exactly know," murmurs eema, grimacing.

"You just came home today and found it missing?"

"Punct."

"What did the police say?"

She shakes her head and begins weeping. I go over and hold her for a very long time. And gradually, she calms down. I pour her some more tea and sit back down in the chair. Then I ask myself why eema wouldn't call the police. And it comes to me.

"There wasn't any break-in, was there?" I murmur.

"No."

"Sondra's handiwork?"

Eema nods, then shakes her head sadly. "We could tell. There's this scent in the air. You remember that distinctive perfume she wore, yes?"

"That stupid ganef!" I exclaim.

"Sha, meydeleh," urges eema, smiling faintly at me. "She's your sister. And who's to say what kind of tsores Sondra has. She needed the money maybe more than we needed the set. Anyway, it's only furniture. It's replaceable. Sondra isn't."

"Sorry. I didn't mean to offend you. But eema, tell me the rest."

"Well, we started to talk about Sondra—abba, Esther, Harry, and me. How could we not with the smell of her perfume everywhere? And Harry got this strange look on his face like he was trying not to let the cat out of the bag. You know that look he gets. Anyway, it was obvious he knew something. And so abba pressed him. And he told us. Clearly, she's back in the city now, yes? But apparently a few years ago, a friend of Harry's saw Sondra on some street in Vancouver. And she was.... She was prostituting. Oy! My poor Sondra!" eema exclaimed, her eyes welling up again.

Again I went and sat beside eema and held her. Then I asked, "but how could Harry have told abba of all people?"

"How? Well, Miriam, he didn't until abba started screaming at him. But abba began hollering, and that's how. Anyway, knowing your abba, you can guess what happened after that. First abba starts calling Harry a pimp. Then he apologizes. Then he calls Sondra a whore and says she'd be better off dead. Next thing you know, he's grilling Harry about their plans. Now Harry keeps changing the subject. But every time he doesn't get a straight answer, abba gets more upset. And finally Harry says, 'Mr. Himmelfarb, we're thinking about Israel, but we have no firm plans.' But all your poor abba hears is 'Israel.' And before you know it, he's back in a world where everyone's dead."

"Oh eema. I'm so sorry."

"He needs to see everyone around so that he can get his bearings again. You'll stay a few weeks, yes?"

"Of course."

"Sweetie, go down and let Harry and Esther know that abba's doing fine. And stay and talk with them. They're upset, yes? I'll just sit here with abba for awhile."

"You sure you're okay, eema?"

Eema nodded. "And you?"

Returning her nod, I looked at the tears in her eyes and the lines in her face and I didn't want to leave. But she insisted.

I entered the living room to find Esther sitting on the couch, her hands over her eyes. Harry was right next to her, his arm around her shoulder, his eyes fixed on her. Feeling touched, I approached the couch, knelt in front of my distraught sister, and whispered, "Esther."

"Oh Miriam, we almost killed him," she wailed, slowly removing her hands and staring into my eyes.

"Sha, sweetie," I said, holding her gaze. "Eema told me to let you know he's going to be okay. He's not sweating and his breathing's regular."

"Is he really okay, Miriam?"

I nodded and sat down cross-legged on the floor at her feet. A few seconds later, Esther and Harry joined me on the floor.

"Miriam," said Harry after a few minutes, "Esther and I've been talking. And we've made a decision. We'll postpone the wedding another year. Then the two of us will move into Sondra's old room. Your father will see us around all the time and so will be calmer. It'll be good. One big happy family," he added, placing his left hand in his jeans pocket.

I couldn't believe my ears. "What planet are you guys on?" I exclaimed. "Get real! It won't be one big happy family. And it's not fair. You've a right to a life too."

"Don't be so negative," Esther objected. "We really don't mind about Israel. Harry's been offered a lectureship in Judaic Studies at York University, and I'm sure I can land a social work job at Jewish Family Services. You remember that 'A' I got on my placement there?"

"Yeah. They hiring?"

"Yes. Actually, they're desperately short-staffed."

"There's a life for you here? And you're prepared to give up Israel? Fine! Zy gezent! But don't keep putting off your marriage. You've already gone way slower than anyone had a right to expect. And one more year won't make enough of a difference. As for moving in here, let me tell you. I can't see it."

"We could make it work," said Harry.

"Sure, but at what cost?" I countered. "You need some distance from abba to have any kind of marriage. Nu? What do you think will happen if you're under his roof? That he'll suddenly become someone who respects privacy? I can see it now: Abba telling you what to do— how to run your marriage, how to raise your children, the whole schtick."

Esther's brow furled. "Of course, you're right, but what choice do we have?"

The three of us brainstormed for the next hour, with me leaving every so often to check on abba. Eventually, Esther came up with a plan. They would say nothing for a month or so while abba recovered. Then they'd look for a place within a few blocks of the Lippincott house and only announce the wedding date once they found something that close.

"What do you think, Harry?" asked Esther.

"I like," answered Harry. "But Miriam," he checked, glancing over at me, "would he be able to handle it? I mean, it would still mean having none of his kids at home."

Now with that question, my world was to shift—shift decisively. "One of them *will* be at home," I answered. "It's my turn now. I'm moving back."

"You sure, Miriam?" asked Esther, her eyes beaming with gratitude. "I'm sure."

Everything went as planned. Abba was close to his normal self in a couple of weeks, though he still had moments. And while he initially got upset when Esther and Harry told him their plans, his eyes receded as they mentioned where they'd be living. And he downright beamed when they announced that they were intending to have a large family.

"I'm so happy for you, sheyneh meydeleh, and you, our Hershele," said eema, going over and hugging each of them in turn. "Yingele," she added, eyeing him tenderly, "I can't tell you how delighted I am to have you in this family. A mother couldn't ask for a better son. And such a wonderful husband and father you're going to make!"

"Is a mechayeh!" exclaimed abba, his eyes coming alive. "Family is gut. And us Jews, we haf to haf kinderlekh—lots of kinderlekh. Six million we lost. Caput. But every kid we haf, is bringing back a little piece of our vorld—another little Liebka, another Shmuel."

"Abba, you're really okay with this?" asked Esther, excitedly.

"Okay? Why vouldn't I be okay when a daughter tells me such news? Still, if you postponed the marriage another six months, vould it make such a very big difference?"

Fortunately, we had read abba right. Abba stopped pushing for a postponement the second I asked if it was all right if I moved back home. It was clear he was thrilled with this new development, though he played his cards cautiously.

"Is not perfect," he responded nonchalantly, leaning back on the beige chair and trying to wipe the grin off his face. "I vould like what my children should be independent, but nu? Are you my kid or what? So you vant to move back, you move back. Only you're in *my* house, you obey *my* rules, which means none of that pot stuff. Farshtey? Vat? You think I don't know you smoked up in that den of iniquity?"

The wedding was at the schul near College. We tried to locate Sondra and Uncle to invite them, but no luck. The reception was at our place. The house was all decked out in Stars of David and lace. And except for Sondra and Uncle, everyone was there—all the campers and the campers' children, Lanie, the Morrisons, Harry's entire clan from parents to cousins twice removed. "Mazel tov, mazel tov," said person after person, kissing the bride, shaking abba's hand, shaking eema's hand, shaking my hand, slapping Harry on the back. "Two children of survivors, like it was meant to be," exclaimed Mrs. Plautsnicki, her hand on her heart. "So, Miriam, how about you?" asked Mr. Schachter from next door. "You're going out with some good Jewish boy, and we'll hear something soon maybe?"

One-and-a-half weeks later, Lanie, Joe, and I were sitting slumped over the harvest table in our Rochdale home, waiting for the moving van. We'd been up packing most the night; there were boxes everywhere—in my bedroom, in the living room, on the tables. Saddened that we would be parting, we said the things people typically say at such times.

"Hey, kiddo, we're really going to miss you," said Lanie, looking bleary-eyed and resting her chin against one of the boxes.

"I'll be around so often, you'll be dying to get rid of me," I joked.

"Promises, promises," exclaimed Joe, yawning.

When the men arrived, we all pitched in, carrying box after box into the van. As I maneuvered a particularly large box onto the elevator, it suddenly dawned on me that I'd not be having that nightmare again; and this wave of relief swept over me. Then I thought of the play I'd been in, the puppet we'd made, those special times with Lanie. And the relief vanished; and I could taste the sadness. The end of an era, I thought to myself. And now what? I'm going to be there again. Waiting for another stick of furniture to go missing. Waiting for the Holocaust to catch up to us, to label us, to put an end to childbirth, to drag us to the camps, to burn us, and to scatter our ashes in ditches throughout the fatherland.

*Image: It is dark. Just barely hanging onto life, two skeletons in rags—a young man and a young woman—sit cross-legged by a foul smelling ditch, talking. The man is holding the woman's hand and peering into her feverish eyes. Pus is oozing from several open sores just above her upper lip. Seemingly not noticing, the man reaches over and kisses the woman on the lips. After a minute or so, he pulls back, puts his bony hand into the pocket of his tattered pants, and takes out a piece of bread. It is green and moldy and crawling with lice.*

*The woman's eyes light up as if she were beholding a banquet and she reaches for it. "Hurry! Someone's coming," whispers a gruff voice from out of the darkness.*

*The man and woman startle, and the bread falls down, sinking deeper and deeper into the sea of mud around them.*

## Chapter Five

## Miriam, ages 28-44

Despite my apprehension about how life would unfold after Harry and Esther wed, and despite real concerns about eema's frequent whimpering at night, in many ways the decades that followed were a mitzvah. Why a mitzvah? For one thing, and this is no small matter, thanks to Esther and Harry, I was soon surrounded by a growing family. Cast your eye down the genogram, and you'll see that I became an aunt three times over. Yes. Three times, kinehora. First came Samantha, with that birthmark under the eye not unlike mine, then freckled-faced Niel, named after Uncle Nathaniel, and finally, little Channa—named after Harry's great aunt, but the spitting image of our Esther. They were often over, the kinderlekh, them plus this heimish little cockerspaniel named "Schmootsy" that Harry and Esther had picked up for Sammy's seventh birthday and that always bounded toward you and gave you a slurpy lick.

I cannot honestly say that this new generation held the same importance to me as my parents' generation. Nor did my own. It was always the survivors that felt central, and the further from the survivors, the less urgent people's existence seemed. Nonetheless, they had a special place in my heart, these grandchildren.

It was strange at first finding myself with an altered identity, not the child, but the adult, not the direct relative, but a relative slightly removed who at times played only a supportive role in the proceedings. But what joy watching this new generation of Jews strive to comprehend the universe! Niel's eyes shone with amazement as eema drew her white lace shawl over her head and lit the Shabbes candles. As eema's steady hands circled the flames again and again, his jaw would drop ever so slightly and his freckled face would peer up at her, beaming. And how he would grin when eema would give the kinderlekh that knowing look and ask, "Sweeties, did I ever tell you about the long white hair your

Aunt Miriam was born with?"

While for the first few Pesachs, everyone had to help her with the difficult words, by the time she was six, the youngest child Channa was asking the fir cashas like an expert. "Mah nish'tanah ha'lilah hazeh," she would sing, looking straight into Harry's eyes, clearly aware that she was the prime mover, that the entire evening was devoted to answering the queries that she had so deftly placed before us.

Now things were different with Samantha, the eldest, named after zeda Shmuel. Esther and Harry never knew what to do with Sam because Sam frequently brooded and would go for days without uttering a word. Esther was particularly distressed by this. One Shabbes shortly after Sammy's seventh birthday, when the family was sitting around the living room, Esther grew so alarmed as she watched Sammy sulking in the corner that she drew eema and me aside and asked, "So, whatchya think? Should we take her to a psychiatrist or what?"

Eema shook her head. "Sheyneh punem," she cooed, "it'll be okay. Remember what you used to say about your great Uncle Yosef? That he was a remarkable man, yes? Well, our Samantha is a remarkable meydeleh."

Though I adored all the children, I felt especially close to Sam, partly because she was troubled, partly because I recognized something of myself in her despite the enormous difference in temperament. The sheer fact that she wore thick glasses, the way she quickened her pace when passing the Uncle Nathaniel, the lightening speed of her mind. Then too, there was her pressing need to ground herself physically—in her case, by rubbing her right fist against her palm ever so gently, feeling her flesh made flesh. And so what if she broods?, I reasoned. Why would someone not brood when all of her great grandparents and most of her great uncles and aunts have been murdered? Could it be awareness we are witnessing pure and simple? Or maybe this brooding child is a sign instructing us to remember. One of those signs the universe drops on you, even without a supreme being at the helm.

The Holocaust, did it crowd in on these children? Did it whisper to them as they went about their daily chores the way that it whispered to Sondra, Esther, and me? At the time, I wasn't sure, though I kept finding myself wondering: How are they managing it? Niel, Channa, and Samantha, are any of them hiding as Sondra and I hid? Do they have a place under the stairs? In the attic, perhaps? And I frequently found myself wanting to protect them. I even found myself wincing and wanting to shush abba when he would rush over and pinch their cheeks, exclaiming in that booming voice of his, "Is a mitzvah. Is the defeat of Hitler. No posthumous victory for that mamzer now." Of course, I didn't shush abba. How could anyone shush a survivor for doing what he must? Despite my urge to shush him, I was happy for abba—for eema too—for they clearly delighted in their growing family. And there were times when abba and I were of one mind. I knew well enough why he proclaimed the defeat of Hitler. I too felt the triumph. Here we were, us Himmelfarbs—and we had not only survived; our numbers were growing. Actually, despite my ongoing struggle to escape my own awareness of the Holocaust, there were even moments—fleeting, to be sure—when I had no interest in protecting the children, myself, or any of us; for I could sense deep in my bones that protection was a ruse. That the Holocaust was part of our facticity—theirs, mine, Harry's, Esther's, abba's, and eema's. And that it could no more be avoided than the darkness at night or the vulnerability of the human soul.

*Image: The sun searing their scab-ridden skin, their eyes sunk into their faces, hundreds of scrawny women in soiled fatigues kneel in rows just to the left of the wooden barracks. The women are on their knees, their puny arms outstretched, their bony palms facing the sky. A pile of bricks lay in front of them. Facing the ghostly rows are two well-fed women in immaculate uniforms, the one on the right holding onto a white Alsation, who is straining on its lead. The woman with the dog points to the kneeling figures and asks, "Wievel stück?"*

*"Two hundred and twelve pieces," replies the assistant in perfect German, her voice matter-of-fact, her words crisp. The woman with the dog tightens her clutch on her whip, then nods to her assistant. The assistant bends down, picks up two bricks, approaches one of the kneeling women, and without a word, dumps a brick in each of the outstretched hands. Half marching, she returns to the pile and picks up two more bricks and places these in the hands of the next women. And so she continues until each of the kneeling figures has a brick in each palm. The task complete, the two officials stand side-by-side, their feet slightly apart, and gaze on in silence, a look of fierce determination in their eyes.*

While the years had rolled by without our seeing Sondra, how very often her presence was felt! Whenever Niel would stick out his tongue at Channa, Sondra would flash through my mind. Also when Sammy was having a good day, for Sammy too was a beauty with blonde hair and a long slender figure, and she looked somewhat like Sondra at such times. Needless to say, every solitary one of us thought of Sondra when things disappeared, as they periodically did, though how abba tried to deny it!

Abba and eema had just returned home from a party at the Morrisons. Eema was all spiffed up in this green velour pants suit. Eager to snap her picture, abba raised his right hand and instructed, "You'll vait while I get the Nikon, yah?" Then he headed to his room. When he returned minutes later, he was pale. "Is gone is the camera," he stammered. Eema exchanged looks with me, a sad knowing smile on her face. Abba paced the living room, then pointed to the drawn blinds and exclaimed in a flat voice demonstrably lacking in conviction, "You left for us the blinds open maybe, Miriam?"

"Abba, it's not the blinds."

"What kind of meshugener vorld are we living in where everywhere there are ganefs," he continued, his voice beginning to come alive, his eyes starting to bulge. "I haf survived Auschvitz so that the neighbours should organize us out of house and home? I... I...." And then he went silent and looked lost in thought.

Now Sondra was not the only one whose absence haunted us during this period—just the only one this intrusive. We still hadn't heard from Uncle Yacov. "But abba," I pointed out one afternoon as we were sitting on the porch, "he can't just have vanished into thin air."

Abba looked away nervously while hastily assuring me, "Leave it to me. Is inquiries I'll make." But though he was a capable man, somehow, he came up with nothing.

And then there was the business with the campers. Aside from Harry's folks and the Plautsnickis, we now saw far less of them. We'd hit a rough spot, and there seemed to be no way around it. It was just after the Yom Kippur war when I first noticed something amiss.

Everyone was at this party at the Plautsnickis. A number of the campers were standing in the centre of the room discussing the Middle East. What should be done about Egypt? About Jordan?" Sitting on a couch to the side, eema and abba were staying out of it. But Mrs. Schugarenski—a camper, roughly eema's age—strutted straight over to eema, placed her hands on her hips, and said, "You have a position I've never understood. You'll clarify it for us maybe?" Eema declined but was pressed so often that she ended up explaining as briefly and delicately as she could. When eema finished, Mrs. Schugarenski narrowed her eyes and exclaimed, "Rachael, you a survivor, and you don't understand the significance of Israel! As my mother the balebosteh used to say, there's no anti-Semite like a Jewish anti-Semite. Farshtey?"

Last but not least, of course, there was Lanie. Oh, we'd visited for a while after I moved back home, but the visits had steadily declined, and within a year or so, they had petered out. In the end, we even stopped phoning one another. Nu? Though neither of us named it, I suspect that on some level, we were both aware that nothing much was possible. I had chosen my family over her, and my relationship with my family just didn't allow room. Oy! Not that I didn't occasionally let myself dream, but then I would set eyes on eema or abba, and I would rejoin the waking world.

My family aside, it was work that most engrossed me during this period. A year before eema's retirement, I was hired by the philosophy department at York University. I began as assistant professor and quickly climbed up through the ranks. "So much better than in my time, when women got bupkes," observed eema.

Harry also had a position at York. Department of Judaic Studies. With Harry living only a few blocks away, he'd give me a lift to work every morning. And we would schmooze along the way about abba, eema, Esther, and the kinderlekh, and now and then university politics. "But Miriam, is he remembering to take his heart medication?" Harry would ask.

"Not to worry," I answered, "but tell me, how's Esther finding working with incest survivors? Pretty big switch for her, eh?"

Nothing in my life suited me quite so well as being a prof. From the beginning, I was a good teacher who cared about my students and who had a sense of how to inspire them. Again and again, I saw the young women and men in my seminars come alive and begin questioning the age old verities. "Professor Himmelfarb, just look at what Cooper calls the philosophic tradition," objected Mohammed. "Europeans, Europeans, and more Europeans."

"Why do Jews have to put on Jew faces to be recognized as Jews?" asked Ida. "Personally, I don't fit the stereotypes, right? But aren't I every bit as much a Jew as the davening Orthodox?"

That said, though I in no way question my contribution as a teacher, as a theorist, I was still missing the mark. And I was hardly alone. It was the dawn of postmodernism, yes?

Postmodernism is this philosophy that had begun to sweep academia. It demands nothing less than the rejection of all high level theory. Nu? For the postmodernist, like Derrida, the order of the day is not absolute truths but the partiality of knowledge. Not plausible interpretation, but the ultimate undecidability of meaning. Not reading that follows the text, but what Yale's Paul de Man—the founder of the deconstructionist method—calls "reading against the grain."

Fascinated by a philosophy that insisted that there were no ultimate truths, in the late '70s I started publishing postmodernist articles in the *American Journal of Philosophical Discourse*. By the early '80s, I had become an internationally renowned expert on the implications of Derrida and de Man for feminist thought. And I was a frequent speaker at postmodernist conferences. What I didn't see, what I didn't want to see, is that postmodernism was not simply the natural progression of my thought, though, to a degree, it was that. However sophisticated and fascinating, it was also a way to escape my own embeddedness. More particularly, like semiotics, it was a way to flee the Holocaust.

Fleeing the Holocaust and being trapped in the Holocaust—that was still the central paradox of my life, whether I was at work or at home. By the mid to late '80s, though, the cocoon I had worked so hard at weaving started to unravel.

✡

I was on my way out of class when I first learned that the legendary survivor and author Primo Levy had killed himself. How come Levy of all people? This survivor unshaken in his belief in humanity. Not sure if eema and abba had heard, I came home early. I found them in the kitchen discussing Levy's suicide. And they didn't look shocked. Not even surprised.

"I see you know," I observed, joining them at the table. "You okay?"

Eema and abba nodded, though their eyes were moist.

"Is a terrible thing," muttered abba, putting down his coffee and shaking his head. "But then again, vat can you expect?"

"Not sure why you say that, abba," I remarked. "Why the man survived, married, had children, became an internationally acclaimed author, by all accounts had a good life."

"Yes, but you know, Miriam," observed eema, looking more at abba than at me, "he wasn't young any more."

I sat there hoping for a fuller explanation. None was offered. Eema and abba just exchanged looks, then changed the topic.

Next day I went to the library and took out Levi's most famous work—*Survival in Auschwitz*. I spent the day rereading it. Yes. Just as I had remembered. Levy was a realist—not a pessimist. So why would he have killed himself after all this time? Also, what were eema and abba getting at? Like, what had eema meant when she said Levy was no longer young?

For the next few weeks I spent every spare moment rereading every single piece that Levy had written, going particularly slowly over anything penned recently. But I found no answers. One evening, I returned the Levy books to the library, plunked myself down at the typewriter, and began tapping away on a review of Lester's latest book on Derrida. And I was back extolling the virtues of postmodernism, but not for long.

It was December 1987. I was in my office, leaning forward in my brown leather chair, making minor adjustments on a manuscript on de Man. De Man had died recently. Knowing that there had been an upsurge of interest in his philosophy since his death, I had no doubt but that the article would be published, but I wanted it to be flawless, yes? I was in the process of rewording a particularly tricky sentence when there was a knock on the door. "It's unlocked," I called out. "Just come in."

The door opened and there was Harry, a concerned look on his face, a newspaper tucked under his arm. I was hardly expecting him, for we'd driven to the university together not two hours ago. "Harry, something wrong?" I asked. "Is abba...?"

"No. Nothing like that," he responded, standing in the doorway. He removed the newspaper, then looked at me sympathetically. "Don't be so jumpy, kiddo. The family's fine."

I smiled, shrugged my shoulders, and gestured for him to come sit down.

"Nope. Got to go. It's just, there's this piece I thought you should look at. Didn't want you submitting your article without... Well, you'll see."

Reiterating that he had to go, Harry handed me the newspaper, then hurried off.

I immediately place my manuscript aside and begin scrutinizing the paper. The *New York Times*. It takes me only seconds to figure out what Harry wants me to see, for the headline is there—bold and unmistakable—"Yale Scholar's Article Found in Nazi Paper." Of all people, it's de Man! I start to feel light-headed but force myself to focus. From 1940 to 1942, says the article, the guru of deconstructionism wrote for a Nazi newspaper. Surely they have it wrong. I grab the phone to check with Leslie Sharpner—a postmodernist colleague that's more in the loop. Before I even have a chance to ask a question, she goes straight to the point.

"Got a class. So forgive me if I just cut to the chase. Yes, it's true."

"We're talking about de Man?"

"Uh huh."

"Oy Gott!"

"I can understand your surprise. Everyone's really shocked."

"Ay yay yay! And Derrida didn't know?"

"Not until very recently. None of us did. Actually, he's taken the matter in hand and begun a detailed examination of the texts. So I think it'll be okay. Miriam, you all right?"

Putting down the phone, not even taking in that I haven't said goodbye, I place the article in front of me on the desk and consider the dates. 1940 to 1942. Where were my parents when de Man was writing for this paper? Abba, vey iz mir! Poor abba was taken to Auschwitz in late 41, yes? But where was eema?

An image of eema sewing Nazi uniforms crystallizes in my mind. It slowly fades and is replaced by an image of something darker. No light. No air. Shadowy figures of women squeezed together. The smell of day old excrement stinging the nostrils. Women relieving themselves. Women wailing. A feeling of motion. Something relentlessly propelling the women forward. But to where? Just a minute. I remember reading it. March 26, 1942—that's the first transport of women from Ravensbrück. Eema herself could have been on her way to Auschwitz. I look down at desk, stare at the article, and shudder.

The rest of the day I was on automatic pilot. I taught a class on Sartre's *Being and Nothingness*, but I couldn't tell you what I said, for I wasn't exactly there.

All the way home, I kept rehearsing what I was going to say to eema and abba. But nothing sounded right. How do you tell survivors that one of their child's primary mentors wrote for a Nazi paper?

As I entered the house and approached the kitchen, I saw eema standing there in the doorway. She was looking at me tenderly.

"Meydeleh," she began, "Harry phoned and told us. Ach! Has to be awful for you, sweetie. I know. I've been there."

"You're meaning Heidegger?"

"Yes."

"Eema, how on earth did you manage?"

"Come, sit with me while I make supper," urged eema.

As I sat down at the table, eema brought me a bowl of soup. Just seeing her there, I could feel my panic lifting.

"Listen to me, meydeleh," she urged, taking a seat across from me and eyeing me intently. "Abba and I, we schmoozed. And we want to be crystal clear about this. We're okay. We're not hurt. And there's no way you've let us down. Not us or anyone else. Think about it, sweetie. From what he published, how could you conceivably detect Nazi sympathies in his distant past?"

"I'm not so sure about that. But it feels good to hear you say it."

Eema smiled at me, reached across the table for her package of Players Light, and lit a cigarette. Taking a few puffs, she reiterated that I'd done nothing wrong and urged me to talk further about my dilemmas over de Man.

"The thing is, I feel so betrayed."

Eema groaned and looked at me forlornly. "Betrayal, yes, Miriam," she exclaimed. "I wish I could help you with that. Ach! If only I had worked through my own tsores over...."

"Please don't feel pressured in any way. But if you were up to talking about Heidegger.... Like, eema, were you actually a student of his?"

"Forgive me, sweetie. It's not that I don't want to talk about it. I just can't."

"It's okay, eema."

"Oy! Since you were a mere toddler, I knew you'd be a philosopher."

"Because of that time I asked you if I was?"

"That, and the way your mind worked. And I couldn't have been more pleased. But I also dreaded something. I could never put my finger on what, but perhaps it was precisely this moment, yes? When you would have to face the betrayal of the mentor."

"You make betrayal sound inevitable."

Eema opened her eyes wider, looked toward the ceiling, and inhaled deeply. "On some level, and at some moments, yes," she answered. "But why am I going on like this? For yourself, you'll see. As for that other issue," she continued, looking at me again, "you know, whatever the man did or didn't do during the Nazi years, you can't just assume that it contaminated the later writings of de Man the scholar."

"But minimally, it's significant that de Man the scholar had this past. Yes. And it's significant that de Man the scholar covered up his own complicity—if he was indeed complicit. All this, of course, I've got to check."

"Of course."

"Then there's my own personal situation," I went on. "You know I've never been a follower of anyone."

Eema put the cigarette in an ashtray and began shelling a small pile of peas. "No," agreed eema, selecting a particularly long pod. "Now I haven't always liked where you've gone, and, to be blunt, I'm no fan of postmodernism, but kinehora, you've always been your own person. Sorry," she added. "This is probably not the time to take a swipe at your school of philosophy."

"Not to worry. It's not as if I've not been having other misgivings of my own. Nonetheless, eema, I'm part of the postmodernist community. So I have a responsibility here."

Eema nodded. For the next few minutes she massaged her sore shoulder. Then she began running her fingers through her whitened hair. Her hair, yes. I found myself staring at eema's hair, then her face, then her hands.

Eema's hair was completely ashen white by now, ashen and wispy; and deep grooves were appearing in her face and hands. Nu? She was seventy-four years old. Was it my imagination or was it getting harder for her to talk about things? And how is it that I hadn't noticed that she was growing old?

Eema took in that I was looking at her and smiled.

"And then there's Derrida," I continued.

"Harry said Derrida didn't know."

"He didn't, eema. But he's the leading figure in postmodernism. So the question is: What'll he say? And if his response is inadequate, what'll I do?"

"What you always do. Assess the situation carefully and do what the situation asks of you, yes? Abba and I, we know how you operate, and we are confident about this. And I must tell you, Miriam, it's a comfort to me. Thankfully, you don't get frozen like me. Know what one of my worst regrets in life is?"

"Something to do with that woman Roza—the one you light the yarhzeit for?" I blurted out foolishly.

Eema turned white, and her chin began to quiver. I was alarmed by what had just happened. How could I have intruded like that! Why, eema had never even spoken to us about Roza. Without fail, early each January, she had simply lit the yarhzeit and quietly uttered the name "Roza," her eyes filled with pain. And every few weeks, she would awake in the middle of the night, screaming, "Roza, vey iz mir, can't anyone help her? Can't anyone do anything about this God forsaken land?" I was shocked that I had barged into the inner recesses of her mind like that, no? The inner recesses of a survivor's mind, it's just not something you violate, not even accidentally.

"Eema, I'm so sorry," I murmured.

Eema recovered her composure and assured me that there was no harm done, but that it was Heidegger that she was thinking about. "The Heidegger controversy, I never had the courage to weigh in on it," eema explained, "and I regret it, though not half as much as I regret not being able to talk to you about it now."

Giving me a reassuring smile and encouraging me to finish my soup, eema headed to the fridge and started pulling together ingredients for a meat loaf—eggs, ground beef, garlic, matzo meal. I removed my shoes, stretched out my legs, and dawdled over the soup in silence. I soon found myself thinking about eema's age again. Then my mind imperceptibly drifted to abba.

Now had that man cheated the grim reaper or what! A man with a serious heart condition, he was seventy-eight years old and still going. Of course, he walked more slowly now. He couldn't bend properly and so had to maneuver himself out of the chair gradually. And he looked his age, his face sagging, and his jet black hair a thing of the past. And who could not see that his heart was continuing to takes its toll. Oy! How often these days he would clutch at his chest and grimace! And yet, kinehora, he was still sitting on NDP committees, still attending meetings, still working for a just society.

I glanced nervously at the clock above the sink. 6:30. I was always a bit uneasy when abba was late. He could be all alone, his heart failing, the world of the Nazis crashing in on him, and none of us there to lend a hand. To my relief, a few minutes later there were three quick knocks on the door.

"Gevalt!" exclaimed abba, as I opened the door. "Is forgetting my key again, yah?"

We talked further about the de Man situation that day, but we didn't discuss it the following day or for the rest of the week. Abba had pressing news that simply took precedence.

We were sitting around the dining room table. We were eating late because abba had been at an NDP committee meeting until almost 8:30. Eema had placed the turkey on a blue serving plate in front of abba; and abba had rolled up his sleeves and begun carving it in long thick slices. Then he stopped, put down his knife, shook his head sadly, and muttered, "Rachaele, Miriam, is an announcement I haf. Vas not vanting to say anything because of Miriam's tsores, but such bad news I haf! Vey iz mir!"

"It's okay, abba. Go ahead," I responded.

"You know Ida Schugarenski."

"Of course, abba. She's one of the campers."

"Not sure how to tell you this, uttered abba, sighing, "but gotenyu, is some time mid-morning, the woman died. At the NDP meeting, I heard about it. Rafal, he told me."

Saying nary a word, her hands trembling, eema instantly rose from her chair and rushed out of the room. Abba and I sat there looking at each other. I was about to suggest that one of us go after her when eema returned, her eyes reddish and swollen. "Ay yay yay, her poor son, Abie!" she moaned, tears rolling down her cheek. "Daniel, when's the funeral?"

"Tomorrow."

"We'll all go, yes?"

Abba grimaced and shook his head. "You and I maybe, but Miriam, nein. And then, you and me only for the service. Vat can I say? They're not vanting a crowd. And is clear instructions they've given. Only the immediate family at the shiva."

Eema's eyes widened. Then she took a deep breath and nodded.

"I didn't even know she was sick!" I exclaimed. "What did she die of?"

"No one said," answered abba. "But, kinehora, she vas seventy-four years old. Is such a big mystery that a woman of seventy-four dies?"

No sooner had abba finished speaking than this terror grabbed at me from the behind my eyes, and as if from out of nowhere, I found myself face-to-face with eema's mortality. Abba's mortality I'd lived with on a daily basis what with his bad heart, but until this point, eema dying had seemed unimaginable. Yet Mrs. Schugarenski was eema's age. And she was gone.

Mrs. Schugarenski was the first of the campers to pass away. Concerned that her death would shake the entire community and struggling with this sense of fragility, that evening I began to phone around, just to check in with people. But people had surprisingly little to say.

"Such a shame," said Moshe. "But what can you do?"

Feeling the need to at least do *something*, the next day I decided to have roses sent to the funeral home. I had just picked up the phone to order them when abba shook his head and said, "Nein. No flowers, but what did they say? Ah yes, donations to the HRA."

"Meydeleh," cautioned eema, looking at me tenderly, "sometimes, you just have to let things be, yes?"

And so it is that I sent a card to the Schugarenskis, wrote out a $500.00 check to Holocaust Remember Association of Greater Toronto, and little by little came to focus again on my own dilemma.

Despite my initial alarm, I was well aware that as a responsible academic, I had to grapple with the de Man situation according to accepted scholarly principles: Research it. Get a sense of the scope. Analyze the pieces in depth. And factor in multiple contexts. In the coming months, I went about the task diligently, taking apart the articles and pouring over accounts of occupied Belgium. De Man was Belgian, you see. And the articles at the centre of the controversy appeared in the Belgian newspaper *Le Soir*.

What did I find out? During the period in question, de Man was a literary columnist for *Le Soir*. Throughout that entire time, *Le Soir* was in the hands of the Nazi occupiers. It had recently been re-opened and was being run in accordance with Nazi principles when de Man accepted the job as columnist. So he knew exactly what he was getting into. De Man wrote 178 articles during the period in question—most of them for *Le Soir*. He did leave *Le Soir* in late '42, and I initially thought that this departure meant a change of heart. However, as I came to realize, by late '42 the tide was turning; the Allies were gaining momentum. And political animal that he was, Paul de Man had deserted the sinking ship.

As for the articles themselves, to be fair, they did not explicitly endorse Naziism or even mention it. What his articles did, though, was mirror the Nazi strategy for quelling Belgian resistance. De-emphasize

Naziism and convince the Belgians that their evolution was dependent on becoming part of a greater German nationalism, such was the Nazis' Belgian strategy. And de Man contributed to it. Again and again, he contrasted French culture with German culture, proclaiming the superiority of the second. And he declared the fall of the decrepit Belgian world a deliverance. He was even writing in this vein when his own countrymen were being rounded up for slave labour.

As regards anti-Semitism, I found no reason to believe that de Man was actively anti-Semitic in his private life. And anti-Semitism *per se* was not at issue in the vast majority of those articles. Nonetheless, as the *Times* had pointed out, one piece was damning—his article "Les Juifs dans la Littérature Actuelle," which appeared in *Le Soir*'s special supplement "The Jews and Us," on March 4, 1941.

One evening the adults in our family got together for the explicit purpose of discussing that article. Well, the adults plus Sammy. Abba had said, "Is up to us to help Miriam come to grips with this meshugah piece, yah?" And quick as can be, eema and Esther had chimed in, "yes." In retrospect, I suspect that the real reason for the discussion was that we needed to talk about it as a family. Helping me, that was a pretext to get around our unspoken rule to keep Holocaust conversation to a minimum. Now barely had the meeting started when it became clear that we were all aghast.

"Ay yay yay! Just look at this!" shouted abba, his eyes bulging, his finger pointing at the paper. "Is calling Jews cold and detached, this de Man person is. Is calling Jews a foreign impediment."

"And what does he mean by 'the solution to the Jewish problem?'" asked Sammy, turning first to Harry, then me. "I don't get it. Just what makes us a problem?"

Important though it was that we schmoozed, the meeting didn't help me make sense of the article. In the days that followed, I continued struggling with it. I couldn't quite get it to come together. However, one evening about a week later, I suddenly realized why. Because I kept thinking of Jews as the primary focus. While Jews may or may not have been primary in his mind, the piece was so structured as to make the fate of the Jews utterly secondary to the fate of literature. Once I accepted this reality, which would have been blatantly obvious to anyone differently situated, the article came together like a dream. Well, hardly a dream.

De Man's underlying premise is that while Jews have badly contaminated European culture generally, they've had little effect on European literature, for very few European writers—and indeed, none of the good ones—are Jewish. This evaluation of Jewish writers and their allegedly negligible significance in the literary scene paves the way for his pièce de la resistance—his literary position on the deportation of European Jewry. Solving the Jewish problem by deporting the Jews, writes de Man, "would not entail, for the literary life of the West, deplorable consequences. The latter would lose, in all, a few personalities of mediocre value and would continue ... to develop according to its great evolutive laws." *

The point was clear. Jews were an expendable commodity whose disappearance involved negligible loss and clear gain. And speaking from the vantage point of literature, the literary expert of *Le Soir* was giving his blessings to the mass deportation of European Jewry. Was I horrified? Absolutely.

For the next few months, I continued researching. Then I began writing the first of a series of articles that lay bare the injury and commented on the possible significance for current postmodernism. Did I probe the other problems with postmodernism that had begun to disturb me? To a degree, yes, but only to a degree. The thing is, I was waiting for Derrida's response. Derrida had already convened a conference to discuss the articles. And he'd readily accepted when the journal *Critical Inquiry* invited him to write about the de Man controversy. To my great relief, he'd declared it his responsibility.

The wait was long by layman's standards, but academia's like that, yes? In early 1988, York U. was abuzz with the news that Derrida's article was appearing in the next issue of *Critical Inquiry*. Excited, I called the library and put in a special request for that issue. And sure enough, in late May, who should call but the librarian, Mrs. Shuft? "Professor Himmelfarb, the spring issue of *Critical Inquiry* is in. And we're holding it at the front desk," she said. Within minutes, I was at the desk, the issue in my hands. I eagerly xeroxed the pages, returned to my office, and began to pour over them.

Initially, I was pleased by Derrida's heart-felt expression of dismay at discovering his friend's past. But my pleasure quickly evaporated.

---

*This quotation is from the subsequent Derrida translation of the passage. For the Derrida translation and for the Derrida article, which is about to be discussed and quoted, see J. Derrida, "Like the Sound of the Sea Within a Shell: Paul de Man's War," Critical Inquiry Vol. 14.*

Using the phrase "on the other hand," Derrida kept putting forward far-fetched interpretations of de Man's article, then insisting that there was no way to decide between his reading and the common sense reading. By the time the article finishes, Derrida has done the unthinkable. He's elevated de Man from collaborationist to anti-fascist, from anti-Semite to opponent of anti-Semitism. And he's vilified the journalists who ran with the de Man story. Gotenyu! He's even compared criticism of de Man to "an exterminating gesture." And he's done it all using time-honoured deconstructionist principles. He has read against the grain.

The weeks that followed were painful ones. I had just seen postmodernism at its most chilling. Being a fair-minded scholar, I was determined not to judge it on such a basis. Nonetheless, the more I thought about it, the more disturbed I became about how comparatively easy it was to use postmodernism this way—to use it to wriggle out of every conceivable problem. And slowly but surely, it became clear to me that Derrida's evasion was indicative of a more fundamental evasion at the heart of postmodernism. Yes. If everything is indecipherable, if nothing has more validity than anything else, there is no foundation, no base from which to proceed, no truth, and, ultimately, no morality.

I soon found myself confronted with an even more disturbing truth: If I was attracted to a philosophy this evasive, there must be something I was desperately trying to avoid. And what could that be if not the Holocaust? Bit by bit, I began tracing my flight from the Holocaust: the focus on performatory utterances, the immersion in semiotics, postmodernism.

"Eema," I said one day over breakfast, "while I've always prided myself on how seriously I struggle with the big philosophic questions, I've been cavalier here. *You* knew how slippery postmodernism was. If *I* didn't, it's because I didn't want to. As a Holocaust survivor, you've never had the luxury to be cavalier about truth, reality—any of it."

"You think you're the only one?" asked eema, her eyes flickering with pain. "Meydeleh, in our own ways, we're all of us running from reality. It's a question of survival, yes?"

In the years that followed, I had to work hard at repositioning myself in the world. I began by making it clear to all of my colleagues that I was no longer a postmodernist. Also, I became more of an activist again. By the early nineties, I was attending anti-racist demos regularly. And I was on the verge of getting involved in Jewish Feminist Antifascist League, JFAFL for short.

Brenda—this York colleague of mine—had phoned and urged,

# Chapter Six

## Miriam, age 44

"Brngg," goes the alarm clock. Oy! How exhausted I feel! Ach! Can't afford these late nights. Can barely pry open my eyes. How can there still be over a hundred pages of that Buber dissertation to read? I reach over to the night table, turn off the alarm, pull a manuscript from my knapsack, and force myself to concentrate.

"Miriam, you up?" comes eema's voice, sounding just a little strained.

"Just barely."

"You'll come downstairs, yes?"

"Yeah, in a minute, eema," I answer, yawning. I put aside the thesis and pull on my jeans.

I quickly brush my teeth, splash water on my face, and head for the kitchen. I peer in. No eema. "In the living room, Miriam," I hear abba call out.

I enter the living room to find abba sitting on one of the beige chairs, looking bewildered. Esther, of all people, is in the other. Her eyes filled with tears, eema is hovering by the couch. Sprawled out on the couch is this disheveled woman in a dirty red dress, her hair in tangles, a bottle of whisky in her hand. Baffled, I take a seat and wait, hoping that someone will enlighten me. But no one does.

"Esther, what you doing here at such an hour?" I finally ask, turning to her. "And Gott in himmel, what's going on?"

"Easy there," answers Esther, her voice hushed. "She called me. So I came. Miriam, we can make it right. We can't change everything. But, Adoshem be praised, at least now we can begin the healing. It's only right, Miriam. Deep down, you have to know that."

I feel strangely off-balance. Like an actor who's been inserted into a play mid-way through without being shown the script.

"Eema…" I try.

Eema does not respond. She is too absorbed with the visitor.

The visitor puts the bottle to her lips, tosses back her head, and takes a slug. Perhaps she's a street person, I think. Eema and abba both advocate for affordable housing and count homeless activists among their friends. But no. This woman doesn't look like an activist. And a friend of abba's and eema's would hardly have called Esther and brought her from her bed. I glance inquisitively at abba, but he doesn't seem to notice. I again look at eema. Though she is still tearing, she is smiling warmly at the figure.

An image from the past, it's seeping, seeping. Now it's past the blood brain barrier. Now it's coursing through my body—into my shoulders, into my nose, into the sinews of my crouching legs. I'm nine years old. I'm under the stairs, hiding. How musty everything is! The mold, it's tickling my nostrils. And I can feel this pressure against my shoulder, this warm moist air on my neck.

I am jolted back by the sound of the visitor coughing. She hacks convulsively for a few minutes. Then she spits a greenish gob into a kleenex, which eema nimbly hands her. Good. Now she's more comfortable. I observe her more closely. Shiker, beyond a doubt, but not so drunk as to be incapacitated. Weaving a little, she sits up, reaches over, fingers a couple of the butts in the ashtray directly in front of her, carefully selects the largest, and takes a drag. The ashtray is filled with smoldering butts. Hmm! Obviously, been here a while. She seems to be oblivious to our presence. She simply goes about her business, coughing, rubbing her eyes, smoking, and taking a belt from the mickey, not addressing anyone or even looking our way. Touched by what I can see of her predicament and wondering if she's capable of responding to us at all, I am just about to ask her whether I can get her anything when her head tilts upward and her nose wrinkles with contempt.

Scene after scene flashes through my head: Sondra calling me "baby." Sondra on the couch with Harry. Sondra smashing eema's broach. Sondra saying that if the Nazis came, she wouldn't save either eema or abba.

The visitor's eyes flutter. Then she looks about purposefully, her gaze finally settling on me.

"Oh, so her majesty's finally deigned to join us? What's the matter, shvester mayn?" the visitor asks, in a voice I would have known anywhere. "What! Don't recognize your own flesh-and-blood? And they call *you* the family historian!"

"So it really is you!" I exclaim, my heart pounding.

"In the flesh. And by the by, that's where I always am—in the flesh. But better to sell it than to sit on it, I always say. Not that this old broad's getting a whole lot of nooky these days."

Eema's hand reaches toward Sondra. Sondra winces. And eema hastily withdraws it. I get the feeling that Sondra is about to say something nasty to eema, but no. Instead, to my surprise, she casts abba a long icy glare.

"But where've you been? And...and...what's happened to you?" I ask.

Sondra shrugs her shoulders and says nothing.

"Sondra, sorry. I don't know what to say. It's been so long."

"Spoken like the loving shvester you've always been. Not exactly overjoyed to see your older sister, are you?"

"It's just that it's all so sudden," I stammer.

Aware that I am not telling the whole truth, I feel guilty. And yet how can I be happy, knowing what tsores she brings: They're old and fragile, these parents of ours. If she hurts them now, who's to say they'll bounce back?

"Oy, Sondra," says eema, her hand on her heart, tears trickling down her face. "Not to worry. She'll come around, our Miriam. You'll see. The important thing is you're back after all these years. And we love you. Sweetie, nothing else matters. You're in trouble? There's this farshtunkener you owe money to? Is what family's for, yes?"

"Is just like eema says," agrees abba. "Sondra, is how much you're needing?"

"Make it out for a cool two grand. And I'll just stick it where the moon don't shine."

Abba winces, leaves the room, and comes back a few minutes later with a cheque. "Zy gezent, Sondra," he murmurs, handing it to her.

Without so much as looking at him, Sondra grabs the cheque from his hand. She examines it and starts roaring with laughter. After fumbling and swearing a number of times, she manages to tuck it inside her bra. Abba's jaw drops. Then he returns to his seat in silence.

Sondra takes another big gulp from the mickey. "No point keeping the johns waiting," she asserts, starting to rise.

"But sweetie, where you staying?" asks eema, her voice cracking. Pausing to compose herself, eema adds, "It's been so long, Sondra. You don't want to see us, sweetie? Fine. But bubeleh, won't you give us a number, or an address, or something? We won't phone or disturb you in any way. I promise. But it would be nice to have, yes?"

"Stuff it," snaps Sondra. Sondra reached for her kleenex and begins to hack again.

"But you'll sit for a minute, yes?"

"Oh, we weren't about to leave. We have something to say to that husband of yours first. And you too, eema. In fact, the whole damn lot of you."

"Sondra, not again," I protest. "What good has all this anger done you? Surely after all this time...."

Her hacking subsiding, Sondra tucks the tissue into her pocket, straightens her body, and raises her head high. For a split second, her eyelids flutter. Then she looks different somehow. While every bit as angry, she no longer strikes me as someone who would make cracks like "better to sell it than sit on it." There is a dignity about her. And you'd almost mistake her for sober.

"After all this time?" she exclaims. "After all this time, I need to speak my peace." "Abba," she continues, her voice absolutely steady, "he was your brother. You knew what that man was like. I was a twelve-year-old child. And I was your daughter. Your own daughter. How could you?"

Abba's eyes widen, and a beseeching look comes over his frail wrinkled face. "But mayn tokhter, what did I do? Is so awful that I vant mayn one remaining bruder with me? Family is important. And is almost everyone what is caput."

"How can you sit there and ask, 'What did I do?'" shrieks Sondra.

"Is what, Sondra?" he pleads.

"You know damn well. You brought a man into the house you had every reason to believe would abuse me. You're a fucking pimp. Worse than a pimp. A pimp's honest."

For about twenty seconds, no one utters a word. I can feel my heart racing. Yacov, he was capable of this? Of course! Just look at how he treated eema. And there is something else, yes. Something tucked away. Something I've relegated for decades to the far corner of my mind. Yes. Yes. I see it:

I'm eleven years old. I'm on my way to my hiding place. I approach the basement door. I turn the handle. Nothing. Doesn't budge. I try again. Nothing. These voices—Sondra's and Uncle's—they're coming from the basement. That's it! That's why that door was locked!

"The history lessons," I exclaim. "They ... they weren't real, were they? ...Oh Sondra, no wonder you lashed out. I can't tell you how sorry I am."

"You believe us then?"

"Us?" I ask.

"Miriam," urges Esther, casting me a sideways glance. "Just answer."

"Of course, I believe you."

"Well, at least that's something. And you, eema?"

"Sheyneh punem, of course. Oy! I suspected. That's why I sent him away. Oh, my poor bubeleh!"

Eema reaches out to fold Sondra in her arms, but Sondra motions her away and stares at abba.

"And you, abba?" Sondra persists.

Abba hesitates. "Is my own daughter what is telling me Yacov has done this. How can I say nein? Ach! That I have survived Ausch..."

"Not another word about your precious Auschwitz," screams Sondra, her eyes aflame. "This is *our* tragedy—not *yours*. And we'll tell you something else. It's not enough that you believe us. Not even close. What did you do about it? Sweet bugger all!"

"Your eema..." began abba.

"We know eema tried to do something—too late, years too late—but not *you*. And you were the one who knew this man. You knew how he was with women, what he did to women."

"Women and Yacov? Ay yay yay! A bisel I knew, but not so much."

"And... and..." abba stammers, avoiding her look, "who vould think a man vould do such a thing to his own flesh-and-blood! A hunt, he is! A meshugener hunt! Why, with my bare hands I could...."

"Damned you, abba!" Sondra interrupts. "You set us up! Uncle Yacov, he's so sad, you said. Uncle Yacov, he needs us to comfort him, you said. Remember? Remember telling me how much I look like bubbeh and what comfort bubbeh was to him? Well, he took comfort from me all right. Day after day, he took comfort from me. Want to know how often, abba? Want to know how many times that darling brother of yours boinked me?"

"Nein, nein," moans abba, covering his eyes. "Vey iz mir! Is not what I meant. Is not what I intended."

"Maybe, maybe not. But you knew the danger. And you let us walk straight into it."

Eema is trembling and looks faint. Her eyes are fixed like a magnet on abba. "Just what did you know about Yacov, Daniel?" she finally asks, her voice uncharacteristically shrill. "What did you know when you brought that paskudnyak into our household? Speak up. Gott in himmel! He's violated your own child and Sondra has a right to an answer. All the women in this family have a right to an answer."

Silence descends on the room. Everyone's staring at abba. Abba fidgets for a few minutes, his eyes lowered. Glimpsing Sondra from the corner of his eyes, he responds sheepishly, "Is very young you were, Sondra. You could haf misinterpreted, no?"

"Gevalt! What's age got to do with anything?" protests eema, her brow raised, her lip curling. "What? You think a young woman can't figure out when she's being taken?"

"But…" pleads abba.

"Just look at what that man has done to her," eema continues, shaking her head and pointing at Sondra. "And to lose Sondra on top of eema, abba, bubbeh, zeda. And so, Daniel, I ask you once again: What did you know?"

"Epes. Some kind of legal entanglement. Is not quite remembering I am. I'm sorry."

For the next fifteen, twenty minutes eema keeps pressing that same question, and abba keeps evading. Then abba lets out a huge sigh, and without another word to anyone, he maneuvers himself out of the chair and slouches out of the room.

"Daniel, you can't run from this," eema warns.

"Runs in the family, this treatment of women, don't ya think, abba?" calls out Sondra, her voice rising above abba's footsteps on the stairs. "You think Uncle didn't tell us about Auschwitz?"

Eema turns white but says nothing.

I look around. We are all of us frozen—unsure what to say. Turning to Sondra, eema just keeps nodding her head over and over again. "Meydeleh, I can't pretend to know what you've been through," she finally utters, her voice soothing, concern in her eyes.

"Eema, don't think it's just abba I'm angry with."

"No, I failed you too. I understand. And you've every right to be furious. And, meydeleh, I want to hear what you have to say."

"I don't need you to tell me what my rights are. I'm not looking for group therapy here. And don't for a second imagine that I'm going to rejoin this Holocaust-ridden family. My pain's not taking a back seat to anyone's ever again."

"Understood. So, what's next?"

"I don't know. I'm really not intending anything. I needed to say my peace. I've got what I came for. And I'm off. No tearful goodbyes. No promises."

Sondra nodded at eema and watched as eema nodded back. Then she got up. For a second there, she hesitated, staring at the remnants of her package of cigarettes, a puzzled look on her face. Then leaving the cigarettes and mickey on the table, she turned around and headed for the door.

"But sweetie, if you're in need, you'll be in touch, yes?" implored eema.

"I can't say, eema," answered Sondra, hovering in the doorway, "but I doubt it. It's not that I don't care, but I can't trust you people. And you can see for yourself I don't belong. What! You think Sondra the whore is really going to fit into this family? This nice Jewish family?"

Eema started to say something, but Sondra didn't wait. Within seconds, the front door closed, and Sondra was gone. Instantly, eema began weeping.

Esther and I did what we could to console eema. I remember stroking her hair, holding her hand. I remember Esther drawing on her social work expertise to reassure eema. Anger, drinking, prostituting—these were ways of coping common to childhood sexual abuse survivors, explained Esther. Confronting the family, that was a critical step forward. "Uh huh," eema would answer, sounding uncertain. But slowly, she began to take Esther's lead.

For the next few hours, the three of sat in that living room trying to make sense of what had happened. We spoke of how traumatized people cope by creating separations, by distancing themselves from their own thoughts, feelings, perceptions, memories. We talked about multiplicity and switching, with Esther pointing out that Sondra had switched personalities three times that morning. We talked a lot about dissociation. I remember, for I recall being embarrassed. I hadn't realized how far eema had penetrated into the inner workings of my mind, but clearly pretty far, for to my surprise, at one point she caught my eye and said, "You know, Miriam, it's probably not so very different than what you do; it's just progressed a bisel further, yes?"

"How long have you known about what I do, eema?" I asked.

"It's been since that time in the schoolyard, yes?"

It goes without saying that we also dissected the Yacov years piece by piece. And we asked each other, "Do you think we'll ever hear from her again?" The one thing we didn't talk about was abba.

Of course, we were all furious with abba. And I suspect that we all knew that something huge had happened between him and us. But beyond that, we didn't know what to think or do. Nu? Abba had always been the substance of our world. We would no more have questioned him than the air we breathe. And now this. We needed time, yes? Time to think it through.

Eventually eema whispered something about being tired and went upstairs.

"Miriam, I should stay the night? Maybe longer?" asked Esther.

"Whatever you can," I answered, nodding. "I've got a bad feeling."

Esther called Harry and arranged everything with him.

"It'll be okay?" I checked. "Harry alone with the kids that long?"

"Why wouldn't it be?"

"Forgive me, Esther. It's been a strange day."

Neither abba nor eema came downstairs for the rest of the day. And neither of them touched supper, though Esther and I threw together some glazed chicken and took it up. At times it was silent upstairs, though more often we could hear eema chastising abba, trying to get him to come clean.

"Daniel, what did you know? Exactly what are these legal entanglements?" eema asked.

"Is sorry I am. I'm an old man. How do you expect me to remember?" wails abba.

"Don't hak mir tshaynik. You think I don't know when you're lying? Is me you're talking to."

From the sound of it, eema was getting nowhere fast. And by 10:00 or so, she had stopped trying.

Abba slept in my study that night, while Esther bedded down on the living room couch. Esther and I brought up the cot from the basement and helped abba fix it up—tucking in the sheets and fluffing the pillow. At one point he looked at me as if he was wanting some assurance, but I didn't offer any. It's not that I didn't feel for him. Of course I did. He looked haggard and lost. And who's to say what Auschwitz nightmares were being stirred up. Moreover, I was well aware that abba wouldn't have intentionally set Sondra up to be abused. But I just couldn't get over how utterly reckless he'd been. Reckless with the entire family! Not once warning us! Not interpreting a single sign. And then trying to stop eema from casting Yacov out. And even now not coming clean!

It was a long hard night. Both of my parents kept waking up screaming.

"Bruder, how could you?" wails abba.

"Oy! Oy! Someone help Sondra," pleads eema.

It seemed as if there was pain everywhere. Even the walls seemed to ache. I wondered where Sondra was and what was happening to the walls around her. Did they moan too? Did they weep at the pity of it all?

The coming days were strained. Nu? It's not that we didn't speak to abba. But he faded into the periphery. Time passed, with the women of the family focusing on Sondra while abba just sat there, his head lowered, saying nothing. He had clearly fallen into a depression, for he had stopped dressing and shaving and was now spending most of his time lying about in his blue pajama bottoms, his chest bare, his head hanging down.

Esther had to go home the morning of the third day. Eema and I continued to discuss Sondra, but eema's focus was beginning to shift. And as she had so often done in the past, she was starting to worry about abba.

"Your abba, he's not looking good," she said over lunch. "You'll try to help him, yes? Me too. Sweetie, he's your abba and my husband and we need to try."

I was relieved to hear her say that, for I too had become worried. Abba's face was getting that bluish tint that always meant trouble. And his hand kept reaching for his heart, pinching it, stroking it.

While abba stayed in the study throughout lunch, he came down to the dining room for supper when he heard me call up, "Abba, dinner's ready." His skin was still bluish; and there were deep rings around his eyes. To my surprise, though, he had on black slacks and a white shirt; he was clean-shaven; and his wispy white hair was neatly combed, a straight part at the side.

"Abba, you're dressed," observed eema, as abba sat down opposite her. "Is good. Better a man should look like a mentsh, yes?"

Abba nodded, but looked away, his head lowered.

"Daniel," continued eema, smiling at him, "you'll move back to the bedroom, yes? And I won't push you for answers for a while. Not that I'm saying things are okay. They're not. But look at me, Daniel. I love you. We all do. And the last thing any of us need is you getting sick."

Abba smiled feebly, then nodded.

"Abba, you'll try some beef?" I asked, cutting him a huge piece.

A tiny moan came out of abba. Then tears streaming down his cheeks, he shook his head and muttered, "Is bad, terribly bad I handled everything."

Abba reached for eema's hand, and for a few seconds there, she let him hold it, squeeze it, but then she abruptly pulled it back. I thought abba was going to say more about what he'd done, but he didn't. He slowly mopped his face with his right hand and composed himself. Then as if from out of nowhere, he announced, "Incidentally, is something I vant you to look at, Miriam. Is still the family historian what you are, no?"

"Sure thing, abba."

"One more thing. I'm going out after dinner," he added. "Is epes I need to do."

"It can't wait for tomorrow, Daniel?" asked eema, once again smiling at him. "Noodnic, come relax with the family. We'll watch TV together. Make popcorn. And tomorrow, if you're feeling better, no argument."

Abba agreed, and the family hung out that evening. I can't say abba perked up much, but he did enjoy reminiscing about his early years as a tailor.

Next morning at breakfast, abba looked a bit better. Still, eema and I didn't like the sound of that breathing. Too laboured.

"Daniel, maybe you'll put off that task of yours another day?" asked eema.

"Nein," insisted abba.

"Till after dinner then? And if you're looking better, zy gezent."

"If it'll make you happy."

"Where you going?"

"What's mit the third degree? A man can't go out any more? Okay, okay, I'll tell you. I'm going to my storage locker, yah? Where I haf the old office papers. Some accounts, they're vorrying me. And I promised Bernie, the new owner."

"But Bernie's owned the business for years," eema pointed out.

"I know. I know," answered abba, taking a bite of his toast. "But is right what I do this."

"Maybe give it another day, abba?" I suggested. "Give yourself a chance to get on your feet."

"Yes, please, Daniel."

"Is on my feet, I am. And is going after dinner," he answered impatiently, his eyes beginning to bulge. Then he stopped short as if surprised by his own tone. His eyes receding, he continued more calmly, "But danke. No vay I deserve such a good vife and daughter."

"How long will you be?" asked eema.

"One, one and a half hours tops."

"You driving?"

"Yah."

"Got some reading I'd like to do at the Scarborough Library," eema observed. "Tell you what, Daniel. How about giving me a lift? And maybe after you've finished your business, you can pick me up, yes? And I'll stop kvetching."

"Bargain," agreed abba, nodding.

"Punct," I said. "And as long as you young whippersnappers are out and about, I think I'll put in a nice long day at the office."

I hitched a lift to work with Harry and updated him on what had been happening over the last few days. "Glad things are calming down," Harry commented, "though I can't say I'm happy with abba."

It was good to be at the office. It gave me the opportunity to respond to my phone messages and even work on the bibliography for my new course, "Philosophies of Memory." I worked straight through without a break, catching up on everything I'd let slide. Then around 10:30 p.m., I called it a day and subwayed home.

When I arrived at Bathurst Station, I stopped to look at the tailor shop on the second level of the subway. Nothing extraordinary. Not like abba's, with those historical pictures of tailors all over the walls. Just this tiny shop with a huge sign in the window which reads "Mend-it." My mind drifted to abba's shop, now called "Bernie's," and then to abba, his face blue, tears in his eyes. I glanced down at my watch. 11:31. They would have been home hours ago, I realized. Probably already in bed.

For a reason that was not at all clear to me, I quickened my pace just as soon as I exited the subway station. As I turned south on Lippincott, I remembered the day at the schoolyard. The kids chanting, "Eenie meanie, miny mo," me breaking through the circle, then awaking to find abba sitting next to my bed, his hand stroking me, a warm smile on his face. Picturing instead that wrinkled discoloured face I'd been looking at nervously these last few days, and reminding myself that he was now eighty-two, I found myself again wishing that I'd reassured him that first night, and I once more picked up my pace.

I arrive home in minutes. Eema is there in the hallway, her eyes strained with worry.

"Where's abba?" I ask, trying to catch my breath.

"If only I knew!"

"But he was supposed to pick you up."

"Exactly. Exactly, Miriam," exclaims eema, her voice panicky. "I don't know what's happened. He drops me off, yes? He says, 'Is picking you up at 8:00.' Eight o'clock comes, but where's abba? So I call Bernie to see if he's dropped in there. But no, Bernie hasn't heard from him for over two years."

"Not for over two years," I murmur, astonished.

"Anyway," continues eema, "so I figure he's lost track of the time. Meydeleh, you know what abba's like with time. But then it's 8:45. They announce, 'the library's closing in fifteen minutes.' I hang around outside for a few more minutes. What else? Then I grab a cab and come home."

"Eema," I observe, "don't mean to worry you, and I know abba's often terribly late, but he could be in trouble somewhere."

"Exactly what I'm thinking. I need to go out and look for him, yes?"

"You're exhausted," I point out, eyeing her tired face. "It's what? After 11:30? And there's not a whole lot of point going out. After all, we haven't a clue where to look."

"We could try his locker. Epes."

"Know which locker company he uses?"

Eema thinks for a moment, then shakes her head.

"Okay then. Let's stay here and keep calm. I'll make some calls. I'll start with the hospitals. If his breathing got worse, he could have gone to the closest emergency."

"Gut, Miriam. But let's not rush into calling hospitals just yet. I've just remembered something. Remember that time a few weeks ago when he was six, six-and-a-half hours late, and it turned out he'd finished his business early and gone to see Rafal?"

"Mr. Plautsnicki, yes. And then he forgot he was supposed to pick you up? Sure do," I answer, beginning to grin.

"Meydeleh, he's an old man and he forgets, yes? So how's about we call some of his friends? They're in his little black book, the numbers."

"And that's where?"

"Bedroom."

I found abba's book on the night table and sat down on the bed and grabbed the phone. I began with the numbers of his closest buddies and worked my way through. No, the Plautsnickis hadn't heard from him. No one home at the Fensters.

The list quickly exhausted, I decide to call Harry and enlist his help. I explain the situation quickly.

"Talk to eema," suggests Harry. "See if she can think of any friends that aren't in the book. With everything that's happened in the last few days, he probably just wanted to talk things over with someone. You say he's exhausted. Maybe he fell asleep and whoever's with him hadn't the heart to wake him. Anyway, you continue to concentrate on friends. Meanwhile, I'll make some other calls."

An image of abba fills my mind. He's in a hospital. He is laying in a bed, a soiled sheet under him, blood gushing from his chest. A tall large-boned nurse is trying to pull off his shoes; and abba is screaming.

"Harry, you'll phone the hospitals? Phone the police?" I ask.

"Don't worry. I'm on it."

"Harry, call if you find out anything. Doesn't matter how late. We're hardly about to go schlufen."

"Of course."

I join eema in the living room; and we put our heads together. For a while, we come up with additional names, but eventually, it becomes obvious we are scraping the bottom of the barrel and are waking people up pointlessly. So we stop.

By 1:30 or so, eema is no longer saying anything to me. Nor is she responding when I address her. She just sits on the living room couch, leaning forward, her hands over her eyes.

Me? I keep nervously checking my watch. 2:00 a.m., no abba; 2:09, no abba; 2:47, still, no abba. A little after 3:00, there are three quick knocks on the front door. I remember that last time abba forgot his key and locked himself out. Also three quick knocks. It could be. Eema and I exchange looks and both rush into the hallway. "Let me," urges eema, her face tense, her hands shaking. Eema struggles with the loose handle and opens the door. In walks Esther and Harry. They hover in the hall in silence, their heads lowered. Then slowly, Harry raises his eyes and looks at eema.

"Don't just stand there," shrieks eema, her eyes fixed on Harry, her hands waving in the air. "Gott in himmel, tell me! He's dead, isn't he?"

*It is dark. An aging silver-haired man in an olive green Toyota sedan is driving down a dimly lit street off the main way. The man's skin is blotchy, and he appears unwell. Suddenly, he contorts. He struggles for breath, perspiration streaming down his body. In seconds, his face turns blue and puffy. Gotenyu! He can't breathe. The car, it starts swerving from one side of the road to the other. The terrified old man removes his foot from the pedal and pulls at the steering wheel, desperately trying to reassert control.*

Whizzing down the street in the opposite direction comes a battered-up old Taurus. A young couple are in the car, the man driving. "What the fuck!" shouts the young man, as he takes in the menace up ahead. The young man floors the break pedal and tries to swerve out of harm's way. The unavoidable hit comes, but it is quite minor and at the side. The young man gets out of his car and examines it. He spots the dent and shrugs. Then he walks over to the other car. To his amazement, the man inside is weaving about, lunging from one side of the car to another. "You coming out?" the young man asks.

Then what does he hear back but words so slurred that he can't make out anything! "Shikh nokh an ambulans," murmurs the Toyota driver, each word slurring into next.

"No point trying to talk to this old geezer," the young man calls out to his partner. "You know, he's in royal shit if I report this. But come to think of it, there's really no need. So many dents in this old baby now, another's hardly going to make a difference. Might as well be a good Samaritan and just let the old fart sleep it off." The young man smiles amiably, hops in his car, and takes off.

His eyes filled with panic, the old man gazes at the deserted street and clutches at his heart. "Nein, not to the left, not to the left," he groans.

# Chapter Seven

## Miriam, age 44

I kept feeling this weight on my chest, like something was crushing me. And I was having trouble breathing. But I was determined to listen carefully. I just had to get a better sense of what had happened to abba in those last hours. If I'd failed to protect him, at least I could do what I'd always done. I could understand.

"You mean he didn't die from the car crash?" I asked, eyeing Harry.

"Sorry, Miriam. I'm so upset, I guess I haven't been clear. The hit, it was bupkes. Had to have been, cause there was no real harm to the car."

Harry and I were in the living room, me on the couch, Harry on the lazyboy. Esther was upstairs with eema, trying to coax her into lying down and sipping some tea. I gripped the arm of the couch and braced myself for the inevitable. "So it was abba's heart," I murmured.

Harry nodded.

"Harry, we always knew it would get him in the end. We've been waiting for it for how long? But not one of us imagined it happening like this."

He shook his head and put his hands in his pockets.

"Why didn't the other driver call for help?" I asked. "Gotenyu! A man was dying!"

"The police weren't sure," he answered. "Tell you what I think, though. You know how abba always started staggering and slurring his words when he was having one of his attacks?"

"Uh huh."

"Well, you can imagine what that must have looked like to someone who didn't know him, especially with abba swerving all over the road. And signs of swerving, that the cops saw."

"You suggesting this other driver thought abba was drunk?"

"Yeah. Even thought so myself the first time I saw him having an

197

attack. So I can see how someone would get the wrong idea."

"So abba died because of a wrong idea? Because of a mistake?"

"Oh Miriam, I know how awful that sounds. And to tell you the truth, I don't really know what to say because Esther and I, we're believers, and you and eema aren't. But even had an ambulance been called, who's to say he'd have pulled through?"

"You know what really gets me, Harry?" I groaned, tears welling up in my eyes. "He was all alone. He'd been alone since the day Sondra told us. And damn it, he was alone when he died. Alone, and I'm sure, terrified."

Fingering his yarmulke, Harry opened his mouth as if about to say something. "Adoshem..." he finally began.

"Please, Harry," I intervened. "Please don't tell me that Adoshem was with him. As far as I can see, if there is any Adoshem, he deserted Jews long before the first smoke went up the chimneys at Birkenau."

Harry smiled faintly and went quiet.

"Sorry. I'm feeling guilty about abba and I'm taking it out on you. The thing is, we've always been so careful around abba, given his bad heart. But when we heard Sondra's story, we..."

"Just hold on there," insisted Harry. "You started reaching out to him days ago. Don't forget that."

"We started to. But things were still pretty strained. If only we'd had more time!"

Harry was starting to say something about Judaism and time when Esther came into the living room, approached the couch, and put her hand on my shoulder. "She's just drifted off," Esther murmured, her eyes melting. "Oh, Miriam, she seems so helpless!" Esther and I hugged. Then assuring me that they would be back in a few hours, Harry and Esther left. I went upstairs and crawled into bed, this enormous sense of guilt weighing on me. And needless to say, eema had an appalling night. Oy! As long as I live, I'll never forget her screams.

"Oy, Daniel!" whimpers eema, "don't let them get you. Gott in himmel, hide! Is coming for you, the sonderkommandos."

I keep hoping eema will fall back asleep, just as she always has, but I soon realize she can't. She's far more upset now, yes? And now there's no abba to comfort her: No one to roll over, smile at her, and say, "Rachaele. Is having those nightmares again? Me too." How on earth is she going to manage without him? Not being able to leave her like that and realizing that it has come down to the two of us, I get out of bed, open the door to her room, and rush to her side.

"Eema, it's okay," I assure her, choking back my tears.

"Daniel—where is he?" shrieks eema. "Ach! Look there! Vat are they doing to him? Vat?"

Eema's head rises from the pillow, and her eyes dart about as if searching for unseen dangers.

"Sha, eema," I urge. "You're at home with me, Miriam. Abba is dead. And we're going to get through this."

"Iz gornit iz okay. Gornit. Oy, di sonderkommandos!"

It took a good ten minutes for eema to get her bearings and over two hours to settle down, for no sooner did she take in where she was than she realized that nothing could save him. After a while, she began blaming herself. "Such a mentsh, he was," she moaned, shaking her head sadly. "For 49 years, we were a support to each other, yes? And then the man's in trouble. The man needs me. The man reaches for my hand. Vey iz mir, Miriam, how could I not take?" Eventually, utterly exhausted, I returned to my room and crawled back into bed.

In the days that followed, Esther, Harry, and I did what we could to comfort eema. But we found ourselves strangely inept. Naturally, eema being in the state she was, the three of us also took charge of the funeral arrangements, though here too we seemed to be lacking. Oh, Esther and I made a reasonable choice of casket and worded the obituary tolerably well. And of course, being observant and all, Harry and Esther covered all the mirrors and put a tear in everyone's garments. But we were hardly on top of things.

✡

It was the wee hours of April 5th—three days after abba died. Contrary to Jewish custom to put off the funeral this long, but somehow, we couldn't get it together any quicker. Until the last minute and even after, confusion reined.

"You mean you didn't call the Morrisons?" I asked Esther, when she phoned.

"I figured eema would," she answered.

"Eema? Why, she can barely drag herself out of bed—never mind make calls!"

"Okay, okay, Miriam. You don't have to snap my head off."

Dressed in black, Harry and Esther arrived at the house at 5:45 a.m.

Well, them, and the kinderlekh, and Schmootsy. Everyone piled into the living room and took a seat. For the first few minutes, the family just sat there looking forlorn. Eventually, it dawned on us that we couldn't all fit into Harry's car. We were thinking with dread that we were going to have to use abba's car—yes, *that* car—when unexpectedly, the Plautsnickis turned up and joined us in the living room. Seeing our confusion, the Plautsnickis took charge and made the decision. The kinderlekh would go with them, and the rest of us would ride with Harry. Then once again everything went quiet. A strange thing. Insofar as we talked at all, we focused on Schmootsy.

"We're going to be at the funeral all morning," said Esther, patting Schmootsy's head, then starting to scratch her big floppy ears, "and we'll be here the rest of the day. So we couldn't exactly leave our favourite doggie at home, now could we, Pooch?"

"Esther, you think Schmootsy's picking up on anything?" asked Harry, walking over, crouching down, and taking the dog's face in his hands. "Looks a bit sad to me," continued Harry. "Dogs are sensitive, you know. You want us to pick up a treat for you, Schmootsy? Poor girl, you were always so fond of abba."

"Ah, poor Schmootsy," echoed Niel.

The service was at Gan Eden. It is this large old-fashioned schul with a solid oak bimah and three columns of oak benches extending almost to the platform. To the left, as we walked in, was a series of stained glass panels, each of them depicting a different part of the Moses story—Moses approaching the burning bush, Moses receiving the Ten Commandments. Nothing about Moses's sister Miriam, I thought to myself, recalling eema's story of my birth. Not that I could any longer even imagine a Promised Land.

There were 120-130 people in attendance—needle trade workers, the campers and their children, activists from abba's anti-fascist days, NDPers. Unionists. Oh yes, and the odd Communist buddy who I'd never met. Like that heavy-set man with the thick moustache and bum knee who hobbled up front to the family section, shook my hand, and said, "My condolences. Knew your pa real well. You must be Sandra. You've no idea how proud your daddy always was of you. I'll tell you, Sandy, I couldn't believe my ears when I heard. Comrade Himmelfarb, of all people!" I cast a quick glance over my shoulder to see if eema had heard any of this. She had kept hoping that Sondra would turn up. And so the last thing she needed was any further reminder of Sondra's absence. Then I just sat there, not even having the presence of mind to thank the man for coming. Eventually he murmured, "Nice to meet you at last, Sandy," and left.

Throughout, I kept wondering what I was supposed to do, where I was supposed to go, what I was supposed to say. And while they had a bit more of a handle on the situation, I could see that Harry and Esther were similarly confused, despite being observant Jews. We were in grief, yes, but that didn't explain everything. Who isn't in grief at funerals? Anyway, we just had to pull ourselves together. The least we could do for abba was get things right.

We spoke nary a word to one another at the service. Nor did I exactly attend to what Rabbi Aaron was saying. When I did catch a sentence here or there, I couldn't relate, for the man he was eulogizing, it just wasn't the man I knew. Why hadn't any of us thought of briefing the rabbi about what abba was really like? Nu? He's just described abba as "a Holocaust survivor who laboured with quiet determination to make the world more just." As if abba had ever been quiet about anything!

After the service, we drove to the cemetery in silence. And in silence, we parked the car, walked past the scattering of birch trees up front, and proceeded past twenty, thirty rows of plots until we turned to the left and came to an abrupt stop at this perfectly rectangular hole in the ground. Once there, we just bumbled through, doing what people told us.

"Mr. Cohan, if you don't mind, go back over there," Rabbi Aaron directed. And Harry went.

"Why don't you stand here?" a woman in a veil urged me.

I remember turning for guidance to a Jewish colleague who had just turned up at the cemetery and was offering her condolences. "Rose," I whispered, giving her a hug, "thanks for coming. Glad you could make it. I need help. Tell me. Is there something I'm supposed to do?"

Rose smiled at me warmly. "Miriam, so sorry about your father. Would've been at the schul, but of all days, the babysitter arrived late. As for your question, this part, it's pretty easy. You just recite the Mourner's Kaddish and stuff like that."

"Yeah," I nodded gratefully. "Now I can't actually recite the Kaddish, but of course, Esther can. Anything else I need to do?"

"What everyone always does." "Don't worry, Miriam," she added, as she took in my confusion. "We're a 3,500-year-old religion and nothing much changes. Just do what your parents did when your grandparents died; and how can you go wrong?"

And that's when it dawns on me. Harry, Esther, and I—not one of us has exactly had grandparents. In fact, except for Uncle Nathaniel—and no one was there for that—not a soul in our family has ever been buried. Relatives vanished. Relatives were pointed toward the left. Relatives mingled with the smoke that spewed out the chimneys of Auschwitz. But no burial, no funeral, no services. No wonder we've been running around in circles without a clue how to proceed!

I remember feeling strangely angry with abba and eema for putting me in this impossible situation. Then suddenly, I realized that I was more than angry. I was furious. And mostly, I was furious at abba. Odd. I'd been feeling guilty not an hour ago.

The graveside service was starting. And I joined the circle that was forming about the opening in the earth, positioning myself just to the left of Esther. A few psalms are read. Eema and Esther recite something or other, but I can't focus on it. Images of abba keep whizzing through my mind. Abba clutching at his heart. Abba's car swerving out of control. As time goes on, I become progressively uneasy about the casket. It's been spooking me ever since the Cohans and Mr. Plautsnicki carried it over, but I've managed to keep it out of my sight, just like I did at the schul. I try to push myself. Miriam, I say to myself, all your life, you've seen abba dead in a casket. Now it's for real and you've got to take it in. I force myself to look. Hmm! How about that! Not as bad as I'd expected. What was I worried about? Why hadn't I realized that the coffin would be closed? But what's happening now? They're lowering it. They're taking him further and further away. *This* I can't watch. Maybe if I look somewhere else.

I glance at the people to my left. A thin bearded man in a black suit and navy windbreaker is holding onto his yarmulke as the wind threatens to blow it away. Mrs. Morrison too is having trouble with the wind and is clutching at her sweater. I look down at myself. Black pants suit. No sweater or jacket. My body trembling. I must be cold. Yes, yes, the wind, it's biting into me. I decide to ignore the cold and cast my eyes further afield, taking in as much of the surroundings as I can. I see mounds of black earth, waiting for lodgers. I see gravestone after gravestone—different sizes, different shapes, most of them stark gray. Heartless, every last one of them. Austere, granite hard, utterly without pity.

I can feel the tears streaming down my face. I glance over at eema. She's crying too. "Abba," I whisper under my breath, "how could you abandon us like this? How could you leave us here, wretched and sobbing, amid these cold grey stones?"

I look back at abba's plot. The casket is all the way down.

Something else is happening now. Someone's put a shovel in my hand. Yes, yes, I've heard about this part. And this time, thank God, I know exactly what I'm supposed to do. Putting my muscles into it, I sink the shovel deep into the pile of earth. I clench my teeth and thrust the dirt onto abba's casket, hear it land with an eerie thud, then hand the shovel to Esther. As she maneuvers the shovel, I recall how abba always hated dirt. "Ay yay yay, Miriam," he would exclaim, "is making us wallow in our own filth, that's vat they did, those farshtunkener Nazis."

I glance over at eema. It's her turn. She has a solid grip on the shovel. But she isn't moving it. Just standing there, holding it, the end of the shovel dangling in the air.

"Eema, it's heavy. Want me to help you?" Harry offers, placing his left hand on the shovel.

"Eema, you don't have to," I whisper. "Just pass it to Harry. It's fine."

Eema nods and hands Harry the shovel.

Images of abba in the house flash through my mind. Abba sweeping under the fridge and bending down to ensure that not a speck of dirt remains. Abba on his knees cleaning the stairs from bottom to top, top to bottom. I feel this nudging at my left shoulder. What? My turn so soon? I reach for the shovel, grasp the cold metal handle. I look down the hole where abba's casket had appeared only moments before. Gone.

Once again, I sink the shovel deep into the earth. But just as I am about to dump the contents into the ever shallower hole, in my mind's eye, I hear the thinnest of wails. Not a wail. More like the echo of a wail. It is coming from under the earth.

Now everything's gone dark. I am somewhere blocked from the sun. I can hear sounds up above—clanging, thumping, praying. And all around me, I can see worms wriggling about. Brown worms. Green worms. And there in the midst of the worms is abba.

The coffin open, abba is lying there, his face blue, blood trickling from his chest, dirt covering him from head to toe. Brownish black dirt matted into what little remains of his white hair. Pieces of earth lodged in his nostrils. Worms crawling up and down his legs. Muddy tears flowing from his eyes. He is groaning piteously. Slowly, and with great effort, he maneuvers himself into a sitting position, then looks at me sadly. His eyes bulging ever so slightly, a look of deep disappointment on his face, he exclaims in a thin wisp of a voice, "Miriam, your own abba? Is throwing muck onto your own abba? For this I haf survived Auschvitz!"

"Abba, forgive me," I murmur.

✡

They were truly nightmarish, those first days of shiva. Oy! Every night, being repeatedly jolted into consciousness by the sound of eema screaming. Every day, facing the endless small talk of those people in black who appeared with the rise of the sun and lingered long after darkness was again upon us. Hour after hour, asking myself: How could I have let this happen to abba? What do I do for abba? For eema? Is there no force in the universe which protects those who have already suffered more than the heart can bear?

Despite my palpable grief, in the early hours of the fifth day of shiva, I did something totally out of a character for a mourner. Something that surprises me to this day. Eema and I were sitting on the couch, and as if from out of nowhere, I found myself getting up, approaching the far left window in the living room, and asking, "Eema, mind if I raise the blind?"

Eema startled. And she instantly protested, "but abba and the ganefs and...." Then she stopped herself and sighed, "but Miriam, it's shiva."

"I know, eema. Just for a minute. I'll lower it before anyone arrives. Promise."

Looking at me knowingly and sighing again, eema nodded. And then, kinehora, I actually did it. At this solemn time when it was blatantly inappropriate, I reached over, gave a tug on the blind, and brought it up. Not a crack, as we sometimes did, but all the way. And in streamed the sunlight. Something that I'd never seen in that room. Something none of us had ever seen in a single room in our house. I looked about in a kind of awe. The darkness around the couch, around the lazyboy, it was gone. Then I pressed my face against the pane and peered through the window into the yard.

The grass was beginning to come alive. Hints of green here and there. And two sparrows were perching on the upper branches of our maple tree. Busy collecting twigs, they seemed to know nothing of this death that had shaken the universe. As a third sparrow flew toward the tree, I shifted my gaze just in time to take in Mrs. Plautsnicki carrying a plate wrapped in tin foil not three houses away. I quickly pulled down the blind.

This stolen moment notwithstanding, abba's death continued to weigh upon me. Seldom did an hour go by when I did not rush to my room to cry. And I didn't dare lose sight of eema for a minute, she was that depressed. Somehow though, the hours passed. And toward the end, I was grateful for the steady stream of kindly visitors who kept arriving, challah and knishes in their hands, ready conversation on their lips. Besides that it relieved us of the necessity of attending to life, it gave us something to do. Epes. And at times, it softened the horror of it. Oy, there was even a moment there when Mr. Plautsnicki was standing by the kitchen table repeating the tale of abba's famous soup trade, that a distinct smile came to eema's lips. Then suddenly, shiva was over. And now there were no people, no distractions, nothing to make eema smile.

As devastated as I still was and as alien as the everyday world had initially seemed, my relationship to the ordinary had imperceptibly shifted during shiva. Though I couldn't imagine keeping regular hours, I felt as if I could manage half days at the office or at least do enough so that my students wishing to go to oral were not held up. But, gotenyu! How could I even think of such a thing with eema so vulnerable? Why even as I would go from one room to the next, I could see the alarm in her eyes. It was as if she feared I'd disappear too. "Be right back, eema," I would assure her.

Realizing that going out was out of the question, on the first day after shiva, I arranged with Rose to pinch hit for me on a thesis committee. Then I resumed everyday chores at home, including dusting the Uncle Nathaniel—an unpleasant task, of course, given my long standing aversion to the picture, but eema wanted it. "Abba's brother should look nice, yes?" she pointed out.

By the second day, the post-shiva duties had set in for real and my time was largely spent attending to the endless minutiae that abba's passing had thrust upon me. Freezing the bank account. Removing abba's clothes from eema's closet. Choosing mementos for people. Rummaging through bills, manifestos, minutes of union meetings, knickknacks, and trying to figure out where everything should go. For the most part, that task was a solitary one. Eema couldn't bring herself to participate and years ago abba had taken me aside and said, "Miriam, you're mayn executioner."

"You mean 'executor,' abba."

"Executioner, executor—from vat does a Jew know? But if something should happen mit me, you'll take care of everything, yah?"

205

Anything related to the Holocaust, anything that would allow abba to bear witness, anything connecting him with life before Auschwitz, I scrupulously saved, assembling it in the top drawer of the dining room bureau. Sadly, it didn't amount to much—just a few papers and pictures. Oh yes, and the old cloth measuring tape, its edges now frayed. Now I wasn't exactly sure why I was holding onto that particular piece, but somehow, it just didn't feel right tossing it.

Almost immediately, of course, I began searching for the will. Unable to find it, I eventually called this lawyer I remembered abba using a few times—old Mr. Fineburg—and I was lucky enough to catch him in. He was sorry to hear about abba. Such tsores! Yes, he had the will. Also a few other documents abba had left for safe keeping. We could come down maybe and sign some papers? No. No need to bother Esther.

Eema and I arrived at Mr. Fineburg's office at 4:00 p.m. sharp the next day. We signed everything he placed before us and listened carefully as Mr. Fineburg explained the will. It was all quite straight forward. I was the executor, just as we had figured. And naturally, eema inherited everything. It wasn't much, the inheritance. Just the house and roughly twenty thousand. But there would be another fifty coming from this insurance policy, no?

"But with his bad heart, how did he get coverage?" I asked.

"Quite a husband you have there, Mrs. Himmelfarb," asserted Mr. Fineburg, adjusting his glasses and peering over at eema. "It was decades ago. I remember because I'd just opened up my practice and in comes this meshugener with a bad heart, asking me how to get insurance. I told him it's not the business I'm in, but I don't see any way. But then off he went from one insurance company to another until he found one that said yes. Ridiculously high premiums, I recall. But he said to me, 'It's for my Rachaele.' He obviously loved you very dearly."

Before we left, Mr. Fineburg handed me a copy of the will, together with a few other papers. I placed them in a red folder in my knapsack. Then eema and I returned home and began dinner.

Eema barely touched dinner that evening, though I coaxed her into a few mouthfuls. After dinner, I went to my room, opened the knapsack, and took out the folder. I gave each of the documents a quick once-over. The will, the insurance policy, the deed to the house. Yes, everything as Mr. Fineburg had explained it. Along with these papers was an empty 10 by 12 inch manila envelope with a rip at the top. I was about to toss it into a throw-away pile when I realized there was something at the very bottom. Reaching inside, I removed a small pink slip of paper with scribbling on it, all of it in red. "April 1, 1991" was written at the top, and yes, the handwriting was abba's. Immediately, I began reading.

"Shalom, Miriam," the note begins. "If you're reading this letter, kinehora, is dead your abba is. I'm hoping it's not of too much importance, the information what I'm giving. I was tempted to get rid of this junk, but nu? What if you should need? Anyway, mayn tokhter, you are the family historian, and what can a family historian do without *all* of the history—even when is not gut? Enclosed please find some papers about your uncle. Always was he having tsores, our Yacov. Be careful, Miriam. You can't assume he did everything what people say. But oy gevalt! Is no question. Our Yacov is not living as a man should. Nein. You'll use your discretion, yah? Your loving abba, Daniel Himmelfarb."

There were no documents attached. Nor had I come across anything related to Uncle earlier, despite having gone through all of abba's papers.

Now I was well aware that these mysterious documents that were nowhere to be found might well shed light on the questions that Sondra had raised. Nonetheless, for the next couple of hours I tried to pretend that the content of the note was no longer significant. I really didn't want to address it. Poor abba was gone. So who gives a flying fuck what Yacov did in the past or what abba knew or didn't know? The whole miserable business, it had already cost abba so dearly. Vowing to throw out the note, I stuffed it in my jeans pocket and busied myself.

I chose two of abba's hats to pass on to the Sally Ann. I began sorting through his ties. No use. I couldn't banish it from my mind. So abba had the goods on Uncle Yacov after all, I recall thinking, and the bit about not remembering was deception pure and simple. I was disappointed in abba, of course, but not exactly surprised. It had been clear ever since that day that Sondra appeared—there was a lot more to know about Uncle. Yes. And abba knew.

Sighing, I went downstairs, made coffee, and joined eema in front of the TV. But I couldn't focus on the program. My mind had begun drifting back to the day before abba's death. Abba had expressed remorse at handling everything so badly. Then he'd added something like, "Incidentally, Miriam, something I vant you to look at. Is still the family historian what you are, no?" At the time, I had thought he was changing topic. But maybe not. With us women feeling as we did, maybe he had finally decided to show us these documents he'd squirreled away. Could that be the urgent business that took him out on that fateful night? Now he couldn't have been to the lawyer's that night. Fineburg would have said. So obviously, he'd removed them earlier. Who knows why? Second thoughts about our ever seeing them, perhaps. And perhaps he simply forgot to remove the note. At any rate, he couldn't bring himself to dispose of these papers. Then, come all the tsimmes over Sondra, he decided to fetch them. He was going to give them to his daughter, the historian. Good. But where were they? Now, there'd been no papers with him in the car. So...

"You seem lost in thought, yes?" comes eema voice. "Anything wrong?"

I glance over at eema. How haggard she looks! "It's okay, eema," I finally answer. "Just thinking about abba's stuff. Eema, you want another cup coffee?"

"If it's not too much trouble, yes. Sheyneh punem," she adds, her eyes beginning to tear, "you've been slaving away all day. Oy, sweetie! I'd help you if I could, but I can't."

"Sha, sha, eema. I know."

I spent a good part of that night asking myself where abba had gone after dropping eema off. It wasn't until morning, as I was pulling on my corduroys, that I recalled the locker. Ach! Now why hadn't I thought of that earlier? Yes, the day of his death abba had announced that he was going to a storage locker. "*My* storage locker," he'd called it. Punct.

As I sat down to breakfast, I vowed once again to let the whole matter drop. Who knows what abba really intended that last day? I reasoned. And how can I risk betraying him yet again? Just an hour later, though, I found myself making phone calls. I phoned every storage company in the greater Toronto area. But no! No one had rented a locker to anyone named "Daniel Himmelfarb." It crossed my mind that the locker might be a fabrication and that we might never locate those papers. But this was my sister, yes? My sister and my mother. And I was not about to give up.

# Chapter Eight

## Miriam, ages 44-50

Try though I did, I couldn't locate the Yacov papers. They weren't in the garage. They weren't with any of the lawyers the family had ever used. But that was the least of our problems. The place was lifeless without abba. For hours on end, the two of us would sit opposite each other at the long dining room table, barely exchanging a word. Eema's eyes seldom flashed with that sparkle of intelligence I had grown to expect and only occasionally connected with me. Oy! And while she would sometimes go to Esther's for Shabbes, and the Cohans would sometimes come to our place, many is the Shabbes eema and I celebrated alone, if you could call it a celebration. Nu? Eema would only peck at the food. And while her hands would go through the motions of lighting the Shabbes candles, the entire operation seemed mechanical, without spirit, without conviction. You'll forgive the comparison, yes? But at such times, the image of the musselmen would flash through my mind, their eyes vacant, the divine spark snuffed out.

I knew older couples where one partner died soon after the other, and witnessing eema's terrible depression, I kept thinking that eema wouldn't last the year. But she did. It was as if a small part of her was holding on. It was a gift, yes? A gift with almost nothing to sustain it. I was grateful for that gift, though I couldn't quite understand it. Nor could I figure out what I was supposed to do. How was I to reach that part of eema that held on? What did it want? What if anything was it trying to bring about?

*Image: Her bones protruding from her starving body, a young woman of about twenty-three is standing alone in a dark room. The room has the unmistakable odor of death; it is littered with objects—hundreds of scraps of clothing, tiny slivers of gold, countless strands of cloth, and collections of what would appear to be human hair. She keeps gazing expectantly toward the door. About half an hour passes. Then light footsteps can be heard. In walks another woman, a few years older, her nose beakish. "I have it," mutters the newcomer. Glancing quickly to one side, the newcomer nervously removes a tiny bundle from the inside of her frock and hands it to the younger woman. From an adjoining room comes a particularly loud cough. Both women startle; the older one scurries into the shadows.*

I can't say that eema ever recovered from abba's death. Nonetheless, for a period, there was a kind of reprieve. And I can date its beginning fairly precisely. Between 3:00 and 4:00 a.m. on the first anniversary of abba's death.

Disturbed by noises throughout the house, I awoke in a panic and leapt out of bed to find eema wandering about in her orange kimono. Her feet bare, her kimono askew, eema was anxiously opening doors, peeping into room after room, almost as if searching for abba. I stood there aghast, terrified that she had lost her all too precarious footing in time. "Eema, you looking for something? Can I help you?" I finally asked. Eema's eyes narrowed. Then without answering, without so much as noticing my presence, she headed to the kitchen. Seemingly oblivious to the fact that I had followed her, she knelt down, opened the drawer next to the sink, and brought out a yarzheit candle. An unusual time of day for lighting one, of course, but such niceties were never important to eema.

Eema placed the yarzheit on the table and struck a match. Then taking a deep breath, she reached over and lit the wick. The wick glowed for a second. Then it looked as if it were about to sputter out. But no, the flame grew and it opened up a space of light about her. Smiling through her tears, eema chanted a few words in Hebrew, ending with "Zichrono livrachah," which means "may his memory be a blessing." Then she closed her eyes, whispered, "Daniel, sweetheart, you'd like me to sing it?" A few seconds later, she began to sing softly—so softly I couldn't initially make out the song. But I soon realized it was Zog Nit Keynmol—Never Say This is the End. The song of the Jewish partisans, yes?

The candle burned for the full twenty-four hours. And for the entire time, except for trips to the washroom and grabbing the odd nash from the fridge, eema sat there keeping vigil over abba's flame; and I sat next to her. I remember looking at the frail figure before me and reminding myself that she was seventy-nine, so was bound to nod off sooner or later, but somehow she didn't. Next day, when the candle flickered out, eema looked straight at me, let out this huge yawn, and smiled. "Miriam," she whispered, reaching over to touch my cheek, "you look absolutely exhausted. We should get some sleep, you and me, yes?"

And with this, a kind of reprieve began.

✡

"Where's Harry?" I yelled into the receiver.

"Oh Miriam!" exclaimed Esther. "So sorry! I was supposed to call you right after Shabbes to let you know. Harry's out of town and so can't pick you up this morning."

"Damn it, Esther, its already 8:15! I'm gonna be late for class. I take it this also means one less supper guest tonight," I added.

"Stupid me! Something else I forgot. The kinderlekh will be with their zeda and bubbeh. But I'm still coming. That's okay, isn't it?"

"Yeah, yeah, if you remember," I quipped, "but I can't talk now. Bye."

Pressing the stop button, I immediately dial Beck's—the one and only cab number I know by heart. "Be at least twenty minutes," advised the dispatcher. "Can't wait. I'll try elsewhere," I answer. I race to the kitchen to look up another number, and it is then that it strikes me. I've had a driver's license since I was sixteen and there's a perfectly good car in the garage. So why not use it? It's not as if it would bother eema. Why she made the very same suggestion not three months ago. And the license plates are good.

Determined, I open the bottom drawer just to the left of the sink and locate the spare key to the Tercel. Then I head for the garage.

I was a bit nervous when I first climbed in, half expecting to see abba's ghost at the wheel. But no. Just that old familiar sight: Raspberry red steering wheel. Red bucket seats with some tears toward the top. I turned the key, pressed down on the pedal, and heard it ignite. I drove to the garage at Dupont and Bathurst, filled the tank, then headed for the university, passing every car I possibly could. As I pulled into Harry's spot just north of Atkinson, I looked at my watch. Whew! Three minutes to spare.

I went through my work day, tickled at having pulled this off. And I was oh so much more relaxed on the way back. Now the car drove like a charm for most of the trip. But a few blocks from home, it started to lurch. For a split second, abba's terrified eyes flashed through my mind. Oy! Is this what he experienced?, I wondered. But no, it's not out of control. Just a flat. The car wobbling along, I continued to drive flat tire and all for the next few blocks. Then I pulled into the garage and opened the trunk.

While it took me almost half an hour, and while I bloodied a finger in the process, I put on the spare tire just as abba had taught me so many years ago. Just as I am about to replace the jack, however, I spot something protruding from a flap in the trunk. I lift up the flap. Jammed in a corner is this blue folder, and clearly, there's something in it. Excited but nervous, I reach for a rag on a shelf nearby and quickly wipe the blood and surface grease off my hands. Then I unwedge the folder and stare at it. There in the bottom left corner in small black letters is the word "Yacov." I look inside. Letters. Also a number of newspaper articles, some neatly cut, others clearly torn out in haste. My heart speeding up, I tuck the folder under my arm, enter the house, and make a bee line for my study.

"That you, Miriam?" comes eema's voice.

"Yeah, eema. I'll be awhile. Something I need to read."

"Take your time, sweetie. A good hour before your sister arrives, yes? And I've everything under control."

With what trepidation I open that folder again! The first item I come across is none other than the letter that abba claimed to have lost—the one explaining Uncle's delay in arriving. I can instantly see why abba hid it. There's a prison stamp smack in the middle of the page. Scanning the letter, I find no reference to prison. So I put it aside and begin on the newspaper articles, hoping that they'll shed some light on the anomaly.

The articles are all about Uncle Yacov, each about some legal conviction. Mostly fraud and robbery, but a few are far more serious. And gevalt! Just look at what it is! Sexually abusing minors! To think that Uncle had hurt other little girls too—an eleven-year-old, it seems, a ten-year-old, and a thirteen-year-old! I instinctively check the dates. Two of the convictions are long after Uncle had left us. One so recent that he's probably still in jail. But Gott in himmel, the date on this one! Uncle was convicted of statutory rape just days after he'd sent abba that letter saying he was coming to live with us. So that's why his arrival was unexpectedly postponed! And that's what Sondra was referring to! Yes. And as was now abundantly clear, abba knew.

I start working my way through the rest of the letters. The ones on foolscap bear a prison stamp—a clear sign that Uncle was an inmate when he penned them. While they also discuss other matters, most refer to some transgression or other, either acknowledging or denying guilt. Now Uncle fesses up to fraud, but he repeatedly insists he has sexually abused no one. Each time I come across a denial, I feel furious. One particular statement, though, turns my blood cold and unsettles the universe as I know it. "As Hashem is my witness," he writes on a piece of foolscap dated April 2, 1988, "I would never. Believe me brother, I wouldn't force myself on an adult—never mind a child. But by the by, as for pushing the envelope just a bisel, now that's a whole different can of worms. Nu, Daniel? We're both men. And we've both seized the opportunities Hashem has brought our way. I have my peccadilloes, and you have your Rachaele, no? Come, Daniel. You're an honest man. Can you honestly say it is so very different—how I get my women and how you got yours?"

As I struggle with these frightful words, the doorbell rings. A few minutes later, eema calls up, "Sheyneh punem, Esther's here. You'll join us, yes?" I take a deep breath, carefully return the manuscripts to the folder, and head down.

The kitchen table is set. Eema and Esther are sitting around it, sipping tea.

"What on earth you been up to?" asks Esther, as I take a seat.

"Just finishing this manuscript."

"But your hands!"

"Sorry, I didn't realize." I go to the sink, scrub the remaining grease off my hands, and return to the table. Esther eyes me curiously, but thankfully, asks nothing further.

I don't know who said what after that, for my mind kept drifting back to Yacov. By the time we started in on the compote, I'd made a decision: I'd tell Esther, but not eema.

To my relief, shortly after nine, eema called it a night. Right there and then I told Esther the whole story—the empty envelope, the search for the missing documents, the flat tire, what I just found in the trunk of abba's car. Esther listened patiently, shaking her head sadly from time to time.

"So hard to believe! Miriam, can I see it?" she finally asked.

"Of course. You've as much right to these documents as I do.

213

They're in my study."

"How about bringing them down?"

"Too risky," I answered. "What if eema gets up and comes downstairs again? Let's go to the study."

Esther nodded; and we tiptoed upstairs, entered the study, and carefully shut the door. Removing my bifocals, I put on my reading glasses, then spread the documents out on the desk. And Esther and I each pulled up a chair.

As Esther read through the documents, we occasionally spoke of different parts and their implications. At one point, Esther excused herself and went to the washroom. I figured she was going to call it a day, for her arthritis was acting up. But when she returned, she kept right on reading.

"Miriam, I can't understand abba," she finally exclaimed. "Yacov, he's an abuser pure and simple. But abba was a decent man. Abba had three young daughters. And yet he let in a known perpetrator."

"I know. It's unbelievable."

For the next half hour, we both kept dipping into the documents, periodically expressing utter dismay. As time went on, I found myself wondering if Esther had taken in that other matter—the accusation Uncle had leveled against abba. I was beginning to think she hadn't, and I decided not to call attention to it, but then she picked up the April 1988 letter and added, "and this thing Uncle says about abba. Just listen to what he writes here: 'Can you honestly say it is so very different—how I get my women and how you got yours?' What's this about? Has to be an empty taunt, don't you think? I mean, we lived in this house with them for all those years. We know how abba was with eema."

"I'm not so sure," I answer.

"Miriam, how can you even think such a thing?"

"I know. I know, Esther. In so many ways, he was wonderful to eema, to all of us. A regular mentsh."

"I can feel a 'but' coming on."

"We don't have to go there."

"Miriam, what?"

"Well, remember that story abba used to tell about how he and eema met?"

"Of course. Why, when they were just little pishers, I would bounce the kinderlekh on my knee and ask them, 'Know how Zeda and Bubbeh Himmelfarb met?' And they would say, 'Oh please, tell us the bread story again.' And then I..."

"Esther," I interrupt, holding her look, "I don't want to scare you, but don't tell that story again. Not to your children. Not to the grand-children yet to be born."

A look of horror spreads across Esther's face. She bites her lip and peers into my eyes. "You say you don't want to scare me. But you *are* scaring me."

"Sorry."

"What's so bad about the story?"

"To begin with, it's not true. Least ways, not all of it. I always knew something was wrong with it, but I couldn't tell what. All this time, we thought abba was like a knight in shining armor saving the damsel in distress. Well, it sure isn't looking that way."

"But eema always liked that story."

"I'm not sure she didn't just go along with it because it pleased abba so. Also, because we all adored it. Anyway, there came a point she wouldn't tolerate it. Remember that day when she ran out of the room as abba was telling it?"

"Actually, no. When was that?" she asked, her eyes scrunching up.

"One afternoon. You must have been eight or nine. The Plautsnickis were over. Playing bridge, it seems to me. Maybe you were too young to notice. Or maybe you were out of the room at the time. I don't know. Just trust me when I tell you that it happened."

"Of course."

"You do remember, though, that abba stopped telling the story?"

"Sure, Meems, but I thought that's because it's a kids' story."

"I wish. It's because of something he told Uncle Yacov—epes, some-thing about what really happened back then."

"But the letter doesn't mention the bread story."

I stop for a second and look at my sister long and hard. There are tears rolling down her face. I feel like a brute persevering. "Esther," I say, "maybe I'm reading too much into everything."

"Don't patronize me," insists Esther, straightening her back. "You know perfectly well you think nothing of the sort. Just go on, Miriam, please. For Pete's sake, I'm a social worker who works with abuse cases."

"Fair enough. But it has to be harder when it's family."

Esther nods. "You can say that again. But I need to face the truth. I owe it to Sondra. And Adoshem expects no less of me."

"Okay then, Esther. Here's the thing. Yacov, he winked at eema just before she ran out of the room that day. It's as if he were taunting her, rubbing her face in something. Now in this letter here," I continue, picking it up again, "Yacov is speaking about how abba ended up with eema and he's implying something. It sounds sexual, yes? But there's something beyond that. Something that feels like pressure. Epes. Now, I don't know exactly what abba...."

"No, you don't," comes a voice from outside the doorway, "but I do."

I look up. Having the wrong glasses on, I see only a blurred figure hovering just outside the room. But I know that it has to be eema and that she is looking our way.

Esther instantly turns to face eema. "Gevalt!" she exclaims. "I must have left the door open when I... Eema, how long you been standing there?"

"Long enough," answers eema. "The two of you, come down to the kitchen, please, and bring those documents with you. I'll put on some tea."

I quickly remove my reading glasses, slip on my bifocals, and focus. Yes. Eema is in her kimono. A few tears are trickling down her cheek. Her eyes are strained, though she seems strangely calm.

"I'm so sorry, it's all my fault; eema, you don't have to..." I stammer.

"Sha. Sha, meydeleh. It's okay. I'm going to my room now and putting some clothes on. I don't want to feel any more naked than I have to, yes? But the three of us, we've got to talk."

Eema got dressed, came downstairs, plugged in the kettle, and brought out the large brown teapot. And for the next hour or so, the three of us sat around the kitchen table, trying to make sense of what had happened. It became clear very quickly that eema had known nothing of Yacov's history. And initially, she was as dumbfounded as us that abba would have let Yacov move in under circumstances this dire.

"It's awful," she moaned, "and Sondra paid for it. I always had this feeling abba was hiding something about Yacov—you know how abba could be, yes?—but something this extreme!"

"How could abba have done this to us?" asked Esther. "It wasn't just his home. It was *our* home. And the three of us were just little girls. Eema, all three of us could have been abused!"

"I know. I know," uttered eema, nodding. "Meydelehs, I'm so sorry. Always that Yacov made my skin crawl. I really let you down."

"Abba let us down," corrected Esther. "What was he thinking of?"

Eema sighed, poured us all some more tea, and sat there thinking for a few minutes. Then she narrowed her eyes and looked at us intently. "This isn't going to make you feel any better," she began, her eyebrow raised, "and it doesn't excuse abba. There's no excuse for what's happened here. But if it helps, I've a pretty good idea what must have gone through abba's head. He'd have believed that Yacov was framed."

Esther shook her head in disbelief. "How? Just look at all this evidence!"

"Because he's a man, yes? And men can more easily delude themselves about such things. Also because he so desperately wanted to believe it. Wanted so much to have this man in his life. So despite overwhelming evidence to the contrary...."

"And despite his responsibility to his wife and kids," added Esther.

"Punct. Despite all that, he convinced himself Yacov was innocent, yes? And what did he do with the doubts he had? The doubts he had to have, because, after all, he was no fool, your abba. He told himself that, regardless, Yacov would never touch his own flesh-and-blood."

"Possibly," acknowledged Esther, "but tell me this. Why didn't he say anything to you—his partner, the mother of his children?"

"Why? Because he knew I'd see it differently, yes? Knew if he breathed a word about any of these charges, that farshtunkener would never set foot in this house."

"And later on when it became clear something was wrong?" Esther persisted.

"I imagine it's very hard to stop covering up once you begin. Also, kinehora, the worse things looked, the more urgently he would have lied to himself about what his brother was capable of."

"Eema," I observed, holding her look, "I think you're right. At the same time, abba held onto all this incriminating evidence. My guess is he wasn't intending us to see it until after he was dead. But he changed his mind that day he took you to the library. He was going to show us the file even though it might mean losing all of us. And that at least is something. Of course, it would hardly be much comfort to Sondra."

Eema nodded, muttering, "It's gut he got the papers, but it's not enough. Oy! Not even close." She sipped her tea. Then she began rubbing her sore shoulder, then her face, then her palms. I could tell she was hesitating. There was one more piece to this puzzle, and she wasn't sure how to tell us.

"I think he figured Yacov was like himself," she finally murmured, her nose wrinkling up. "Someone who'd crossed the line but would only go so far. You know, meydeleh," she continued, looking directly at me and smiling sadly, "they were dead on, your suspicions about the bread story. The story isn't right."

"But he didn't just make it up, did he, eema?"

"Not exactly. He mixed fact and fiction—actually, prettied it all up. And yes, I went along with the story because everyone loved it. Hmm! Actually, strange though this may sound, the time came when abba had told it so often, I ended up half believing it myself. Then too, I was something of a coward, yes? Going along with the fiction felt easier than facing the truth. Not that the discrepancy didn't gnaw at me from time to time. Now years ago you asked me not to keep secrets. What can I say? It never looked like something a mother should share with her kinderlekh. But things have a strange way of coming back at us, yes?"

"So abba didn't save your life?" asks Esther.

"Oh, on the contrary. In the long run, I've every reason to believe he did. The fact is, that man gave me food again and again, and I probably wouldn't have survived Auschwitz without him. And make no mistake about it. It cost him, yes? We all had so little, it was an incredible sacrifice depleting your own meager stock to give a scrap of bread, a gulp of water, epes. We were being literally starved to death, every last one of us, don't forget. The thing is, though, while I was deliriously hungry, I wasn't on the verge of dying when he first gave me bread. And while every bone in my body ached, and while it was a struggle holding onto consciousness, I was no musselman. I wasn't wandering aimlessly, didn't slobber, didn't have snot trickling down my face. And while, of course, none of us could ever be sure of anything, I would probably have survived the next selection, yes? So it wasn't an immediate question of life and death. But more than that, initially, the bread, it was no gift. You see, he could tell I was desperate and there was something he wanted. You understand what I'm trying to tell you?" she asked, her eyes focusing in on me.

"This was one of abba's trades?" I ask, dumbfounded.

Eema nods. I'm getting a sick feeling. I glance at Esther. She looks back at me and shudders.

"Sex for bread," said eema, scrupulously avoiding our eyes. "It happened to us women. Not often, let me be clear, for in Auschwitz, inmates seldom had sex on their mind. Satisfying hunger and thirst, meydelehs, these were the instincts which drove inmates day and night—not sex. But this other thing, it happened. A man would get lonely. A man would see a woman—a woman oozing with pus, a woman who stank of urine and foeces, a woman you couldn't imagine a fellow inmate looking at with any feeling other than compassion or horror. But sometimes a very different feeling would come over a man. And sometimes, even when the woman clearly didn't want it, a man would put his everyday scruples aside and a trade like this occurred. And it entered into the mix of degradation, of course. Something, I suspect, the Nazis were only too happy about, may even have planned, for they did everything they could to undermine our fundamental sense of decency, our respect for ourselves and each other. You know," she said, shaking her head, "we talk about survivors as if men and women had the same experience, yes? It was awful for all of us, of course. Awful beyond anything I can describe. But the same? No."

"I understand about needing bread, eema," responds Esther, her teeth clenched, her eyes angrier than I've ever seen them. "And I understand your taking the trade. But later on, you married him. Married a perp."

"A perp?" asks eema.

"Perpetrator," Esther clarifies.

I stare at Esther in astonishment. "Esther, for God's sake!" I exclaim.

"Easy, Esther," cautions eema, looking straight at her. "Don't forget who we're talking about here. Abba. Not some monster. A man who made bad mistakes to be sure, but a man who cared for everyone and who was facing a horror worse than anything you're ever likely to contend with, kinehora. What abba did here, I hate. And both at the time and afterward, we had dreadful arguments about it, abba and me. But remember, I agreed to it. And think about it, Esther. Compared with everything that was happening to us—the daily beatings, the endless insults, the purposeful starving, sending us up through the chimneys, just how significant do you think it was that a man would exact a trade of this nature? *Now*—that's another matter—but at the time? To tell you the truth, there were even moments I found it touching. That a starving man should want intimacy so badly he would give up his own food. And you have to understand, it only happened at the beginning. As time went on, he gave me bread and asked nothing in return. Actually, despite those occasional trades, which he always boasted so much about, abba gave to everyone. And this is the man I fell in love with and married, yes? Not some perp."

Esther sniffles and says nothing.

"Now, of course, with the coming of the women's movement, I found myself struggling once again with the beginning of our relationship. Oy! You can imagine. And when Yacov winked at me that day, and I.... Well, Miriam," she adds, catching my eye, "you saw for yourself, yes?"

"Yeah, eema."

"Anyway, we worked it out. I told him he couldn't ever tell the story again and, kinehora, he stopped. That's what we did, abba and me. We worked things out. And clearly, that's been both a strength and a weakness, yes? It gave us a life, though I now suspect it also gave him the message nothing men do to women in everyday life is all that bad. And I suspect that too played a part in him letting Yacov in. Vey iz mir, if I'd been a little less agreeable, perhaps Sondra would be an actress right now touring the world instead of...anyway, that's what happened."

"Eema," I utter hesitantly, "I know this is terribly personal and I don't want you to talk about anything you don't want to, but you lived with the man for decades, shared a bed with him. It must have bothered you at night when..."

Eema closes her eyes and says nothing for a few minutes. Esther and I exchange looks but remain perfectly still. "Sometimes when he'd touch me," she murmurs, her words more like a whimper than a communication, "I would flash back to those days, and I would cringe. He would get hurt, abba, yes? And his eyes would start to bulge, you know, like they did, but there was no way I could let him near me. Don't mistake me here, meydelehs. Mostly, we had a good sex life, abba and me. But, oy, every so often when he would put his hand on my shoulder or even look at me with desire, I would find myself back again, sitting next to one of those putrid ditches, this strange man who I didn't even like leering at me, starting to grope me. I would blink my eyes, but when I opened them again, the ditch was still there. And there this foul-smelling man would be, dangling bread in front of me, telling me my scruples were pointless, and reminding me of my obligation to get my strength back. Ach! What can I say, Miriam? He was right. Frighteningly right. And he was wrong. Appallingly wrong. And a woman doesn't get over something like that."

Eema pauses, opens her eyes, and takes a few sips of tea. Then at long last, she looks at us again. "If there's anything else either of you need me to clarify, please ask me now—not tomorrow, not the next day, yes? Forgive me, kinderlekh, but I really can't talk about this again. About abba's letting Uncle Yacov into this house, and about me failing to act when God knows I should have, yes. But about the trade, no. Gott in himmel! The man was my husband—my beloved husband—for almost fifty years. And you, you're my children," she sighs, tears welling up in her eyes.

"It's okay, eema," I answer. "It's enough. And, eema, please understand. We love you and respect you."

Esther nodded.

"And how about your abba?" asked eema, looking straight at Esther. "You still love and respect him too, yes?"

Several minutes passed, but Esther just stood there. I turned to eema. "Eema," I urged, "we need time." She smiled faintly. I glanced at Esther, hoping she would say something, but no. Then I reached over and hugged eema.

Eema was exhausted by this point, and after checking to see if we were okay, giving Esther a kiss, and expressing concerns about Sondra, she headed for bed. Esther and I entered her room a few minutes later and sat with eema as she slept. The last thing we wanted was for her to wake up and find herself alone. After Esther left, I stayed a bit longer. I remember listening to eema's unsteady breathing, wondering if she was perhaps getting sick. Then I went to my room, crawled into bed, and switched off the light.

I couldn't sleep though. And it wasn't simply eema's nocturnal screaming that kept me up. Hour after hour, this terrible picture played over and over again in my mind—abba dangling a crumb of bread in front of a starving eema and asking, "Is vanting it, you are? Come, we'll make a trade, yah?" I can't keep facing that image. I flick on the light, go to my bookshelf, and take out this book on women and the Holocaust. I flip through the pages; and sure enough, I find one or two references to such man-woman trades, but only in throw-away lines. I read through a few first person testimonials. Then I turn off the light.

No sooner is the room dark than the image is back. A few seconds later, it fades, and I see abba and Uncle hanging out on the living room couch, the two of them grinning as abba says, "Is such a good story, bruder, but I've got one that'll tops yours. Ever tell you about the time I met my Rachaele." Eventually, this image too fades, and it is replaced by one of eema, her body a thing of bones, her eyes feverish, a look of deep disappointment on her face. Then slowly, the eema image drifts into a corner, and my mind expands to take in a large spectrum of women inmates—young, old, white, of colour, German, Polish, Roma, heterosexual, lesbian, all of them grievously violated. I see tearful mothers, screeching in protest as their children are snatched from their bosom and hurled head-first into the flames. I see young girls—not even Channa's age—trembling as they are paraded naked in front of the male functionaries. I see hands searching through vaginas, x-ray machines burning into ovaries, naked women stacked in cages, one cage on top of the other, the foeces and urine from the higher cages pouring onto the heads of those below. Gott in himmel! What else has happened to the women?, I ask myself. What horrors they dare not name? And how come so many more women than men?

Just as I ask that question, one final figure makes its appearance. I recognize her instantly. Same face as in that photo abba used to carry around in his wallet. Same dark brown hair, same squared chin, but ever so much thinner, the teeth rotten, the cheeks hollow, the eyes burning. The woman opens her mouth. "Niece," she cries out, her voice hoarse, her tone desperate. "What? Haven't you ever wondered why Yacov and Nathaniel were sent to safety but not me? Don't you know about the extra value placed on the boys? Didn't anyone ever tell you that...." Feeling too drained to face anything further, I whisper, "not yet," and I pull the covers over my head. And slowly, slowly, the curtain of consciousness falls and the specter of Auntie Miriam vanishes.

For the next few weeks, I watched eema nervously, fearing that we had gone too far. Though she never once mentioned that evening or any of the revelations associated with it, many is the night she screamed abba's name repeatedly. Nonetheless, to my surprise, during the day, eema stayed pretty level, or at least, showed no signs of being in difficulty. She got up early, read seventy, eighty pages, and watched her favourite TV programs. Also, she surfed the Internet, tapping into libraries all over the world. Additionally, she started seeing more of Sammy, who was fifteen now, needing the freedom to be her own person, and who would turn to eema for support. And how eema rose to the occasion!

✡

It had drizzled a few hours earlier, but the sun was now blazing, baking the already tinged grass, soaking into our all-too-eager skin. Clad in shorts, the family was in Esther's and Harry's backyard. Most of us were sitting on the padded lawn chairs about halfway between the house and the garage, admiring the blush-red peiris bushes. A few feet closer to the house, Harry and Sammy were hovering over the barbecue. Harry was flipping the patties, Sammy dabbing them with her special barbecue sauce. I don't know how it started, but a quarrel broke out.

"Fuck! I don't want to go to schul with you and mom," objected Sammy, scowling.

"Sweetheart, I understand. But schul's important," insisted Harry. "When you're older, you can decide for yourself, but right now, you gotta go."

"Remember that one time Sarrah came with me?" asked Sammy. "Know what she said later? That it really sucked. Totally heterosexist."

"So where is it written you have to go everywhere with your special friend Sarrah?" asked Harry. "Now our temple's a bit behind the times, sure, but we're working on it."

Sammy winced.

At that very moment, eema took out her cigarettes and lit one. And as if for no reason, she began to talk about a few of the newer synagogues in town, betraying a knowledge that rather surprised all of us, given eema's unwavering commitment to atheism. Then she inhaled deeply and noted, "Yes, and there's a newer one too. Hershel, you heard about that new schul in Kensington? Whatsitsname?"

"Temple Ruth. Yeah," answered Harry. "Part of Jewish renewal, right?"

Eema and Harry continued to schmooze, with eema commenting on how Jewish renewal was speaking to alienated Jewish youth all over the world. Now while eema made her points tactfully, who's to say how Harry would have responded had it been anyone else? He'd always had serious qualms about Jewish renewal. But Harry adored eema.

"So, Hershel, what you think?" eema finally asked. "Would it be all right if Sammy went to Temple Ruth instead?"

"Hardly my cup of tea, eema," he observed, smiling half-heartedly at her. "But I see your point. And better Temple Ruth than nothing."

"Well, meydeleh, how about it?" asked eema, turning to Sammy.

"But bubbeh," exclaimed Sammy, "why would I want to go there?"

"I think maybe you and Sarrah would like it," she responded, smoke drifting out her nostrils. "The congregation, it's progressive. Come, humour an old woman. I'll go with you and introduce you to the chazan. A friend of mine, yes?"

Next Shabbes, Sarrah, Sammy, and eema went to Temple Ruth. Sammy was genuinely impressed by its Jewish renewal philosophy. And she raved on and on about how participatory the service was. However, as we discovered over dinner the following Shabbes, it wasn't only this that delighted her.

"Can you believe it?" exclaims Sammy. "The rabbi's a dyke, the chazen's a woman, and about sixty per cent of the congregation is queer, bi, or trans. Pretty wicked, eh Aunt Miriam?"

"Sure is," I reply, unable to stop myself from grinning despite the somber look on Harry's face.

"Absolutely," agrees eema. "Esther, Harry, you want to join us next week? It's based on a revolutionary commitment to Tikkun olam—the sacred obligation to gather up the sparks and repair the world. You might find it interesting."

Esther looks uneasy as she glances over at Harry. Harry nods, and then a smile breaks out on Esther's face. "Yes, that'd be nice," she agrees. "Some of my clients are excited by Jewish renewal and, in all honesty, I'm curious."

"Gut," eema declares. "And Sammy, you'll ask your ... now just what *do* you and Sarrah call each other?"

"Partners," asserts Sammy.

"Punct. And you'll ask your partner Sarrah if she'll join us for Shabbes dinner as well? And Harry, if you like, ask your folks. Ask your brother and his partner too. Once in a while, it's good that all the family should get together, yes?"

Now there were a few awkward moments, for no one had exactly acknowledged the nature of Sammy's and Sarrah's relationship before. Nonetheless, the dinner went surprisingly well, with eema graciously drawing out Sarrah at every turn. Of course, contrary to eema's description, it wasn't the entire family that turned up. And as people kept making toasts and exclaiming how good it was to have everyone present, even I was painfully aware that someone was missing. Not that I any longer wanted her to return. Not now.

Stuff was going missing again, you see. The laser printer in the study, the radio in the kitchen. I couldn't believe that Sondra had started up again. And I couldn't stand to see what it did to eema. Every single time she would weep the entire night. I wanted to act, to put a stop to the theft once and for all, but eema and I were hardly of one mind.

✡

Eema and I had been at Esther's for dinner. As I pulled up to the curb in front of our house, I saw Sondra on her way out the front door, our toaster under her arm.

"Just what do you think you're doing?" I yell, exiting the car and rushing toward the stairs.

"Miriam, leave her be. If she needs, she should take, yes?" I hear eema call out.

I step in front of Sondra and force her to look at me. "Sondra, abba's dead," I stammer. "Eema's all alone. And she's almost eighty, for God's sake! Now I'm sorry you were abused. But if you can't treat eema properly, you're not welcome in this house!"

Sondra scowls, pushes me aside, and walks off.

Eema cried for hours that night. And we bickered next morning over breakfast.

"We've got to change the locks," I insisted.

"No way I'm locking my daughter out of my house," answered eema, her voice determined. "Miriam, she's a survivor. You've got to make allowances, yes?"

"*You're* a survivor. And look at the effect she's having on you. You were screaming most the night. And what about me? I've just lost one parent. You think I want to lose another?"

Needless to say, eema won. What else? The locks weren't changed. And so periodically, something new would go missing. Furniture, appliances, epes. And oy, everytime it did, eema would have one of those awful nights.

Then something happened that shook eema even more fundamentally. Something totally natural. Something whose very inevitability made it all the more agonizing. Mrs. Plautsnicki called to say that another camper had passed away. This time, Gisella.

"Oy, meydeleh," groaned eema, shaking her head forlornly, "one by one they're being snatched away—just like at Auschwitz!" And what a grievous time she had that night!

"Gevalt!" she screamed. "Where have they taken my eema, my abba? What have they done to Daniel? Gisella? Roza? Regina? Alla? Onika?

Volya? Shmuel? Lionel? Chaim?" Every few minutes, she would call out a new series of names—German names, Polish names, Russian names, many of them ones I'd never heard before. It's as if the whole six million were in her head. And one by one, she was watching them disappear.

Now I couldn't have slept more than a couple of hours, what with tending to eema. But in the little time I did, I dreamt of Auntie Miriam. In the dream, we were standing a few feet away from this utterly ordinary looking building. Suddenly, I hear this terrible high-pitched wailing rising from within. Not human. Surely, it couldn't be human.

"What's that?" I ask.

"The screams of women," she answers.

"Gevalt! What's happening?"

"One of the Block 10 experiments. Careful. You don't want to come any closer to Block 10, niece. Know what happened to me after I was sterilized in Block 10?"

"Please, I'm not yet ready."

"But, Miriam, I'm your guide."

Even as we speak, a gaunt man appears, dragging the naked remains of a woman. The corpse is almost all bones. She has no breasts, no pubic hair, and there's blood near her genitals, blood dripping down her poor withered legs. I reach over and touch the bony face that droops out of the trunk. Still warm. Bending down, I examine the face carefully. It too seems to be Auntie Miriam, but ever so much thinner than the woman serving as my guide. I can feel a hand on my shoulder. I cringe, glance to the side, and see that it belongs to my guide.

"They did this to you?" I ask.

For a second there, my guide says nothing, just stares at me forlornly. "Well? What you waiting for—the Moshiah?" she finally spits out, her lip curling, her eyes coming alive. "For all the women survivors and their children to die off so no one's left to tell our story?"

"Just a little more time."

"Hurray up, niece," she cautions. Removing the watch from off the arm of the man to our side, she grasps it by the buckle, leans toward me, and dangles it in front of my eyes. "Look," she instructs, her index finger pointing to the minute hand. "Time is running out."

Gisella's death set off an alarm deep inside me. And that very week, I began writing a grant application for a proposed research project. "Women and the Shoah," it was called, yes? WATS, for short. There were two parts to WATS. The one I felt most passionate about involved students interviewing women relatives who had been through the Holocaust. Mothers, grandmothers, aunts, sisters, epes. Part II was other interviews with women survivors.

About four months after mailing in the application, I received notification. I was being funded for both parts. In short order, I set up the infrastructure and informed the student body. And WATS was under way.

In the first year of WATS, I was extremely busy, but oh so gratified. We came across a few stories in which a male inmate pressured a female into a bread-for-sex trade. Third person accounts, of course, for who's likely to divulge something like this about themselves? Nonetheless, I quickly came to see that eema was right. Such incidents were pretty rare. On the other hand, dozens of women spoke of their brothers being sent to safety while they were left behind. Auntie Miriam's situation, eema confirmed. Naturally, the bulk of everyone's story was Nazi atrocities, with both male and female inmates periodically coming to their aid. I could see the common plight of all survivors in the testimony. At the same time, the gender difference also struck me—having one's breast repeatedly cut open by whips, being forced to defecate in front of male functionaries.

I conducted follow-up interviews with those few women who had been part of the organized resistance. And it was in the middle of one of these interviews that I again found myself wondering about eema's involvement. "Know what?" asked Gerta, about fifty minutes into the interview, "though everything was hush-hush, I knew a thing or two about Roza and the explosives." No sooner were these words out of Gerta's lips than an image of eema lighting the memorial candles flitted through my mind. Could this be the Roza whose yarhzeit eema has so dutifully lit year after year?

Now my interviewees and I were frequently on TV at that point; and I was hoping that the enormous excitement which the project was generating would move eema to say something more about her own experiences. But no. She carefully kept her distance, though she was clearly delighted with the witnessing.

"A real mitzvah," she called it one morning, her hand reaching for my cheek. "And I can't tell you how proud I am."

"Thanks, eema."

"Though be careful, meydeleh," she cautioned. "The Holocaust, it can take hold of a person."

Over the next year, I listened to and began coding almost a hundred survivor tapes. And I was thrilled by the depth of what was emerging. My one regret was that eema wasn't able to be a part of it. But there it was. Eema said nary a word. And so we continued on our separate paths.

I was uneasy as I went about my work that day. Mrs. Plautsnicki was in hospital again. Now she was getting out this afternoon, and as promised, eema was just staying home and watching television and letting Mrs. Plautsnicki's own kids take care of things for a change. Nonetheless, eema was so distraught over how terrified Mrs. Plautsnicki had become that I regretted not being able to take the day off and keep her company.

When I arrived home, I could see that eema wasn't downstairs watching television. So I sucked in my breath, climbed the stairs, and approached her bedroom.

The door is open. Eema is inside sitting at the computer, her forehead furled, what I take as a stunned expression on her face. Again, I am struck by the wrinkles on her aging face and feel this sweet sadness coming over me. She's eighty-two now, yes? And who's to say how much longer she'll live?

"Eema," I say.

She doesn't respond.

"Eema," I try once more.

Again, no response. But by now, it's clear that eema isn't so much stunned as riveted. She is focused on the screen. Eema clicks the mouse. And almost instantly, I hear the familiar hum of the printer. I glance at the top of the printer. There's at least a couple of hundred printed pages sitting there.

"Eema," I try a third time.

"Miriam, a moment, please. I'm in the middle of something, yes?"

"You want me to leave?"

"No, just give me a few minutes, but while you're waiting, meydeleh, you might take a gander at what I've already printed, yes?"

I pick up the top half of the pile, make myself comfortable on the bed, and begin reading: "In 1942," states this one writer, "Red Cross officials inspected and fixed all the showers in the camps. Were the showers fake, the officials would surely have discovered the discrepancy, and commentary on it would have appeared in their report. It does not."

"As Leuchter testified," declares another author, "Zyklon B or hydrogen cyanide—the supposed agent of mass murder—chemically unites with brick to create Prussian blue. Zyklon B is a standard insecticide. And so there are naturally traces of Prussian blue in the delousing chambers. However, it obviously requires more Zyklon B to kill a human being than a louse. And yet exhaustive chemical analyses of samples taken from the respective chambers indicate far more Prussian blue in the delousing chambers than in the alleged homicidal gas chambers. So the chambers in question could not conceivably have been used for murdering human beings."

Meshugah, I tell myself as I stare at the sheets. Why the camps inspected by the Red Cross were regular concentration camps—not death camps. And as every student of the Holocaust knows, it takes far less hydrogen cyanide to kill a human than a louse. But that is hardly the point. Why...

"They could convince someone who knew bupkes, yes?" comes eema's voice.

I look up and see eema eyeing me.

"Exactly. But, eema, it's worse than that. Even a person with average knowledge could get confused by this."

"And that's just *one* strain of Holocaust denial," points out eema. "I've come across others. Look at this," she urges, handing me the sheet on her clipboard. "This Moshekapoyer here argues that there's countless ways to read the documents which inform current orthodoxy. And that it's elitest to prioritize the Jewish Interpretation."

I immediately recall my postmodernist years and feel embarrassed, for the logic is all too similar. Not that my postmodernist colleagues would be likely to swallow this particular brand of shit.

"Miriam, you know how to construct websites?" checks eema.

"Enough to get by. Whatchya got in mind?"

"What else? Creating my own website and posting detailed refutations of all the standard arguments."

I looked at eema in utter amazement. I didn't know how long it would last, but I had the old eema back. Rachael Himmelfarb—the fighter. Rachael Himmelfarb—the social activist. And it felt good.

The very next morning, we began preparations in earnest. Eema started drafting refutations complete with scholarly references. And I brushed up on hypertext markup. And within no time, www.shoah.ca was under way.

✡

It was just before sundown on January 5th, 1996. I'd been in my study working on some photos for the web page. I feel a tickle at the back of my throat and come down to the kitchen for a glass of water. I find a yarhzeit burning in the centre of the table, eema sitting in front of it. She has on the same black pants suit she's worn all day, but now a black lace kerchief is drawn over her head. Her eyes are closed, and she is swaying ever so slightly. And over and over again, she is muttering the name "Roza."

I sit down opposite her and remain silent. Although I can't exactly say why, I have this feeling that she is aware of my presence and wants me to stay. Fifteen, twenty minutes pass. Then eema opens her eyes and nods.

"Meydeleh," she says, looking at me without a hint of surprise. "Thought I heard you. Tea?"

"Yeah, thanks."

Eema pours us both a cup, then asks me to fetch my cassette recorder. Without another word exchanged, I go upstairs, return with it, plug in the external mike, and sit back down. Eema reaches over, removes the cassette, scribbles on the label, and hands it to me. "WATS Interview with Rachael Himmelfarb," it reads.

"Eema, you sure?" I ask.

"Meydeleh," she answers, her eyes meeting mine, "us survivors, we're rapidly dying off. What's going to happen when we're all gone? The Holocaust deniers, they're persuading people as it is. So please, Miriam, interview me, yes?"

"Of course. It'd be an honour. But we can't just rush into it. You see, there's these documents.... "

"It's okay, sweetie. I've read the research protocol. I fully understand my rights. And the signed consent, you'll find it in the top drawer of your desk."

Eema gives me a knowing smile, then instructs me to insert the cassette and turn on the machine. Far more nervous than I've been with any other interview, and well aware that eema has assumed control, I take a deep breath and do as she instructs.

I begin by asking her about the early years just after Hitler's ascension to power. About this, she says little, though she does emphasize how devastating it was to live through the Nazi buildup.

"Though none of us had a clue how bad it would be," she explains, "most of my friends and I, we were pretty astute Communists, yes? And we picked up the signs of impending disaster early on. The Schlageter affair, the banning of the unions, outlawing the party, the burning of the books."

"So being a Communist heightened your awareness?"

"To a point. Epes. Being a Jew at least as much, though I can't tell you how many who should have known better were in denial. In some ways, that was the most frightening part, yes? Seeing friends and relatives fooling themselves, calling it a mere blip. Know what my cousin Norman said? 'What do you mean resist? In a democratic country, when an election's held, you accept the results. So, it'll be bad for a few years! Since when have things not been bad for Jews?' And can you believe it? He was singing this same tune even after we were stripped of citizenship."

"Must have been utterly exasperating."

"To say the least. Especially when they dragged 17,000 of my bubbeh's Polish countrymen to the border.* But did I know that we were in serious trouble? Absolutely."

"Eema, I can hear you were experiencing everything as a Jew, as a Communist, as someone with Polish heritage. How about as a woman? What did you think when the first abortion law was passed?"

"What can I tell you?" she answered, her eyebrow arching. "I knew it was outrageous. But I never focused on it. I didn't exactly have what you would call a feminist consciousness at that point. I thought like a Communist and I acted like a Communist. I attended these illegal meetings where we discussed how to keep the unions alive."

"And that's why the Gestapo came for you?"

"Yes and no. On the surface of it at least, it was because of this poster encouraging the workers to organize. My friend Frieda had been distributing it, yes? But somehow, *I* was picked up. I said nothing that would implicate anyone, thankfully. Now it was soon apparent even to the Gestapo that they had the wrong person. But did they release me? No. They sent me to Ravensbrück."

Eema went into a detailed description of what it was like being at Ravensbrück—not knowing whether or not her family had been picked up, having to sew Nazi uniforms hour after hour. Then she took a sip of tea and started to massage her sore shoulder, and her eyes began to tear.

*In 1938, Poland issued an edict stating that all Polish citizens who had been absent from Poland for more than five years would have their citizenship revoked unless they got a special stamp. Polish Jews in Germany were refused that stamp. Nazi Germany responded by dragging 17,000 Jews with Polish passports to the Polish border.*

"I was beaten badly once at Ravensbrück," she resumes, her voice cracking. "And for what? Bupkes. Did I hurt anybody? Did I refuse to work? No. I stopped to wipe some sweat off my brow, yes? Oy! I didn't see it coming. Suddenly, I can feel this terrible blow. And my shoulder feels like it's shattered—caput—and then there's another blow, and another. I am down on the ground, my eyes closed, and I can feel kicks everywhere—my arm, my leg, my kishke. Some time later, I open my eyes and try to move my arm. But it just hangs there like a broken wing, yes?"

"Eema, I'm so sorry. So that's what happened with your shoulder?"

Eema nods. "But the worst thing," she adds, "is the business about memory. Remembering family. Remembering friends. Slipping into daydreams, hopes for the future, only to have them shattered again and again by the grim reality about me. Night—that was the most dangerous time. I would fall asleep, and despite my best intentions, these images would creep into my head—my eema at a picnic laughing, my cousin Norman and I at a movie. Then I would hear someone shout, 'Raus!' And I would open my eyes, confused and heartbroken."

"It's awful."

"Awful, yes, Miriam. Ravensbrück was awful. But Auschwitz was worse. There's nothing, nothing that can prepare a person for Auschwitz."

"You up to talking about it?"

Eema nods. "March 26, 1942," she begins, "was the day women were first transported from Ravensbrück to Auschwitz, yes? We didn't know where we were going or what was going to happen to us. And, meydeleh, what a harrowing journey it was! Locked inside this boxcar, no light, no air, no water, just a bucket for relieving ourselves. And when the car finally stopped, nothing got better. It got worse—way worse. Even as I was stumbling out of that car, I knew I'd left the world of the living and entered hell." "You think I'm speaking metaphorically?" she asks, her eyes seeking mine. "Miriam, when you write this up, I want you to be absolutely clear. Most of my adult life, I've been an English professor, yes? And I know from metaphor. We were literally in Hell."

"Oh eema!"

"Instantly, I found myself in the midst of this infernal commotion. Oy! Such a din! There seemed to be no way to focus. Yet I knew if I lost my concentration—lost it even for a second—anything could happen. Gotenyu! Alsations growling, officials with rifles running in all directions and barking orders at us, faces filled with contempt commanding us to line up, to take off all our clothes, to go to the right, to go to the left. Rifles firing. And everywhere, the sound of women wailing. And right from the beginning, again and again, they forced nakedness upon us, yes? It's as if they were hell bent on eradicating any sense of privacy, any sense we were individual human beings. Naked, as the hair was shorn from our heads. Naked, as we stood in lines. Ach! I remember a few hours after arriving, not a stitch of clothes on, straddling these two chairs for God knows what reason, as two men in uniforms pointed at me, snickering at my withered breasts, one of them quipping, 'it really doesn't matter. Like the rest of your miserable race, you'll be dead soon enough.'"

Even without my prompting, eema would frequently reflect on gender.

"Robbed of family," explained eema, "we turned the women around us into sisters, mothers, daughters. And you know, meydeleh, the women were somewhat better at this than the men. We would gather together, share food, make Shabbes. We didn't have candles, of course. So we would say the barucha over the light bulb instead. Epes. Also we would share our favourite recipes, reciting each and every ingredient with great care. What was most important of all, we looked out for each other. We would warn each other if a kapo was near. If a woman couldn't hold herself up, two of us would get on either side and prop her up so that the Nazis didn't notice. Not that men didn't come to the aid of others. And not that women didn't descend into individuality and greed.

Eema spoke a fair amount about abba, but she said nothing that would reflect badly on him. And in all honesty, I was relieved.

Now I asked eema several times about her role in the Resistance, but somehow, the answer kept circling back to abba—how he struck names off official records and ensured that Resistance members got what they needed from the warehouse named "Canada." Then at one point, eema lowers her head and when next she raises it, I see this determined look on her face. Seconds later, she leans forward, eyes me intently, and asks, "Miriam, know why I'm talking about Auschwitz today?"

"Something to do with the yarhzeit, eema?"

"Punct. Any of your interviewees mention a Roza?"

"Roza Robota?"

"Roza Robota, yes," she answers, her eyes lighting up.

"One did. She didn't go into details. But I know that Roza Robota was involved in the Revolt of the Sonderkommandos."

"Roza was a hero. So were they all. All the women. All the men. It was truly extraordinary—the Revolt of the Sonderkommandos, yes? But

Miriam," she adds, leaning forward, "it's important to remember: The women were pivotal."

"You involved, eema?"

Eema closes her eyes, steadies her shaking hands, then opens her eyes again. "I never talked about it. Partly because I didn't want to upstage abba, partly because it's scary. But yes."

"So, eema," I ask, my heart pounding, "what happened?"

"The Resistance was planning a large scale revolt. And at the centre of the revolt was the sonderkommandos. These tragic men who shoved their own people into the gas chambers and stuffed the corpses into the furnaces, they were actually going to rise up, yes? Blow up the crematoriums. The question is, with what? And that's where the women came in.

I was at Auschwitz One at the time. I was assigned to this factory called 'the Weichelsall Metall-Union Werke.' We made verzögerung there. That's delayed action fuses for bombs, yes? And what special ingredient is used in the making of verzögerung? Gunpowder. Punct. You see the point. The Nazis, of course, they watched us like hawks. And there were tight controls. Each worker was given a precise amount of gunpowder. They knew exactly how much gunpowder went into each fuse, and if at the end of the shift, the number of fuses and the remaining powder didn't tally, there was major trouble.

A few of us talked—Anna Heilman, Estusia Wacjblum, Rose Meth, Alla Gärtner, and me. And we decided that this would be our contribution to the Resistance. We would smuggle gunpowder from the factory and give it to the Sonderkommandos. We would approach Roza Robota, for she was strategically placed. She worked at the sorting warehouse attached to Crematorium IV, yes? But first we needed to figure out how to remove gunpowder without the missing powder being detected.

Meydeleh, it took us a few days to work out a plan, but it was brilliant. Whenever the powder is pressed down, there is abfall—overfill, waste. That's powder that falls out, is no longer good, and is supposed to be thrown away. Farshtey?"

"Yes."

"So we asked ourselves: What if the women working in the Powder Room occasionally filled the tiny cavity in the fuse with abfall while stealing an equal amount of good powder. The amounts would still tally, yes? And the Nazis would be none the wiser. We even devised a method for dumping the powder if the worker was about to be body-searched.

With an amount so miniscule, kinehora, it wasn't difficult. With great trepidation, we tested the plan. It worked. The next hurdle was finding enough women in the gunpowder room willing to take the risk. Also, we needed women to act as couriers. The crematorium, you see, was over in Auschwitz II. Anyway, right away Roza signed on, yes? So did a few of the women in the Powder Room. I helped Anna round up couriers and agreed to be one myself. Approaching women with such a proposition was no easy matter, of course. What if our assessment of a woman's loyalty was wrong and she set us up? What if we overestimated her strength and she broke down under torture?

Now the operation took a long time, for even on a good day, the most we could smuggle out was two teaspoons of gunpowder; and many is the time the fruits of our labour had to be dumped because of a body search. But we persisted. For eight long months, women hid gunpowder on their person; women passed gunpowder to other women, and Roza Robota passed the gunpowder on to this sonderkommando named 'Wrobel.' And on October 7 1944, the revolt happened. Explosives were set off in Crematorium IV. Gotenyu! They actually blew it up! Seeing the flames, the sonderkommandos in Crematorium II rose up and destroyed large parts of that crematorium as well. Not a bad job, all and all. The brave men paid with their lives. Vey iz mir, you know, they were all slated for extinction in the next few days, and they knew it. That's why they rose up on that particular day, earlier than the general revolt planned by Battle Group Auschwitz. They wanted to strike a blow, yes? To make their death count. And they succeeded. And the women had made it possible."

"Eema, I can't thank you enough for this," I uttered, deeply moved.

"It's vital. And for me personally, well, you have no idea how long I've waited to hear this. But let me ask you something. Any chance you were linked a bit more closely with the sonderkommandos?"

"A strange question, meydeleh," observed eema, her eyes widening.

"You see, I used to have a vision where you were smuggling something to this sonderkommando."

"How you could have known that, Miriam?" she asked, eyeing me curiously.

"Something Uncle said."

"That day on the lawn when you got sick?"

"Yeah."

Eema grimaced. "Ach!" she exclaimed. "Lest I forget, that man

235

abused two of my daughters—not one. Though there's no name for what happened to you."

"But eema, *did* you work more closely with them?"

"It was nothing, and far too much has been made of it."

"Be honest here. If it were some other person—any other person—would you still call it nothing?"

A smile of recognition comes across eema's face. She thinks for a few seconds, takes a couple more sips of tea, then nods. "After I was transferred out of Union Werke and was back again in Auschwitz II," she resumes, "I became backup for Roza, yes? At this point, I was delivering the gunpowder directly to Roza. If anything happened, if ever she was too sick, it was up to me to get the gunpowder to Wrobel. It didn't occur often," eema adds, taking a deep breath. "But I remember being petrified each and every time, for there were always a number of people milling about and vey iz mir! If someone should see! Now I was almost caught once, but I was lucky. A kapo is approaching, yes? And just in the nick of time, I dart behind this bin ... and ... and...."

Eema stares at the tape recorder, bites her lip, and begins wringing her hands.

"Eema," I say, "if you're starting to feel that old terror...."

"It's not that. It's that I haven't finished the story."

"Take all the time you need."

"I... I can't stand how it ends," stammers eema.

"If you want to stop...."

Eema shakes her head. "You have to understand, after the revolt," she continues, her voice getting ever so much thinner, "they started interrogating women, torturing women, for they knew that we were the only ones with access to gunpowder."

"Eema, were you...?"

"No, Miriam. Gotenyu! Everytime I heard a sound outside, I thought they were coming for me, but I was never picked up. But so many were, including Roza. The wait was terrible. What's happening to them?, I kept wondering. Eventually, they let everyone go, for they had no real evidence. Oy, sweetie," exclaims eema, tears beginning to stream down her face, "as long as I live, I'll never forget the sight of our Roza after they released her from Block 11—dozens of broken bones, her face smashed in, her body, one gigantic bruise. They had hit her, and hit her, and hit her, but God help us, we'd made our choices wisely, yes? She let on nothing, jeopardized none of us. Neither did Estusia or any of the other women. But eyes had seen things, yes? And ears had heard things. And it was only a matter of time.

Just before Christmas, the authorities came once again—this time for these three amazing women—my sisters in struggle, Roza Robota, Estusia Wajsblum, and Alla Gärtner, also, for poor Regina Saperstein, who had done nothing. And on January 6," murmurs eema, her voice barely audible, "they assembled all of the women prisoners together and forced us to watch this public execution in the name of the Führer, in the name of the German nation, in the name of the law. Did they manage to intimidate Roza? No. Not even then. Oy, Miriam, even as they placed the noose around her neck, a snarl on her mangled face, Roza looked around at her sisters and hissed out the single word 'revenge.' And then... and then...."

Eema is sobbing at this point. I turn off the machine, reach over, and hold her. I tell her how very fortunate I am to have such a brave soul for a mother. Then we just sit in silence, watching the yarhzeit flicker.

As time passes, the flame takes shape. I can see courageous women hiding something underneath their frocks. I see women exchanging looks and passing the powder. And eema is among them.

I have no question that eema derived something important from that interview. To this day, however, I can't really assess what it cost her. What I do know is that she wept for hours that night. I remember wondering if she was going to pull back, but she didn't. In fact, less than a week later she took the next major hurdle. What a surprise coming downstairs and finding eema stretched out on the sofa, a book about Heidegger in her hands!

"Eema, you're reading about Heidegger?" I asked in amazement.

"Uh huh. And writing about him."

"You all right?" I checked, noticing the tears in her eyes.

"Not sure. We'll just have to see. You know, meydeleh," she re-marked, peering up at me, "we were so excited when this radical new thinker became rector at Freiburg. And we waited with baited breath to find out what he would say in his incoming rectorate address. Know what he said?"

I shook my head.

"He pronounced academic freedom banished. Declared the Fuhrerprinzip the essence of the university."

"That what you writing about?"

"No. Trying to lay to rest that meshugahs about Heidegger being a Nazi for nine months only. If only! Why in '35 he was still proclaiming his absolute faith in Hitler. Such a shame, though, sweetie," she added, shaking her head sadly. "To think that but a few years earlier, he penned something as remarkable as *Being and Time*."

"*Being and Time*, it's the book you love the most, isn't it? It's not Shakespeare."

"That's the pity of it," sighed eema, sucking in her lips.

I know that eema wrote an article on Heidegger around that time, for the article appeared in *Mind and Society* about a year-and-a-half later. But she didn't mention Heidegger again. Clearly, it was not Heidegger but Holocaust denial that preoccupied her. Eager to aid the new generation of antifascists, she had her heart set on making her website a critical resource.

For the next year or so, eema and I continued working on our respective projects, me analyzing the interviews, eema adding to the website. Frequently, however, I would give eema a hand, for many a claim required extensive investigation. Take that macabre proposition that it would have taken sixty years to dispose of the six million because it takes six to eight hours to incinerate a corpse. Dealing with it meant obtaining detailed diagrams of every single one of the Auschwitz furnaces, spreading them out on the dining room table, and going though them bit by bit. "See. There's three muzzles on this furnace here," eema observed, her finger pointing to the diagram on the far left. "And the denial literature assumes one."

"Yes," I answered, "and given emaciated corpses, they could have easily squeezed in three bodies per muzzle." Then we both shook our heads, as if trying to dislodge some terrible image that had just been added to the portfolios of our minds.

Eema's health was not as good as I would have liked during this period. She often complained of pains, and she frequently went to the doctor, though she was uncharacteristically tight-lipped about what Dr. Epstein had to say. "Eema," I recall saying, "I'm really concerned."

Eema just shrugged her shoulders and answered, "It's okay, Miriam. I'm managing. You know who you really should be worrying about? Molka. Molka Plautsnicki. Oy! Always, that poor woman's coming down with one thing or the other."

It's hard to pinpoint when it first dawned on me that eema's spirit was again plummeting. Gotenyu! I don't think it was until eema started avoiding the Internet entirely, even neglecting her own website. But in retrospect, the signs were there earlier. The nightly screams increasing, the long days where eema pulled the covers over her head and didn't budge. But there came a time when I could no longer fool myself about eema. Actually, about either of us.

✡

"Gevalt!" eema was screaming. "Look at her face. They're smashing it! Killing her! Murderers!"

It was the fourth time that night, and I was exhausted, but eema's screech was so piercing, her words so urgent, I just had to try to help her calm down. I went to her room, gently woke her up, and tried to orient her. But a few orienting remarks did nothing. Over and over again, I had to repeat, "Eema, it's okay. It's me, Miriam. And we're at home on Lippincott."

And oy! When she finally did grasp where she was, she just looked at me sadly and muttered, "Is gut that you care. But maybe you should stay in bed, meydeleh? What's the point of interrupting your sleep to come to my aid? I'm going to end up back there regardless."

"Eema, is there no way to fight it?"

"Ach."

I was thrown by eema's response and too distraught to get back to sleep. So I sat down at my desk, and began re-coding interviews. For a while, the coding was going well. And then something shifted.

I was reading this account by a Russian woman—Milovna. I was particularly interested in this story, for Milovna was like eema and abba—one of those very few who survived more than a year in a death camp. I was coding this section on the crude lavatory, when the image came alive, and I saw her there:

There are deep lines under Milovna's eyes. Crouching on two trembling feet, she is perched precariously over the plank and is struggling with her clothes, trying to get everything out of the way. A woman in a uniform watches, a nasty grin on her face. Then she snickers, struts over, and kicks Milovna in the hip. Milovna groans and starts to slip into the reeking muck below. She recovers her balance just in the nick of time. Again comes a kick to the hip. And the poor woman loses her footing and begins to fall.

There's a bitter taste in my mouth. Ach! Not up to an image like this, I tell myself. I put down the transcript and pick up another. But, gotenyu! Something's wrong with the transcript. Where did that come from? How did shit get smeared all over it? Better clean it up. I go to the washroom and get a rag. I turn on the tap so that I can dampen it. But just look at this water! Brown, putrid, gurgling.

Can't be, I assure myself. Just tired, and the old noggin's playing tricks. Just need rest.

Ah, good, back in my room. Need to open the window. Need to get rid of that terrible stench. And sleep. Yes, Miriam. Close your eyes. Just close your eyes.

Nu? I must have fallen asleep, for day was dawning when the screaming awoke me. Ay! Fifth time tonight, I recall thinking. Don't have the strength, but poor eema, I just can't leave her like that. I start to pull off the blanket when the door opens and there is eema, her black nightgown on, her eyes flickering with worry. I can still hear the screaming. But strangely, eema's mouth is closed.

"Sweetie," she murmurs, sitting down next to me on the bed and stroking my hair, "it's okay. Everything's all right. Come now, Miriam. No more screaming. Just breathe."

I take a deep breath, and the screaming stops.

"It was *me?*" I ask, utterly astounded. "*I* was screaming?"

Eema nods. "Meydeleh, you're not being careful. Neither of us were. You've got to give it a break. Oy! I'm so frightened for you."

"Oh eema," I groan. "What have I done to us?"

"Not *us*, Miriam. *You.* I made my own choices, yes? I went too far too, but I've pulled back. You know, Miriam, I haven't touched the website for over six months."

"Didn't realize it had been that long. But eema, in that case, how come…"

"How come I'm sinking?"

"Well, something like that."

"Surely after all these interviews, you've begun to suspect. No survivor gets to cheat Auschwitz forever. But never mind about that now. I'm worried about you. There may be things that can't be helped; and clearly, we've hurt you, abba and me. But you don't have to be where I am. And I won't have it." Eema cushioned my face in her wrinkled hands, kissed both my cheeks, then looked at me tenderly. "Sweetie, take a break from the interviews, yes?" she asked. "A long long break. And do it now."

"Okay, eema. I'll take care of it."

"Promise?"

"Promise."

While it took me several months to stabilize, I was as good as my word. Within two weeks, I'd arranged for a six month leave. And I had brought in this assistant—Becky Shapiro—who'd be in charge of WATS during my absence and would shoulder part of the burden thereafter. Somehow, I'd lost sight of my own vulnerability, yes? And I had just received a rude awakening.

Now eema was clearly pleased by the difference that she saw in me. But did it stop her slide downward? No. Poor eema, she rarely came down for breakfast now. She just lay there in her bed, like a prisoner who'd lost her will and was putting in time.

I was hoping for some kind of good news. Epes. Even Sondra turning up to steal again was starting to look good. Anything that would rekindle eema's interest in life.

It was about a month or so after my leave ended. Eema had dragged herself out of bed early that morning and gone to the hospital to see Mrs. Plautsnicki. When I returned that night, I found eema sitting in the kitchen, her hands covering her head.

"Eema, it's bad, yes?" I asked.

Eema lowered her hands, peered up at me, and nodded. "Been there all day. And got to go back first thing tomorrow. Molka needs me."

"I don't have any classes tomorrow. Want me to come with you?"

Eema shook her head. "Thank you, but no, meydeleh. Better you shouldn't. Better it be just us survivors."

Next morning, I offered once again, then set off for the university. Just as soon as I arrived, I started in on my yearly progress report. A little after 3:00, Harry turned up at my office, that grim look of his on his face.

"Miriam, we'd better go. Something's happened."

"Mrs. Plautsnicki?"

"Yeah," he nodded. "Passed away a couple of hours ago. Eema, she was with her at the end and she's a bit unsteady."

Now Harry had grossly understated eema's reaction, no doubt to give me time to adjust. Why, eema could barely speak. She didn't recover in time for the funeral the next day. Though everyone expected eema to give some sort of address, she just sat on the bench, weeping. Nor did the following days bring any improvement.

For the next several months, eema spent more of the day upstairs than downstairs. She never came down for meals anymore. And aside from going to the doctor's, she seldom went out. I would make supper and take it up, imploring her to eat. And I would watch as she got thinner and thinner.

Eema's depression wasn't the only problem. Worse was the terror. The night fears continued to escalate. But daytime itself seemed to have lost its safety. We would be doing something innocuous like discussing finances when suddenly, her eyes would cloud over or startle, and I could tell she wasn't with me.

I remember, one evening, I'd carried up two plates of turkey and kasha so that we could eat together. As I entered the bedroom, she gave me that faint-hearted smile I'd come to expect, then took her plate and began picking away at the turkey. By sheer fluke, I gazed up at the ceiling and noticed that some of the white paint was peeling. Not two years ago, I'd paid a professional to paint it; and so I was irritated. "Look at the lousy job!" I exclaimed, pointing to the problem area.

Instantly, eema's eyes startled; and she visibly cringed. "I'll do better," she pleaded, shielding her bad shoulder with her other arm. "Please don't hit me."

Awful as such times were, they were not that much worse than what was happening routinely. Most of the time now, eema was precariously balanced between life in Toronto and life in Auschwitz, with Auschwitz progressively winning out. And insofar as she spoke at all, she would talk about the lager—but not like someone trying to bear witness, more like somebody who could think of nothing else. "It's six o'clock," she announced one evening. "Gevalt! You any idea what happens in the lager at 6:00?"

I was beginning to think she was fated to plod through her final years miserable and frightened. But one day a change happened—a truly incredible change. Somehow, and without our help, eema had come to a different place inside. And she was about to propel the entire family down a course that was to have a profound impact on each and every one of us.

It began simply enough. It was 7:00 a.m., Sunday, November 15, 1998. Though eema had been screaming a good part of the night, when I arrived in the kitchen, to my surprise, I found her standing next to the counter, dressed in her turquoise pants suit. Eggs and home fries were sizzling in the cast iron frying pan on the front left burner. The toast had just popped out of the toaster, and eema was picking it up and putting it on the table. Eema's eyes caught mine, and she smiled tenderly. I stared at her in disbelief. Did that woman look fantastic or what! Why I hadn't seen her this way for ages—her eyes clear, her muscles relaxed, a look of keen interest on her face.

Good old eema, I thought to myself. Who'd have thought it? Just when I was counting her out, she's bounced back, and everything's going to be okay.

"Sholem Aleykhem, meydeleh," she said cheerfully.

"Aleykhem Sholem," I responded. "Good to see you up, eema. And mazel tov."

Eema nodded, and the two of us set the table together, then sat down opposite each other. While eema's eyes flickered with fear now and again, she did indeed seem to be her old self. As we nashed, she talked about world events. She asked about Esther, Harry, and the kinderlekh. And she took a keen interest in Sammy and Sarrah, clearly registering what I was saying, albeit I had tried to talk to her about them a few weeks ago, and she'd taken in bupkes.

"So, they're still together, yes?"

"Uh huh."

"Such a mitzvah," exclaimed eema. "To find someone that loves her so. And such a sweet meydeleh too."

"You may have forgotten my mentioning it, but they announced the news about a month ago. Sammy's pregnant."

"Artificial insemination?" asked eema, an unmistakable twinkle in her eyes.

"Yes."

"Well, good for them. And how wonderful we're starting a whole new generation of Himmelfarbs. Abba would be so pleased. Why I can almost hear him saying it, yes? 'Is no posthumous victory for Hitler now.' Incidentally, where they living these days?"

"Moved in with Esther and Harry a few weeks ago. But as you can imagine, it's pretty tense. The thing is, they're making so little, and with a baby coming, they really need to save on the rent."

"Might be better off living here. And I know they'd prefer it. Even mentioned the idea to me about a year ago. But it's up to you, Miriam.

Totally up to you."

"Why me? Why not both of us?"

Eema hesitates for a few seconds as if unsure how to answer. Then she leans forward in her chair. "Actually, sheyneh punem," she finally responds, "that brings me to a larger question. I've made a decision, yes? A very important decision. And you and I, we need to schmooze."

"Nu? What's up?"

Eema reaches over and strokes my cheek. Then she purses her lips and looks at me intently, her eyes holding mine. "Miriam," continues eema, pacing her words slowly, "I've thought about it for many months now. And I know what I'm doing. Now I know you're going to be shocked, but there's no way around this."

"Eema, what is it?"

Eema pulls out a cigarette, lights it, and inhales deeply. "I want to die," she answers, exhaling the smoke ever so slowly. "And I want to die *now*."

## Chapter Nine

# Miriam, age 50

*It is mid-afternoon in the lager, and the air is rife with the stench of burning and decay. Her head bald, eyes dazed, hands trembling, a young girl in fatigues is standing out in the open, in the middle of a sea of mud. She appears to be about thirteen. She must have arrived fairly recently, for you can still see roundness, the bulging of the breasts, recognizable flesh tones. Again and again, her hands finger the top of her head, searching through that vulnerable baldness where the hair should have been. Shaking her head and gazing about frantically, she whimpers, "Mommy, where are you? Daddy, where? Manachem? Sweet Daniel? Lillian? Adonoi? Anybody?" Her hands pause for a second, and she remains perfectly still, though tears stream down her face. Could it be that she is expecting a reply? Does she not know that this land is outside God's dominion? Suddenly, a piercing cry issues from her lips. And her fingers digging into her skull, she begins to run toward the electrified fence up ahead.*

I need a moment of quiet here. Yes. And I need to be as clear as possible as I relay what unfolded on this day and the days immediately following, for I don't want to lose you. Am I forgetting that you may have different beliefs, different bottom lines, different commitments? Honestly not. Nor, for that matter, was the family itself of one mind. Nonetheless, I know that something beautiful transpired here. In this very house. Yes, this Holocaust-ridden house where the Himmelfarb family lived these many years.

I know as well that there are moments when well-worn rules and guidelines don't serve us. We desperately want them to, yes? And we turn to them just as we would turn to a trustworthy old friend. But we find ourselves strangely adrift.

Eema had just uttered words which I instinctively knew would be seared into my memory. And all the while she was looking me straight in the face like someone who knew exactly what she was about. What does a daughter do with words like that? With words uttered by a woman like that? What can she possibly say? Even if I objected on principle to people ending their lives—and I do not—surely eema had a right. At the same time, what a finality those words conveyed! Vey iz mir! If I acknowledged them even for a second, the world as I knew it, as the entire Himmelfarb-Cohan family knew it, would be changed forever. A spark would be snuffed out that neither Esther, nor I, nor Sammy, nor Channa, nor Niel, nor even eema herself could ever re-ignite.

For what seemed like an eternity, I sat at that kitchen table, my mouth open, unable to find words, unable even to find direction.

"Eema," I finally respond, my eyes moistening, "I'm scared."

"Me too, sweetie."

"You *are* saying what I think you're saying?"

"That I want to kill myself? Yes," asserts eema. "Oy, Miriam," she adds, reaching over and stroking my cheek, "knowing you as I do, I shudder to think what images must be chasing about in your head."

"Not something for you to worry about, mamenyu."

Eema reaches over and takes my hand; and for the next few minutes, we sit in silence. Then she lets go of it and once more regards me intently.

"Oh eema, I don't know what to say," I whisper.

"Sorry, meydeleh. It's terrible for you, I know. If I could spare you, I would, yes? But the thing is, no matter what I do, I'll be causing my kinderlekh pain."

"Please don't worry about that part. Now I know you've been in serious trouble for a long time," I begin cautiously. "And Gott knows, for ages now, I've been useless as a support. But there're people who understand Holocaust trauma far better than me. Would you consider letting me look for help? I don't mean the shrinks, of course. But there are feminists—feminist therapists."

"And I wish them well, yes?" answers eema calmly, "but please understand. I've thought about this carefully. And I'm not sad about what I'm planning. And I'm not looking for professional services. Miriam, I'm not wanting anyone to diagnose me, or empathize with me, or analyze me, or teach me the latest coping skills."

"And could you tell me, eema. What *are* you looking for?"

"Your blessing."

"You're asking me to bless a suicide?"

"I think of it as a deliverance, but essentially yes."

"Deliverance, I understand. Can I ask you something?"

"Of course, meydeleh."

"Let me just say first, I'd never stop you from killing yourself. Nor would I let anyone else interfere. And, kinehora, I'll be with you in those final moments, no matter what. But what if I can't bring myself to give my blessing? You able to manage?"

"Manage? For sure. I have pills and am hardly helpless. But you think I'd do that to my kinderlekh? Unless my daughters are truly okay with it, there's no way I'll proceed."

"So you need Esther's blessing too?"

Eema nodded. "And sweetie, don't misunderstand me," she added. "I don't want anyone to be untrue to themselves."

Eema reached for the butter. I passed it over, the toast as well, then asked, "eema, you be offended if I checked some stuff out?"

She shook her head, poured us both a cup coffee, and began sipping hers. Oy! And for the next hour or so, I kept looking for a way around this. I inquired about her health. And learning that she had breast cancer, I suggested a lumpectomy. Eema shook her head. I asked her if loneliness was getting to her. And discovering that it was, I suggested bringing more people to the house. Ignoring the various fallings-out, I even offered to create weekly gatherings for the campers. Still she shook her head, though this time, she groaned, "More reminders of the Holocaust, oy, Miriam, that's the last thing I need."

I was about to make yet another suggestion when I noticed the flicker of pain in her eyes and instead asked, "Eema, what's happened to you?"

"Your interviewees," she asks, reaching for a cigarette and lighting it, "they didn't talk about age?"

"Some."

"Sheyneh punem, you know what happens to memory as you grow old?"

"It falters?"

"That too," she answers, her eyes narrowing. "But there's something else, yes? Something terribly important. It becomes your dwelling place. Pleasant enough if your past is filled with happy memories. But look at *my* past! Look where I'm forced to go."

"So that's why you don't want to see other survivors. It'd just trap you further?"

Eema nods. "Miriam, you suggested seeing a professional."

"It's okay. You said no, and I respect that."

"No, no. Hear me out, because I don't want you to have regrets later. Did you know Molka saw one?"

"I didn't. No."

"Well, she did. Ida Schugarenski too. And though I'm sure everyone did their best, afterward their problems were greatly exacerbated. Gevalt! Terror and flashbacks like you wouldn't believe. And is it surprising? No. Think about it. What do therapists want of us? For us to face our experiences. What did Molka's therapist call it? Work through the trauma. Punct. But I tell you are surely as I am sitting in this chair, while this may work for all kinds of tsores, there are some things so horrid that they cannot be faced, cannot be worked through."

"The Nazis, they really did rob you of your life. We... we..." I stammered, tears flowing down my face, "we let you down. Not just Sondra. Esther and me too. It was up to us to...."

I stopped in mid sentence, shocked by what I was thinking. Picking up on my meaning, eema leaned forward in her chair, a look of deep compassion on her face. "Oy, meydeleh," she exclaimed, her eyes holding mine, "up to you to make up for what the Nazis did to us? That's what you were going to say, wasn't it?"

"Sounds stupid, doesn't it?"

Eema reached over and stroked my cheek. "Stupid or not, it's very sweet of you, yes?" she answered. "But it wasn't even vaguely possible. What's more, it wasn't your job. And I can't tell you how sorry I am for everything abba and I did to make you feel that it was."

"You did bupkes, eema."

"Bupkes? Hardly. Was it bupkes to yammer on about the Shoah day in, day out? Bupkes to make you feel you couldn't leave this house?"

"That was abba," I insist. "Not you."

"Come now, Miriam. We're both of us too old for this. The truth, that's all we really have time for now."

I take a deep breath, catch her eye, and nod. "You're right, of course. I *was* affected by things you said. By the meetings too. But you know, I do remember you trying to protect me."

"Oh, I'm not saying there was no difference. And yes, I tried to protect you. But the difference, it's not as big as you think. Look around, meydeleh. Is no abba here. Hasn't been for years, yes? Yet here you are."

"Ah, but that's my doing. My choice."

"You saying that this choice of yours had nothing to do with having a survivor for a mother?"

"How can I answer that? I stayed because I love you. And who's to say who I'd be even if I didn't have a survivor for a mother? But that hardly makes you responsible."

"Oy, I'm not saying I was a bad parent. Nor abba either. And I'm certainly not blaming us, kinehora. You injure people the way abba and I were injured, and you'd better believe that it will affect the next generation, yes? And the next. Now fortunately, Esther, she got some distance. Sondra too in her own way. But not you. Think I don't know how you ended up with so few friends? Why you and Lanie had no chance for a relationship?"

"You understood about Lanie?"

Eema nodded. "Miriam, think about what I'm saying, yes? If not now, after I'm gone. I love you and want you should have a fuller life."

"I will," I answered, "but please don't go to the grave lamenting my life. Now I'm not saying there's no problem. But as lives go, mine's hardly been shabby. Caring family. Meaningful work. Research that matters— almost all of which I owe to you, incidentally."

"Point taken," answered eema.

"And meshugah though it is, eema, how could I not want to make things up to you? It's been so hard, your life."

"Now who's lamenting needlessly?" she asks, her brow raising. "While some survivors never had much of a life after Auschwitz, abba and I did, yes? Naches like I can't tell you. But was it by working things through? No. Know what we did?"

"The two worlds," I hear myself murmur under my breath.

Eema looks at me inquisitively, her eyebrow arched. "Oy Gott, you know about this too! You do, don't you?"

"Sort of."

"Ach! It's as if you too have been living in the shadow of Auschwitz. The other kinderlekh also. Vey iz mir, Miriam, what a frightful legacy we've bequeathed to you!"

"You've bequeathed love, a sense of duty, a genuine comprehension of the world."

"*And* the Holocaust," she insists.

249

"*And* the Holocaust," I reiterate pointedly. "And for sure, I've been hurt by it. But you think for a second I regret being your daughter?"

Eema's face melts; and once again, she reaches over and strokes my cheek. Then, a single tear trickling down her face, she asks, "Sweetie, you mentioned two worlds. Clearly, you figured something out, yes? Saw how we got by. Tell me. What did you see?"

"A number of times I heard abba refer to two worlds—*Auschwitz* and *now*. And at times I could see them clearly—one stinking of mud and filled with starving people in rags, the other comprised of family, students, this house, abba's shop. And I could tell you were in trouble whenever those worlds collided."

"Sorry you had to experience that, sheyneh punem," said eema, a sad sort of smile on her face, "but essentially, you're right. For want of a better metaphor, it's as if we inhabit parallel universes, us survivors. And we need to keep them separate, yes? Dwell in Auschwitz for this moment, then put Auschwitz aside and dwell in Toronto. This is the routine, this the juggling act we had to master."

"And abba had a harder time. That's why he blew up when we left the lights on or forgot to pick stuff up."

Eema nods. "Of course not all survivors were as lucky as abba and me," she resumed. "Those who tried to banish Auschwitz altogether found Auschwitz assaulting them at every turn, yes? Those who got stuck in Auschwitz drowned. But those of us fortunate enough to be adept at juggling, we had a good life. And me, I surely did. But oy, how that's changed!"

Eema stubs her cigarette in the ashtray and begins massaging her sore shoulder. And it looks like she's going to say no more.

"Eema?" I ask.

"Is what age does," she explains, looking up at me again. "I can't juggle like I used to, can't distract myself for long. And so the stench of excrement in my nostrils, the sight of my dear Roza, her face mangled beyond description, once again this is my daily reality, yes? This the hell in which I find myself."

"Oh eema! So when I urge you to bear up, you must feel as if I'm condemning you to Auschwitz!"

"Well, I wouldn't quite put it that way. But when we get down to the nitty-gritty, does 'bearing up' mean bearing Auschwitz? Yes. And, of course, the first time round, there was reason to bear up, yes? England, Russia, the U.S. were doing battle with the Third Reich. There was hope of liberation. But now? Look at me, meydeleh. I'm eighty-five years old. There's no new life to look forward to. And there'll be no Allies landing."

I let myself stare at eema. I saw an old woman with white hair and wrinkles massaging a shoulder that was just barely functioning. Her skin was leathery and dotted with brown blotches. There were saggy folds under her eyes and scaly patches on her face, neck, and arms. I could still make out those facial expressions that I'd adored all my life—the ironic rise of her eyebrow, the tender smiles—but it was as if the aging skin was covering over this wonderful woman, was blurring those beloved features, was already taking her away.

'Eema," I finally murmur, my voice hushed, "I'm so sorry for continuing to put you through all this. And please don't take this as any kind of criticism of you, cause it honestly isn't. But there are survivors who go through old age without everything getting this bad."

"Is it worse for me than others? Maybe yes, maybe no. And if it is, perhaps it's because I spent an exceptionally long time in those hellholes. But remember, Miriam, many survivors kill themselves in old age. You were amazed when an optimist like Primo Levy killed himself, yes?"

"I remember."

"Well, Levy was hardly alone. In massive numbers, aging survivors kill themselves and for precisely the reasons I've described. We hide these acts, yes? Is like this secret that we don't want out. Who wants to admit that so very many survivors end their lives in despair? How undermining of current paradigms which construct everything as fixable! How inconvenient for those who see Jews as oppressors only! What a threat to Jews themselves—especially those frightened souls who hide everything that could be interpreted as Hitler achieving a posthumous victory! But hiding this terrible truth does not change it. And hiding it does not help those of us who are at the end of our rope."

I nodded. And we again fell silent. Eventually, eema began picking away at her food. I tried a mouthful of toast, a sliver of egg, but nothing tasted right. So I put aside my plate and kept eema company as she ate. Once she was done, I said that I needed time to think and assured her I'd get back to her as quickly as I could. Then as hard as it was to leave her, I kissed her on the forehead, and went upstairs.

I spent a good part of the morning on the orange chair in my study staring up at the ceiling replaying eema's words. After a while, without exactly knowing why, I found myself hearkening back to Mrs. Schugarenski's death, trying to piece together what my family said that day. I had wanted to pay my respects. And what had abba said? "Only the immediate family at the shiva." But, there was something before that as well. Or was it after? Abba had been evasive when I inquired what she'd died of. What had he answered? "Kinehora, she vas seventy-four years old. Is such a big mystery that a woman of seventy-four dies?" And eema, she'd said something that surprised me too. Something about letting things be. Like they were hiding something. Of course! That's what it was all about! Ida Schugarenski had killed herself just like Primo Levy and who knows how many other aging survivors throughout the world!

I left the study, went to the bedroom, and laid down, my running shoes still on. I closed my eyes, and at first, I went blank. But then this image of a havdalah candle slowly takes shape in my mind:

There is less than an inch of the candle left, and some of it has lost its shape, but oh, you can still make out its white braided form. It sputters from time to time but continues to burn, its light reaching out to embrace me. How precious these last moments and how hard to let go of Shabbes! Then I imagine a huge hand descending from on high, the thumb and index finger coming together as they approach the wick. Then the flame, it's out. Snuffed out, just like that, before its last sweet flicker has faded and Shabbes is over. And this wave of horror comes over me. And nu? Sure enough, I start to draw the inevitable comparison. After a few minutes, though, I stop. The hand that will be coming down on eema's flame is not someone else's but her own, I remember. And eema is not an inanimate object but a human being in agony, yes? And who's to say I wouldn't feel differently about the havdalah candle itself if I could hear its call. If I could enter more fully into its last melting moments? If I could reach into its heart and discover its pain?

Opening my eyes, I linger a while longer. Hearing eema in the living room about half an hour later, I take a deep breath, walk downstairs, and stand in the doorway watching her.

Eema is sitting on one of the beige chairs, the green family photo album in her hands, her head bent over it. The photo she's examining must be of Sondra, for she repeatedly murmurs, "Sondra, mayn kind." After a few minutes, a half smile appears on her face. Then, glimpsing me from the corner of her eye, she places the album on her lap and looks over, her eyes beckoning.

"Eema," I say, my voice steady, "you have my blessing. My blessing and my help."

Eema lost no time. By noon, she had phoned Esther, saying that she had something urgent to discuss. Esther hurried over. And for about twenty minutes, the two of them were closeted together in eema's bedroom. I was downstairs on the couch, worrying about how the tête-à-tête was going, but it was soon obvious.

"Just forget it," came Esther's voice, loud, desperate. Seconds later, a door slammed. There were footsteps on the stairs. Then Esther burst into the living room, her face white, her body stiff.

"Sorry to let you just walk into that," I said, eyeing Esther. "I'd have warned you, but eema really needed to break it to you herself."

Glancing at me from the corner of her eye, Esther plunked herself down on the lazyboy and folded her arms. Then she stared at me, her mouth open. "She says she wants to kill herself," she stated, her voice tense.

"I know."

"And when I asked her what you thought, she changed the topic a few times, but eventually, know what she said? That you're okay with this. Miriam, tell me eema's misunderstood you."

"Oh Esther, I know how awful this must sound to you, but I *am* okay with it."

"I was afraid of that."

"It isn't easy. Not for me either. Initially, I did try to talk eema out of it. But...."

"But what?" snaps Esther, her eyes flaring. "A clinically depressed woman says she wants to kill herself. Says she has a plan. Says she has means. And not only do you do nothing to get her to hospital, you tell her it's okay. Well, it's not okay. And I intend to hospitalize her whether you like it or not."

"I understand you being upset, but eema knows what she's doing. You don't approve? That's fine, and it's your right. And if you continue to disapprove, she won't proceed. But hospitalization? No way!"

"What's the point of talking to you?" she retorts, rising from her chair. "We've played it your way up till now and just look where we've ended up!" Then she heads out of the room.

I immediately get up. "Esther," I call out as she approaches the door. She turns around and looks at me, her body still tense but her face gentler.

"I love you, Esther, but this just isn't right."

"Be reasonable," she pleads. "This is an emergency."

"How? If you say no, she's not going to do anything."

"And you're prepared to take her word for that? The word of someone clinically depressed?"

"Esther, let's slow down, okay?"

Our eyes meet and Esther nods.

"You know that eema's opposed psychiatry all her life, yes? So it would mean imposing something alien on her. And you know how survivors react to hospitals. As for her going ahead without your blessing, do consider. She's depressed, yes. But this is eema we're talking about. You honestly think she'll break her word?"

Esther thinks for a moment, then shakes her head and lets out a huge sigh. Then, tears welling up in her eyes, she looks at me forlornly and whimpers, "I'm sorry, Miriam. No, she wouldn't go back on her word. And I know this isn't your fault."

"Sha. It's okay, sweetie," I assure her, going over and hugging her.

Esther cried for a few minutes. Then we both sat back down, and she cried some more. The tears clearly resolved something, for she visibly softened, and it wasn't long before she agreed to drop the whole issue of psychiatry. She's just gotten scared, she assured me. Esther urged me to consider other professional help, but she genuinely listened as I relayed what eema had said. We talked about survivors and old age. About Levy, about Mrs. Schugarenski. Inevitably, of course, we found ourselves speaking about Mrs. Plautsnicki.

"You know, I offered to accompany eema to hospital that last week of Mrs. Plautsnicki's life. Know what eema said?" I asked. "That it would be better if just survivors visit. Now at the time, I wasn't sure why she was restricting access, but I think I do now. My guess is that Mrs. Plautsnicki had become utterly desperate."

"You saying eema was protecting you?" Esther asks.

"Yeah, and I suspect protecting Mrs. Plautsnicki too."

"You think eema's trying to protect us now? Like she'd rather kill herself than have us see her in such a state?"

"Could well be a part of it. But believe me, it's not simply us. She's eighty-five and in agony. She's seen how bad it can get. And she doesn't want to hang in any longer. Can you blame her?"

Esther looks taken back. "Of course not," she utters. "For the love of Gott, Miriam, you think I'm heartless? It's just that I can't say it's right. Life's not ours to take. It's a gift from Adoshem."

"Ah, but you're a believer. Eema and I aren't."

"Come now, Meems. You may be an atheist, but I've watched you all my life. Shabbes after Shabbes. And I can tell you believe in holiness. You and eema both."

"In a way."

"So, is it holy to waste the last breath of life? To pit individual will against the ways of the universe?"

"We're different, Esther. For me, almost everything eema's ever done is holy. And, yes, I can find holiness here. In the love she's showing us, in the incredible care with which she approaches death. But do I understand that deliverance conflicts with your basic beliefs? Of course."

Esther's eyes widened. "You think it's just me and my beliefs? My *personal* beliefs? If only! What eema is contemplating violates Jewish law, violates halacha."

For the next few minutes Esther explained the significance of halacha to Jewish life, calling obeying the laws a mitzvah and suggesting that all real blessing begins here. When she finished, I let her know that I could see why she couldn't give her blessing.

"You've got me wrong," said Esther. "I wasn't saying no. I was telling you I *should* be saying no."

"You saying yes?" I asked, astonished.

"No. I'm saying, this is my mother. She's miserable. And I'll think about it. Just don't expect much."

"Esther, maybe the contradictions aren't as absolute as they seem. With halacha, there are exceptions, yes?"

"Sure, but the sanctity of life, now that's basic Judaism."

"Perhaps Harry knows something. He's the Judaic scholar."

Esther shook her head. "For the time being, this is between the three of us. He'd be just too shocked."

I was uneasy about holding out on Harry, but I wasn't about to push. And to be honest, I too had fallen into thinking about eema's deliverance as something between eema, Esther, and me. But it wasn't long before the penny dropped.

Mid-afternoon the following day eema was sitting up in bed clarifying everything to Esther and me. Seated on a chair to the side, Esther had just promised to consider the matter more carefully. Then she bent over, kissed eema on the cheek, and asked, "So, eema, let me be clear. You're going through with it if I give my blessing, but not otherwise."

"Not exactly," answered eema, her eyes narrowing.

"Now just hold on," Esther objected.

"Not to worry, meydeleh," eema assured her. "As I've said all along, I won't proceed without my daughters' blessings."

Now these words were virtually identical to the ones eema uttered earlier, yes? This time, though, the proverbial wool was out of my ears, and I was hearing them as if for the first time. "Eema, you're not saying what I think you're saying?" I ask.

Eema nods. "Punct. I mean *all* my daughters. What, Miriam, you think I'm going to kill myself without letting my first born have her say?"

While Esther looked pleased, I immediately thought of Sondra availing herself of this last opportunity to torment eema and started to say, "but." And then it sank in. Sondra is indeed eema's daughter. And this may well be the last chance eema will ever have to get her back. "Let's try to find her," I respond, catching eema's eye.

"Sheyneh punem, thank you," says eema, her eyes moist. "Now I'm not sure where to begin cause she didn't leave any contact information. I asked. But my poor bubeleh, she couldn't bring herself to give. She didn't feel safe, yes?"

I sat down and took out my pen. And for next half-hour, eema and I brainstormed places Sondra might be. We came up with names of soup kitchens, women's drop-ins, clinics. Esther said nothing the entire time. Just stared at the floor, now and again fumbling with the top buttons of her turquoise sweater. But as eema called out, "The Hassle-Free Clinic," Esther looked up. "Please stop," she urged, her face crinkling, her hands rising. "It's pointless."

I put down the pen and stare at her. "Esther, what?" I ask. "She's not...."

"Oh no!" wails eema.

"Oh eema, I'm sorry," says Esther. "You too, Miriam. I didn't mean to scare anybody. No, it's nothing like that. It's just that ... well, you're not going to find her that way. And, actually, I've a number."

For a second there, no one utters a word. Then her eyes brightening, eema asks, "Sheyneh punem, this number of yours, you think it's good?"

"Sure of it."

"You've been in touch with Sondra," I murmur.

Esther nods. "For some time now, but she asked me not to tell."

"Of course!" I exclaim. "That morning she reappeared, I asked you what you were doing here, and you said she'd called."

"Oh sheyneh punem," murmurs eema, looking at Esther imploringly, "that was just before abba died, yes?"

"Sorry, eema."

"Sondra wasn't at the funeral. Nor at the shiva. Did she know? Did she..."

"She couldn't come, eema," explains Esther, returning her look. "She just couldn't. You saw the state she was in. She was too angry. Too hurt. I don't know that she'll come now. But I'll ask."

"And just how long have you..." I begin to ask.

"Over twenty years," Esther answers.

"You kept eema and abba in the dark for twenty years!"

"Is okay, meydeleh," eema coos. "That my bubeleh wasn't totally alone, that my bubeleh had somebody, this is gut, yes?"

"Thank you, eema," Esther murmurs, gratitude beaming in her eyes. "You know, I never saw much of her, but she would call from time to time, often in a very sorry state. Anyway, we'd talk and it would seem to do her good. The time came when I truly valued our talks, when it was something I was doing for me, though, at first it was obligation, right? Well obligation and guilt. I mean, look at my life compared to hers. And Harry, after all, had been *her* boyfriend. Not that she was angry about that."

"You seem to be the one family member she doesn't hate," I observed.

"Actually, Miriam, it's not as bad as all that. She's not as angry as she used to be. And she's just fine with Harry. Now Harry, he helped her too. You know how Harry is. Cares for everyone, but especially family. And Sondra he's always felt this special responsibility for."

"Cause of that time on the living room couch?" asked eema.

Esther flinched but quickly recovered. "I guess," she answered. "Anyway, he would come to her aid whenever there was trouble. Give her money. Drive her to the hospital when she o-d'd. Mind you, that was a while back. She's been fine for a long time now."

I remember looking at Esther and feeling proud of her. Don't mistake me. I was very uneasy over her keeping eema and abba in the dark all that time. But I was moved by the kindness she'd shown Sondra, yes? And even more, I was struck by her inner strength. For over twenty years she'd pursued her own path, kept her own counsel. Clearly, there are sides to this woman I don't know, I realized.

Esther told us more about Sondra. About how she'd gotten her own apartment and had pulled her life together. Now while I was pleased, eema was positively ecstatic. I was delighted to see eema come alive like that. For a moment there, I even began thinking that this turn of events might pull eema out of that terrible state and she'd forget all about deliverance. But within an hour, you could see the old familiar signs. Could see Auschwitz in the terror that flickered in her eyes. Could hear Auschwitz in her cautious whisper, "Did anyone see you come in? The kapo, did she see?" Eema herself must have realized that she was losing touch, for just after making this inquiry, she shook her head, put her hand on Esther's shoulder, and announced, "kinderlekh, time for me to get some shut-eye. You'll forgive an old woman if her mind wanders and she needs to rest, yes?" Moments later, Esther and I left the room.

The next few days were difficult. Eema kept making a heroic effort during the day—getting up, having breakfast, even once venturing out to lunch with Sammy. But come night, she would inevitably start screaming. And it would literally take her hours to calm down.

Esther dropped by every single day to visit. And every time, she would be bearing little culinary gifts—her own special cherry strudel, large meat knishes, tanned perfectly and still warm from the oven; and eema would purse her lips and take a few bites, and exclaim, "Oy, Esther, such a mechayeh!"

And then she'd wait patiently. But the news was always the same. Sondra didn't want to get involved in any way. "Not any way," Esther emphasized, slowly shaking her head. And she herself was still unsure.

One day, Esther failed to put in her customary appearance. While eema said nothing about it, she stayed up especially late as if hoping that Esther would finally show. I remember wondering if Esther had decided she couldn't give her blessing and was now having trouble facing eema. As I awoke the next morning, I determined to check in if we hadn't heard from her by evening. It was unnecessary, however. Nu? No sooner had we sat down for breakfast, than Esther turned up. "Hey guys," she said, pulling up a seat at the kitchen table, "sorry about not visiting yesterday. An emergency with one of my clients." Minutes later she placed her elbows on the table and announced, "'Fraid I still haven't come to a decision. But I have news."

Eema's eyes lit up and she leaned forward.

"Sondra called late last night," Esther continued, looking straight at eema. "She'll meet with Miriam and me at 2:00 tomorrow."

Eema proceeded to ask a flurry of questions. But Esther had few answers. About the only thing she was able to clarify was that Sondra would come to the house but wouldn't actually meet with eema. Just Esther and me.

"Truthfully, Esther, you really think she's going to show?" I asked.

"Yes."

"Is gut," declared eema, her hand reaching for her heart.

✡

Eema slept little that night. Nonetheless, she looked strangely relaxed when she appeared for breakfast next morning. She was dressed in that sleeveless blue frock that she often wore when cleaning. I found my eyes drifting toward her tattoo. As usual, my vision blurred as I tried to take in the number, but I did notice the wrinkles in and about it.

We said little during breakfast. After breakfast, eema grabbed a broom from the cold room, and using her one good arm, started hobbling about the house sweeping. I joined in, even dusting the Uncle Nathaniel. And within hours, the place was spotless. A little after 1:30, as I was putting away the duster, eema reached over and put her hands on either side of my face. "Miriam," she murmured, staring lovingly into my eyes, "I'm going to my room now, yes? You don't have to worry. I'll stay put."

"Eema, I'll do my best," I promised.

"Just remember, bubeleh, what happens to me, that's not what's important. You'll let Sondra have space, yes?"

Eema kissed me on the forehead and headed upstairs. Minutes later, Esther arrived, bearing a huge bag of pumpernickel bagels fresh from Harbord Bakery. I put them in the kitchen and the two of us made ourselves comfortable in the living room, each taking one of the beige chairs. I must have been more nervous than I realized, for at one point, Esther said, "Take it easy, Miriam. She's just a person." Then she began talking about Sammy's pregnancy, I suspect to cut the tension. Time ticked on, but just as I was beginning to think that Sondra wasn't coming after all, the bell rang. I started to get up. "Let me," Esther urged, catching my eye and making her way to the door. I sat back down. Seconds later, I heard the door opening and loud voices in the hall. Is she drunk?, I suddenly found myself wondering. Now I was in for many surprises that day, but it all started here.

Esther reappeared with a dignified looking woman at her side. "Hi there, Miriam," said the woman, looking straight at me. "I apologize for being late. And sorry to be meeting you at such a difficult time."

"Hi yourself," I responded, "and thanks for coming. It can't have been easy."

As she sat down on the lazyboy, I took in the woman before me. She was decidedly not drunk. She did not appear to be in any trouble. She hadn't used the word "we" when referring to herself. She was polite. But what most surprised me, while years of drinking had taken their toll, she looked stunning, her figure slim, her eyes bright, her long gray hair freshly washed and smelling of lilac, her brown pants suit showing nary a wrinkle.

For a few seconds, no one spoke. "Sondra," I found myself asking, "can I get you something? Tea? Coffee? Epes?"

"Coffee, black."

"You, Esther?"

"Yes, coffee."

I got up, plugged in the kettle, and returned with three cups. Then I asked Sondra if she'd like me to say something about where we are and how we got there.

"No need," she answered. "Esther's filled me in. Now I'm sure everyone's wondering what I'm thinking of it all. And I wish I could be clear. But to tell you the truth, I'm not sure myself. When Esther called and told me, at first I was pissed. Not at the idea. I mean, having lived on the street for years, I've seen enough people do themselves in. I was pissed at being asked. I've calmed down since then, but do I understand why I'm being asked? Frankly, no. Now I don't want to be callous, but it's like I'm being dragged into somebody else's mess. Most of my life, I've not been a member of this family. What's changed?"

"Eema can't see her way clear to die unless all her daughters approve," I answered.

"But that's just it. I'm not her daughter anymore. Haven't been for ages."

"I understand, but you know, Sondra, in her eyes, you're her daughter. Her bubeleh. Always have been."

Sondra nodded, and for a split second her eyes teared. "Yeah, I've known that for some time. Haven't always been honest with myself about it, but I've known it. And in *your* eyes, Miriam?"

"I'm grateful you've come. And now that you're here, it seems only right, yes? But I can't pretend I've been open to you. It's rotten, I know, but I haven't been."

"I've sensed that," said Sondra, her body tensing. "And I don't mind telling you, it's hurt. You've seen me as nothing but a pain in the butt, haven't you?"

"I wish I could say you're wrong. But in all honesty, it's been as if you weren't my sister. Just this threat to eema. And I agree, that wasn't good, but there *was* a problem."

"And now?" asked Sondra.

"I'm not in the same place any more. But I still don't know who we are to each other. The only thing I'm sure of is we've got a family emergency on our hands. And, of course, I know you don't consider yourself family, and I respect that, but I'm hoping we can find a way to pull together. Epes."

"For eema's sake?"

"Yes, but...."

"But don't you see?" asks Sondra, her voice rising, her nostrils beginning to flare, "as always, this is about protecting eema. What about *my* feelings? Almost all my life, you reject me; and now, when eema needs something, you open the door. Correction: You let Esther open the door. Didn't fuckin' bother to do it yourself."

I glance at Esther. Esther looks confused. I find myself bristling even though I'm beginning to understand Sondra's anger. "I get your point," I answer, an edge in my voice. "But Sondra, eema always reached out to you. And you didn't just reject eema. You rejected me. And it's not like you were trying to be a member of this family."

"I was abused," objects Sondra.

"Absolutely. I'm not questioning that. But eema didn't abuse you. And I didn't abuse you. And when you did come back, what did you come for?"

"Go ahead, say it" she snaps, her face turning white. "You're obviously thinking it. Came to steal. Well, yes, Sondra the ganef came to steal. But I was desperate. Not that you would know anything about that. And anyway, as long as we're dredging up history, let's get it right. You rejected me decades earlier. Remember what you said that day I left? 'You do this, Sondra, and you're no sister of mine. I mean it, Sondra. Take one more step in this direction and I'm through with you.' Loud and clear you said it."

I look over at Esther. "Miriam, it is what you said," she points out. The words are familiar all right. But how horrid they sound now! "Sondra, I'm so sorry," I exclaim. "What I said was awful."

"Yup. And here you had everyone thinking you were the sensitive one. Go figure."

"It *was* awful," Esther acknowledges, turning to Sondra. "But hold on there. Miriam *is* sensitive. And don't forget what you were doing at the time. Systematically stealing and destroying eema's things. Declaring that you wouldn't save either eema or abba if the Nazis came. Denouncing both of them! Disowning both of them!"

"Damn it, I was a child, and I was hurting."

"So was Miriam," insists Esther. "And Miriam didn't just make up the bit about eema and abba being vulnerable. All our lives, they really have been vulnerable. You know that."

"And on top of being a survivor, abba had a bad heart," I add. "Gevalt! He almost died that night."

I instantly regret those words. I brace myself for Sondra's reaction, but she doesn't lash out. Nor does she fall apart. Covering her eyes, she goes quiet for a moment. Then she mutters, "I didn't know about the heart attack at the time. But later, yes. And yes, I acted badly. But abba had betrayed me."

"I know," I answer.

"And of course I knew eema and abba were vulnerable!" she continues, putting her hands down and looking at me again, "but don't you see? That was always the problem. Like they'd been through so much, anything that ever happened to me seemed unimportant. You understand that much, don't you, Miriam?"

I nod.

"My problems always seemed so puny by comparison. Barely worth mentioning, certainly nothing you'd feel right mentioning to a survivor."

"Even abuse," I murmur.

"Yeah," she answered. "But something I've come to over the years. Much as I've always blamed them, it's me. Fuck! *I* couldn't take my pain seriously because of theirs. Funny how furious I got with eema when she was the only person who actually did something to protect me. Not that I realized the abuse had anything to do with her kicking Yacov out. Thought it was all because of you. You know, cause of what happened that day on the lawn."

"At the time, me too."

Sondra sighed, then began talking about how her life had unfolded since that abrupt departure oh so many years ago, in the process, letting drop that she's been in touch with Uncle, whom she described as old, sick, and just out of jail. Now I was beginning to think we'd gotten through our impasse when suddenly, the focus shifted back to me.

"You know," she mused, "I was somewhat taken back when Esther reminded me that you were a child too. Which is surprising given that you were always such a baby. Ach!" she exclaimed, her nose crinkling up, "you've no idea how I've resented you."

"Because of Yacov and the history lessons?"

"Sure part of it. You know, the bugger only wanted me for my body. But you he wanted to talk to. Like, you he actually respected. To this day, I still remember the two of you, your heads together, huddled over the dining room table like I didn't exist. Shit! You know what he once called out in his sleep? I mean right after fucking me?"

I shake my head, dreading Sondra's next words.

"Hashem, help me get through to my favourite niece. Baruch Hashem, help me get through to Miriam."

"Sondra, I'm really sorry."

"And it's not just him," Sondra continues, a pained look on her face. "You any idea what it means always being the other daughter?"

"The 'other' daughter?"

"From the moment you were born, you were eema's favourite. You were the one she invented that idiotic story about, remember?"

"The story of my birth?"

"Precisely. And you were the one who was brilliant like her. Like two peas in a pod. How could I conceivably compete? How could either of us compete? Right, Esther?"

"It was different for me," Esther explains, returning her look. "Adoshem be praised, I always felt there was love enough to go around. But was Miriam eema's favourite? No question. And was I often clueless what the two of them were yammering on about? You bet. But then again, I was the youngest."

"Well, I was the oldest," asserts Sondra lighting a cigarette, "and frankly, I was displaced."

"The oldest often feels that way," observes Esther.

"Fuck!" exclaims Sondra, the cigarette dangling from her lips. "No more social work crap, *p-l-ease!*"

"Easy there, shvester. I'm not exactly disagreeing. There always was this special bond between Miriam and eema, and you couldn't help being aware of it."

"And getting hurt by it," adds Sondra.

"That's more you than me," Esther points out.

"There you go taking her side. As usual."

"I'm not taking anyone's side," Esther retorts, her face flushed. "And incidentally, in case no one's noticed, I've never once taken sides. All these years, I've kept everyone's confidences, sided with no one while the two of you fumed away at each other like a couple of farbisiners. So don't make me the bad guy here."

Sondra bit her lip. I could tell she regretted what she'd said to Esther, but she wasn't a woman given to apologies. I glanced at Esther. She didn't appear to need one.

"Sondra, I never realized how much my closeness with eema was affecting you," I say, facing Sondra again. "As I saw it, eema adored everyone. And the two of us just had this extra something because our minds worked similarly. Now Esther I worried about because the family banter kept going over her head. But did I worry about *you?* Honestly not."

"And why not?"

"You were older. And you always seemed so powerful."

"Bull! I didn't have any power."

"But you did, Sondra," Esther points out. "You'd order us about. Remember? Call the kids' meetings. Change the results of votes you didn't agree with."

"But that was nothing," protests Sondra. "I was the eldest, and some things were simply my responsibility." Sondra looks confused for a few seconds. Then she begins talking again about eema preferring me. "And no one likes feeling second best," she points out.

"Now this may surprise you," I say, "but I felt the same way. Abba preferred you, remember?"

"Dream on!" she exclaims, her nose crinkling.

"He did. You remember how he'd go on about you reminding him of bubbeh."

"Yeah, and you remember what happened with that? I was encouraged to comfort Yacov because I reminded everyone of bubbeh. I got boinked because I reminded everyone of bubbeh."

"I'm truly sorry about that, Sondra. But our history together didn't begin with the abuse. Remember how things were before? How abba always wanted you around? And it wasn't just abba. You were the popular one, the beautiful one, the one all the kids on the street adored. Me? I was the nerdy kid sister with the thick glasses who was always spaced out, always lost in the images in her head."

Sondra's eyes widen. And she nods.

"And you weren't exactly a welcoming sister," I continue.

"Actually, I have this vague recollection of liking you way back when."

"Me too. But things changed. It's like you became my personal tormenter. Calling me names, kicking me."

"What did I call you?"

"Baby. Nimrod. Public Enemy Number One."

Sondra nodded again. Then a broad grin broke out on her face. Esther's too. For a split second, I felt irritated—the way children do when they think no one's taking them seriously. Then I found myself smiling too. And the three of us began chortling.

We laughed for some time. Then realizing with a start that eema was trapped upstairs without food, I excused myself, went to the kitchen, made her a tuna sandwich, and brought it up. Eema asked how things were going, then said something about needing the music louder to ensure she didn't fall asleep and start screaming. So I turned the radio up, then returned to the kitchen and pulled together some food. And before long, the three of us are together again, plates with bagels, lox, and cream cheese before us.

For the next hour or so, we nash and continue schmoozing about our childhood, sometimes getting angry with each other, sometimes apologizing. Then slowly, the conversation shifts back to our adult lives.

"Miriam," Sondra points out, taking a puff of her cigarette, "You've been an adult most of your life. I was abused. And like, for years, you didn't exactly worry about it."

"Sorry. But remember, until you told us, I didn't know."

"Bullshit! If you didn't know," insists Sondra, looking at me accusatorily, "it's because you didn't want to know. Be real, Miriam. You telling me abuse never once dawned on you?"

"Obviously, it should have dawned on me. And I can't explain why it didn't. But it didn't."

"Damn it! This is my life. So don't fuck with me. I've misread plenty.

And as Esther over there keeps reminding me, projected plenty. And if it's just my craziness, I've got the balls to face that. But don't lie to me."

Precisely at that moment, Esther rose. I thought she wanted to be closer to Sondra, for she walked straight over to Sondra, leaned forward, and kissed her cheek. But then Esther turned, approached me, knelt on her knees, and looked into my eyes. "You've been doing fine, Miriam," she begins. "You and Sondra both. Far more open to each other than I thought either of you could be. Now this is important to Sondra. So please think about it, Meems," she urged, putting a hand on my shoulder. "You yourself told us how shocked you were at finding the basement door locked. When you thought back on it later, didn't you ever wonder why it was locked?"

I lowered my head and forced myself to think. I pushed past the fog, felt my way into the corners of memory. And there it was. I'd been cleaning the basement, yes? And for the umpteenth time it struck me as odd that Uncle would have given Hebrew lessons to Sondra of all people! Oy, and to use the basement of all places! And to lock it even! Could it have been abuse?, I asked myself. But I quickly dismissed the idea as farfetched when it was anything but. I really didn't want to know. Maybe because I'd been fond of Uncle. Maybe because I'd been furious with Sondra for such a very long time. "You're right," I acknowledge, tears trickling down my cheeks.

"Oh Miriam, thank you," murmured Sondra. "I needed to hear that." And for a moment there, Sondra's face softened.

For the next little while, we stuck to safe topics—Sammy's pregnancy, Esther's health. Then slowly, we began challenging each other again. Now I often found myself holding back, but there was one issue I just couldn't back away from—Sondra turning up again and again to steal.

At first, Sondra maintained that she only did it because she was destitute. But Esther pointed out that she and Harry always gave whenever Sondra asked. Then she insisted that she knew nothing about any of the thefts, claiming it was the personality Sarah that stole—not her. Now I had seen the multiplicity with my own eyes. Nonetheless, Sondra's story just didn't feel right.

"Come on, Sondra," I asked, looking straight at her, "you telling me you had absolutely no knowledge of stealing?"

"I'm multiple, for God's sake. I've far more control now, granted. But then? That's a whole different kettle of fish."

"So it was all Sarah," I stated, obvious incredulity in my voice. "None of it was ever Sondra."

"That's right," Sondra asserted, her eyes scrupulously avoiding mine.

"Sondra never knew a thing? And even if she did, she couldn't change a thing?"

Sondra eyes began flitting about the room as if searching for an escape route.

Esther lifted her hands up and looked at me pointedly. "Miriam, enough," she urged "If you knew anything about multiplicity…"

"No, no," cried Sondra, her eyes anguished but once again focused on me. "Miriam is right. Some of the time, I *did* know. And some of the time, it *was* me. I was angry and I wanted to hurt them. Both of them. Actually, you too, Miriam." And with this, she began to weep.

I walked over and put my hand on Sondra's shoulder. Remembering how Sondra shrank from eema every time eema reached out to her, I half expected Sondra to recoil. But she didn't. Sondra stopped crying after a few minutes. I returned to my seat. And none of us said a word until Sondra regained her composure, sat up, and asked with her customary edge, "So what the fuck we waiting for—the Moshiah?"

"Sondra, can I ask something?" I check.

"Like I could really stop you."

"There came a point when you knew you were hurting eema and that it was wrong?"

"In a way, I always knew."

"How come you continued?"

"Ach! You think that helped? The guiltier I felt, the more shit I gave everyone. That sound crazy to you, Miriam?"

"No. Just painful, yes?"

Tears again began streaming down Sondra's face. I remember staring at her and seeing a distraught child. "Sondra, you wouldn't by any chance want to change your mind and look in on eema?" I ask.

Sondra shook her head. "No, but I'd like to go the john. Think I can do that without disturbing her?"

"Yeah. Just go on up."

The second Sondra was out of the room, Esther and I took one look at each other and heaved a collective sigh of relief. You see, it had been a hard conversation, and we both figured we were now getting a break. But we were soon disabused of this illusion.

Sondra was gone longer than we expected. And somehow, Esther and I ended up discussing childhood sexual abuse. Now I don't recall how she got there, but at one point Esther said, "You and Harry have always been great friends, but you have been suspicious of him, haven't you?"

"Oh, Esther, it's nothing," I assured her. "Harry's wonderful. As abba used to say, an absolute mentsh."

"And?"

"And I have enormous respect for him. Surely you know that."

"Oh I know that all right," she answered, shaking her head. "Not that this mutual admiration society of yours hasn't been a problem too."

"Esther?" I asked.

"If he needs an opinion on something, guess who he goes to? Eema or you! Not me! Exactly the same with you. Who did you turn to when abba died? Harry. Why not me?"

While I relied on Esther far more than she realized, I could see what she meant, and I acknowledged that I tended to underestimate her. Now I was hoping we'd continue to focus on that. Inevitably, though, the conversation returned to my "suspicions."

"Please don't, Esther," I urged, as she pressed the topic again. "It's my meshugahs—nothing more."

"I know there's something. When the kinderlekh were young, whenever a crisis kept me here over night, know what you'd ask? 'Sure it's okay? I mean Harry being alone with the kinderlekh.' It's as if you didn't trust him with the kids."

"He's a wonderful father."

"Oh, I know that, and I know you know it. But something's always bothered you. Epes. And it's sexual, yes? I can feel it."

"Believe me, Esther," I said, eyeing her intently, "whatever you're picking up on, it's residue from the past. Nothing more. Nothing I believe in."

"It's that incident on the living room couch, isn't it?" she asked, pursing her lips.

"I won't lie to you. I think about it from time to time. But I know it's foolish of me. He was just a teenager. And what was it after all? Bupkes! Typical teenage behaviour!"

For some time now, Esther had been squirming in her seat. "Oy, what a hypocrite I am!" she suddenly exclaimed. "Adoshem, forgive me."

"Esther, what's wrong?"

"Here I am giving you a hard time! And what about me? I have this absolutely terrific partner. And yet this thing with Sondra, it's niggled away at me. Not because it's a big megileh, cause it isn't. But know something? Over twenty years we've been married, right? And not once has he been willing to talk about it. Now I'm sure there could be thousands of perfectly good explanations for this, but I keep asking myself: What could the man be so ashamed of that he can't even tell a wife who loves him?"

"Hold on there," comes a voice from the doorway. I look over and there is Sondra, once again looking composed.

Esther takes one look at Sondra and turns beet red. "Oy, Sondra!" she utters. "We shouldn't have been talking about this."

"Don't get your nickers in a knot on my account," Sondra responds, looking vaguely bemused. "I'm fine, though obviously, I need to clear this up."

"You were pretty shiker," notes Esther. "You remember very much of that night?"

Sondra comes in, sits back down, and tosses her hair back. "Well, enough to know it wasn't Harry."

"Just what are you saying?" asks Esther, her eyes widening.

"I was using sex to get at eema. Harry was just the means, right?"

"You *planned* it?"

"Sure did," Sondra answers leaning back in her chair and making this clicking sound with her tongue. "I intended to get us both blotto and grease the weasel in full view of everyone. Now Harry was all for smooching. What teenaged boy isn't? And we smooched. Even stroked each other. But he didn't go further. And every time I reached for his dick, he pulled away. *I* took my clothes off. *I* grabbed the bottle. *I* kept unbuttoning his shirt. *I* kept pulling him on top of me. Like the whole scene, it was something I engineered. The fact that it looked a whole lot worse than it was, hey, icing on the cake."

"But he was so shame-faced," I exclaim. "And what he said to eema and abba!"

"He'd been caught fooling around, and in a home where he was a guest. So of course he felt guilty! But that bubbehmeiseh about it all being his fault and him plying me with liquor? Pure fiction. Harry's attempt to take the heat off me, right?"

Esther sighed with relief.

"Hold on, guys," I urged, rising from my chair. "There's one more piece to this puzzle." In short order, I went upstairs, returned with Yacov's letter, and read aloud that postscript about Harry.

"That mamzer!" uttered Sondra, her face reddening.

"Sondra," I asked, catching her eye, "just what happened between the two of them?"

"Harry caught Yacov groping me in the basement of the temple."

"The basement of the what?" asked Esther.

"Temple. Chill, won't you? We only used it a couple of times, Esther."

"But it's a holy place!" Esther protested.

"Let's not worry about that right now," I urged, picking up on Sondra's exasperation. "Sondra, go on."

"Well, Harry really lit into Yacov. Told Yacov what he was doing was wrong. Said he was going to tell abba. Yacov wept. Pleaded with him not to. Said it was only a kiss and it wouldn't happen again. But nothing deterred Harry until I warned him that abba could have a heart attack. And with that, he agreed to hold his peace. But he told Yacov in no uncertain terms what he would do to him if he so much as touched me again."

Esther nodded, and a warm smile came across her face.

"And Yacov?" I asked. "How did he react to it all?"

"Remorseful at first, right? Even got down on his knees and asked Hashem for forgiveness."

"You said 'at first.'"

Sondra shrugged. "Within a few days the bugger was after me again. And a week hadn't passed before he accused me of balling Harry behind his back."

"So that's what's behind this idiotic postscript," I muttered.

I was relieved that the mystery was finally solved. However, as I told my sisters, I felt like an idiot for ever giving any credence to Uncle's words.

Now it was going on 5:00 at this point. And we clearly needed a break. Esther let out a huge yawn, got up, stomped the pins-and-needles out of her foot, then suggested we get some air. Sondra and I readily agreed. I went upstairs and told eema. Then we bundled up, Sondra putting on this long mauve coat with raglan sleeves I'd not seen before; and we stepped out.

What a relief to be out! No more chatter. Just taking in the beauty of the day. And it was beautiful. It was a brisk November afternoon. The wind was not the kind that whipped you raw. More the kind that teased you, whispering gently in your ear that the universe is alive. The light was already fading, yes?, but the darkness was soft, reassuring, the shadows, a place of rest. I enjoyed the feeling of motion as we stepped down the cement stairs at the front of the house. And I got this strange sense of déjà vu as we strode down the sidewalk three abreast, every so often making room for a passer-by, but always joining up with each other again.

I could tell that none of the neighbours recognized Sondra. Not even Katie Morrison, who came upon us on her way home from work. Smiling the second she spotted Esther, Katie stopped and exchanged a few words with Esther and me. How's our mother? Had we heard about Akimbola's new granddaughter? But she just gave Sondra this impersonal nod—the one people sometimes give strangers that they feel obliged to acknowledge but who mean nothing to them. And no one else so much as nodded at her. Not that there was more than a handful who had lived in the neighbourhood long enough to remember that there were once three sisters in the Himmelfarb house.

We didn't discuss where we were going. And I don't remember having any destination in mind. To this day, neither do either of my sisters. Yet I cannot help but feel that we walked in the one direction we needed to go. Onto the north side of Bloor. Then west on Bloor. Past Bathurst. Past Tasty's Restaurant. Until we found ourselves on the outskirts of Christie Pits.

While still on the sidewalk, we came upon a large rectangular sign with big letters which read "Discovery Walk." I nodded with approval as we approached the sign, but my eyes instinctively searched for a very different sign—a sign that demonstrably didn't exist. That never existed despite eema's and abba's lobbying. The one bearing witness to the Riot at Christie Pits—the largest riot in Toronto's history.* Then Sondra called out, "let's do it," and we stepped onto the grass and began the descent.

The park was deserted except for a lone runner in a blue-and-white track suit, his breath visible in the cold November air. The flowers were gone for the year. The trees looked strangely denuded. Red and gold leaves were scattered about, covering much of the grass, softening our steps. I looked far off in the distance and to the left and took in the green

---

*On August 13, 1933 anti-Semitic slogans were shouted and a swastika flag displayed at a baseball game at Christie Pits between a Jewish team and a Catholic team. A riot involving thousands ensued.*

roof of the pavilion. Not far from it, I made out the tip of the changing room. Then I cast my eyes to the right. And there it was—the playing field. And, vey iz mir! Despite the urgency of the current situation, images from yesteryear began flitting through my head: Youth on Camel's Hump unfurling a swastika flag. Spectators leaping to their feet screaming in unison, "Kill the Jews." But I'm forced to redirect my attention to my footing as the decline gets sharper and I feel my body propelled downward.

The three of us make our way down the slope with difficulty, me pausing after each step, Esther audibly panting and occasionally lunging, Sondra bending her knees to get a better grip. To think we were once young enough to bound down it! The steepness, it takes my breath away! Oy, if one of us should fall! But we keep our balance, kinehora. As we near the bottom, I once again think of the non-existent sign and realize with a certain sadness that eema won't live to see it materialize. Gotenyu! Perhaps me neither. Or Sammy. Or Sammy's unborn child.

As we near the pavilion, a very different image flashes through my mind—a picnic from decades ago. The red table cloths. The large spread of food—knishes, gefilte fish, hard boiled eggs, herring. Men at one table, women at the other.

Esther, Sondra, and I turn just in front of the pavilion and start bearing west again. We have trouble finding a table, for by this time of year, most have been removed. "Oy, my legs are giving out. Not as healthy as I used to be," Esther mutters, still out of breath from the descent. Sondra and I immediately slacken our pace and the three of us consider just sitting on the ground. Spotting a weathered green picnic table at the foot of an oak not ten yards away, however, Sondra points it out; and we trudge on. "Finally!" Esther exclaims, as we reach it. Esther places one hand on the table and pauses to catch her breath. Sondra and I immediately sit down, me on one side of the table, Sondra directly opposite. Now Esther is standing on Sondra's side, and so the most natural thing in the world would be for her to sit down beside Sondra, yes? But she doesn't. She walks around the table and plunks herself next to me, her legs folded in front of her, a puzzled look on her face. And for a moment, no one speaks.

"You thinking what I'm thinking?" I asked, my elbows on the table, my chin resting in my hands.

"About the time we had to choose between eema and abba?" asked Sondra.

"Uh huh."

"Yes."

We again fell silent. Now while I can't say with any certainty what Sondra and Esther were thinking, it was all coming back to me: Mrs. Weitzman saying to eema, "I swear you were one of the bravest women in all of Auschwitz II." Sondra, Esther, and I leaving and coming upon Harry seated on this small boulder, his hands in his jeans pocket, all the children scattered on the ground about him. Harry telling us that the Nazis are coming and that we have to give up one of our parents. Me taking Esther's hand, and the three of us walking away in a daze and sitting down at a table very like this one, Esther and I on one side, Sondra on the other. Then us struggling with each other, the weight of that awful decision on our shoulders.

"Do we dare talk about it?" asked Esther.

"Think we might have to," I answered. "You?"

"Uh huh."

"That makes three of us," concurs Sondra.

"Could someone else begin?" asks Esther.

Again, no one utters a word.

"Miriam?" asks Esther, looking at me imploringly.

"Okay," I offer, removing my elbows from the table and taking a deep breath. "Now the whole thing was ghoulish, of course. But we sincerely believed Harry's story, right?"

Sondra nodded.

"Insofar as I could follow it," Esther qualified.

"And none of us were exactly gung-ho over proceeding. I mean, who wants to betray a parent? Now, Esther, of course," I continued, turning to her, "you were too young to be responsible for anything."

"So it's me you're pissed at," concludes Sondra. "C'mon, Miriam, we've been through a lot together today. And I'm a tough old broad who can take it. Just spit it out."

"Well, yes, I *was* angry at you."

"Was? Didn't you stay angry?"

"Sure did. It's like I've been in this time warp. Not able to get distance."

"Welcome to the club." Sondra says, looking at me meaningfully.

"You too, Sondra?"

"Yeah, Miriam. So don't go all even-handed on us. Just tell us what it was like for you."

"Okay. I was appalled by Harry's directions, yes? And I came to the conclusion I couldn't conceivably go along. More than that. I shouldn't. I'd rather face losing both of them than betray either of them. And once we actually sat down and schmoozed about it, I told you as much. Told you over and over again, in fact. Kept saying, 'You don't choose between people—and certainly not eema and abba.' But damn it! As always, you didn't listen. You just kept pushing me. Remember? Insisting I had to choose. Insisting that I had to vote. Glaring at me. Telling me to stop being a baby, when you knew full well how name-calling undermined me. Quoting Harry's take on it as if it were gospel. And finally, I broke down. Did something I knew was wrong. Because of you, I betrayed abba. And yes, I've resented you for it all these years. A strong reaction I admit, but you've got to understand, Sondra, I felt like a traitor every time abba's heart twinges started up again. I'd even get these images of abba in a coffin bleeding, wailing that his daughter Miriam had done this to him."

"I didn't know," said Sondra. "Actually, never could understand about you and your images. Well, leastwise not until after the abuse. That's when I started dissociating, right? But by then, I was too fucking pissed to give a damn. Now as for that bit about forcing you to vote, let me tell you something," she continued, eyeing me intently. "I've been bitter about that too."

"I felt that, but why?"

"That little pisher over there," she answered, pointing at Esther, "she was too young. But you, I had a right to expect help from."

"Not sure I follow."

"Harry had been clear. We had to choose. And his rationale made sense. Like it seemed preposterous letting both eema and abba die when we could save one of them. As you describe it now, I can appreciate that there's another way of looking at it. But for me at the time, it was absolutely straight forward. As the eldest, it was my responsibility to ensure that we did what we had to. Now I looked to you to share the burden and the responsibility. Even recall thinking to myself: thank God one of them isn't a baby. But you didn't help. You kept refusing to budge the way you sometimes did, right? Forcing me to insult you. Forcing me to apply pressure. And by doing that, you made sure all the guilt fell on me."

"You felt forced?"

"I *was* fucking forced."

"Sondra, I understand that. Sort of. And I can understand why you felt the burden fell on you. But not the shtick about the guilt. How can you say it all fell on you when we both voted?"

"Hardly rocket science. By forcing me to pressure you, you ensured that I was the only one who voted freely. So ultimately, I was the one responsible."

"Come on, Sondra. I felt responsible too."

"Of course. But face it, Miriam. You could always say: I didn't mean it. My evil sister Sondra made me do it. But me, I had no way of wriggling out of it."

"I can see that," I responded, surprised by this new perspective. "But look at it this way. You could always say: 'I stuck to my guns and did the right thing.' But I knew full well I had betrayed abba, yes? And I'd done it for one reason and one reason only. When push came to shove, I didn't have what it takes to stand up to my older sister."

Sondra nodded and looked at me with a compassion I never imagined her capable of. Then the two of us continued to talk. Now I thought that the significance of her crush on Harry would be a major bone of contention, but no. I hadn't so much as raised it when she remarked, "Incidentally, sorry I was so gaga over Harry. If I hadn't been, who knows? Maybe I'd have seen things differently."

"Sondra," I said, "the way you just spit things like that out, it's gutsy."

Sondra grinned, but to my surprise, while Esther had seemed thrilled with our progress earlier, she was now looking irritated.

"How nice that the two you can come to such easy accommodation," Esther muttered, her voice dripping with sarcasm.

Not fully taking in the sarcasm, I turned to her and replied, "Didn't mean to leave you out. What about you? Which of us you angry with?"

"Who says I have to choose?" she objects, her face tense, her tone sharp.

"Sweetie, what is it?"

"For the love of Gott," Esther exclaims, glaring at me, then Sondra. "I was a mere toddler. Barely able to see over the top of the table. You were my sisters! My older sisters! What could you conceivably be thinking of?"

Sondra startles, opens her mouth as if to say something, then closes it again.

"Aren't you going to say anything?" asks Esther.

"As we saw it, it was an emergency," Sondra points out. "Just what did you expect us to do?"

"Protect me from your meshugahs—that's what!"

"But we didn't know it was meshugahs," protests Sondra. "We really believed the Nazis were coming."

"How could you not have known?"

"Shit!" mutters Sondra, her face reddening.

"Esther," I suggest, "maybe it would help if you told us what you remember."

Esther takes a deep breath and places her elbows on the table. "Okay. I was at this picnic eating these yummy blintzes, right? Then, Miriam, you take my hand and drag me off somewhere. For years, I thought it was to a completely different park, but obviously not. Anyway, next thing I know Harry is demanding that we hand over one of our parents. Then you hold some kind of vote. Now I largely ignore it, cause I know voting's mostly an older kid thing. But all of a sudden, Miriam, you're looking down at me, asking me who to keep—abba or eema. Then you ask me if I understand what's going on. Now I said yes, cause who wants to always be the stupid one? But all I really understood is the bogeyman was after our parents and only one parent could be spared. Then you looked in my eyes and assured me that I didn't have to vote if I didn't want to. Remember, Meems?"

"Yeah, Es."

"I figured that was just the kind of thing older people say. So I voted. And for months, I kept worrying the bogeyman was coming for abba."

"I never checked in with you afterward, did I?"

Esther shakes her head.

"My mistake. But I do remember keeping an eye on you the next few days and you seemed just fine."

"The story of my life!" says Esther, her hands raised. "I've always seemed 'just fine.' Not like the two of you. Clearly in trouble. Clearly traumatized. Well, I admit it. Shoot me! I've had a comparatively easy life. Great kids, wonderful husband, the whole shtick. But I haven't always been fine. And incidentally, having sisters who've never had a decent word for each other hasn't exactly helped."

Esther proceeded to talk about the difficulty of her position—being the youngest, being the only truly religious one, getting caught between Sondra and me. While we often agreed with her, at one point Sondra rolled her eyes and exclaimed, "Give me a break! You saying you never got just a little enjoyment out of being the only one in everyone's good books?" Esther blushed, then focused back on the vote.

"Esther, can I clarify something?" I asked.

"Sure."

"Just why did you vote after I said it was okay if you didn't?"

"You wanted me to. I could tell."

"And that's really why?"

"Of course, Meems. I loved you," she responded, her face softening. "You were the one who looked out for me. If you needed me to do something, how could I say no?"

"I see."

Esther leaned forward and folded her arms. "Okay now," she said, "that explains me. But what about you guys? Why did you drag a little one into this meshugahs? I mean you were my older sisters, and you were supposed to protect me."

"Esther, no question, you were very young," I reply. "And no question, you shouldn't have been dragged into it. But don't forget. We were just kids ourselves. Me, nine, Sondra, ten. And we were born into a very particular community. A community whose hearts and minds were shaped by a very particular horror. It was all around us. It was there in the silence of the night. There in the table talk. There in abba's sighs. There in eema's screams. Is it so surprising that it crept into the fantasies of little children?"

Esther nods. "Funny, I never exactly thought of either of you as being little," she muses. "But, of course, you were. Tell me something. How come I never thought the Nazis were coming when you farshtopterkops were always so sure?"

"Don't know. Maybe because you were younger when Harry told that story. Or maybe you just responded differently to eema and abba. How *did* you cope when you heard them screaming at night?"

"I remember hearing them now and then and getting upset and all, but I just told myself that if I was extra nice, everything'd be okay."

"You heard them *now and then*!" says Sondra, her jaw dropping. "You gotta be kidding! They screamed almost every night."

At this, an image of Esther fast asleep in the next bed flashes through my mind. Oh yeah!" I exclaimed. "You're the heavy sleeper. You slept through it all. But your dreams, it must have entered them."

"I guess."

"You did have nightmares, yes?"

"Sure, but not a regular basis. And not about eema and abba."

"Just what did you dream about?"

"You guys. Forcing me to hide under the stairs. Now I never did hide, I know. But how you pestered me about it! And I'd always been scared of dark places, and I was afraid that some day…"

"Sorry, Esther," I respond.

"You know, Miriam," she observes, "you haven't exactly answered my question. That vote, just why did you drag me into it?"

"Sondra voted to save eema, remember?"

"Yes."

"Then I did too. That made it two-to-nothing for eema. Which meant abba was a goner, yes? Now I was horrified I'd betrayed abba. And I didn't know what to do. And that's when it dawned on me. What if I insisted you be allowed to vote? And what if I stipulated that the vote be unanimous? You see, if you voted for abba, then…"

"But Miriam," says Esther, her eyes narrowing, "you couldn't have honestly believed I'd choose my father over my mother. What kid would?"

"Hold your horses," pipes up Sondra, unexpectedly coming to my aid. "Who's to say what was in Miriam's mind?"

"No, Sondra," I answer, "she's right. Somewhere down deep I had to know that she wouldn't vote for abba. So just why would I involve her?"

Sondra pulls out a cigarette and pops it into her mouth. "Simple," she answers, lighting it. "Because it meant less responsibility falling on you."

"Yes, of course!"

"But it wasn't just Miriam, was it?" asks Esther looking straight at Sondra.

"Oh no you don't, Esther Himmelfarb-Cohan," Sondra objects. "Forcing a little squirt to vote wasn't my idea."

"But you figured it out too quickly," ´Esther points out.

"What the fuck you mean by that?"

"Miriam's real motive, you knew it. Knew it instantly."

Sondra's nostrils start to flare like she's about to lash out.

"Sondra, let's try to do this," I urge. "Just think back. You always took charge of the voting. Remember?"

"Well, I was the oldest."

"Punct. And as the oldest, how often did you reopen any matter you considered decided?"

Sondra mulls the question over for a few minutes. "Almost never," she finally answers, shaking her head. "You're right. While involving Esther didn't occur to me, once you suggested it, I sort of jumped at it."

"Cause it meant divvying up the responsibility one more way?"

"Yeah. Who'd have thunk it? Fuck a duck!"

Esther looked relieved at this point. And it occurred to me that we might be able to start talking about eema. But then Esther asked, "While we're on the topic of the Nazis coming, maybe you can clear up something else that's always confused me. Miriam, how come you continued hiding after Sondra stopped?"

Sondra eyes opened wide. "Miriam, I... I..." she stammered.

"It's okay, Sondra," I assured her. "I know."

"And you're not pissed?"

"Not any more."

"I don't know what to say."

"Somebody enlighten me," urged Esther.

"The story about the Nazis coming," began Sondra, looking shamefaced, "about a year later, Harry told me he discovered it was bogus. I was supposed to tell Miriam. But I didn't. Like purposively didn't."

Esther turned pale. "But Miriam was always so vulnerable when it came to anything to do with the Holocaust," she murmured. "And that means..."

Not wanting us to get scuttled here, I caught Sondra's eye and stated firmly, "It's over. We've all made mistakes." For a second there, Sondra just shook her head. But gradually, her demeanor changed, and she began to smile. Esther clearly settled something inside herself as well, for before long, the frown disappeared from her face, and the three of us were sitting there enjoying each other and the silence.

I must have sat for a good twenty minutes just breathing in the old familiar scent of Sondra's perfume. Then I began gazing about. How dark it had become! Couldn't even make out the pavilion now. Just the odd shadowy figure, the sense of motion, and the suggestion of trees. Then gradually, my eyes closed, and I found myself marveling first at us, then at eema.

Quite something she's cooked up, I mused. All three daughters called upon to bless this deliverance. But the daughters are divided. How can they possibly do what she's asked? Obviously, they can't unless they first come to terms with each other. All of our lives, eema's given to us. And this, this is her parting gift.

I opened my eyes to find Sondra staring at me curiously.

"Miriam, I'm ready to talk about eema now."

"Esther, you?" I asked.

"Yup."

I took a deep breath and braced myself for an even harder conversation. But it soon became clear I'd misjudged. And in short order one more daughter declared her position. I remember.

Finding it difficult to keep sitting on the hard cold wood, Esther had had gotten up and stood just in front of the table, her right foot pressed firmly against the edge of the bench. And we'd all begun commenting on the parallels between this decision and that infamous vote. "But this time," said Sondra, "let's make damn sure that no one's pressured."

"Meems, you really going to be okay no matter what?" asked Esther.

"Really am."

"Well, I've given it a lot of thought. And it was touch-and-go for awhile. But eema, she has my blessing."

"You found a halachic ruling?" I ask, surprised by this abrupt shift.

"Nothing that helps," says Esther. "It really is forbidden."

"So Esther, how…?"

"Can't put my finger on it, but, epes, it started to feel right. And if there aren't responsas on the unique position of aging survivors, well maybe there should be."

"And Adoshem?"

Esther shook her head. "That's the point," she answered. "I just can't believe Adoshem sits in judgment over survivors easing their pain."

"You sure about this, Es?" I ask, gazing up into her eyes.

"No. But know something, Meems? Sitting with it all this time, that's what I've come to realize. Making this choice means taking a leap beyond what I'm sure of. And I've made it."

I nod. Esther sits back down. And we find ourselves turning to Sondra.

"'Fraid I'm going to have to disappoint you chickadees once again," says Sondra. And with this, she begins explaining why she can't give her blessing. She says its none of her business. That she's not really a member of the family. Then she trots out the Shakespeare quote, "the readiness is all," and suggests that eema probably isn't ready. I can see the desperation in Sondra's body. The raised shoulders. The hurried speech, the darting looks. Catching her eye, I murmur, "Sondra. Not being a member of the family, eema's readiness—that's not what's really bothering you, is it?"

Her eyes filling with tears, Sondra lets out this high-pitched howl and shakes her head. "Miriam, I'm not ready for her to die," she whimpers. "I've been robbed—robbed of a life with eema. And those years, I fuckin' want them back."

I rise from the table, walk around, and sit next to Sondra. "Sondra," I say, my voice hushed, "we can't get back those years. But maybe you'd like to see eema now?"

Sondra looks up and nods. Esther suggests we go now. And the three of us rise and start making our way though the darkness.

✡

The music was blaring as we stepped into the house. Esther and I immediately unzipped our jackets, but Sondra just stood there, her face pale. Esther put her hand on Sondra's shoulder. Next thing I knew, I could feel something rushing past me. Then Sondra was half way up the stairs, calling out, "Eema, eema."

Esther and I stood in the hallway frozen to the spot as Sondra disappeared from view. Seconds later, we heard eema yell out, "Mayn kind." Then we could hear sobs over the music. And then the music was gone. And the sound of weeping filled the house.

Not picking up any sign of trouble, we exchanged looks and went to the kitchen and waited. At first, we kept glancing nervously at the ceiling. So transfixed that we couldn't even bring ourselves to answer the phone despite its ringing repeatedly. But eventually we settled down, made coffee, retired to the living room couch, and began schmoozing about how we'd manage if Sondra couldn't bring herself to let eema go.

We both agreed straight off that eema shouldn't ever be alone in the house. And we quickly dismissed the idea of outside help. Esther offered to cut back her hours at JFS so that she could be around more. And she suggested that Harry, Sammy, Channa, and Niel do some sleepovers. "Meems," she pointed out, "you need a good night sleep once in a while, no?" Now I knew that eema wouldn't want her grandchildren hearing her screams. And I was just beginning to explain the dilemma when we heard eema calling.

"Eema?" I answered.

"The two of you, you'll come up now, yes?"

We arrived to find eema in bed, propped up on her pillow, Sondra on the blue chair next to her. Sondra's eyes were red and puffy, but there was a kind of serenity in her face. Eema looked exhausted, but she was beaming. She was at the edge of the bed, about as close as she could get to Sondra, and she was holding Sondra's hand, squeezing so firmly that her knuckles were standing out.

"Sheyneh punems," exclaimed eema, "this is a mechayeh, yes? Your sister here like this!"

Esther and I sat down, Esther on eema's other side, me at the foot of the bed. And before long, we were reminiscing about the early days. About how we'd all pile into the battered-up chevy and head for the movies. About how us kids would hunt for the afikomen at Pesach, abba rapping our knuckles the moment our fingers neared it, eema sneaking it to us, a conspiratorial smile on her face. Then a sadness came over Sondra and she began talking about how much she'd missed us.

"You know," she observed, shaking her head, "there were times I was on the verge of coming over. I mean for a real visit. Even had my coat on, right? But I just couldn't. Too ashamed."

"Gotenyu!" exclaimed eema.

With eema's urging, Sondra began telling us more about her life without us. I could see there was a genuine life here—one with its own dignity and depth. She spoke of running a paper supply business, of looking out for her friends, of getting involved in a sex trade workers' union and doing this action where they actually locked out the brothel owners, forcing them to bargain in good faith.

"But you always seemed in such difficulty!" exclaimed Esther, obviously surprised by what she was hearing.

"At times I was," Sondra clarified, "especially during my days on the street. And I guess that's when I would show up. Like the time I started shooting up again. That was just after Sperm-Whale started forcing himself on me, right? Now, there was a real piece of work. Liked to really hurt girls, if you know what I mean."

"I remember your talking about that guy," Esther said. "He was a pimp, right?"

"A cop."

Esther's eyes widened. "You never told me that. And you didn't charge the chazer?"

"You got to be kidding! When it comes to Toronto's finest, you think a sex trade worker has a chance? And I'll tell you, I wasn't alone. The s.o.b. took whoever he wanted. Try to make a stink about it. And guess what! Bingo! Just like that you're charged with communicating."

"Is a terrible thing," uttered eema. "The women, Sondra," she asked, her eye brow raising, "they're organizing now, yes?"

Now I figured Sondra and eema hadn't discussed the one issue that had brought us together. And, nu? I wasn't about to ask. About an hour into the conversation, however, Sondra looked intently at Esther and me. "Miriam, Esther," she said, "thanks for helping me get eema back. And the shortness of the time, I can handle it. Really."

"The shortness of the time?" I asked, looking at Sondra, then eema. "Sheyneh punem, Sondra's given her blessing," eema explained. "But why don't I let Sondra tell you about it?" Then she maneuvered herself out of bed and headed for the washroom.

"You saw your way clear, Sondra?" I asked, truly surprised.

Sondra nodded. "Something about being in this room and remembering that screaming. Like, I'm not about to cause eema any more pain. Anyway, it's like you said. Those years, I can't exactly bring them back."

"You've just found eema again. How you going to manage?"

"Don't know, but at least it's not going to happen today. You know what eema's talking about? Holding off one more week. To give us a bit of time, you know."

"It's not a lot of time," observed Esther sadly.

"No," agreed Sondra. "But I'm a pragmatist, right? And it's a week I didn't have a few hours ago."

I started to feel this pressure building up in my chest. I glanced at Esther. She was pale. So she's struck by it too, I realized. Before, eema's death was pure conjecture. But now, not only are all the daughters onside, there's a time line. An actual time line. The end of eema, it exists as a temporal phenomenon. Something toward which we're moving step by step.

I was struggling with the enormity of this shift when eema hobbled back into the room. "Sondra's been explaining, yes?" she asked, repositioning the pillows, then sitting down on the bed.

"Yeah, eema," I answer.

"A week, would it work for you, Miriam?"

"We'll make it work."

"And you, Esther?"

"Yes."

"It's okay that you're upset, sweetie," says eema, focusing in on me. Then her eyes scrunch up, and she lets out this huge yawn.

Remembering that she barely slept last night, I suggest calling it a day.

Eema shakes her head. "Miriam, okay if Sondra comes by every day from now on?"

"Of course."

"Punct. So that's what we'll do. Spend time with each other. Give each other what support we can, yes?"

"Absolutely," I answer.

Eema leans forward and looks at us intently. "Now listen to me, my meydelehs," she continues. "There's a few more things the four of us need to get clear on."

"We're listening, mamenyu," says Esther, her eyes riveted on eema. "Well, first of all...."

Eema doesn't so much as finish this sentence when the door bell rings. And not just once. Repeatedly, and in rapid succession. Like we're being summoned.

Reminded that there is a world around us, we look at each other nervously and freeze, almost as if we expected a cop to barge in and charge us with conspiracy to commit matricide.

"Vey iz mir! Who would just turn up at such an hour? And without even calling?" eema eventually asks.

Vaguely recollecting that the phone was ringing earlier, I get up, intending to rush downstairs, but I'm not half way across the floor when there are sounds on the stairs. Then the bedroom door swings open. And in walks Harry, his black leather coat on, his yarmulke askew, a key in his hand, his face flushed.

"What in the name of Gott's going on here?" he exclaims, looking at one of us, then another.

"Oh, Harry, I'm so sorry," murmurs Esther.

"You any idea what I've been through," asks Harry, angrier than I've ever seen him. "Six different times I called. Six," he reiterates, raising six fingers in the air. "And did anyone answer? No. Then like a dumkopf, out I go into the cold looking for you. I think to myself: Harry, maybe they've gone for a walk and run into trouble. Maybe they've taken the car and been in an accident like abba, Adoshem forbid. I even think of dialing the hospitals to see if something's happened to eema. And...and...Sondra, you're here?" asks Harry incredulously, as if just registering the novelty of her presence.

"Yes, Harry."

"Happy to see the family together, of course," he continues, "but now I'm really worried."

"Esther, what is all this?" he asks, facing Esther once again. "For almost a week now, you're here most every day. Then today you say you're going to eema's for a couple of hours. And over eight hours pass. And you don't even answer the phone."

Esther apologized and instantly launched into an explanation. Harry stood there listening, his legs slightly apart, his hands in his coat pocket. His eyes widened as he learned of eema's plan. "Eema, you're actually going to kill yourself?" he asked, turning toward her, his lips quivering.

"Mayn yingele, what a horrid way for you to find out!"

"And you were gonna go through with it without saying anything to me? I'd just wake one morning, and you'd be gone?"

"No, Hershel," said eema, her tone gentle. "I'd never do anything like that to you. Promise. You'll listen to Esther now, yes?"

Harry calmed himself, turned to Esther, and nodded sadly as she continued her explanation. He sighed when he heard that Esther had given her blessing. And he glanced at eema uneasily from the corner of his eye when Esther brought up the time line. But he didn't interrupt.

"And I didn't want to say anything until we were sure," added Esther, walking over and squeezing his hand. "I was worried you wouldn't understand. Also, that it would bring up stuff for you. You know, Harry. Like around Bubbeh and Zeda Cohan."

Harry pulled his hand away, looked at Esther, and shook his head. "Look. I need to know when something's up," he pointed out. "And while I've always understood about the daughters' wishes counting more, I have a right to an opinion too. What did you think? That you could just work around me and everything would be okay? And Esther, I'm your husband. I would have thought...."

Esther blushed and lowered her head. Then Harry walked over and sat down on the bed beside eema and looked into her eyes. "Eema," he murmured, his voice gentle, his eyes pleading, "I love you like you were my own mother. My very own eema. And I've been a member of this family for a long time. If I've made some mistake I don't know about, if I've been insensitive..."

"Oy, my Hershel! A better son-in-law, who could ask for?"

"Or a better husband," adds Esther.

"I love you too," says eema, gently stroking his hand. "So does everyone. And yes, we should have said epes. Quite a family you married into, Hershel," she adds, her eyes connecting with his. "Us women, we have a terrible habit of leaving you out, don't we?"

"You've got to understand. The women of this family, you're my life."

"You think we don't know that?"

"Oh eema, I really don't want to lose you," he murmurs, tears rolling down his face.

Eema smiles warmly at Harry, removes his glasses, wipes away his tears, then kisses his moist cheek. "The rest of you, go now," she urges, carefully positioning his glasses back on his face. "Mayn yingele, I need time alone with mayn yingele."

Esther caught Harry's eye and nodded. And without another word, the three of us headed downstairs. Sondra took off home only minutes later, assuring us she would be back by noon tomorrow. Then Esther and I sat down in the living room and began speaking of Harry.

"Keeping him in the dark like that, I really blew it there," muttered Esther. "What can I possibly say to the man?"

"Oh Esther," I responded. "He loves you. He just needs to know that he'll always be in the loop. Keeping things from each other, it's caused a whole lot more problems in this family than it's ever solved. Of course, us sisters, we needed this time together, and who knows what would have happened with one more person involved?"

Esther said something about things never being simple, then began talking once again about her difficulty juggling loyalties. She was in the middle of describing how she keeps getting caught between Harry and Sammy when Harry came downstairs, walked up to her, and took her hand. I immediately excused myself and went to check on eema.

When I opened the door, I found a woman so tired she could barely keep her eyes open. For some time, she muttered on about Nazis. I just kept nodding and trying to help her orient herself.

"Eema, everything okay between Harry and you?" I finally asked.

Eema looked confused for a second, but then her face relaxed and she nodded. "Yes, meydeleh," she answered, "but oy! We have to be more sensitive."

"Agreed. Incidentally, you and Harry, where did you leave things?"

"Told him I'd like his blessing too," she answered, letting out a big yawn.

"That's good, eema. We need to include Harry. But you're not saying everything's now contingent on him?"

"Nope. The decision, that's between me and my daughters. And it's been made, yes? And Hershel, he accepts that."

"So the blessing?"

"Something he needed to be asked for and something I'd like to have."

"I take it he didn't give it?"

"Says he needs to consider halacha," she answered, yawning again. "Says...." And at this, eema's words became garbled; then she stopped talking altogether and her eyelids fluttered down.

I knelt over her and checked to see if she was breathing. Just a superstition, yes? She was fine. Except for this odor. It was faint, but unmistakable. How's she dealing with it?, I wondered. Once again living with the stench of urine in her nostrils. Realizing that there was only one place it could take her, and shuddering at the horror of it, I changed her nightgown, pulled her onto the blue chair, replaced the bedding, then laid her down again. She didn't waken, though at one point she cringed and called out, "Won't happen again. Gevalt! Don't strike me." She calmed down in a few minutes, and I was about to leave, but then became bothered by that sore shoulder. Wasn't properly supported. And much of her weight was on it. So I came back and started to reposition her. As I lifted that bony arm, I again caught a glimpse of the tattoo. And my vision blurred as always. Then I turned her over, slipped a pillow under her arm, and returned to the living room.

Harry was on the couch, his coat slung over his shoulder. No sign of Esther.

"Miriam, Esther's gone home to rustle us up something to nash on," Harry explained. "Me, I was just staying long enough to make sure eema's okay."

"You and Esther all right?" I asked.

"Yeah. Just a bump."

"You seemed pretty angry for a while there."

"Oh, it was more than 'seemed.' I was angry all right. You've got to admit, keeping me in the dark on something this serious, it was over the top."

"You're right. It was."

"Anyway, enough said. How's eema doing?"

"Pretty good, Hersh."

"Haven't seen her this alert in over a year. Maybe she's turned a corner."

"We'd all like to think that. But your parents are aging survivors. You know it doesn't just turn around."

Harry nodded, and his eyes filled with pain. "Tell you something. Just before they restricted access, I visited Mrs. Plautsnicki at the hospital. Adoshem forgive me, I hadn't a clue it could get that bad."

"To tell you the truth, Harry, I'm not sure there's a whole lot of dignity in most deaths. And if eema's found another way, I say, mazel tov."

Seeing Harry tense, I sat down and said something about how hard this must be for him, and before long we were commiserating with each other. Then I apologized for saying nothing to him earlier.

"Not to worry," he assured me.

"Good of you to say so, but it does worry me. And there's something else I'm sorry about," I continued, feeling my face flush. "You're my good and dear friend—my very best friend, yes? But I've not always been fair to you."

"Hold on there, Miriam. I wasn't meaning you when I referred to people working around me. You don't."

"No. It's something else. I've always had this idiotic suspicion niggling away at the back of my mind. Well, until Sondra set us straight."

"Oh, the thing around Sondra? And Yacov's letter, right?"

"You know?" I asked.

Harry nodded. "Esther just filled me in. But I always knew there was something. Oh Miriam, don't fret about it," he added, taking in my agitation. "My not saying anything, that's what created the confusion in the first place."

"I'd have thought I bore some responsibility here too. But can I ask you something, Hersh?"

"Shoot."

"I understand you were protecting Sondra. Also that promises were made. But once we knew about the abuse, why didn't you set the record straight? I mean, rather than letting us go on wondering about you?"

Harry ran his fingers through his whiskers and considered for a minute. "Stupid of me to stay silent, perhaps," he finally answered. "And obviously it caused Esther and you tsores, right? But I'm not the kind of man who takes promises lightly. And I figured: Who am I to presume to know what it might mean to Sondra? I mean, Miriam, how would you feel if I started breaking my word to you just cause a lot of time had passed and it no longer seemed important?"

I realized even as Harry was speaking that he was leaving out something crucial. How being the eldest of the campers' children set him up. But I also knew not to probe. Maintaining his privacy, that was Harry's way, yes?

"You're a sweet and honourable man, Harry Cohan," I observed. "Actually, you and Esther are not all that different in how you handle things. Now it's been a difficult day. And I know you want to get home to your wife."

Harry nodded and mumbled something about needing to examine halachic texts. Then reminding me that he and Esther were there if we needed them, he got up and started to leave.

"Harry," I called out after him.

"Yeah, Miriam," he answered, turning around again.

"Promise me something: If ever you make me a promise that causes you or anyone else grief, you'll at least talk to me about it."

"Promise," he replies, a shit-eating grin on his face.

I felt the exhaustion hit me as the front door closed. And I staggered upstairs and crawled into bed almost immediately. But oy! What trouble I had falling asleep that night! Even before my head hit the pillow, I started worrying about eema. Then eema began shrieking in Yiddish, "The Gestapo! Hide! Hide!" And I could feel my skin go clammy and my eyeballs ache. How will she feel if Harry can't give his blessing? And how in the world is she going to manage everything else facing her?

As I ponder these questions, the events of the day begin flashing through my mind—Esther sitting next to me at the picnic table exclaiming, "What could the two of you conceivably be thinking of?" Sondra running upstairs to eema.

Kinehora, we've come a long way, I muse. But look at the confusion, the web of misunderstandings, the pain. And look at me. All my life trying to be sensitive, and yet, vey iz mir, how very often I've faltered! Dodged what I couldn't face. Misread situations totally. Even with Esther. Not that I'm any different than anyone else. Good intentions and all, we've each of us contributed to the tsimmes, no? Perhaps eema also, I think to myself.

Nu? She's no fool, eema. She might well have seen through Harry's story that evening but said nothing. Perhaps because she wasn't really sure. Perhaps because she figured it'd cause less trouble in the long run.

At this, my mind drifted back to eema. I imaged a much younger eema blessing the candles, her white laced kerchief wrapped around her head, her hands forming this warm cocoon around us. I saw an even younger eema cradling me in her arms. And once again, I started to feel this pressure in my chest. And once again, I began dreading the prospect of losing her.

Then even the prospect of falling asleep started to unnerve me. Nu? The last thing I wanted was a nightmare about eema. But eventually, I did fall sleep. Yes. And eventually, I did dream. And it was a nightmare, sure enough. But not at all the one I was expecting:

Eema must have just died, for decked in black, family and friends are mulling about the living room, even people long dead. And everyone is abuzz about how wonderful eema was. "A lomed vovnik if ever there was one," declares Chavela Fenster, nodding her head vigorously. "Am I right or am I right?" Dressed in a stunning mauve evening gown, Sondra suddenly appears in the doorway. She is holding up this book and smiling. I walk over and take a peek. "Women and the Shoah," it is titled. "We're all so very proud of Miriam," she announces.

Then the letters lift from the pages, stream into the air, and turn into this large black tornado. The tornado, I can feel it pulling at me. I back away in horror, grab the arm of the couch, and hold on for dear life. No use. My grip on the couch, it starts to loosen. And now I am up high. Dangling in the air. And in I go, yes? Right into the centre. Then everything's a blur. And I'm getting dizzier and dizzier.

Suddenly, I come to a stop. And I see a tall figure in front of me. At first, the figure is fuzzy, but as my focus returns, it becomes clear that it's Harry. Dressed in a black tuxedo, he is standing in the middle of a ballroom, his right arm stretched out in front of him, his index finger pointing. I turn around and walk in the direction of the pointing finger and find myself in the far corner of our living room. Glancing downward, I notice a huge bulge in the carpet just before the tassels. I kneel down, stretch out my hands, and pull back the edge of the carpet to discover a long shallow box, the pine weathered, the sides coming loose. I peer in. And there he is: Abba, much of his body rotted away. His legs green and festering. Worms slithering in and out of the hole in his chest. Horrified, I am about to turn away when abba sits up in his coffin.

"Ach! Take it away! Cover it up!" shrieks person after person.

"What, Miriam, is invisible what I haf to be?" moans abba, his voice low and mournful. "In this imperfect family, there isn't room for an abba too?"

# Chapter Ten

## Miriam, age 50

*Image: In the middle of Poland stands an innocuous brick building, accessible only by a ponderous iron gate. No sign marks it, but ask any veteran, leastwise when no one's looking, and they will surely tell you it is the dreaded bunker 25. The hated station where unfortunates are held after Selection. Selection? Nu? If the index finger points to the right, it means torture, starvation, humiliation, otherwise known as life. Should it point to the left, it's off to bunker 25 with you. Either way, you're trapped. Trapped like a rat in a snare.*

*Guarding the bunker on this day in August 1944 are seven men in crisp SS attire, their heads high, their boots freshly polished. They look on amused as women in tattered clothes and kerchiefed heads hover in front of the bunker, straining to see through its tiny barred windows. It would seem a very young woman is trapped within, for an older women is peering through one of the windows, urging, "Daughter, don't worry! I'll get you out of here." Mad with grief and sobbing hysterically, the older woman reaches for one of the bars and begins pulling at it. A young SS officer but a foot away observes her with disgust, but says nothing. For a good five minutes, she continues to assail the bar, her wounds reopening as her already scabby fingers pull, bang, scratch at it. Eventually, she collapses in exhaustion. The young officer clears his throat. She hears, takes note of her situation, and slowly but surely pulls herself to her knees and crawls toward him. "Please," she implores, peering up at the officer. "Don't let mayn kind die alone. Take me too. Take me too." A smirk spreads across the man's face, and he raises his whip.*

*Fourteen hours pass amid screams and whimpers. Then, with a push, the iron gate swings open; and one hundred and forty-six terrified human beings are marched out of the bunker, some dragged, some whipped, all assured that they are just going to be disinfected.*

*"Schnell! Schnell! Laufen! Laufen!" the men in green uniforms shriek. Two more hours pass. The old woman brings her hands to her face and winces, her nostrils stinging from the thick black smoke which now fills the air.*

*Image: It is a sunny but windy day in the late 1990s in the city of Toronto. In a cemetery in a far northern part of the city stands a youth and three middle-aged men, black yarmulkes on their heads, all but the youth bearded. There is a freshly made gape in the earth about twelve yards yonder. A few tears escaping from their reddened eyes, a bleached pine coffin on their shoulders, the men walk slowly toward the opening in the earth. Gotenyu! Who are these forlorn folk? And what poor soul has been taken from them? And how can the poor bleeding earth be made whole? Their hands steady, their jaws set, they hold what has been entrusted to them carefully, yes? Five times at least, the eldest had cautioned them: "Be gentle. Gentle. Don't fumble. Don't tip it to one side. Wouldn't want her to get sick. Wouldn't want her to start off on a bad footing." And clearly, they have heard. It's as they're ushering a newborn into the world, so tender are they with this human torah, this arc of the covenant. Not uttering a word, keeping the coffin absolutely steady, they measure their steps together. One, two, three.*

*Assembled just to the right of the opening in the earth, a crowd looks their way in anticipation, chanting in unison, "Shall dust praise you? Shall it decline thy truth?" The chanting is not the only sound here today. Overhead are sparrows chirping. Be still, listen with your heart, and you can also make out a thin almost voiceless wail. Something in the wind. Something moaning, "Rachaele, Rachaele."*

*The pallbearers, for such they are, have now taken five steps. They take one more, then suddenly stop and just stand there, the coffin still on their shoulders, even though a long distance still remains between them and the wounded earth. Are they reluctant to continue? Reluctant to relinquish what they hold so dear?*

*Next to the opening in the earth stands a tall middle-aged woman with long raven black hair and a thin angular face. A gold embroidered tallis draped over her shoulders, a matching gold yarmulke on her head, she is holding a slate grey bowl in front of her. Reciting a psalm, she lifts the bowl over her head. As the bowl rises, mouths instinctively open; a hush descends on the gathering. Women, men, children suck in their breath and all eyes focus on her. She looks over at the eldest pallbearer, the one leading and on the left. Seemingly signaling that he is ready, he nods. The woman nods back, then deftly brings the bowl crashing to the ground. It lands with a bang and shatters, sending grey shards everywhere. "The snare is broken and we have escaped," the woman proclaims.*

We were on a strict timetable, yes? Countdown to death. I could feel its stranglehold as I rolled out of bed next morning and slipped into my corduroys. I felt it every morning as I arose. Yes, and at night too as I pulled the warm blue comforter over my shoulders and shut my eyes, knowing that yet another day had slipped away. First there were seven days, then six, then five. Oy! Interesting number, that seven, yes? It took the God in whom I do not believe seven days to create the world. We had seven days to undo one. No. Not just undo it. Help eema in her heroic struggle to bring it to as good an end as possible, to gather in what could be reaped in this her final harvesting. And how diligently we toiled! Sondra, Esther, and Harry were there hour after hour every day, planning, learning, comforting, attending to details. And eema? She was nothing short of remarkable, repeatedly putting aside her terror to instruct, attend, make concrete decisions: "Have Rabbi Pat deliver the eulogy, yes? But not a long one, kinderlekh. Better everyone should get a chance to talk. The Shalom Funeral Home, it'll do, Hershel? Make it the Rabbi's Kaddish at the graveside, not the standard Mourner's Kaddish. My students, it'll mean something to them, farshtey?" Little of this happened, mind you, until we heard from Harry.

✡

It was shortly after supper on the first day, and we were all nervously awaiting word from Harry. You see, the rest of the family still hadn't been notified. "Got to first give Hersh a chance to find out where he stands, yes?" eema had said. Now we'd just retired to living room, and eema had been saying something about including abba in the eulogy when, unexpectedly, Sondra uttered, "So about Yacov...." Eema cringed. Esther bristled. And I braced myself for trouble.

"How can you even think of bringing up that man at such a time," snapped Esther.

"Can it ... will you?" rejoined Sondra. "The thing is, Uncle...."

Exactly at that moment the door bell rang. Worried about what

Sondra had in mind, I promised myself to check it out. But I utterly forgot, what with the frenzy of activity that almost instantly ensued.

It was Harry. Bleary-eyed from having been up all night combing through texts, he walked straight over to eema, took her hand, and smiled.

"It's okay?" she asked, her face brightening.

"You have my blessing," he announced. "Eema, with all my heart."

Harry walked away almost immediately. And so none of us had a chance to ask him about it.

"Hersh," I inquired, finding myself alone with him in the living room about half an hour later, "this morning, you weren't exactly sounding hopeful. What happened?"

Harry leaned forward in his chair and shook his head. "I kept looking, but bupkes. Now I'd come upon something late last night. But it's fairly flimsy; and so I really didn't want to rely on it. But in the end, it's all I had."

"It's been hard on you, hasn't it?"

Harry nodded. "Yeah. But know what it ultimately came down to?"

"What, Hersh?"

"How desperate eema has been. When a person's this desperate, you don't say no unless you absolutely have to. Now at first I thought I had to, because while I'll stretch halacha, even believe in stretching it in certain instances, I won't go against it. But, Adoshem be praised, there was just enough of an opening."

"Something that permits suicide in certain cases?"

"Not exactly. In Judaism, suicide's considered a what-do-you-call it? Desecration of creation. But as a philosopher, you know everything comes down to definitions. Now according to Reb Isaac, a suicide is someone who kills himself out of a cynical disregard for human life. And anyone who kills himself in any other way is not a suicide. You get my drift?" he asked, catching my eye.

"Eema hasn't a cynical bone in her body."

"Precisely. And never have I known anyone with a higher regard for life."

"Harry, thanks," I murmured. "You okay with this?"

"I'd have preferred something more solid. But yes. Meems?"

"Yeah."

"Thanks for pulling this out of me. Thought I didn't want to talk about it, but hey, obviously, I did."

It was Harry's uncertainty that had kept eema from informing the next generation. The coast now clear, that very evening she got on the blower and called each of her grandchildren, making appointments with Sammy and Niel and leaving a message for Channa. Then she called Sarrah—Sammy's partner, yes? Following that, a number of the campers. And for the next several days, she was incessantly meeting with people, always making sure, of course, she put aside lots of time for Sondra.

"Sheyneh punem, I know I'm spending more time with Sondra than you," she said to me one morning over breakfast. "You see, she's had so little of me, and I of her. You understand, Miriam, yes?"

"Sha, eema. Of course."

If eema had postponed her death to spend more time with us, Shabbes figured centrally in her plans. She wanted one last family Shabbes together. And so did the rest of us. We began the preparations well in advance. While Sondra and eema visited, early Thursday afternoon Esther and I set out for Chaim's Meat Market on Harbord, then proceeded to Adele's fishery two doors down. We brought back enough supplies to feed the proverbial army. By evening, we were already stooped over the kitchen counter, rolling, chopping, grinding, taking care to cook all the favourite foods and to get them right. Gefilte fish with the bones ground in, those light potato knishes of Esther's that melt in your mouth, chopped liver with extra onions, just the way eema likes it. Harry, meanwhile, had hopped in his car and driven to Israel's to buy tallises for the women in accordance with eema's specification. "Now none of those flimsy women's pieces, yingele," she'd insisted, a twinkle in her eye. "Real tallises for real human beings with substance, yes?"

It was a remarkable Shabbes. Two bridge tables were added to accommodate the large gathering, each covered with a crimson cloth with silver inlay. Except for Harry's brother Eric, who'd announced, "I really can't go along with this, just can't," everyone was there—the immediate family, the kinderlekh, Niel's girlfriend, Sarrah and her parents, Mr. and Mrs. Cohan senior, and Mr. Plautsnicki. Ah yes, and old Mr. Morrison too. We were squeezed together tightly, yes? But that only added to the intimacy. Now the food and the schmoozing warmed us, of course, but it was eema's blessing that most nourished us.

Decked in a cobalt blue tallis that enfolded her like the sky, with Harry's help, eema rose to her feet to bless the candles. No longer steady, her wrinkled old hands shook as she brought them again and again from the candles to herself, from the candles to herself. The tallis quivering with her, it was as if the blessing was setting off ripples throughout the firmament. Like everything was connected, and eema's barucha was a cosmic caress. As she brought her hands back the last time and placed her palms upright over her eyes, she let out a long sonorous "omeyn." For several minutes, she stood there, swaying slightly, her hands still cacooning her eyes. When she finally removed them, she was looking straight at Sammy's rounded form and smiling. She proceeded to tell us all what a blessing Sammy was and what Sammy was giving this family. "A real shame, don't you think, that every Canadian family does not have a brilliant radical dyke to shake us all up, to give us kinderlekh, and to tell it like it really is, yes?" she exclaimed. Then, one by one, eema celebrated every single person there, ending with Sondra. "My sweeties," she concluded, her eyes now moist, her voice beginning to crack, "gut Shabbes."

As blessed as this week was, of course, it was also hard. Everyone had their own vulnerabilities, needs, limits. Now and again tempers flared, Sondra once stomping off and not returning until the next day. And, what was particularly distressing, on the very day leading up to the big Shabbes dinner, myself excepted, every member of the family privately told eema that they just couldn't be present at the actual act. Fortunately, eema already knew and had accepted.

"Eema, Miriam," Esther said, her head shaking forlornly, "I feel like the rest of us are letting you down. Deserting you."

"You call all this desertion, do you?" asked eema, her eyes keen. "All eemas facing death should be so deserted by their kinderlekh."

Of course, it was eema who was most vulnerable. And while she kept putting aside her terror to give and to connect, many is the time she would shriek half the night and tremble during the day. Death, that's where the vulnerability lies, and inevitably, it was all tangled up with the past. Like she was caught in this snare. Life had narrowed down so far that there was little else left but the Nazis, and so she was killing herself. Now as far as humanly possible, she was giving herself a good death. But, nu? How could the Nazis possibly be kept at bay at such a moment?

"Oy meydeleh!" she uttered one evening, bolting straight up in her bed. "Gotenyu! The Nazis, they're waiting for me. What if they catch hold of me as I breathe my very last breath? If a zig heil is the last thing I see? 'Raus' the last sound I hear?"

"I'll be there, eema, I assured her, gazing into her petrified eyes. "I'll be right at your bedside. Try to stay focused on me." Had she seen family members make comparable promises at Auschwitz?, I wondered.

✡

So heimish, ushering out Shabbes like this. Eema's eyes aglow, a broad smile on her face, she'd urged, "Come, my sweeties," and we'd all gathered together to light the braided havdalah candle. Enjoying each other's presence, raising our wine glasses to toast each other, mesmerized by the sweet tangy aroma of the havdalah spices, we'd sat in the living room, watching the candle get smaller and smaller. And now it was out, and Shabbes was over. Such a mechaya!

We hadn't discussed the concrete details of eema's passing for over a day now, for Esther had looked at us earnestly and asked, "Would it be okay if we go quiet now? Adoshem be praised, let's open up space for the Shabbes soul." We did as Esther urged, and I was glad for it, for it gave me a chance to settle more into myself. To go deep. To rest. The candle now out, I gave myself permission to return to practicalities.

I began with a quick mental inventory. Yes, most everything had been worked out. We would have a quiet family day tomorrow. Everyone who wished would say their last goodbye to eema in the early evening. Eema and I would stay up late. "So she'll be too pooped to pucker," as Sondra put it. "A good time to leaf through the family photos and schmooze, yes?" eema had added. Eema would take the pills at 1:00 a.m. Once she had drifted off, I would go to bed and stay in my room till a few minutes past 9:00. Then I would get up, check in on eema, discover the dead body, and immediately dial Harry, telling him that eema had died in her sleep. Then Harry would call Dr. Silverberg—this doctor the Schugarenskis had used. From there on in, it's all pretty standard. Notify the rest of the family that eema has died in her sleep. Call the funeral home. Make arrangements with Rabbi Pat.

Realizing that eema might want the security of hearing it all again, I turned to her and asked, "Eema, you want me to go over everything one more time, or you comfortable letting it be?"

"One more time, if you don't mind, meydeleh."

I rattled off what everyone would be doing when. Eema kept nodding until I got to the place about calling the funeral home. Then her eyes narrowed and she began wringing her hands.

"What is it, eema?" I ask.

"The funeral home, it's strangers!"

"I know, but we're kind of stuck with that."

"Really don't want to be alone with strangers," she mutters, her lips beginning to quiver.

"Don't do this!" I blurted out, the burden of it getting to me. "We've done everything we can. Just what do you expect of us?"

Instantly, tears begin streaming down eema's face. I take a deep breath and get a grip on myself. "I'm so sorry, eema," I utter. "It's okay. We'll figure out something."

Eema looks up at me and begins to calm down.

"Maybe this is the time to bring in a therapist," suggests Esther.

"For Christ sake, Esther," snaps Sondra. "Like, do you really have to act like an idiot?"

I glance over at Harry, hoping he knows the territory well enough to help. Harry rises from the couch and begins to pace.

"Harry?" I ask.

"Just thinking," he muses, looking over at eema. "We could appoint a member of the family as a shomer. Except for the Orthodox, shomers have largely fallen out of use, but hey, it's traditional."

I glance at Esther. I can tell by her expression that she's familiar with the custom.

"You mind explaining, Hershel?" asks eema.

"It's someone who performs the mitzvah of watching over the goss."

"Goss? Like, you're referring to the corpse, right?" asks Sondra.

"Yes and no. Corpse—that's not a Jewish conceptualization. The person is called a 'goss' at this point. You see, while a 'corpse' is thought of as dead, a 'goss' is hovering between life and death."

"Gobbledygook!" exclaims Sondra, a look of incredulity on her face. "Dead is dead, and the person's dead at this point. Dead as a door-knob."

"Not according to Judaism," Harry counters. "According to Judaism, she's *in transition.*"

"Must remember to tell the johns about this one when they lose their load too quickly," Sondra chortles, her eyes rolling. "No, no. You aren't *spent,* you poor misguided souls. You're in transition!"

Eema had been looking calmer for a while there, but not now. I can tell by the terror in her eyes that this in-between world spells danger. Oy! Whether we joke about it like Sondra or cloak ourselves in scholarship like Harry, like every solitary one of us, she's totally vulnerable in the face of death, though in eema's case, it's not exactly unfathomable. It's all inextricably bound up with that place, that name, that history. Gevalt! Just look at her! She's thinking that this may be the opportune moment for the Nazis to sneak up and grab hold of her. Yes, even though she doesn't believe in souls or gosses. Nu? She believes in Auschwitz. And in the nightmare world of Auschwitz, of what conceivable help is our reason, our philosophy, our daytime convictions? And what solace for the atheist survivor as she inches toward the betwixt-and-between?

"The shomer, Harry," I ask, hoping to offer her something, however symbolic, "she protects the goss, right?"

"Precisely, Miriam. The shomer ensures that no one carries the goss off and that no one, well, does anything untoward."

"Eema," I ask, "I know this is awkward since neither of us believes, but tradition can be comforting. You'd like a shomer maybe? A family shomer who can look out for you?"

Eema nods. The muscles in her back relax, and each of us starts to breathe more easily.

"No offence, Hershele," she observes, "but I'd feel more comfortable with a woman, yes?"

"None taken. And if it's okay with you, eema, let's make it someone young and energetic. After all, it'll mean being awake and on guard for what? Upward of eighteen hours easily."

Sammy immediately offers, but we all agree that it shouldn't be a pregnant woman. We start coming up with other names. "What? Am I invisible or something?" objects Channa. "How come no one ever thinks of me?" To Channa's obvious delight, eema gives her a warm smile and declares she'd be perfect. Sitting back down, Harry offers to make all the arrangements. And for a moment there, the problem appears to be solved. But then I notice eema's chin quivering.

I sit down on the floor in front of eema and look up into her eyes. "There's something else, isn't there, eema?" I ask.

Tears rolling down her cheeks, she utters, "Oh meydeleh, I don't know what to do. I'm stuck. Oy Gott! And that I should be burdening you with all this meshugahs."

"Sorry I got impatient with you earlier. We're your family and want to help. So please, tell us."

Eema says nothing for several minutes while the rest of us sit there nervously. "I don't want strangers touching me," she finally whimpers.

My heart aching, I get an image of this young SS officer taking a club to eema's shoulder. Pound. Crack. I see other officers ordering her to snap to attention as she stands naked in the cold, then pointing to her withered breasts and snickering. Then the bread story flashes into my mind; I think of her removing her tattered rags—the modicum of decorum she had left—and giving herself to this stranger that she didn't even like to keep life and limb together. I glance over at Sondra. There are tears in Sondra's eyes. Ah yes, Sondra understands about abuse.

I reach over and cradle eema's head in my hands. "Eema, we'll find another way," I assure her.

"What other way?" she asks, slowly drawing her head back. "At the funeral home, officials touch the body, yes? Dress it, make it ready."

"So we won't send you to a funeral home. Where is it written the dead have to be sent to a funeral home?"

"Oy! Meydeleh, whatever you're thinking, forget it. I have to be sent there, yes? And once I'm there, strangers will touch me, like it or not."

Once again hoping he knows something, I start to glance over at Harry, but then recalling Esther's words the other day, I shift my gaze. "Esther, do they really have to touch her?" I ask.

"Not necessarily."

As Esther gathers her thoughts, Harry starts to say something. Now whether or not eema picked up on the dynamic, I couldn't say even now, but just at this moment eema turns to Esther and asks, "Meydeleh, you can help us here, yes?"

"What I'm thinking of, eema, it's called a 'tahara.' Now I'm no maven. But I know a bit about it from one of my Judaic studies lessons, and it just might be the answer."

Esther proceeds to explain. An old Orthodox custom, she informs us, the tahara is the sacred ceremony of purification—the cleaning and wrapping of the body. While more commonly handled by funeral home personnel, even in these days it is still performed by community members who take on the mitzvah of being members of a Chevra Kaddisha.

"And family can serve as members?" asks eema.

"No, eema. Sorry. Except for one brief moment, family can't even be present. But friends can serve."

"I'm not sure," murmurs Harry, grimacing. "For us to go out of our way to perform an Orthodox ceremony, and a particularly sacred one at that, when eema doesn't believe. Honestly, not trying to make waves here, but how can this be right?"

"But Judaism doesn't require belief," Esther points out, looking at him intently. "And if we do it respectfully, Harry? And if it's for a survivor?"

"For a survivor, yes," Harry concedes.

While the libraries are now closed and while neither Harry nor Esther have copies of the text in its entirety, it occurs to me that one of my colleagues—Lena Gottlieb—just might. And as luck would have it, she does. "No. No problem with picking it up now," she assures me.

A few hours later, my sisters, Harry, eema, and I were sitting around the kitchen table, sipping coffee, nashing on cold knishes, and passing around this small black book, its pages yellowed and smelling of must. Esther had been flipping through it for the last few minutes. "Want a turn?" she asks. "Yeah," I answer, reaching for the book. I take a package of pink stick-its from my pants pocket and open it. Then removing my glasses and positioning the book inches from my eyes, I begin leafing through it, placing a stick-it on any passage that seems problematic. "Eema," I observe, peering up from the text dozens of prayers later, "many of the prayers centre on Israel. Okay if we leave in some of them?"

"Not to worry, sweetie. Lot of ways Israel can be interpreted, yes? Symbolically, historically, mythically, epes."

"Got you," I answer. I flip to the last page. "Now in this part here, your eldest child comes in to place dust in your eyes."

"Right in my eyes?"

"Yeah. I assume that's out."

"You assume correctly."

"Good. Now something more general. How about all those places where it's one thing for a man and another for a woman?"

Eema polishes off the last knish, then reaches for her carton of cigarettes, and lights up. "If everything's more or less equal, follow the instructions for women. If not," she stipulates, the smoke trickling out her nostrils, "what else? The instructions for men."

With so much still to cover and so much else to do, we decided to divvy up the work. Harry, Esther, and I headed upstairs to continue combing through the ceremony, leaving Sondra and eema in the kitchen giving further thought to the Chevra Kaddisha.

When we entered the living room a couple of hours later, we found eema exhausted but beaming. "Kinderlekh, Sammy's Sarrah has taken on the mitzvah," she announced. "Two of her cousins also. The Chevra Kaddisha, we have it."

Not long after, eema reached for Harry's arm and Harry helped her upstairs and into her bed. Then everyone left. My heart heavy at the thought that this would be eema's last full night on earth, I turned in as well, leaving my khakis and t-shirt on and burrowing deep under the covers.

Surprisingly, I did catch some shut-eye that night, though ominous figures wrapped in linen from head to foot inhabited my dreams. Around 2:00, I awoke from a deep sleep to hear eema screaming, "Gott in himmel, the greens! Duck down! Duck down!" And I rushed to her side. It took some time for her to orient herself, but eventually, her eyes cleared and she answered, "Oh, it's you, meydeleh. So sorry."

"Nothing to be sorry about," I assured her, bending over and kissing her worn face.

"Long day tomorrow. You'll go schlufen now, sweetie, yes?"

"I'm staying right here," I answered, crawling in next to her. "Don't want you to be alone with the nightmares—not even for a second. Any way, it gives me time with you and there's so little time left."

Eema smiled, carefully drew the cover over my shoulders, and rolled over.

"Sweetie," she called out just as I thought she was drifting off.

"Yeah, eema."

"You ever talk to Sammy and Sarrah about Israel?"

"Israel?" I asked, giggling at the thought of her bringing up a subject like this at such a time. "No. Why?"

"Bet you're worried you'll be the only non-Zionist in this family after I'm gone. Well, you may be in for a pleasant surprise. Just check in with them, yes?"

For the rest of the night, I lie there, occasionally dozing off, but mostly watching over eema as she slept, helping her break free from the Nazis whenever they stole upon her, taking joy in the wheezing sound of her breath, marveling at the way her eyelids would flutter, then go still. But soon, too soon, the sun began peeping through the sides of the blinds, and the phone began ringing. D-Day, I reminded myself, shaking off my exhaustion and rushing to answer.

I saw less of eema than I wished in the morning and afternoon. Propped up on her pillows, she lay in bed, sometimes reading, more often having a tête-a-tête with some family member, generally Sondra. As much for myself as her, I would pop my head in from time to time just to make sure everything was okay, but I didn't stay long. Sondra and eema, they needed time.

Shortly after three I approached the door for the fourth time that day, just to do a quick check. And oy! What a surprise! A thick blue book in her hands, eema was reading as before. But gotenyu! What she was reading!

"Eema, you're reading *Heidegger*?" I asked, truly astonished.

"If not now, when?" she answers, looking up from her book, her eyebrow raising. "And if not me, who? Anyway, sheyneh punem, you know how he defines human existence: Being-toward-death. Rather apropos, wouldn't you say?"

Around 6:00, without help and without a word to anyone, eema hobbled downstairs for the very last time, taking each step slowly, cautiously. Opening the front door, she walked out without jacket or even shoes on and stood on the porch for a few minutes, as best I could make out, first taking in the maple tree with its magnificent branches, then the gate with its broken latch, now raising her eyes to the darkening sky. Then, breathing heavily, she somehow made her way off the porch and down the steps. Then she turned left and disappeared from view.

"What on earth's she doing?" Esther whispers to me as we stand there peering through the open door. "So chilly out. Shouldn't we go after her?"

"Es, just let her be."

"For the love of Gott, she'll catch her death."

Esther notices the absurdity, looks at me, and in an instant, we burst out laughing.

I don't know where eema went, but my guess is that she was in the backyard, bidding farewell to all those bushes that she and abba had planted. After a few minutes, she reappears and sits down on one of the rocking chairs—the one where abba would sit, yes? And she begins to rock.

We didn't fuss over dinner that night. Nor did we talk much. Though, kinehora, everyone stayed, even the kinderlekh, and everyone's eyes were fixed on eema. Not long after 7:00, eema said something about being tired. Sondra helped eema back into bed. And once eema had slipped into her kimono, we gathered at the bedside and reminisced, sometimes weeping, sometimes laughing. Then one by one, people rose to take their leave.

"Eema, you know you'll always be in my heart," says Harry, his eyes holding hers.

"Eema, I love you," Sondra murmurs.

Now I was grateful to be alone with eema at long last. But I couldn't help wondering: In the years to come, what if leaving is the one decision they regret? Eema must have been observing me, for she placed her hand on my shoulder. "Not to worry, meydeleh," she urged, smiling at me warmly. "Come, we'll look at the photos, yes?"

I found each of the six albums and deposited them at the foot of the bed. Then I crawled into bed beside eema. And for most of the evening we sat there, propped up on pillows, working our way through the pictures and schmoozing. "Oy, remember this one, meydeleh?" gushed eema, pointing to a black-and-white shot of Sondra and me in jeans, a marble rolling from Sondra's outstretched hand. "What were you, sweetie? Five maybe? A bisel older? And such a punem! Oy, look here," she urged, pointing to an image of a remarkably young abba standing in front of his shop, his hair black and wavy, his shirt starched, his old cloth measuring tape dangling from his neck. "See the measuring tape? Quintessential abba! Oh Miriam, you'll remember to light the yarhzeit for abba each year, yes?"

"Of course, eema," I answered.

By chance, just at that moment my eyes drifted to the picture next to abba's. And there he was. Even in a faded old picture, kinehora, how those eyes of his danced! Eema noticed the picture of Uncle Yacov and remarked, "Strange how life unfolds. You really have made a fine family historian." At this, I suddenly remembered Sondra's worrisome reference to Yacov and vowed to take care.

Letting out a giant yawn, eema checked her watch just after picking up the fifth album. "Getting late now," she murmured, giving me a sad smile and putting the album aside. She reached over and kissed me, then began running her fingers through my hair. "Sweetie," she mused, looking deep into my eyes, "if there were a way for me to stay here with you, I would."

"I know, eema."

"And I can tell you, if I'm conscious at all after I'm dead, I'm going to miss you. An eema, she's not supposed to have favourites, right? And the fact that I did clearly caused tsores, yes?" "But Miriam," she continued, a tear rolling down her cheek, "the unvarnished truth is, always you were special to me."

"And you, eema, you've been my world."

"Oy! How hard this going to be for you, sweetie," she uttered, her eyes narrowing. Eema removed her hands from my hair and hugged me. Then she thanked me for being there all these years. Then slowly, calmly, she began making suggestions, giving last minute information, expressing wishes: "I've left you the house, and it's fine to live here," she pointed out, "but meydeleh, remember, is a whole world out there. The gelt, it's all going to Sondra," she informed me. "You understand, yes? When you talk to Rabbi Pat, remind her about abba," she added moments later.

"Eema," I said, at one point, just after she'd made some passing reference to this last week, "using your death to bring us all together, I don't know how you dreamed up such an idea, but thank-you."

Eema gave me that smile she always gave when she realized I'd understood something she hadn't intended me to. Then she kissed me and asked if I could bring her a glass of water. I hurried to the kitchen, filled a tall green glass, and brought it back. I re-entered the room to find the photo albums stacked in a pile on the dresser. And there in plain view on the nightstand sat three bottles of pills and a small blue plate.

I glanced at my watch. Gotenyu! 12:45 already? I stopped breathing for a second there. Then reminding myself to breathe and staying as calm as I could, I placed the glass next to the pills and sat back down on the bed. Eema smiled, pursed her lips, then started to say something about how she'd felt when she first saw me dissociate. "You know, sweetie," she began, "I could tell you were somewhere else. Not that I hadn't already taken in how very vulnerable you...." Eema cocked her head. The front door, we could hear it creaking. And within seconds, there's this knock on the bedroom door.

"Eema, Miriam," comes Harry's voice. "Okay if we come in?"

Tears of gratitude streaming down eema's face, we both call out "yes." And in walks Harry, Esther, and Sondra.

"Just when you thought you'd seen the last of us, eh eema?" says Sondra.

"What can I say?" exclaims Harry, looking into eema's eyes. "You just can't keep us away."

Everyone comes over and embraces eema, then takes a seat, Harry and Esther on the chairs, Sondra at the foot of the bed.

"Eema, I thought I couldn't be here," Esther explains. "But know what I found out?"

"What, sheyneh punem?"

"That this is the only place I could be."

Eema thanks everyone and wishes everyone "zy gezent." "But you know what, mayn kinderlekh?" she asks. "I'm getting tired, yes? So I hope no one minds if I just take a few pills."

"No problem, mamenyu," murmurs Esther, her voice quivering. "Okay if we stay till you drift off?"

Eema nods, then begins opening the bottles. Once the bottles are open, she pours all the pills onto the plate and places the plate on her lap. Then she reaches for the glass.

I hold my breath as she pops the first few pills into her mouth and takes a gulp of water. Yes. Good. She's swallowed. And again. And again. So that's how you do it. You don't think. Just reach and swallow. Reach and swallow.

The pile of pills, it's getting smaller. Only nine pills now. Now only four. And now the plate is empty, and without a moment's thought, eema takes the last gulp and swallows. Now she places the glass back on the night table and starts to reminisce. She speaks of being fourteen and looking forward to university. "Martin Heidegger, he'd introduced this new philosophy, yes?" She speaks of the early days with her mother and father—the picnics, the debates, Shabbes, her eema blessing the candles, her abba picking up his tallis bag and trudging off to schul. And she's looking fine, even inspired. But what's happening now? Her face is white, her eyes wide, her lips beginning to quiver. "Oy! Where's mameh?" she starts screaming. "Nein! Nein! The greens, they're here. Helf mir! Helf mir!" My heart aching, I put my arms around her, determined she's not going like this.

"Eema, you're with me, Miriam. Look at me," I urge, gently turning her toward me.

"Ach! The hunts, they're snarling."

"Eema, it's your daughter, Miriam. And you're in our house on Lippincott."

"Gott in himmel!"

"Eema, look at me! Look at me!"

Eema's eyes begin to focus. "Miriam?" she asks.

"Yeah, eema. You okay?"

"Okay, yes," she answers, but her lips begin to tremble again. And once again, she pleads, "Helf mir!"

"Eema, stay with me here," I urge, my voice firm but gentle. "There's something I want you to tell me."

"Meydeleh?"

"Yeah," I answered. Then I asked about the details of the will, and she began rattling them off, all the while yawning and rubbing her swollen eyes. It was good, yes? But we ended too soon. And once again, her lips started to quiver.

Now it's hard to explain what happened next, but ever after, whenever any of us told the story of eema's last days, we would get a wistful look in our eyes when we got to this part—even Sondra. For we could all sense that it was as if eema's and my entire life together prepared us for this moment.

"Something else, eema," I found myself saying. "Remember... remember how I was born with long white hair?"

"Long white hair?" she chuckled. "Kinehora, so you were, meydeleh."

"Was it really long?"

"Really long."

"Punct. Just how long was it?"

Eema looked directly at me, clear recognition in her eyes, as if she knew exactly what I was about and was summoning all her resources to go with it. Then she nodded, and without a moment's hesitation just fell into the story like the needle on the record player finding the groove. "How long, meydeleh?" she begins, putting her head on her pillow and shutting her eyes. "Two, no, three, no, four times the length of your body. Oy, had it been a long pregnancy! Two weeks overdue I was if I was a day, yes? And every bone—nay, every sinew in my body ached. Finally, I go into labour. And the labour...." And at this point, eema's voice starts to trail off, and well before the punch line, she's in a deep sleep.

After a few minutes, I felt this hand on my shoulder and heard Harry whispering, "Miriam, we're going now. Hang in there, kiddo. But call if you need anything."

I heard myself answer, "No problem." Then as if from far in the distance, I could make out movement on the floor.

Eema tossed and moaned frequently for the next hour or so, and whenever she did, I gently stroked her hair. Then knowing there was no way I would leave her alone now, I got up, found her alarm clock on the dresser, set it for 9:00 a.m., closed the light, and crawled back into the bed. And my arms around her, I drifted off.

Now though I was lying next to a dead body, it wasn't easy getting up next morning. Oy! How could I part from her? How? And having laid next to her so often since her depression set in, what could be more natural that lying next to her now? And, gotenyu! To actually hand her over to I know-not-what. The tahara, I was beginning to worry about it, yes? What if they didn't do it right? What if somehow she was aware and mistook them for Nazis? But while I stretched out the moment just as long as I could, and while there were hundreds of seemingly good reasons to keep delaying, the second the alarm rang, I braced myself, peeled off the blanket, and walked over to the phone. And oy! Like millions of daughters before me, and I'm sure millions after me, I released my eema into other people's hands.

✡

We'd just had a private schmooze with Rabbi Pat. She'd cried with us, put a tear in our garments, agreed to changes in the traditional order of the procession, asked, "anything else you want me to know about your eema?" The bimah directly before us, the family was seated in the front left row of Temple Ruth, me at the extreme right, then Esther, then Harry, then Sondra, then the kinderlekh. Already, most of the seats were filled. I remember looking about, touched by the kindness around me.

Good that the benches and the bima are plain oak—no curlicues, no flourishes, I thought to myself. And the placement of the family, so much better than with abba's funeral. With the family in a regular row like everyone else, well-wishers are feeling easier about coming over and offering their condolences. And quietly, respectfully, people did approach us. People who I'd seen often over the years like Mr. Plautsnicki, Mrs. Schwartz, Mr. Morrison. "Miriam," murmured Mr. Plautsnicki, shaking his head sadly, "how long have I known you? All your life, right? And I can't tell you how my heart weeps for you."

"Just like Chavella used to say," noted Mrs. Schwartz, bending forward and whispering in my ear, "a lomed vovnik, that eema of yours."

Present in even larger numbers were men and women whom none of us had seen in years but who'd clearly made the effort because at some point or other, eema meant something to them—Joe Jackson and Nira Feldmann, for example. All of it a timely reminder that eema had lived a long life, and that this life had touched so many others. What was also gratifying, there were people who had come largely because they knew one of the children or the grandchildren. Like Lanie. Actually, it was shortly after I entered the schul that I spotted her, and about fifteen minutes later, she caught my eye and made her way over.

"Meems," she uttered, putting her hand on my shoulder, her voice low and gentle. "I'm so sorry. I know how close the two of you always were."

"Good of you to come," I answered. "And after all these years." I got up, and Lanie and I hugged.

"Was she sick for long?"

"She was, yes."

"If I'm not intruding, what did she die of?"

For some time now, I'd been finding myself uneasy with the official line. "Honestly?" I now find myself responding.

"Yeah."

"I know this may sound strange," I answered, tears rolling down my cheeks, "but so help me, she died of Auschwitz."

Lanie looked at me inquisitively, then nodded. "Whatever I might imagine," she replied, "I know it's a pale reflection of what you're telling me. And I'm so sorry for everything you and your family must have gone through."

Lanie gave me another hug, mentioned that her parents had died a few years ago, then gestured toward this tall angular woman in her late fifties standing next to her. "Please, let me introduce my partner Doris McLaren."

We exchanged a few more words. Then Lanie and Doris left. I found myself thinking about what eema had said about Lanie and me as I watched them navigate the aisle, turn right, then take their seat. Then my eyes drifted to where their row continues on the other side of the aisle. And that's when I saw him.

There on the very first seat is this skinny old man with a wizened face, a navy coat wrapped round him, a blue yarmulke on his head. And there can be no mistake about it. He's eyeing me, almost beckoning me. For a while I can't place him, for his hair is grey, his beard scraggly, his eyes blood-shot, his skin blotchy, but there's something about how his body sways. Oy Gott!, I suddenly realize, Yacov! And in all likelihood, Sondra's involved in some way. Told him, invited him, epes. I take note of a freckled-faced girl of about eleven a couple of seats over from him and shudder. I immediately rise and make my way toward him, upset that after all these years I should have to encounter him today of all days. It takes me a while, for a number of people rush over to express their condolences, but I do finally reach him.

"Didn't see you come in," I say, standing just to the right of his seat. "You're well, I hope."

"Baruch Hashem," he answers. "And you, sport?"

"It's a terrible time, as you can imagine. Surprised you recognize me. I was just a kid when you last saw me."

"Not recognize you! How could an uncle not recognize his favourite niece? Come, give your uncle a big hug," he urges, rising with difficulty and opening his arms wide.

As Uncle starts to draw me toward him, I pull away. "Sorry. I just can't."

Looking wounded, Uncle sits back down. "Miriam, you remember the history lessons," he asks, glancing up at me, his eyes suddenly lighting up again.

"Absolutely. And thank you for them, but there's other things I remember too."

"Don't exactly seem happy to see me," he complains, his face assuming that familiar hang-dog expression. "And, nu? It wounds me deeply, for how I've been looking forward to seeing you! Ach! Such a thinker you always were, Miriam! Sharp as a whip! Now I know I wasn't always fair to your poor eema. What can I say? A man does things. But in my heart, I always admired the woman. Sport, I'm sincerely sorry at her passing. Now you may be wondering why I came, but really, as Hashem is my witness, I've just here to pay my respects. A man, he should pay his respects, wouldn't you say?"

"Respect!" I exclaim, astonished at the speech. "When she was alive, you never showed eema one iota of respect. And how can you expect me to be happy to see you? You any idea how you've hurt Sondra? Any idea what you've done to this family?"

"Sorry. A mistake, no?"

"That's what you call abusing your own niece! And if this is a mistake, what do you call the others?"

"Others?"

"Uncle, I know you were in jail for statutory rape."

"*One* accusation. And a smart girl like you, you know a man can get framed."

"I've seen the newspaper stories. Four different children. How could you?" I ask, my voice rising despite my effort to keep it hushed. "And to actually ravish your brother's daughter! Gotenyu! And here you are after all this time—still denying. And you want me to feel good about you because of some history lessons!"

Yacov looked as if he were going to trot out some rationalization. But then he started to pale, and his lips began to tremble. "Ach! I know. I know," he moans, covering his eyes. "A mentsh, I'm not. Not like your abba, may his name be forever remembered. Never was. Sport," he asks, slowly lowering his hands and once again eyeing me intently, "you want me to leave?"

"No. You're here to pay your respects and that's fine. But you've got to understand, you can't come to the house for shiva. There are kinderlekh, and this is my responsibility."

"There's no place in your heart for a sinner? Hashem forbid, I'm not all bad, you know."

I flash to this image of Uncle at the kitchen table, meticulously explaining the details of zeda Shmuel's work. "Oh Uncle, I know," I answer. "And I hope you'll get some help for yourself. And if ever you need money, I'll see what I can do. Don't turn up, though, because I *will* send you away."

For a second there, I was worried Uncle would say something horrid. Such as "like mother, like daughter," epes, but he didn't. He just bit his lip and nodded, whether in approval or simple acknowledgment, I wasn't sure. I nodded in turn and started to leave. But oy! That young freckled-faced child, she was still there. I cast my eyes about the room, hoping to find someone other than Harry who could keep an eye on Yacov. Spotting Moshe a few rows down, I walked over, motioned for him to come to the aisle, then asked him to sit beside Uncle. "And Moshe, keep him away from children. From Harry too. One more thing, don't let him out of your sight," I added.

I returned to my seat, shaken by the experience but determined that this man who had so plagued all of our lives would not be a blight on eema's funeral.

"Meems?" asked Esther, "who was that fellow you were talking to for so long?"

"A lonely old man that unfortunately can't be trusted."

"An old friend of eema's?"

"Later," I answered.

When the service began a few minutes later, sadly, I wasn't able to pay attention. While I was vaguely aware that psalms were being chanted, I kept wondering what kind of hold Uncle had over Sondra. I glanced at her a number of times only to find her engrossed in the service. Once

Rabbi Pat began speaking, though, somehow I did what I had to do. I actually let go.

In accordance with eema's wishes, Rabbi Pat kept the eulogy short. But no question about it. You could recognize eema in the eulogy: What a caring mother and wife eema was. How eema was one of a small handful of courageous women who smuggled the dynamite which the sondercommandos used to blow up Crematorium IV. How Rachael Himmelfarb and her husband Daniel Himmelfarb were not only both survivors but both activists who fought against oppression everywhere. How Rachael was a remarkable feminist educator. Then Rabbi Pat began to discuss the Holocaust. Then she did something that truly surprised me. Pleased me too. In the middle of a eulogy no less, she spoke of Holocaust denial and the importance of vigilance. "Rachael devoted her life to combating anti-Semitism," the rabbi affirmed. "And let us heed her warning. As Rachael so often pointed out," Rabbi Pat continued, her eyes on fire, her body leaning forward, her voice rising to a crescendo, "Holocaust denial is the centre of virulent anti-Semitism; it is dramatically on the rise; and it is successful. Why, did you know that in a recent poll, over 30 per cent of Americans said the Holocaust might not have happened? And make no mistake about it, if those who forget history are doomed to repeat it, those who deny history are intending to repeat it."

As Rabbi Pat finished, she spread her arms out wide, the stretched-out gold tallis in which she was clad making her look like some magnificent bird readying herself for flight, and she announced, "Our Rachaele did not want a long eulogy. Participatory in death as in life, she wanted you, the people she loved, to take control of this funeral. So please, everyone, come to the bimah and share a thought, a moment, a maiseh."

At this invitation, a seemingly endless stream of people approached the bimah to speak, most of them students or survivors.

"It was my first year, and I'd just flunked the mid-term," announced a plump black woman in her early sixties, "and know what Professor Himmelfarb did? Spent an entire afternoon with me, explaining what sort of answers fly and what don't." "She always had a kind word for my sick grandmother," said this young woman who lives a few doors down on Lippincott. "I was on this steering committee with her husband Daniel," explained Joe Flex. "And so we called ourselves the campers," observed Harry's mother. "Miriam, her daughter, she interviewed me for this piece of research she's doing. Mit the university, yes?"

clarifies Ida Kaminsky. "Like me, my wife was a survivor," Mr. Plautsnicki pointed out; "now Rachael Himmelfarb was the only person my wife really trusted, and everyone who has so much as met Rachael knows why." "And ever after," concluded a white middle-aged man, a slight wheeze in his voice, "whenever I would read a Shakespeare sonnet, the words would sing."

The last person to speak was this wizened old man with a bald head and bad hip who had never met eema or even read a word she'd written but who knew he'd be welcome. Helped up to the bimah by Rabbi Pat, he stood there for a long while, not uttering a word. Then adjusting his spectacles, his eyes reaching far into the back rows, he began, "My name is Chaim Poules. I was born in Salonica. My number is 116, 213. And I want you should listen as I tell you about what happened to me years ago in a country that was not my own, in a place called a 'lager.'"

I could feel the muscles in my back loosening and this wave of relief rippling through me. Fitting, it should end like this, I thought. I glanced over at Sondra just to check if the emphasis on the Holocaust was starting to rattle her. It wasn't. So even for her, this is of a whole different dimension, yes?

The graveyard service was next, and that meant a long drive north. Sammy and Sarrah in the backseat and old Mr. Plautsnicki next to me, I turned on the ignition and took Bathurst north to the Allen Expressway, but we were delayed because of a three-car pileup a few yards into the Allen. No serious injuries, thankfully, and nothing I hadn't seen before, but strangely ominous for people on the way to a burial.

Though we arrived a bit on the late side, it didn't feel right or even possible to rush. My arm supporting Mr. Plautsnicki, who was having trouble with his leg, Sarrah giving a hand to her pregnant partner, we tread slowly past the first few rows of graves. When we got to abba's row, I asked everyone for a moment, walked over to abba's tombstone, looked down, and murmured underneath my breath, "Watch, abba. Just watch." Then I rejoined the others. And even more slowly, we navigated this small incline where the ivy had woven its way though the grass. Then there they were—the Rabbi, Esther, Sondra, Channa, Niel, Lanie, and indeed, almost everyone who'd spoken at the funeral.

The crowd is hushed, everyone's head lowered. A gesture of respect, yes? But there's something else. Nu? As if everyone were anticipating some danger that none of us dare put into words. Tears flowing from my eyes, I walk over to my two weeping sisters, and the three of us hold each other, not uttering a word. Then I look down. And there it is. This terrible wound in the earth. My body aching, my very sinews seem to understand what's happened here. The earth, it has been ravished, broken open. And somehow, it has to be made whole.

Lifting up my eyes a few minutes later, I spot them in the distance—four men, facing us, a plain pine box on their shoulders. Harry is upfront and on the left, the lead pallbearer. And I would recognize that expression on his face anywhere—that exact same look of compassion and care he'd had that day in the hospital, when he cradled his crying first born in his arms and cooed, "Sha, sha, little one." Now the pallbearers, they're starting to move, very carefully, their steps measured, their heads high. All the while, the people around me are chanting, "Shall dust praise you? Shall it decline thy truth?" And now for no apparent reason, the pallbearers stop. I hear a psalm being chanted somewhere to my side, recognize Rabbi Pat's rich throaty voice, and turn toward her. As she chants, her body sways ever so slightly back and forth, back and forth. She is holding this large earthenware bowl almost at arm's length in front of her. Just as she finishes the psalm, she raises the bowl high above her head, then stands there poised. Harry nods. Everyone around me sucks in their breath. Then in one uninterrupted motion, she brings the bowl crashing to the ground. "The snare is broken and we have escaped," she proclaims.

I can hear Esther and Sondra breathing again and see bodies about me beginning to relax. Like some terrible danger has passed. But what is the snare that's broken and who is the "we" that is free? Eema, without doubt. Punct! The Nazis can hardly get hold of her now. But, gevalt! It isn't only eema that was in danger, was it? "The snare is broken and *we* have escaped." Yes. Yes. I can feel it in the rush of my blood, in the pounding of my heart. Death is here in our midst, not inches away. I take a long deep breath, strangely relieved at being alive.

The pallbearers start up again, yes? They take one step forward, then stop and just stand there. Are they reluctant to continue? Reluctant to bury this remarkable woman? Now Harry's leg, it's edging forward. And now they're taking another step. And now once again, they stop and linger. And so they continue. Step, stop, linger. Step, stop, linger. My own reluctance to bury eema, I can see it writ large in the ritualized movement of the pallbearers, and I can feel myself melding with it, validated by it. No. We can't part with her. Hold on just a little longer. Just a little longer. Just....

Now they are placing the coffin on the bier. And now, we actually do it. Together, Sondra, Esther, and I step forward. "Inside this coffin lying next to eema is our abba's old cloth measuring tape," I announce. "No one was more important to eema than abba. And eema needs something of abba's with her because they've always faced everything together: Auschwitz, immigration, the needs of a growing family, the neonazis. And my sisters and I know of nothing more fitting than the measuring tape. You see, it was always dangling from his neck because he was a tailor. And it is only because he was a tailor that eema and abba were able to come to this new land. It was 1947, yes? And Canada's doors were still barred to Jews. And then, because of the needs of industry, an exception was made. Jews in the needle trade. Eema, this measuring tape brought you and abba to this land. Take it with you now."

As I step back, I can feel this hand on my shoulder and can sense that it is Esther. And now the coffin is being lowered, and all about me people are singing the Song of the Partisans. And now it is time to shovel the earth into the grave, each of us taking our turn.

While I was just barely aware of it at the time, like so much else at this funeral, shoveling the earth was different than at abba's funeral. Besides that I didn't get swamped with images, we used the back of the shovel. If ever you've used the back of a shovel, you'll know that very little dirt fits there, and it's hard to maneuver. A kind of trick, I guess, but inverting the shovel slowed us down, gave us the time we needed.

After we've all been shoveling for a very long while, I peer into the opening in the earth. The coffin is invisible. And the wound in the earth, it's healing.

Around this time, to my discomfort, everything speeded up. The grave half filled, Rabbi Pat placed the shovel on the ground. At Rabbi Pat's invitation, Esther, Sondra, and I read the Kaddish. Then the mourners started to disperse.

"Everyone ready to go?" asked Harry. "Not meaning to rush anyone, but if we don't hurry, the guests'll beat us home."

I feel a lump in my throat. "Who's going to finish filling in the grave?" I asked.

"Nothing to worry about, Miriam," Harry assured me. "The officials, they always take care of it."

And that's when my sisters and I made the most critical decision of the day. Turning to Harry and Esther, I ask, "Guys, mind taking care of the shiva guests without me for the next hour or so? I'm not quite ready to leave."

"You're gonna fill in the grave, aren't you?" asks Esther, her eyes seeking out mine.

I nod.

"That makes two of us," she asserts.

"Three," corrects Sondra.

Putting her hand on his shoulder, Esther asks Harry if he'll tend to everything on the home front.

"No problem," he answers, running his finger through his beard, "but you sure you're going to be...?"

By this point, Sondra, Esther and I are looking at each other, smiling through our tears. From the corner of my eye, I see Harry take note and nod. Then he walks over to Sammy and Sarrah, puts his arm around Sammy, and whispers something in her ear. I suspect he approached Mr. Plautsnicki too. Be that as it may, within minutes, everyone is gone.

The second we were alone, Esther picked up the shovel, inverted it as before, and handed it to me. And for the next long while, the three of us passed the shovel between us, slowing but surely filling in our eema's grave.

Light was turning into half-light as we finished; the air was damp and the wind was whooshing though our clothes. There was nary another human being in sight. Just grave after grave, tombstone after tombstone, the grass on the ground, the birch trees far off to our right. Exhausted from our long labour, we took one look at each other, and without a word, coats and all, sank onto the cold firm earth and rested, Esther and Sondra on their sides, me a few feet away, my back hugging the earth.

I remember this dreadful emptiness coming upon me as I lay there asking myself: Is this all? Is this the end of it? Nu? But I also remember the satisfaction of knowing we'd done it. Kinehora, we'd helped her die. And right up to the last smidgen of earth, we'd buried her. I closed my eyes and thought of eema, our family, our story. Then I began thinking about the funeral. And for the first time that day, I was able to acknowledge to myself that despite the many wonderful touches, for me at any rate, something was missing. Yes. That eema had killed herself and why eema had killed herself.

Don't get me wrong. It's not that I wanted it to overshadow everything else. Nor was I unaware that blinkers have a totally legitimate purpose: To help humanity in its vulnerability tread the earth without being overcome by mind-chilling terror. But, gotenyu! I could see only too clearly that it was integral to who eema was. This is what the Holocaust had done to her, yes? And this is what we'd all lived through. Also, after everything this family had been through, I really didn't want to be keeping secrets any more.

Feeling lighter, the way one does when something befuddled has become clearer, I opened my eyes. I began gazing about, taking in row after row of tombstones and wondering what stories lay hidden just beneath those ponderous grey stones. Who are these people? And what's happened in their family? What caring acts? Betrayals? Mistakes? Reconciliations? Did they celebrate Shabbes? Pesach? Which of them are survivors? How did they live? How did they cope in the middle of the night? And how did they die?

Absent-mindedly, as I was staring at this charcoal gray tombstone to my left, I squeezed something in my hand. I felt the sting of a sliver entering my palm, realized I was still holding onto the shovel, and instinctively tightened my grip. Oy! In retrospect, I guess I still needed something tangible to hold onto—something that would connect me with eema and the earth where she lay. Yes, and with this act of love we'd just performed, for an act of love it most assuredly was. Also, I needed time. So did my sisters. And so it is that Sondra Himmelfarb, Esther Cohan, and myself, Miriam Himmelfarb—daughters of a woman who had just killed herself because of that atrocity called "the Holocaust"—continued to lie next to her freshly covered grave, the crescent moon beaming down, the shadow of Auschwitz upon us.

It seemed as if hours passed, though in point of fact, it was considerably less. Sondra was the first to break the silence.

"Think she's okay now?" asked Sondra, turning to Esther.

"Eema?" Esther clarified.

"Yes."

"Well, we've done what we can. And now, it's in Adoshem's hands."

"Not that 'Adoshem' stuff again!" exclaimed Sondra, sitting upright.

"You're coming back with us to the house now, aren't you, Sondra?" asked Esther, seemingly, not offended.

Sondra shook her head and began picking brambles out of her hair. "Nothing personal, but like, I've seen more of this family over this past week than I have for the last three and a half decades. And trust me, it's about all the family I can handle for awhile. You weren't expecting me to just blend in now, were you?"

Though I'd been imagining something very different, and I felt disappointed, I knew, of course, that she was right. She had left years ago and created a life for herself. And as the entire course of our family had demonstrated, we can none of us undo history. Something had shifted, without a doubt. But she had a life with its own landscape, its own rhythms, and only time would tell what Sondra was going to be to us and us to her.

"Guys," I asked a few minutes later, "I don't want to keep pretending that eema died of natural causes. You?"

Sondra shook her head, as did Esther. "Now Harry, I'm not sure about," added Esther.

The difficult question broached, we proceeded to discuss moments in the funeral we really liked when, to my surprise, Esther looked at me knowingly and added, "and of course, there was that section we added to the Kaddish." Not sure what she meant, I answered, "Sorry, sweetie. What section?"

"Eema wanted the Rabbi's Kaddish, not the Mourner's Kaddish. Remember?"

"To be honest," I answered, "it sounded the same to me. But you know me and Hebrew."

A look of disappointment comes over Esther's face. "Well, essentially the Rabbi's Kaddish is the same as the Mourner's Kaddish," she explains, "but there's this one extra passage."

"Tell me."

"Pray for the scholars, their students, and their students' students."

As Esther utters these words, I think of the scholars in the Himmelfarb-Cohan family—eema, Harry, me, and in her own way, Esther. Then I think of the students who spoke at the service. Then I start to imagine the thousands of minds, young and old, that eema has touched over the years. And tears coming to my eyes, I hear myself responding, "amen."

"Just one fuckin' moment there," calls out Sondra, a mischievous grin on her face, her index finger pointing to Esther. "It's bad enough hearing religious crap from this one. Surely, not from the atheist."

"Point taken," I answer.

"Now don't anyone pay attention to me. I mean, I'm just the in-house hooker. But, like, don't you gals have shiva guests to get back to?"

Esther and I take one look at each other and crack up. Then at long last, I lay down the shovel. And the three of us rise, dust ourselves off, and head for the car.

# Miriam's Epilogue

We're back at the beginning, yes? Back at eema's death. Back as well to those pressing questions that have so haunted me—about identity, direction, meaning. This story is my answer. Also, my way of finding answers. I've been writing it for almost three years now. I began writing about a week after shiva ended. Esther's idea.

She was worried about this depression I'd fallen into. While thankfully, it proved to be temporary, I'd gone into what looked like an unstoppable tailspin. Esther put her hand on my shoulder, knit up her brow, and urged, "You're a writer, Meems. Maybe if you write something." The next day I found myself sitting at my desk jotting down notes for a piece tentatively titled "Miriam's Prologue," though if you'd asked me what it was prologue *to*, I wouldn't have been able to answer. Given the state I was in, not just desperation, but disorientation leaked into that prologue, and I'd leave it as is sensing that this too needed to be heard, but it wasn't long before clarity set in.

Now the family had yet to breathe a word to others about how eema had really died. But spurred on by the writing, I called a family meeting. Harry must have been struggling with the whole question of privacy, for he was far more receptive to the idea than any of us had anticipated. In fact, it was Harry himself who actually got us moving. "This is important, see," he asserted, his eyes coming alive. "For us. People like us. People like my folks too, right? It'll be hard, sure, but let's do it." And so at long last, we began telling people. Of course, some were shocked, but oh so many were relieved. "Not that I didn't suspect," acknowledged Mrs. Schwartz, "but how can a person ask?" "You mean we can actually talk about this!" exclaimed Moshe, his shoulders lowering for the first time in years.

All this witnessing I'm doing, it's meaningful and I feel good about it. But have I gotten back my life?, you may be wondering. And beyond that, have I achieved the balance that eema so wished for me? Please hear me on this, for our time together is rapidly drawing to an end and I don't want us to squander the moment. Let's face up to the reality of multigenerational trauma. Do anything less as individuals, and we lose an opportunity for tikkun olam—the healing of the world. Do anything less as a species, and we'll continue to commit atrocities with consequences that will reverberate through the generations.

The fact is, Auschwitz does not permit Hollywood-type endings. I cannot be someone who is not haunted by images of emaciated figures. I cannot walk away from the Shoah. And balance is not a term that will ever adequately describe me. Being a second generation survivor who struggles with a terrible legacy is simply fundamental to who I am.

That said, the universe is complex. Even where it seems impossible, we can sometimes achieve a semblance of balance. And at times we find gifts where we least expect them. And so it has been for me around eema's death. Eema's passing was a kind of opening—an opportunity to take stock and make changes. And I took eema's advice to heart and reached for it. The upshot? Nothing dramatic. But something sound. Those workaday changes that are the stuff of life. Getting out more, reconnecting with people, putting energy back into teaching and activism. I made a new friend last year—first one in decades, yes? This semester my colleague Rose and I are spearheading a new course on the use of art in witnessing. And what an interesting experience co-teaching is proving to be! Ah yes, and at long last, I've joined Jewish and Palestinian Women Against the Occupation—Sammy and Sarrah along with me. Now Sammy and Sarrah, they've somewhat turned my life topsy-turvy, but in a good heimish sort of way.

Sammy was six-and-a-half months pregnant when eema made her fateful decision. In due course, she gave birth to a baby boy. Eight pounds, three ounces, his full name is "Avromi Daniel Czerniak-Cohan." "Daniel" after abba, and "Avromi" after both Sarrah's uncle and abba's father, though we quickly fell into calling him "Baby Abe." Now if Sammy and Esther had trouble living under one roof before, after Baby Abe arrived on the scene, everything went absolutely meshugah. After a whole lot of screaming and kvetching and a few interminable family meetings, it was finally agreed that the arrangement was "not working." And so it is that Sammy, Sarrah, and Baby Abe came to live in the Lippincott house, Sammy and Sarrah taking eema's room, my study going to Baby

Abe, the dining room doubling as a study. Now it feels a bit crowded at times, but it's good to have a growing family within these walls again. Also instructive.

Coming out of the washroom one afternoon, I happened upon Sammy standing in the hall, her eyes on the hated Uncle Nathaniel. I'd long been in the habit of averting my eyes when passing that picture, but with Sammy staring at it, I instinctively glanced in the direction she was looking. And ach! There he was, his nostrils flaring, his hazel eyes following me, his hand on the rifle.

"Just why do you keep the goddam picture, Aunt Miriam?" asked Sammy, looking over at me.

"You see," I started explaining, "your zeda needed the picture up because so much of his family died in the Holocaust."

"Then why didn't he put up a picture of one of the victims?" counters Sammy, her eyes narrowing. "Why a settler? Any way, Auntie, I don't mean to be disrespectful or anything, but zeda's dead."

That very day I did something I'd longed to do lo these last fifty years. I took that picture down. "Good for you, Aunt Miriam," exclaimed Sammy. Three weeks later as we set out for the Anti-racist Action demo, Sammy and I were still congratulating each other over the change.

The demo had been terrifying. Taking a page from their American counterparts, police on horses had charged at the demonstrators. Blinkers on the horses, the cops had proceeded relentlessly toward us, giving no thought whatever to who was old, who was disabled, who might not be able to move away quickly. I had tripped while scurrying out of the way and had come within inches of being trampled. After the demo, I went straight home. Still shaking from the narrow escape, I lay down in bed and closed my eyes. To my surprise, within seconds, I found myself suddenly worrying again about eema's tahara. Could she have been hurt after all? Feeling woozy and more than a little disconcerted over where my mind was going, I opened my eyes to try to ground myself. Then sensing I shouldn't fight this, I closed them once more. And that's when I saw it:

Stretched out on a table, covered by a sheet, the remains of an aged woman is being washed by three young women, all of them handling the body tenderly, taking special care not to bruise it, not to disturb it, not to upset that precarious balance which befits the betwixt-and-between.

Sarrah and her cousins Becky and Menya, for such they are, go about their task reverently, methodically. Now they're uncovering the right foot, carefully scrubbing the flesh, using toothpicks to get in under the nails. Now they cover it back up. And now they're uncovering the right leg. And so they wash every part—abdomen, shoulders, legs, arms, head—never letting a speck of dirt escape their attention, never leaving anything uncovered long.

When they arrive at the upper part of the face, I instinctively look into the eyes. Oy! Eema's not looking back! I can't find her in those glassy eyes. But neither do I see any sign of terror.

The women continue. And once they have cleaned everywhere, they proceed to yet another stage of cleaning. Sarrah fills three large aqua blue jugs with water, places two at her feet, then picks up the third. Then one on either side of her, Becky and Menya begin to prop eema up. Gott! It's as if she were rising, standing in our midst once again! Once they have her steady, Sarrah lifts the jug above eema's head and begins to pour. The clear glistening water, it's streaming down eema's head, down her body, massaging that poor injured shoulder, soothing her blistered feet. Even as Sarrah finishes pouring the first jug, she is already on the second, and as she finishes the second, she is on third so that eema is being immersed in one long uninterrupted flow. That initial scrubbing, it left eema physically clean. But *this* water! It's as if it were getting at something more ethereal. Washing away the residue of terror. Washing away the screams in the middle of the night. Washing away the infections of Auschwitz—the lice, the excrement, the beatings, the sneers, the threats. And now eema's being dried. And this spotless white cloak is being drawn around her and tied at the waist. And now she is in the casket, wrapped in white linen from head to foot: clean, warm, protected.

I sighed with relief as I emerged from this vision. Then I got up, sat down in a chair, and began to cry. I sat in that chair weeping for what seemed like hours, these convulsive sobs shaking me from head to foot. Then I became calm. Feeling lighter, I headed for the kitchen, made myself a cup coffee, then went to the living room, turned on the radio, and nestled down on the couch. But I couldn't concentrate on the program. I kept getting this vague feeling I'd seen more than I knew. And so it is that the CBC blaring in the background, I willed myself back into the vision.

I get to the place where eema is on the table and they're working on her right side. Section by section, they uncover and wash, uncover and wash, all the while reciting the Song of Songs. Then they turn her over and begin on the left side. Now they're scrubbing her left hand. And now they're beginning to uncover the left arm. And there it is—eema's tattoo. It starts to blur, as always, but then surprisingly, it reverses and comes into focus. And yes, yes. I can make it out: "379," it reads. I know instantly that it makes sense, for eema was one of the very first— one of the 999 women who arrived on that initial transport from Ravensbrück.

It's as if something inside of me had unblocked, letting my mind take in what my eyes had always seen; and I'm grateful that it did. A gift, yes? But even this inexplicable gift is not what most stands out for me when I think about what I've come to regard as the "post-eema era." It's the simple and seemingly obvious fact that the world did not end. All these years I felt as if there would be nothing after eema was gone. And while for me, certainly, something irreplaceably dear is missing, I've discovered what every mourner must: That life continues. So it has always been. And so it shall always be.

Strange. Oftentimes when I awake in the middle of the night, I can swear I'm hearing whispers of yesteryear, rising, crackling, like the rustling of leaves on a breezy autumn day: "Is Auschvitz, you are thinking of, Rachael, yah?"

"Auschwitz, yes. The smell of excrement and rotting flesh. Ach. Like an odor from Hell."

And I know these whispers will always be with me. And yet, though I dwell in the shadow of Auschwitz, I have continued, sometimes in joy, sometimes in sorrow. And, kinehora! So has the family—Esther, Harry, everyone. Making Shabbes. Lighting yarhzeits. Living, dying, giving birth, arguing, celebrating, worrying, protesting, teaching, learning.

Nu? Esther is now pursuing rabbinical studies. While Sammy rolls her eyes at this, and Harry's clearly worried she won't cut it as a rabbi, I have a feeling that everyone's in for a surprise. Sammy's expecting again. And though she wasn't concerned the first time round, she's really bothered now. "Aunt Miriam?" she asked me not a week ago, "like, do they really expect it to affect the fourth generation?" A respectable activist in her own right, Sarrah can be found every Thursday demonstrating against the occupation, interestingly enough, as a Zionist. Last year Harry became head of Judaic Studies. His colleagues expected him to be on the conservative side. However, a semester hadn't gone by before he began pushing the department to hire a feminist scholar. Ten months ago, Harry's father passed away. Strictly natural causes, though we're not sure what's going to happen with Harry's mother, for much to our consternation, not long after her husband's death, she began having severe flashbacks. An ardent Zionist, Channa emigrated to Israel a year-and-a-half ago. Now Harry and Esther were initially delighted, but even they became aghast when she decided to settle in Hebron. Niel married a Buddhist woman from New Delhi some months back, and by way of accommodation, already Esther and I have incorporated meditation into Shabbes. "Ma, what do you think? That Jews don't meditate too?" pointed out Esther when Mrs. Cohan senior started to object. And two and a half years ago, on February 4th 1999, after suffering a second coronary, Uncle Yacov passed away. His last words, apparently, were "baruch Hashem," but whether uttered in desperation or peacefully, none of the hospital staff seemed to know.

Lest I forget to mention it, the neo-nazis and other virulent anti-Semites have also continued. Why in the very year of Uncle Yacov's death, Aryan Nations follower Bufford O'Neal Furrow Junior sprayed North Valley Jewish Community Center with seventy bullets, calling it "a wakeup call to America to kill Jews." Two hundred and nineteen Jewish graves were desecrated in the quiet prairie city of Winnipeg. In Toronto, elderly Jewish men—including Holocaust survivors—were pelted with stones as they made their way to temple. And in France, an unprecedented number of synagogues were set ablaze. "Biggest upsurge in anti-Semitism since the '30s," Esther lamented one evening as the family was sitting around her dining room table.

"And every sign it's going to worsen," added Niel.

Sondra just rolled her eyes and said nothing, I suspect thinking, "here they go again," or painfully aware of how much less air time is given to the ongoing murder of sex trade workers.

Now about Sondra's life, we none of us know all that much. I have the impression she's currently making a video on police violence against sex trade workers, but for some reason that's not at all clear to me she hasn't exactly said that. Nor do we see her often. Disappointing, of course, but I can see we've a tendency to rub her the wrong way, yes? And I knew that visits would be infrequent from what she'd said that day at the graveside. Nonetheless, every four, five months she joins the family for Shabbes, sometimes being a joy, sometimes a pain, inevitably adding her indefatigable humour into the mix. And once every long while Sondra,

Esther, and I spend an entire afternoon and evening together. Schmoozing, kvetching, laughing, epes. We're sisters, right? And we're joined together by early history—that precious week, those final moments at the graveside, the ongoing saga in which we participate.

As I understand it and as Jewish tradition instructs me, I'm joined to you also. You who have had the heart and taken the time to hear this story. Internal witness is extremely important, yes? But witnessing is not complete without the other. More like an inclination until somebody performs the mitzvah of noticing and saying, "Thou."

Now in those early days, when we were of us all young, sometimes as eema would draw her kerchief over her head and ready herself to light a yarhzeit, she would pause, gaze tenderly into our eyes, and remark, "Meydelehs, know what's special about mitzvahs? Everyone receives, yes? Giver and receiver alike." If eema is right, you will have received in turn or will yet receive. And such is my parting wish.

I thank you. My family thanks you. A blessing on you.

# Author's Note

Having recently finished a book-length manuscript on fascism, I had been thinking about writing a book about trauma in Holocaust survivor families. Then an image came to mind: Two Holocaust survivor-activists and their three daughters. Sensing something with potential there, I held onto that image. And out of that image, this novel grew.

I am grateful to the people who helped it grow. Those who have written on the Holocaust and its aftermath, especially those who have provided first-person accounts. You are the giants on whose shoulders I stand. My friend Margôt Smith, who listened diligently to every chapter after it was written, and who provided the ongoing feedback for which authors yearn. Margôt, if you had not pushed me to develop Sondra further, where would I be now? My terrific editor, Luciana Ricciutelli, who believed in this book and had the courage of her convictions. Freda Forman for her generous help with words. The ever attentive House on Lippincott committee—Don Weitz, Jeff Myers, Teresa Hibbert, and Shaindl Diamond. Psychotherapy clients of mine who are survivors or children of survivors. You have taught me so much.

It has been an exciting if daunting task bringing this novel to fruition. To be able to bring into the open the daily struggles and yearnings of survivors and their children. To give people who may not be Jewish a glimpse of what it can be like navigating the world as a Jew.

While, like most authors, I have tried to capture the universal in the particular, I would caution readers not to generalize too readily from the characters here to all survivors or all children of survivors. While a fair amount of what I have shown is common, some is not, and in some instances, there are diametrically opposite responses that are also common. Additionally, no two people cope in exactly the same way. I would also caution readers not to mistake the Himmelfarb family for typical

German Jews. Besides that the parents are both Auschwitz survivors, which is highly unusual, this family's speech and mannerisms are largely shaped by eema's and abba's Polish heritage, by the family's Slavic Jewish neighbours, and by the Polish Holocaust survivors that figured so centrally in their world. Yacov, additionally, lived in New York from very early on, and his style of speech conforms to the speech of the Orthodox Jews with whom he associated.

Besides worrying that I would fall flat on my face, my biggest fear in writing a novel of this sort is that I might sometimes misinterpret historical information, err in emphasis or nuance, put my faith in a source that is mistaken despite being generally accepted as definitive. Given human fallibility, these are common failings that are inevitable, at least to some extent, but they have an added import here because of the enormous sensitivity of the subject. For errors in judgment which I have made that offend anyone, I apologize.

I apologize as well for any pain which fictionalizing history has caused. I am aware, for example, that I have provided fictional characters with tattoo numbers that would inevitably have been inflicted on real people. Using the *Auschwitz Chronicle* by Danuta Czech (New York: Henry Holt and Company, 1990), I chose each of the two numbers at random from within the set that would be possible for the characters in question given their origin and arrival date. My assurance that no disrespect is intended.

While the characters are fictional, for the most part, the historical events that weave through the novel are real, and the details are accurate. All of the various North American nazi and fascist figures and groups portrayed or alluded to did exist, and the actions attributed to them happened. By contrast, some of the antifascist groups are fictional (e.g., Youth Against Nazis, Antifa Toronto, and Committee to Investigate Nazism in Canada). Nonetheless, the actions in which they engaged were common in antifascist circles in that era. For a good discussion of nazi and fascist groups in North America during this period, see Stanley Barrett, *Is God a Racist?* (Toronto: University of Toronto Press, 1987).

For an authoritative account of the Christie Pits riot and its aftermath, see Cyril Levitt and William Shaffir, *The Riots at Christie Pits* (Toronto: Lester and Orpen Dennys, 1987). For details on Canada's lamentable record vis-a-vis Jewish refugees, see Irving Abella and Harold Troper, *None is Too Many* (Toronto: Lester Publishing, 1991). For another excellent account of Canadian immigration policy and for a description of the early life of Holocaust survivor immigrants, see Franklin Bialystok, *Delayed Impact* (Montreal: McGill Queen's University Press, 2000).

Works on the trauma of survivors or their children which have especially informed this novel include: D. Laub, "Truth and Testimony," in C. Caruth (Ed.), *Trauma: Explorations in Memory* (Baltimore: The Hopkins University Press, 1995, pp. 61-75); Helen Epstein, *Children of the Holocaust* (Toronto: Penguin Books, 1988); and Yael Danieli (Ed.), *International Handbook of Multigenerational Legacies of Trauma* (New York: Plenum, 1998).

While the explicit Holocaust content in Miriam's flashbacks or the various characters' speeches is sometimes fictitious and sometimes not, even when fictitious, I attempted to make it reflective of everyday life within the lager. For the description of the musselman, my understanding of "organizing," as well as for the idea of someone at Auschwitz telling an inmate that there is no "why" here, I am profoundly indebted to Primo Levy, *Survival at Auschwitz* (New York: Simon and Schuster, 1996). Other writings on general life within the lager to which I am indebted include: Terrence Des Pres, *The Survivors* (Oxford: Oxford University Press, 1976), and Yisrael Gutman and Michael Berenbaum (Eds.), *Anatomy of the Auschwitz Death Camp* (Indiana: Indiana University Press, 1998). For details on the specificity of injury to women, I am principally indebted to first-person accounts by women survivors, especially the accounts in Carol Rittner and John Roth (Eds.), *Women and the Holocaust: Different Voices* (New York: Paragon House, 1993).

Uncle Yacov's reference T4 is accurate. For detailed discussion of T4, see Robert Lifton, *The Nazi Doctors* (New York: Harper and Row, 1986).

I deviated only in minor ways from historical accounts of the smuggling of the dynamite. Besides simplifying the description, my major modification is the addition of eema. Additionally, contrary to the impression I have created, as far as I can discern, no one other than Roza Robota ever delivered the dynamite to the sonderkommandos. For the most part, where discrepancies exist between different accounts of the smuggling operation, I have followed the version provided by survivor and participant Anna Heilman in *Never Far Away* (Calgary: University of Calgary Press, 2001). See also the accounts by Anna Heilman and by Ruth Meth in Rittner and Roth (1993); and Israel Gutman, *Smoke and Ashes* (Israel: Sifriyat Poalim, 1957).

The Eichmann interrogation is based on transcripts from the archives of the Israeli police. My representation of the problems of Holocaust survivors in old age is based on an extensive review of the psychological literature as well as my own therapeutic work with Holocaust survivors.

The fair use/fair dealing quotation from "Gerontion" is from T.S. Eliot, *Collected Poems, 1909-1962* (London: Faber and Faber, 1963). It should be pointed out that while Lanie's reference to Pound and his literary influence on Eliot is accurate, no suggestion is being made that Eliot himself had fascist sympathies. For the fair use/fair dealing quotations from Derrida, see J. Derrida, "Like the Sound the Sea Within a Shell: Paul de Man's War," *Critical Inquiry* Vol. 14.

While many of Miriam's opinions and insights on the de Man-Derrida controversy are original, her position draws heavily on the scholarly responses found in articles in *Critical Inquiry* Vol. 15. (See the subsequent volume for Derrida's response to the critiques.) It should also be pointed out that different scholars have very different views on the controversy. Readers are encouraged to go to the sources and make up their own minds.

Eema and Miriam have their own interpretations of Heidegger's Nazi involvement. These most certainly can be debated. Nonetheless, the historical details which they allege are accurate.

Although the specific Holocaust-denial quotations given in the novel are fictitious, they are standard arguments that can be found on almost any Holocaust denial site. The various claims are likewise standard. As Miriam suggests, current articles and the points which they make are largely regurgitations of the positions taken by earlier writers. For the prototype on the argument based on the Red Cross inspection of the camps, see Richard Harwood, *Did Six Million Really Die?* (London: Historical Review Press: n.d.). For the prototype of the Zyklon B argument, see Fred Leuchter, *The Leuchter Report* (Toronto: Samisdat Publishing: n.d.). For methodical refutations of these and other denier positions, see Deborah Lipstadt, *Denying the Holocaust* (New York: Penguin, 1994).

All references to the Toronto police are fictional. And any resemblance to any real officer is coincidental.

# Glossary of Yiddish and Hebrew Expressions

*Regarding the spelling of terms, it should be noted, wherever there is one or more alternate spellings, I have chosen a spelling and stayed with it. Additionally, where I felt that the standard spelling would result in many non-Jewish readers mispronouncing the word, I have altered the spelling so as to avoid this problem. For example, while the name for grandmother is standardly "bubbe," I use "bubbeh." Similar decisions have been made with some proper names.*

| | |
|---|---|
| *abba* | father |
| *Adonoi* | God |
| *Adoshem* | God. In line with the idea that the name of God is too holy to be uttered, only the first three letters coincides with the name of God. "Shem," with which this term ends means "name." Similar to "Adonoi" and less careful than "Hashem." |
| *afikomen* | the broken part of the matzo which is hidden during the Passover seder |
| *ata* | thou, you |
| *ay yay yay* | oh my! |
| *balebosteh* | good homemaker |
| *baruch* | blessed |

| | |
|---|---|
| *barucha* | blessing |
| *bimah* | reader's stand in synagogue |
| *bisel* | little |
| *blintz* | pastry containing cheese, generally eaten with sour cream |
| *boytshik* | little boy. Can be used derogatorily. |
| *bruder* | brother |
| *bubbeh* | grandmother |
| *bubbehmeiseh* | sexist word that connotes a far-fetched or superstitious story. A tall tale. Literal meaning: grandmother's story. |
| *bubeleh* | term of affection, generally for someone younger. Roughly similar to "baby." |
| *bupkes* | If you can imagine the word "nothing" accompanied by thrown up hands and a declamatory tone, such is the sense conveyed by "bupkes." |
| *caput* | dead, turned into nothing |
| *challah* | bread traditionally used on Sabbath and holidays |
| *charoset* | mixture of grape juice and almonds which appears on the Passover plate. |
| *chazen* | cantor |
| *chazer* | pig |
| *Chevra Kaddisha* | burial society; the small group of people who come together to prepare the corpse. |

| | |
|---|---|
| *chutzpah* | nerve, guts, often used pejoratively |
| *cvetch* | complain |
| *danke* | thanks |
| *daven* | pray |
| *di* | the |
| *eema* | mother |
| *epes* | A multipurpose word, "epes" means "something," also "somehow." It often denotes things beyond those listed or "anything" as in, "Pick me up cake, cookies, epes." |
| *erev* | the evening before |
| *farbisiner* | a bitter person |
| *farshtey* | understand |
| *farshtopterkop* | a stuffed up head or someone who is dense |
| *farshtunkener* | a bad person or stinker. Literally: someone who stinks. |
| *fir cashas* | the four questions asked by the youngest child at the beginning of the Passover service |
| *gai schlufen* | go to sleep |
| *ganef* | thief |
| *gelt* | money |
| *gevalt* | a scream, a cry, an expression of fear or shock, a desperate appeal for help |

| | |
|---|---|
| *gornit* | nothing |
| *gotenyu* | roughly similar to "My God!" |
| *Gott* | God |
| *goy, goyim, goyishe* | non-Jew, non-Jews, gentile-like |
| *goyisher-kop* | someone who thinks like a non-Jew. Literally: a gentile head. Bigoted derogatory term intended as an insult to the Jew in question. |
| *gut* | good |
| *gut Shabbes* | good Sabbath |
| *gut yontif* | happy holiday |
| *haggadah* | text read at the Passover service |
| *Hak mir nit keyn tshaynik* or *don't hak mir tshaynik* | literally: Chop me no tea kettle. Similar meaning to "Stop pulling my leg," or "Stop putting me on." |
| *halacha* | Jewish law |
| *Hashem* | commonly used among the Orthodox, a term for God that is so respectful that nothing of God's name is in it. Literally means "the name." See "Adoshem." |
| *havdalah* | literally: separation. Can refer to the ceremony that ushers out Shabbes or the Sabbath or to the special braided candle burned in ushering out Shabbes, which is called the havdalah candle. |
| *helf mir* | help me |

| | |
|---|---|
| *heimish* | home-like |
| *himmel* | heaven |
| *hunt* | dog |
| *ingele* | little boy. A term of affection generally used to refer to little boys, but can also be used to refer to a man if uttered by someone considerably older. |
| *iz* | is |
| *kaddish* | Aramaic for "holy," it refers to specific prayers for the dead. |
| *kiddush* | blessing over the wine |
| *kind* | child |
| *kinderlekh* | darling children |
| *kinehora* | literally, "with no evil eye." Original intent was to ward off the evil eye, and it was generally uttered after commenting on something nice, as in "The girls look so beautiful, kinehora." Now used regardless of belief and often by people unaware that they are doing anything more than adding emphasis. |
| *kishkeh* | gut |
| *kneidel* | matzo balls |
| *knishes* | rounded baked good, always involving flour and generally either potatoes, meat, or cheese |
| *kvetch* | complain |
| *landsman* | countryman |

| | |
|---|---|
| *lila tov* | good night |
| *lokshen* | noodles; sometimes used to refer to a noodle dish |
| *lomed vovnik* | religious term. One of the righteous on whom the well-being of the world depends. |
| *mah nish'tanah ha'lilah hazeh* | the beginning of the first question which the youngest child asks at the Passover service. The whole question is, "Why is this night different from all other nights?" See "fir cashas." |
| *maiseh* | story |
| *mameh* | mother |
| *mamenyu* | affectionate term for mother, more often used with young mothers. Literally: little mother. |
| *mamzer* | bastard |
| *matzo* | unleavened bread |
| *matzo meal* | matzo in powder form, used for flour |
| *maven* | expert |
| *mayn* | my |
| *mazel tov* | congratulations. Literally means "good luck." |
| *machzor, machzorim* | prayer book, prayer books used on High Holidays |
| *mechayeh* | pleasure, wonderful thing |
| *megileh* | scroll. Generally used colloquially to refer to a story, a very lengthy account, a big deal. Also refers to a complicated happening with long-term |

consequences.

| | |
|---|---|
| *mentsh* | literally: man. Used to connote a decent human being. |
| *meshugah* | crazy or nutty |
| *meshugahs* | craziness or nuttiness |
| *meshugener* | a crazy person, a nutty person, or an eccentric |
| *meydeleh* | girl, often used as a term of affection |
| *mir* | me |
| *mishpocheh* | family |
| *mit* | with |
| *mitzvah* | a blessing thing, a good and righteous deed |
| *mogen Dovid* | star of David |
| *moror* | bitter herb |
| *Moshekapoyer* | someone who gets everything backward. Literally: Moses upside-down. |
| *Moshiah* | messiah |
| *naches* | pleasure |
| *nash* | v. eat. n. a snack |
| *nebbish* | a weak pitiable person. Similar to "loser." |
| *niggun* | wordless melody |
| *noodnic* | nuisance. Mildly pejorative term which is sometimes |

used affectionately.

| | |
|---|---|
| *nu* | A common word, often sprinkled liberally through out people's speech, "nu" means something close to "now," "well," or "so." It can be a question, a sigh, an insinuation, the beginning of an explanation, an invitation. |
| *omeyn* | amen |
| *oy* | oh |
| *oy Gott* | Oh God! |
| *oy vey* | literally: oh woe! An exclamation connoting trouble or misery. See "vey iz mir." |
| *paskudnyak* | a disgusting or evil person |
| *Pesach* | Passover |
| *pisher* | one who pees. Used to refer to small children. |
| *pogrom* | mass roundup and murder of Jews (once common through out Christian Europe) |
| *punct* | precisely |
| *pu pu pu* | an expression often accompanied by spitting to imply disgust, sometimes to ward off evil |
| *rebbe* | rabbi, generally only used for Hassidic rabbis |
| *responsa* | legal opinion or ruling written by Talmudic scholar |
| *schlemiel* | jerk |
| *schlep* | to drag something |

| | |
|---|---|
| *schlufen* | sleep |
| *schlump* | To call someone a "schlump" is like calling them "a nothing." |
| *schmaltz* | fat. Also used to refer to something very sentimental. |
| *schmata* | rag. Also used to refer to clothing which is meager as in, "What have I got to wear? Nothing. Just this schmata." |
| *schmeck* | penis |
| *schmendrik* | jerk |
| *schmuck* | jerk |
| *schmooze* | talk, chat, gossip |
| *schmutz* | filth, dirt |
| *schtick* | piece or bit, trick, the routine someone does, especially a comic's |
| *schul* | synagogue |
| *seder* | Passover service |
| *Sha!* | hush |
| *Shabbes, Shabbat* | Sabbath (Friday at sundown to Saturday at sundown) |
| *sheyneh meydeleh* | beautiful little girl. A term of affection used by adults when addressing young girls. |
| *sheyneh punem* | literally: beautiful face. Term of affection for young girls. |

| | |
|---|---|
| *shikh nokh an ambulans* | call an ambulance |
| *shiker* | adj. drunk. v. to make drunk |
| *shiva* | the seven days of mourning that follow a funeral |
| *sh'ma* | central Jewish prayer, put over entrances to houses, and worn on the top of the head by observant Jews (traditionally male) when doing morning prayers. See "tefillin." |
| *Shoah* | Holocaust |
| *Sholem, Sholem Aleykham* | Peace, peace be with you. Used as a greeting. |
| *shteltl* | literally, "little city." Generally used to refer to the little villages or the ghettos where Jews lived throughout Europe. |
| *shtick* | piece, trick, someone's routine, especially a comic |
| *shvester* | sister |
| *sonder-kommandos* | Nazi term for the special squad of prisoners responsible for leading prisoners to the gas chambers and loading the dead bodies into the furnaces. |
| *tallis* | prayer shawl, traditionally worn by men only |
| *tateh* | father |
| *teffiln* | phylacteries or cubes attached by straps to the arms and head of observant (traditionally male) Jews. Contains biblical quotations and are used in morning prayer. See "sh'ma." |

| | |
|---|---|
| *tikkun olam* | healing of the world |
| *tokhes* | rear end |
| *tokhter* | daughter |
| *tsimmes* | a sweet dish multiple food groups mixed together. Also refers to confusion or a mix-up, or problematic episode. |
| *tsores* | troubles |
| *tzedakah* | justice, righteous giving |
| *vey iz mir* | literally: woe is me. See "oy vey." |
| *vos* | what, who, which |
| *yarhzeit* | anniversary of a person's death. Often used to refer to the twenty-four hour memorial candle which is burnt to commemorate the anniversary. |
| *yarmulke* | religious skullcap traditionally worn by men |
| *yenta* | someone who gossips |
| *yeshuv* | Jewish settlement in Israel prior to statehood. |
| *Yiddishkeit* | essence of Jewishness |
| *yingele* | see "ingele" |
| *Yom Kippur* | Day of Atonement. Part of Jewish New Year. |
| *yontif* | holiday |
| *zaddic* | righteous. Generally refers to sage religious figures. |
| *zeda* | grandfather |

*zoftig*     juicy, rounded, or sensuous

*zy gezent*     be well

# More Praise for *The House on Lippincott*

"From the camps of Nazi Germany to the streets of Toronto, *The House on Lippincott* is a complex family drama, a vivid exploration of the intersection of world history and everyday lives. A novel which I highly recommend, Burstow's groundbreaking work is at once a fascinating read and an important foray into the personal and the social, into trauma and resilience."

—Persimmon Blackbridge is a writer and an artist. Her novel *Sunnybrook* won the Ferro Grumley Fiction Prize (New York City) and, an earlier book, *Her Tongue on My Theory*, won a Lambda Literary Award (Washington, DC).

"Bonnie Burstow's wide-ranging novel explores and reveals the aftermath of the Holocaust: its tenacious hold on survivors as well as their second and third generation descendents. This multi-dimensional work moves between memory and contemporary Jewish experience: all shades of feminism, left politics, and religious observance are represented, as are contemporary philosophic disputes. Burstow is to be commended for including in her novel the disturbing truth of Canada's heartless response to the victims of the Holocaust."

—Freda Forman is the founder and coordinator of the Women's Educational Resources Centre, OISE/UT. She is the editor of the anthologies *Taking Our Time: Feminist Perspectives on Temporality* and *Found Treasures: Stories by Yiddish Women Writers*.

"Genocide is an event whose boundaries are unstable. This is particularly so for survivors and their families. The inheritance of Holocaust memories are indeterminate because they presume a difficult, personally confrontational question: how will you live when histories of violence and violation cannot be contained? How will you live within the presence of Auschwitz? Burstow provides a compelling portrait of the Himmelfarb family as it struggles with the everyday realities of this question. *The House on Lippincott* is an important, imaginative contribution to our understanding of how violent histories unsettle lives across generations."

—Roger I. Simon, Director of the University of Toronto's Centre for Media and Culture in Education and author of *The Touch of the Past: Remembrance, Learning, and Ethics*.

*Photo: Mark MacDonald*

A Jew born in north end Winnipeg toward the end of world war two, Bonnie Burstow is an activist, a feminist psychotherapist, a trauma specialist, a videographer, an academic, and a prolific author. Her most well-known book, *Radical Feminist Therapy*, is a recognized classic which was recently translated into Croatian by the Centre for War Victims in Zagreb and placed in every women's shelter throughout Croatia, Bosnia, Serbia, and Slovenia. Bonnie has worked for decades as an ally in the struggles of marginalized populations, especially psychiatric survivors. She has received numerous awards, including the City of Toronto's Constance E. Hamilton Award. She is currently a faculty member in the Department of Adult Education and Counselling Psychology at Ontario Institute for Studies in Education of the University of Toronto.